SACHIKO

WEATHERHEAD BOOKS ON ASIA

WEATHERHEAD BOOKS ON ASIA
Weatherhead East Asian Institute, Columbia University

For a complete list of titles in the series, see page 409.

ENDŌ SHŪSAKU

Sachiko

A NOVEL

TRANSLATED BY VAN C. GESSEL

COLUMBIA UNIVERSITY PRESS
New York

Columbia University Press
Publishers Since 1893
New York   Chichester, West Sussex
cup.columbia.edu

Copyright © 1982 Asahi Shimbunsha
Translation copyright © 2020 The estate of Endō Shūsaku
All rights reserved

Library of Congress Cataloging-in-Publication Data
Names: Endō, Shūsaku, 1923–1996 author. | Gessel,
Van C., translator.
Title: Sachiko : a novel / Endō Shūsaku ; translated by
Van C. Gessel.
Other titles: Onna no isshō. English
Description: New York : Columbia University Press, [2020] |
Series: Weatherhead books on Asia
Identifiers: LCCN 2019057063 (print) | LCCN 2019057064
(ebook) | ISBN 9780231197304 (hardback) | ISBN 9780231197311
(trade paperback) | ISBN 9780231552103 (ebook)
Classification: LCC PL849.N4 O613 2020 (print) |
LCC PL849.N4 (ebook) | DDC 895.6/35—dc23
LC record available at https://lccn.loc.gov/2019057063
LC ebook record available at https://lccn.loc.gov/2019057064

Columbia University Press books are printed on permanent
and durable acid-free paper.
Printed in the United States of America

Cover design: Julia Kushnirsky
Cover photograph: © Alamy

See page 411 for acknowledgments of the subsidies and grants
that have supported the publication of this book.

*To my cherished colleagues and friends in the
Department of Asian and Near Eastern Languages at
Brigham Young University, along with thirty years
of outstanding students.*

CONTENTS

TRANSLATOR'S INTRODUCTION

THE JAPANESE PREMIERE in early 2017 of Martin Scorsese's film adaptation of Endō Shūsaku's novel *Silence* was awaited with great anticipation. Audiences were eager to see how faithful the American director had been to the original work—one of the most widely read and highly esteemed novels of the modern period—and to ascertain how "Japanese" it felt. They needn't have been concerned. Critical and viewer reaction to the film was almost universally enthusiastic. One critic effused, "I was moved by how deeply the director understood the novel. . . . This is the first time that anyone has displayed this splendid level of accuracy in understanding the true meaning of *Silence* as a [literary] work. . . . Director Scorsese has almost perfectly realized in film the intentions of Endō Shūsaku."[1]

Such a response to the film echoed the enduring popularity of Endō's historical novels in Japan. Many of these works focus on the persecution of Japanese Christians, beginning with the violent tortures and killings in the early seventeenth century as portrayed in *Silence*. In *Kiku's Prayer* (1982; trans. 2013), Endō

---

1   Katō Muneya, quoted in Darren J. N. Middleton and Mark W. Dennis, "The Global Afterlives of Silence," in *Scorsese and Religion*, ed. Christopher B. Barnett and Clark J. Elliston (Leiden: Brill, 2019), pp. 305, 307.

examines the final martyrdoms of hidden Christians in Japan that were carried out in the 1870s, just as the country was coming out of its two-hundred-year seclusion period.[2]

This novel, *Sachiko*, is among the most popular and beloved of his writings, no doubt in part because Endō brings his compassionate consideration of the sufferings of Japanese Christians into more recent times: the dark years of military aggression between 1930 and 1945. Like *Kiku's Prayer*, *Sachiko* is set in Nagasaki, a city that Tokyo-born Endō would ultimately call his "heart's home" (*kokoro no furusato*). He was drawn back to the city, which has played a central role in the history of Christianity in Japan, time and again for materials and characters to include in his writings.

In *Sachiko*, Endō concentrates on the impact of World War II on ordinary people, both the men who were shipped off to battle—often unwillingly—and the women who were left behind to endure pain and loss in very different ways. Unlike the martyrs of earlier times, the Christians of wartime Japan were subjected to psychological torture. The leaders of Japan questioned the loyalty of those citizens who believed in a "foreign" religion as they laid their plans to expel foreign ideologies and set the stage for war with the nations of the West.

The ultimate pain of war inflicted on Nagasaki came when hundreds of thousands of its citizens died as a result of the atomic bombing on August 9, 1945. The ironies of this cataclysmic tragedy have not been lost on the Japanese: the bomb, nicknamed "Fat Man," was dropped by combatants from a presumably "Christian" nation, and the epicenter of the explosion was almost directly above the largest Catholic church in the city, the Urakami Cathedral.

---

2   A synopsis of *Kiku's Prayer* can be found in the appendix to this volume.

Endō chronicled these several periods of pain in his writings, concentrating on the egoism, both individual and institutional, that causes so much of human suffering. Though he was not so naïve as to think there were easy fixes for the core problem of human selfishness and governmental cruelty, Endō found what for him was the ultimate source of consolation amid so much agony—a Christ-like "companion" who never left the side of the sufferer, who was always willing to share in the grief of the weak who are trodden upon by those who wield power over them. Sachiko emerges as such a character in this novel.

Endō, too, seems to suffer alongside his characters. I would suggest to the readers of *Sachiko* that Shūhei, the other central character in the novel, is an imaginative amalgamation of Endō and his older brother, Shōsuke. Both of these sons of a divorced mother were baptized into the Catholic Church at a young age. Shōsuke was a bright, highly successful student who went on to an executive career with Nippon Telegraph and Telephone Public Corporation. In contrast, Shūsaku was an idle underachiever in school, far more adroit at carrying out pranks than at pursuing his studies. Had it not been for a mother who doted on him, loving and encouraging him despite his failings, it is highly unlikely that he would have turned into one of postwar Japan's best-known and most highly lauded authors.

The chapters in the novel that take place during Shūhei's youth and his closest interactions with Sachiko come very close to describing incidents from Endō's own adolescent days. The same could be said about Shūhei's early days at Keiō University in Tokyo, the school Endō attended, and his stay at a Catholic dormitory at Shinano-machi where Endō lived while in school. Unlike Shūhei, however, when the war came, chronic lung problems kept Endō from the military draft and he spent his days of conscript service working in a factory that produced airplane parts. Shōsuke, on the other hand, was drafted into the Japanese

Navy—just like Shūhei—where he advanced to the rank of lieu-tenant paymaster and saw out the end of the war in Singapore.

The Endō brothers survived the war physically, but the psy-chological scars that were inflicted upon them during those years were deep and long-lasting. Shūsaku at the factory and Shōsuke in the payroll office were both subjected to incessant torment because of their Christian affiliation. They were repeatedly ac-cused of being traitors to their country, of worshiping a being more exalted than Japan's "divine" emperor, of following an alien religion that made them somehow less Japanese. This emotional persecution was exacerbated by Shūsaku's inability to accept the Catholic Church's silence on the question of whether it was ac-ceptable for Christian draftees to kill on the battlefield. Neither Shūsaku nor Shōsuke hit upon answers to these questions that satisfied either themselves or those who intimidated them, just as is the case in the character of Shūhei. As *Sachiko* progresses, it is fairly easy to see how Shūhei's experiences closely parallel those of the Endō brothers—up to a certain point.

This novel is also a fine example of Endō's ability to inter-weave seemingly unrelated story lines until at a certain point he brings them subtly and persuasively into juxtaposition. Mingled with the lives of Sachiko and Shūhei is the factual narrative of Saint Maximilian Maria Kolbe (1894–1941). Father Kolbe la-bored in Japan from 1931 to 1932 and founded the press where a Japanese edition of the small missionary booklet *Knights of the Immaculata* was published. The story of his final days in the Aus-chwitz concentration camp closely follows the historical facts. The sacrifice he chose to make in the name of love more than adequately justifies his 1982 canonization as "a martyr of charity."

In *Sachiko*, the struggles of the main characters, the emotional and spiritual traumas they experience, and the unanswerable questions about the taciturnity of God and the church in the face of mortal trials share much in common with the great religious novels that make up Endō's informal trilogy: *Silence, The Samurai,* and *Deep River. Sachiko* puts Endō's celebrated talents of literary construction on prominent display as his nameless narrator searches the chilling landscapes of wartime Japan and even of Auschwitz in search of someone—anyone—who will choose love over cruelty, sacrifice over manipulation.

ACKNOWLEDGMENTS

THE TRANSLATOR WOULD like to express his gratitude to the following people, who have assisted in the often challenging task of making a novel available to readers: to the late Endō Shūsaku, whose extraordinary gifts as a writer have always moved and challenged me, and whose support and dearly missed friendship are the primary reasons I have had a career as a translator; to Endō Ryūnosuke, who kindly granted permission for me to translate his father's novel; to Braedon Rodenberg, for help in the initial stages of research; to the College of Humanities at Brigham Young University and Dean J. Scott Miller, who approved an academic leave to complete the translation and subsequently provided a generous publication subvention grant; to the three anonymous readers, who gave encouragement and helped me refine the translation; and to Christine Dunbar of Columbia University Press, for her support and patience in shepherding this manuscript into final book form. To each of them, no blame for any errors or infelicities in my translation, but only sincere appreciation for their unwavering assistance.

SACHIKO

1

HIS ARRIVAL

APRIL 24, 1930 . . .

The rain that had begun to fall late the previous night intensified near dawn, waking the sleeping populace of Nagasaki. With torrential hammering it pelted the roofs of the houses, the trees, and the shrubbery in the gardens.

Tamaki Kōjirō, who lived in Narutaki, was stirred from sleep by the deluge.

"What a terrible downpour," he exclaimed to his wife, who lay beside him in bed. "You're sure you closed the rain shutters upstairs tightly?"

"Uh-huh," she responded drowsily.

"Maybe this rain will put an end to the drought."

The dry weather had been ideal for kite-flying on Mount Kazagashira, but the newspapers were reporting that the long stretch of days without any rain had significantly reduced levels in the Hongōchi reservoir, which supplied water to the city. But it seemed likely that with this rain, the citizens could stop worrying about a drought.

It'll be the Nagasaki-Maru *coming in to port today.* As he listened to the rain, Tamaki's thoughts turned to the ship that would be arriving today from Shanghai. It was Tamaki's duty, as chief customs inspector for Nagasaki, to examine carefully the identification papers of every foreign passenger on ships that docked in Nagasaki.

Some Japanese tried to smuggle in opium and other illegal substances from Shanghai, and because Nagasaki was a fortified defense zone, these ships might also be carrying foreigners who came as spies.

With all this rain, the Nagasaki-Maru *must've hit some rough waters in the East China Sea. Probably a lot of passengers with seasickness . . .*

With that thought, Tamaki drifted back to sleep.

That morning the rains, whipped up by wind velocities as high as forty miles an hour, continued heavy but subsided somewhat in the afternoon, turning intermittent by the time the *Nagasaki-Maru* reached port at 1:30.

The *Nagasaki-Maru* carried 262 passengers—72 in first class and 190 in third class—with perhaps a score of foreigners mixed in among them.

With their usual formality, Tamaki and the members of his staff boarded the *Nagasaki-Maru*. Several other officials were already on deck, comparing the faces of the passengers with the photos in their passports.

The passengers formed a long line to wait their turns. Guardedly they studied the Nagasaki Police detectives, who stood in strategic locations along the edge of the deck, trying to keep out of the rain.

After they received reports from the ship's captain and purser, Tamaki and Detective Kaneda searched the trunks and bags in every first-class compartment. It was the duty of the staffers to inspect the third-class cabins.

A staffer emerged from belowdecks to report: "There are five foreigners in third class."

"Foreigners—in third class?" Except for the Chinese, virtually every foreigner traveled in a first-class cabin. "What sort of foreigners?"

"Sir, the purser says they are Christian missionaries. But they've got three cameras with them."

Tamaki instinctively sensed something suspicious. His role as chief inspector made him responsible for examining all of the foreigners.

The air in the third-class cabin was clouded with the smells of paint and oil and the aroma of pickled radish wafting from the mess hall, mixed with the dank odors from bodies crowded together in a narrow space.

The cramped cabin was furnished with nothing more than blankets and pillows. Tamaki imagined that Japanese people could spend any number of days crammed together in here like sardines, but he could scarcely bring himself to believe that foreigners, lacking any means to communicate with those around them, could endure such conditions.

"See—it's those foreigners over there." Once they reached the bottom of the ladder, the staffer pointed toward a corner of the large cabin.

Indeed, five foreigners stood together in the corner, each with close-cropped hair and all dressed in black robes. One of them was trying to communicate with the Japanese near him using body language and hand gestures.

"Do they speak Japanese?"

"Very little."

"What a bother! Get an interpreter from up on deck."

"They actually can't speak much English."

"Where are they from?"

"They're Polish."

What are Poles doing here in Japan? Tamaki's suspicions mounted.

"Well anyway, find some kind of interpreter. And Detective Kaneda from the Nagasaki Police is up on deck. Could you inform him?" With these orders, he approached the foreigners by himself.

"I'm from customs." Tamaki pointed to his uniform cap. "Do you understand Japanese?"

Each of them had his head shaved nearly bald, while two of them had beards, which made it difficult for Tamaki to guess their ages by looking at their faces.

The five Polish men simply smiled at him, conveying in their expressions that they did not speak Japanese.

"Please open up your luggage." Tamaki pointed to their weathered steamer trunks and gestured for them to open them.

There was the sound of footsteps on the ladder just then, and Detective Kaneda appeared.

Foreigners with cameras demanded special scrutiny. Nagasaki had been designated a defense perimeter, which meant that unauthorized photography anywhere in this area was prohibited.

"Mr. Kaneda," Tamaki said as the detective approached him, "These are men from Poland who don't speak Japanese. Three of them have cameras. And they don't speak English."

"That's a problem. We've got an English interpreter, but nobody connected with our station knows any Polish." With piercing eyes, Kaneda studied each of the foreigners. If these men had anything to hide, they would surely react in some way to his penetrating gaze.

There was a reaction.

One of the men—scrawny, pale-complexioned, his upper lip and chin covered by whiskers, with round glasses perched on his nose—took an envelope from his pocket and timidly held it out to Tamaki.

The customs inspector pulled a sheet of paper from the envelope and read, "These five men are Christian priests and friars from Poland. This document is to certify that they have come to Japan to carry out religious activities in Nagasaki. Please be aware that their guarantor is the Catholic Church at Ōura." It was signed, "Ōsaki Jōkichi, consular minister, Shanghai."

Tamaki thrust the document toward Detective Kaneda.

Without hesitation, Kaneda—who had a weakness for official documents—nodded broadly. "Nothing suspicious about this."

With a sigh of relief, Tamaki asked the men, "Will you be going to the church at Ōura, then?"

One of the men unexpectedly answered in Japanese, "Yes, yes."

"Oh, you understand Japanese, do you?"

"Yes, yes."

"That's a relief. I wasn't sure what to do, since I figured you didn't. Now, who do those cameras belong to?"

"Yes, yes."

"Are they yours?"

"Yes, yes."

"You aren't allowed to take any pictures in this area. This is a defense zone. Do you understand what a defense zone is?"

"Yes, yes."

"What is your name?"

"Yes, yes."

Deflated, Tamaki peered into the man's face. He returned Tamaki's gaze with a smile of unvarnished decency. Tamaki scowled and said to the detective, "I give up. I can't find anything questionable about these men."

Their steamer trunks, all but empty except for two or three books and some changes of underwear, had been thoroughly searched without locating anything suspicious.

"Fine."

Tamaki and Detective Kaneda scampered up the ladder out of third class.

The passengers began disembarking around 3:30 p.m. Pullers of rickshaws that formed a straight queue in front of the customs office at the pier kept their eyes peeled, watching for clients they could load, along with their belongings, and cart off to their destinations.

Detective Kaneda was about to return to his station when he noticed the five Polish men still standing aimlessly at the wharf. Each carried his own trunk; they seemed lost, but gave no indication that they planned to use a rickshaw.

"You there!" the detective called out.

"Yes, yes."

"You're going to the Ōura Church, right? It's that way."

"Yes, yes." The Yes-Yes foreigner gazed into Detective Kaneda's face and grinned. The remaining four, each with their own smile, were lined up behind him like a flock of little birds.

The nearly tearful smiles on the faces of the five men convinced the detective that he was going to have to lead the group to Ōura himself.

"Bunch of troublesome, beastly foreigners," he grumbled. "Never had to deal with anybody this bad before."

"Yes, yes."

Detective Kaneda grew surlier by degrees as he led the five non-Japanese-speaking Polish men up the hill toward Ōura.

They may not be suspicious, but they certainly are an annoyance!

The foreigners, carrying their trunks as the rain pelted them, panted their way up the hill, while the detective, holding the only umbrella, charged ahead, making no attempt to speak or turn back to look at them. They passed an old, deserted Western-style building with a sign reading "Amenomori Hospital." They caught sight of the ashen-colored church perched at the top of the slope. To their left stood a Buddhist temple.

Many years earlier, a man named Itō Seizaemon, a low-ranking official from the Nagasaki magistrate's office who performed functions much like those of Kaneda, had walked up and down this same hill every day. Kaneda knew nothing of Itō's existence. In those days, Itō had despised the Kirishitans;[1] Kaneda, too, felt that those Japanese who believed in the religion of the foreigners had bartered away half of their souls. Japan had its own unique way of the gods; those whom the Japanese revered as gods were the emperors who had ruled in an unbroken line throughout history.

"This is it." Breathing heavily as he reached the top of the hill, the detective looked back disparagingly at the foreigners who followed him. Having walked without a rest all the way from the harbor to this spot, carrying their trunks, the five Polish men were drenched by the rain. The man with the round glasses, moustache, and beard, evidently the oldest of the group, seemed to have some sort of health problem: his breathing was particularly labored.

"I'm heading back now," Detective Kaneda said.

"Yes, yes," the oldest man nodded and smiled. "Arigato . . . gozarimasu."

"Hmm . . . those must be the only words you know. Anyway, try to settle in here without causing too much trouble for us at police headquarters."

"Yes, yes."

---

1 Itō Seizaemon is a central character in Endō's novel *Kiku's Prayer*. Kirishitan is the Japanese term for the sixteenth- and seventeenth-century Christians in Japan, many of whom were persecuted and executed for their faith. A significant number, known as Kakure Kirishitan (hidden Christians), continued to practice their faith in secret throughout the seclusion period, but lacking the guidance of a priest, many of their rituals and beliefs diverged from orthodox Catholicism. A few Kakure remain in the vicinity of Nagasaki today. The term is used in Japanese to refer to the earliest Christian converts, from the mid-sixteenth through mid-seventeenth centuries.

After watching Kaneda's black umbrella start down the slope, the five Polish men picked up their trunks and climbed the stairs to the church.

✳ ✳ ✳

They knelt down, crossed themselves, and knit their fingers together to pray. After several moments of prayer, the man with the round glasses stood up and walked over to the statue of the Blessed Mother Mary beside the altar. He gazed intently at this image of Santa Maria.

Just then the door to the chancel opened and a Japanese nun peered in. When she noticed the five Polish men, she muttered, "Oh, goodness!" and quickly disappeared.

Soon an elderly Japanese priest, his back rather hunched, came in. He was exceedingly old.

"My, my. I hadn't thought you'd be here already. . . . The bishop and the other fathers aren't here today. . . . There was a funeral at Naka-machi." He stopped himself, remembering that these men did not understand Japanese, so in rather shaky Latin he explained to them that he was the only cleric at the church today.

"This statue of Our Lady, . . ." the bespectacled man said, "we read about this in Poland."

Piecing together some Latin words, the aged Japanese priest was, after a fashion, able to provide them with the following explanation.

"Well, you see, it's thanks to this statue of the Blessed Mother that Father Petitjean was able to locate the Japanese hidden Christians some sixty-three years ago."

Like sparrows lined up on an electrical wire, the five foreigners lifted their faces as one and looked up at the statue of Santa Maria. The Blessed Mother, with an expression as cherubic as that of a young girl, cradled her Child.

The bearded man in the round spectacles responded, "Our Order is known as the Knights of the Immaculate. We labor on behalf of Our Lady."

The aged priest had a room prepared for the men to the left of the staircase on the second floor of the rectory. The room offered a view of Nagasaki Bay and the Mitsubishi Shipyard.

"I'm sure you're exhausted. You should just rest until evening." With those words of encouragement, the old priest left them in their room.

Through the window affixed with shutters, the men took their first curious looks at the scenery of Japan.

The rain had finally stopped, and white clouds that had replaced the earlier dark clouds began to gather over the bay. Steam swirled like smoke above Mount Inasa.

A young girl with bobbed hair, her kimono tied with a lovely obi, stood by herself outside the gate of the church. She seemed to be waiting for someone.

The young Polish priest who had kept saying "yes, yes" to Detective Kaneda noticed the girl and broke into a grin. He was apparently very fond of children, and with quiet steps, so that he wouldn't be noticed by his compatriots, he left the room.

"Father Kolbe. Brother Zeno[2] has slipped away again," one of the young men—all of whom were smiling—reported to their superior.

The slender, bespectacled priest, also smiling, said, "Let him be. Talking with children is the best way to learn Japanese."

Young Brother Zeno left the rectory and went to talk to the girl.

"Goodorning."

---

2   This is Zeno Żebrowski (1898–1982), a Franciscan monk who was known for many great acts of charity toward the Japanese people, among whom he labored until his death.

What was evidently meant to be "Good morning," he mispronounced as "Goodorning." The girl looked up at the tall man warily.

"I called, Zeno." He tried reciting the Japanese phrase he had struggled to memorize before coming to Japan. "I, Zeno."

The frightened girl took a few steps backward.

"I, Zeno."

He heard footsteps, and the nun who had earlier peeked into the chancel and then gone to summon the aged priest came hurrying down the stone steps.

When the girl saw her, she ran frantically from Zeno's side, clung to the knees of the nun, and began to cry.

"Don't cry. Don't cry. I'm sorry about this," the nun awkwardly apologized to Zeno, who was looking very sad.

"Why don't you tell him your name. You can tell him that, can't you?" she prodded the girl, both arms wrapped around her like a mother hen shielding her chick with her wings. "Come now, say it."

"O-ku-ka-wa Sa-chi-ko." Peering up at Brother Zeno between the nun's arms, the girl pronounced each syllable distinctly.

"There, you said it. What a bright child!"

Emboldened by the praise, the girl loudly repeated her name. "Okukawa Sachiko."

Once Zeno realized that the child had announced her own name, he pointed to himself and jubilantly repeated, "I, Zeno. Zeno."

"This is my niece, Father."

Zeno was a brother, but the nun assumed he was a priest.

"The girl's mother is my younger sister. All of our family were born in Urakami, but this child lives with her parents in Nagasaki now."

She seemed to have made up her mind that Zeno could understand Japanese, so she rattled on at him with an affable smile.

"Sachiko, why don't you sing a song for the Father? She just loves songs, and she sings all kinds. She'd often sing for Father Matsukawa when he was here. You did, didn't you, Sachiko?"

At her aunt's urging, Sachiko launched into a Japanese song for Brother Zeno.

The sun is setting,
Glowing red;
On the hill
The temple bell is ringing.
Come take my hand
And let's all go home

Brother Zeno crouched down and closed his eyes to listen as the first Japanese girl he had ever met performed this children's song with gusto. Hearing the girl's voice in this foreign city just as the sun was setting, he felt somehow that he was experiencing authentic life. And he sensed with certainty that he had traveled from Europe to a far, far distant land.

"The sum is smetting," he sang, trying to mimic the words the girl had sung in her language. "On the hill, the temple bell is ringing."

"You remembered that very well!" The nun was impressed. Though she wore the robes of a nun, her tanned face still retained the look of a kindly, middle-aged farm woman working in the fields.

She turned at the sound of someone approaching. Another foreigner—this one thin, pasty-faced, with a beard and round glasses—stood there smiling at them. His smile was tinged with sorrow.

He directed that sad smile toward the young girl as well. Still in the nun's arms, Sachiko stopped singing and stared at the foreigner.

It was Sachiko's first meeting with this man.

2

SACHIKO

EVERYONE SAID THAT Sachiko more closely resembled her grandmother, Mitsu, than she did her own parents. It wasn't just her face. Sometimes even her mother would nod appreciatively and whisper that something Sachiko had done was "Exactly like Granny!"

But Sachiko was never pleased by such comments. "Stop saying that I look like Granny!" She would puff out her cheeks in protest. "I'm not a wrinkly old woman!"

Sachiko's family was Catholic, so instead of a Buddhist altar in their home, they had placed a crucifix on top of the dish cabinet in the parlor. Next to the crucifix was a photograph of her late grandfather and grandmother.

Her grandfather was Okukawa Kumazō, her grandmother Okukawa Mitsu. The photo had yellowed somewhat with age, but in the blurred image her grandfather, dressed in a formal haori jacket, had an exceedingly somber look on his face, while Granny was looking out at the viewer with a bashful gaze.

"The older a person gets, the more their face starts looking the way it did when they were a child," Sachiko's father explained to her. "That's why Granny's face seems childlike."

Sachiko's memories of her grandmother Mitsu's face were dim.

She did remember that once, when they were living in Motofurukawa-machi, she had been sitting on Granny's lap on the veranda, watching a puppy play. Mother had often said that Granny was the sort of person who couldn't simply walk by when she saw some abandoned creature, be it a puppy or a kitten. "There were times she'd sneak her own dinner to a stray cat," Sachiko reminisced.

Curiously, the only stories Sachiko had heard from Granny that lingered in her memory were the ones she had related as Sachiko sat on her lap watching the frolicking puppy.

"I was about the same age you are now, Sachiko. In the Nakano district of Urakami, Kiku and I found a stray dog and brought it home, but our folks wouldn't let us keep it, so we did the only thing we could do: Kiku and I secretly took care of the puppy."

"Who was Kiku?"

Granny looked suddenly distressed and whispered as she looked at her granddaughter. "Kiku was my cousin, a few years older than me."

"Wow, then she must be *really* old!"

"She's not really old. A long time ago, Santa Maria at the Ōura Church took Kiku to heaven."

"The Santa Maria at the Ōura Church?"

"That's right. That Santa Maria." Granny nodded forcefully, confidently, as she spoke.

Sachiko still clearly remembered that conversation with her grandmother. And every Sunday when she went to mass with her parents and brother at the Ōura Church and saw that statue of the Blessed Mother to the right of the altar, she thought of that conversation.

One day she asked her mother, "Did you ever meet Kiku?"

"I didn't," her mother responded with a suspicious glance. "Who told you about Kiku?"

"Tell me about her."

Sachiko couldn't clearly remember when she had started pestering her mother to hear more about Kiku. But often at Sunday mass, as she knelt with her parents in prayer, she would gaze at the statue of the Blessed Mother and think about Kiku.

"I'll tell you about Kiku once you've grown up," her mother had told her.

"Why won't you tell me now?"

"You're still too young."

A comment like that only fanned Sachiko's curiosity. Granny had whispered to her that Santa Maria had taken Kiku to heaven. What sort of bond had existed between Santa Maria and Kiku?

Those were the thoughts in Sachiko's head as she gazed at the Blessed Mother, who nestled the Baby Jesus in her arms and looked down at Him with girlish, angelic eyes. The expression on the face of the Blessed Mother changed when viewed from different angles.

An innocent face. A startled face. A quizzical face. A joyful face. A lonely face.

When she mentioned to her mother, "That Blessed Mother has lots of different faces, doesn't she?" her mother's response was an indifferent "Oh, really?"

Their homeward route after mass took them down the slope from the church past the Amenomori Hospital. Sachiko liked walking this path. There was something in the atmosphere of this area that made it seem as though it wasn't Japan, but instead some foreign land.

"The director of this hospital has a daughter who plays the piano extremely well," her mother told Sachiko. Both of Sachiko's parents were Catholic, and since childhood they, as Sachiko did now, had climbed this slope every Sunday to participate in the mass at the Ōura Church. They were well acquainted with the history of the area.

"One of the foreigners ran a hotel here. It was called the Cliff House Hotel. After she died, the residence was bought by Doctor Amenomori, who turned it into a hospital."[1]

When Sachiko was three or four years old, the Amenomori Hospital was moved to Shin-machi. Later, several foreign priests and monks started up a printing operation in the vacated building.

One of those monks was Brother Zeno, the one Sachiko had taught the children's song to. Another was the man with the round spectacles who always looked exhausted.

One Sunday after mass, Brother Zeno noticed Sachiko walking by, and with a broad smile on his face, he poked his head out the window and called "Sachiko-san, hello!" He was wearing an apron.

"My job, making food for everyone here. Busy, busy!" he told Sachiko, as though he were conveying some vital secret. Brother Zeno was often heard saying, "Busy, busy!" Sometimes, when Brother Zeno talked with Sachiko through the window, she caught a glimpse of the bespectacled old priest peering out at her with a forlorn expression on his face.

There was hardly room to walk inside the printing building, which was crammed with tables piled with movable type, printing presses, and stacks of pamphlets tied in bundles. The old priest sometimes looked like an ominous shadow in that dark, greasy-smelling room.

In all honesty, Sachiko preferred the cheerful Brother Zeno to the old priest. The older man seemed kindly, but there was something sorrowful about him.

Sometimes the priest would say to her, "Sachiko, please love Blessed Mother Mary." But his Japanese was so much worse than

---

1 Charlotte Walker established the hotel in 1896; it was sold to Doctor Amenomori in 1922.

that of Brother Zeno that she wasn't really sure what he was saying.

"I don't like that priest very much," she confided to her mother.

"Why not?"

"He always looks like he's about to cry. Brother Zeno's a lot more fun!"

"The priest's name is Father Kolbe. He's come to Japan from very far away, so I'm sure he's quite lonely. That must be why he always looks so sad."

That made Sachiko feel as though she had said something very bad.

One Sunday Father Kolbe called to Sachiko through the window. "Sachiko, give you this." He gave her a bookmark with a sacred image on it, one of many such bookmarks imprinted with a famous painting of Jesus or a portrait of Mary, with scriptures from the Bible written underneath.

The bookmark that Father Kolbe gave her had a depiction of the Blessed Mother gazing with pained eyes at the body of Jesus, which had been taken down from the cross. A scripture in Japanese read, "Greater love than this no man hath, that a man lay down his life for his friends."[2]

Sachiko was only six at the time, so it was impossible for her to grasp the meaning of the scripture. But an image given by a Father was not to be treated carelessly in the homes of believers, so Sachiko carefully placed it in her little box of treasures. It was actually a chocolate box, its lid decorated with a snowy scene from Switzerland, a place she had never seen.

---

2   I have used the Douay-Rheims translation of the Bible, taken from the Latin Vulgate, for renditions of scriptural quotations in the novel. The Douay-Rheims has long been one of the favorite Bible translations in the English-speaking Catholic Church. This particular verse reads the same in both the Douay-Rheims and the Challoner revision.

Eventually Father Kolbe, along with Brother Zeno and his other followers, moved out of the building on the Ōura hill. Their move took place in May, when Nagasaki's landscape was virtually buried beneath green leaves.

On the Sunday prior to their move, Sachiko was talking with Brother Zeno after mass.

"Sachiko-san. You know Hongōchi?"

"Nope."

"I move to Hongōchi."

As always, the bespectacled old priest with the sad smile listened in the background to their conversation.

After their move, every time Sachiko walked past the empty building she felt a loss, as though a decayed tooth had been yanked from her mouth. But with time, as she grew accustomed to the feeling of emptiness, she eventually forgot all about Father Kolbe and Brother Zeno.

She had forgotten them, but the bookmark with the holy image was still carefully preserved in her chocolate box. The bookmark with the scripture, "Greater love than this no man hath, that a man lay down his life for his friends."

Although it wasn't due to the influence of this verse, in the spring when Sachiko entered third grade, she startled the adults by doing something courageous on her way home from mass.

That day after mass, Sachiko's mother said to her, "You can make it home alone, can't you? Your father and I have something we need to talk to the priest about, so can you go on ahead and make breakfast?"

As a third grader, she was already able to look after her younger brother, Mitsuo. With help from her mother, she could also boil rice and heat up the miso soup.

"Uh-huh."

"Be careful not to start a fire."

Mitsuo wanted to stay with their mother, so Sachiko headed down the hill by herself.

It was spring, and petals from the cherry trees danced in the wind. From the top of the hill she saw that a large ship had docked in Nagasaki Bay.

Just as she was passing the old wooden building where Brother Zeno and Father Kolbe had once lived, she heard the yapping of a dog and someone's frantic wailing. The clamor was coming from the garden of the old deserted building.

A foreign boy was backed up against the crumbling wall, his tear-streaked face contorted in fear. A large black stray dog with a wrinkled snout was baying at him.

It was certain that the black dog would pounce on him if the foreign boy tried to flee.

Sachiko froze in alarm. The moment she realized what was happening, she turned to look for an adult to help.

But she couldn't see a single adult on the hill where the cherry petals danced. The more the boy wailed, the more the stray bared its sharp fangs and yelped.

Sachiko's parents had often told her, "You have to help your brother or any other little child who needs help." And in meetings with the children, the priests had taught, "Helping the weak is what we as Christians do."

But it wasn't because of what her parents or the priests had taught her that Sachiko positioned herself between the foreign boy and the dog.

She simply had to do something to help whenever she saw a pitiful person or a wretched animal. Apparently, the blood of her Granny Mitsu flowed in her veins as well, impelling her to try to help the foreign boy.

But Sachiko was still in the third grade. Her first response to tangling with a dog was fear, and she wasn't sure what she should do. So she hugged the foreign boy tightly and screamed along with him. Then she frantically hurled rocks at the dog.

One rock struck the dog's snout. At first it recoiled and backed away, but then it came charging back at them with increased ferocity.

Just then, several adults came running to help. After they chased the dog away, they were startled when Sachiko, who was still clinging to the foreign boy, broke into an ear-splitting wail herself. It was her way of saying, "I'm safe!"

"Don't cry. The dog has run away." Dumbfounded, the adults tried unsuccessfully to calm Sachiko, and their consternation mounted when the foreign boy in her arms began to howl.

Sachiko was supposed to be headed home, but instead she ran back to the church.

"What in the world is wrong with you? Haven't you gone home yet?" Her mother scolded her, but after she heard Sachiko's story, she said, "That dog didn't bite you . . . because of the mercy of Lord Jesus. It would have been awful if that had been a rabid dog."

That afternoon, while Sachiko was playing in front of her house with her brother and some of the other children from the neighborhood, a foreign woman appeared, led there by a Japanese man. The man was one of the adults who had rescued Sachiko and the boy from the dog attack.

"Ah, that's the girl there," the man said, and then said something to the foreign woman. A beaming smile spread across the woman's face, and after jabbering something incomprehensible to Sachiko, she suddenly hugged the girl and kissed her on the cheek.

The other children watched this scene in incredulity.

"Where's your house? You have a father and mother, don't you?" the Japanese man asked. Sachiko did not respond, but her brother pointed to their house and said, "It's that one."

The two adults went into Sachiko's house. She had never been so ashamed of how small and run-down their house was.

A few minutes later, Sachiko and the neighborhood children watched wide-eyed as her grateful parents escorted the two visitors from the house, bowing to them over and over again. The foreign woman gave Sachiko another kiss and waved goodbye before leaving with the Japanese man.

Sachiko's grinning father said, "That foreign woman is the mother of the boy you helped today. She gave us a big box of chocolates!"

That evening, Sachiko and her brother got into an argument about ownership rights to the box of chocolates and were reprimanded by their parents.

An incident occurred foreshadowing the dark period that would come to Japan domestically and overseas. This was the year the Japanese Army, which had already occupied Manchuria, laid plans to invade northern China.

But Sachiko knew nothing about such things. Besides, as Christmas approached, she received an unexpected invitation.

It came from the foreign family. A letter arrived inviting her to visit them on the afternoon of Christmas Day. The letter was written in impeccable Japanese, but it was a different hand that had signed "Mrs. Walker" in English. Mrs. Walker was, of course, the mother of the boy Sachiko had rescued.

In the homes of Christian families such as Sachiko's, even though they were Japanese, Christmas was a more enjoyable and important holiday than New Year's.

It was the usual practice for Christian families to attend church on the day before Christmas. Inside small enclosures in one corner of the sanctuary, they would each confess their sins to the priest. One by one, Sachiko and her brother knelt in the confessional of the Ōura Church and related to the best of their recollection their wrongdoings: "I talked back to my parents,"

"I got into a fight with my brother," "I got into a fight with my sister." Since Sachiko had very few transgressions that she could remember, the priest asked irritably, "Is there nothing else?"

All she could think of in response was a made-up fault: "Well . . . I had too much to eat." The priest rebuked her for mentioning something so trivial.

Near midnight, as the bell of the church echoed in the starry sky, Sachiko and her family climbed the hill. It was an hour when ordinarily they would be sleeping, but Sachiko and her brother were in high spirits because of their excitement over Christmas Eve.

Deep in the night prior to Christmas Day, the priest offered up mass. The flames of many candles flickered at the altar, and the church was tightly packed with believers while the nuns, including Sachiko's aunt, sang hymns. Surrounded by the singing voices and the lights from the candles, the statue of the Blessed Mother Mary faced the congregation, her large eyes opened wide. Included among the worshipers were some who had come from Urakami; their grandparents had similarly joined their hands in prayer at the feet of the statue of the Blessed Mother. Three generations of Sachiko's family had shared a fondness for this church, this altar, and this image of the Immaculata.

When the midnight mass was over, they returned to their homes and fell into a deep sleep. But Sachiko awakened early that morning, her heart pounding with anticipation and anxiety when she thought about her invitation to the home of the foreigners this Sabbath afternoon.

That afternoon her father, carrying a bag of mandarin oranges as a thank-you gift, helped Sachiko locate the Walker family home near the church. The sound of a piano playing and the laughter of children echoed from the Western-style wooden house.

"Thank you . . . thank you for coming!" Mrs. Walker greeted them in stumbling Japanese at the doorway. Behind her, Sachiko recognized the curiosity-filled face of the boy she had helped, along with his older brother. To her young mind, the bag of oranges that her father handed to their host seemed all too poor a gift.

Besides the foreign boys, there were several Japanese children dressed in Sunday finery waiting in the parlor. At first Sachiko held back, but she joined in as Mrs. Walker played the piano, then stopped, and the children scrambled to flop down in chairs, and soon she was completely caught up in the lively atmosphere.

When her father came to pick her up that evening, she proudly called out the names of the foreign boys, "Bye-bye, Van![3] Bye-bye, Jim!"

For the next two or three days, all she could talk about with her friends at school, the neighborhood children, and her parents was the good time she had had at the Walker home.

In the parlor where the children had played were sofas the likes of which Sachiko had never sat on, tables, and a chandelier hanging from the ceiling with dozens of little candlesticks.

The neighboring room was a dining room with a large, glass-doored china cabinet. It was filled with Japanese plates and vases that Mrs. Walker had collected.

"The boy who was crying because of the barking dog is named Van. He's such a brat. But he's cute. He hung onto my arm with both hands, and he took to me right away. His brother Jim's two years older than me. He's quiet, but his Japanese is amazing!"

She repeated the same stories so often that her brother and friends, who had initially looked on her with envy, began avoiding her.

---

3 Endō frequently inserted the names of his friends and associates—including his translator—into his stories as a sort of inside joke.

"You've got to stop. We're all tired of hearing about it," her mother admonished Sachiko with a droll smile. Still, she was pleased that these Americans had substituted for God in giving Sachiko the best Christmas present ever.

On New Year's Eve, it was so warm in the morning that the sun was blinding, but the temperature dropped abruptly in the afternoon and white flakes began swirling from the sky. It was the first snow of the year.

Sachiko went with her mother to do shopping for the New Year's celebrations. Street stalls had been set up all around, selling fat round mochi cakes, pine-branch decorations for doorways, persimmons on skewers, and forked ferns.[4] Women wearing shawls and carrying shopping bags, and men shrouded in Inverness capes clustered at shops where New Year's delicacies were sold. A record shop was playing a song performed by Fujiyama Ichirō.[5]

Her mother was trying to decide whether to buy a particular pine-branch decoration when Sachiko tugged on her sleeve.

"Over there! Isn't that Father Kolbe and Brother Zeno over there?"

Her mother looked in the direction Sachiko was pointing. There in the midst of a large crowd of people, Father Kolbe and Brother Zeno, dressed in their cassocks, were handing out pamphlets to the passersby.

"Is this free?" one man asked Brother Zeno.

"Yes, yes, free."

---

4 These items are all associated with the celebration of the New Year's holidays in Japan; the mochi pounded rice, pines, and ferns symbolize offerings to the gods and prayers for a prosperous year to come.

5 Fujiyama (1911–1993) was a popular singer and composer noted for his high baritone voice and sentimental lyrics.

"I'll take one if it's free. But even if I read it, I'm not becoming one of you Amen types. Japan has its own Japanese religion." The man scornfully poked the pamphlet into the pocket of his cape and walked off.

Some glanced briefly at the pamphlet and handed it back, while others tossed it away as they continued on. Still others trampled on the discarded pamphlets with their muddy wooden geta clogs as they scurried past.

"Father Kolbe looks just as sickly as ever, doesn't he?" Sachiko said to her mother, sighing.

"Go and say hello to them."

Sachiko was embarrassed, but she stood up straight and approached the two men.

"Oh, it's Sachiko!" Brother Zeno noticed her and called out in a voice filled with joy and nostalgia. Hearing that, Father Kolbe narrowed his eyes behind his round glasses and, with a smile, said, "Sachiko, konichiwa!"

The passersby stared at Sachiko. She felt very awkward.

"Sachiko, you say your prayers?"

"Yes."

"You speak with the Blessed Mother?"

Sachiko did not reply.

"You must speak with Blessed Mother. Children . . . love . . . mothers. We . . . love . . . Blessed Mother."

Father Kolbe became aware of the Japanese looking strangely at them and continued handing out pamphlets, "Read please. Please."

"What's this about?" a middle-aged man asked Brother Zeno.

"Many good things written here."

"I don't know what you mean by 'good things.' What good things does it talk about?"

Brother Zeno became aware of the man's foul breath and said, "You smell liquor. You smell. Liquor . . . no good. Your tummy cry. Milk good."

"What gibberish!" The middle-aged man angrily hurled the pamphlet away and disappeared into the throng.

"Bye-bye, Father Kolbe, Brother Zeno."

"Sachiko, pray to Blessed Mother!" Father Kolbe repeated.

As Sachiko and her mother were about to leave, the middle-aged man who reeked of liquor suddenly reappeared and called out to them, "Are you part of that Amen bunch?"

Sachiko's mother looked at the man fearfully and tugged on her daughter's arm. "Let's go," and tried to walk away.

"Christianity is a foreign religion. How wonderful for you to follow the religion of the foreigners while our troops are bleeding and dying in Manchuria. Don't you feel any guilt toward them?"

The man's breath reeked of stale sake, just as Brother Zeno had said.

"Come on, let's go." This time, Sachiko's mother pulled more firmly at her arm.

"It won't be long before you Amen bunch'll be labeled as traitors!" The man screamed his final insult.

As young as she was, even Sachiko felt deeply wounded. Walking alongside her mother, she asked, "Why would he say something like that?" Her mother was silent.

That evening, her father invited Sachiko to go to the public bath with him. Carrying their soap and towels as they headed toward the bathhouse, Sachiko asked, "What does 'traitor' mean?"

"'Traitor'?" Her father stopped in surprise. He was a docile man, a shipyard laborer who tried earnestly to live his Catholic beliefs. "Where do you come up with questions like that?"

Sachiko explained what she and her mother had experienced that day.

"Are we traitors for going to church?"

"Don't be silly. What could be traitorous about that? Just laugh that nonsense off."

"But then, why did that man say that people who go to church are traitors?"

But as her father soaked alongside Sachiko in the bathhouse tub, a dark shadow crossed his face as he pondered what his daughter had said. In the three years since war had broken out in Manchuria, some of his coworkers at the shipyard had started saying the same sorts of things about the Christian employees. Since several of the locals among the laborers came from families who had practiced Christianity for generations, they banded together to counter these taunts, but the attacks would no doubt intensify over the coming days.

"Sachiko," her father said on their way home from the bathhouse, "You know that your Gramps and Granny come from Urakami, don't you?"

"I know."

"But you haven't heard about the trek of the Urakami exiles, have you?"

"No. What's that?"

"I'll tell you about it tonight."

That night, Sachiko's father told her and her younger brother (although Mitsuo fell asleep halfway through the story) about the fourth raid on Urakami.[6]

"The Christians in Urakami endured a lot of suffering. They were exiled to places all over Japan, and every day was filled with pain for them." He seemed to be less telling Sachiko than trying to give courage to his own heart. "But they never gave up their belief in Lord Jesus and the Blessed Mother."

---

6   As one of the centers of the underground practice of Christianity after the religion was banned by the Tokugawa shogunate, Urakami was first raided by the authorities in 1790, followed by raids in 1839 and 1856. The fourth and final raid occurred in 1867, just as Japan was opening its doors to foreign nations. Despite pressure from Western governments to end the ban, scores of hidden Christians were exiled and tortured until the prohibition was lifted in 1873. This fourth raid is detailed in Endō's novel *Kiku's Prayer*.

"Then," Sachiko, her eyes ablaze, asked, "Gramps kept his belief, too?"

"Ah, Gramps . . ." Her father was unnerved for a moment, but then made up his mind, "Actually, at first he got scared and ran away. But then he became a believer again, and everyone was very proud of him."

"And Granny?"

"Granny became a Christian after she married Gramps."

"What about Kiku?"

Her father hadn't been expecting that question.

"I don't know much of Kiku's story. You'd better ask your mother."

His aim had been to tell his daughter and son about all the undeserved persecution and indignities that their ancestors had endured to preserve their faith. But Sachiko wasted no time turning the subject of the conversation to Kiku.

She rushed into the kitchen where her mother was working and badgered her, "Tell me about Kiku! Papa told me to ask you about her."

"Kiku was your Granny's older cousin." While drying the dishes, she had overheard her husband explaining to their children what had happened at Urakami, so she began to tell Kiku's story. There was no longer any reason to keep it from Sachiko now that she was in the third grade.

"When she was a young girl, Kiku fell in love with a fellow named Seikichi from the Nakano District of Urakami."

"Seikichi?"

"That's right. After she grew to be a young woman, she started working at a shop in Nagasaki, but she didn't ever forget Seikichi."

"Really?!" As she listened to her mother, Sachiko felt somehow both astonished and uncomfortable. A girl her own age had fallen in love with a young man.

Sachiko had experienced such feelings for boys from time to time, but they never lasted long. When they ended up in different classes at school or the boys moved away, she soon forgot them.

As she turned the faucet on and off and wiped off the dishes, Sachiko's mother related the story of Kiku's brief life. Since her daughter was still in third grade, however, she skipped over portions of the narrative that needed to be appropriately concealed.

Tears began to collect in Sachiko's eyes as she listened to the story. They reached the part where Seikichi was put into a cell at Tsuwano. There he worked himself to the bone, to the point of becoming ill, just so that he could send little gifts to Kiku.

"Then what? Then what?" she breathlessly pleaded with her mother to continue.

"That's when the Blessed Mother Mary at Ōura took Kiku to heaven. Kiku wasn't a Christian, but we heard that Kiku died at the feet of the statue of Mary in the church. The Blessed Mother would never abandon her after that."

"So you mean that Kiku is in heaven now?"

"Of course she is."

"Then Kiku died for Seikichi, the man she loved? And she's in heaven now?"

Sachiko remembered the tiny picture she had received from Father Kolbe. Now that she was in the third grade, she was able to read the words from the Bible that were written beneath that image: "Greater love than this no man hath, that a man lay down his life for his friends."

It was difficult for a ten-year-old girl to grasp the meaning of those words. But in her own way, Sachiko decided that they somehow described Kiku.

"Mom, loving someone is different from just caring about them, isn't it?"

There were times recently when Sachiko would blurt out some unusual question like this, surprising and confounding her parents.

"A child your age doesn't need to understand such things."

"I'm asking because the priests are always talking about love." Sachiko purposely unnerved her mother by insisting that the Fathers frequently used the word "love" in their sermons at mass. In truth, she already knew the occasions when adults used the word "love." The songs performed on radios in the village by Fujiyama Ichirō and Watanabe Hamako[7] often sang of "love," and boys at her school would often tease girls by announcing, "I love you!"

But her mother's face was serious as she said, "Love. . . . So let's say, when you or your brother gets sick, Momma worries about you, right? And we pray to God that you will be good children. And I make dinner for all of you every day. That's the kind of love a parent has for her children."

"So it's the same as caring about us, huh?"

"Well, yes, it's the same. But caring very deeply about someone is called love."

"Then, Kiku . . ." To satisfy her own curiosity, and to see her mother's reaction, Sachiko asked, "Then Kiku loved Seikichi, didn't she?"

Her mother said nothing.

"She did, didn't she? She really loved him."

With a peculiar look on her face, Sachiko's mother gave no response. She wasn't sure whether Sachiko was innocent and understood nothing, or whether she was mocking her mother.

---

7 Watanabe (1910–1999), a native of Yokohama, was a singer whose popularity extended from the prewar through the postwar periods.

Sachiko still didn't know what to make of the word "love." But the word definitely had something about it that made her heart pound, while at the same time making her feel embarrassed.

Each Sunday thereafter, when she went to the Ōura Church with her parents and brother, she would look at the statue of the Blessed Mother and think about how Kiku had died for Seikichi.

I wonder what she looked like. She had heard that Granny would often talk about how pretty Kiku was, with her almond-shaped eyes.

What kind of young man was this Seikichi that this pretty girl had loved so much?

Kneeling in the posture of prayer, Sachiko thought about the couple. But then she would realize that her mind was caught up with something other than the words of the mass, and she would blush with shame.

"If Kiku has gone to heaven," she muttered to herself, "then I'm going to ask the Blessed Mother to help me study and have lots of good things happen to me."

The Blessed Mother, at whose feet Kiku had died, looked out with a pure and cherubic gaze at the congregants in the church.

3

A SPY

AT A YAKITORI street stall jammed among many others along the riverbank, Detectives Kaneda and Ono were chomping on yakitori skewers and watching the old chef wash up his cooking utensils.

"Would you officers watch the stall for just a minute? I've got to go draw some water." He was holding a bucket in each hand.

"Sure."

"I'll be right back."

After the old man had disappeared, Kaneda sucked on his sauce-covered fingers. "Ono, I assume the chief talked to you today. About infiltrating that operation run by the Polish priests."

"Yes, he gave me my orders," Ono, a young officer, nodded. He was slender-faced, with a pasty complexion; no one would have taken him for a police detective.

"When those priests arrived in Nagasaki from Shanghai, I took them up to the Ōura Church."

"You did?"

"I didn't think there was anything suspicious about them at the time. But now that we've had that letter . . . I'm the one who recommended to the chief that you worm your way in there and find out what they're up to."

"That's what he told me. Do you think there's much substance to what the letter said?"

"Dunno. But times being what they are, we can't let our guard down with foreigners just because they look harmless on the surface." Kaneda downed a cup of saké in one gulp as he lectured his young comrade. "Before you came to the Nagasaki Station, there was this Simonov affair. He was a Russian defector who'd lived a long time in Nagasaki, and all the Japanese called him 'Simonov-san, Simonov-san,' . . . He opened a tea shop at Hama-no-machi and sold sweets. But we got a letter with accusations about him, so we looked into it, and it turned out that he was taking all kinds of photographs of Nagasaki Bay and the Sasebo Naval Station, so he was deported. No matter how courteous they look, no matter how smooth they are, you never know what's going on behind the scenes. You read the complaint about the priests, didn't you?"

"Yes, I did."

"The letter claims they're getting together in the middle of the night and doing something in secret. And that they're handing out pamphlets they've printed trying to stir up antiwar sentiments. Of course, half of these kinds of complaints come from people who think everything they see is a bogeyman, but the other half generally have some truth to them."

"Yes, sir." Detective Ono nodded deferentially, but he was only half-listening to this aimless sermon. He knew that Kaneda was using this opportunity to impart his admonitions as a means of dispelling many years of melancholy. Detective Kaneda had been a police officer for a great while, but he had never been a great officer.

"Since we've received a complaint, we can't just ignore it."

"No, sir."

"So, do your best."

Ono could barely contain his amusement when Detective Kaneda spoke as though he were the station chief himself.

The old cook returned. The two policemen quickly changed the topic of their conversation to a discussion of this year's Kunchi Festival.[1]

✳ ✳ ✳

On Saturday afternoon, Ono put on a gray uniform with a stand-up collar, picked up a stack of books wrapped in a furoshiki cloth, and set out for Nishihama-no-machi. He knew that anyone seeing him with his shaved head and uniform would take him for an earnest struggling student or a shipyard worker.

At Nishihama-no-machi, the foreigners were handing out pamphlets to the passersby. Ono reasoned that the most natural, least suspicious way to insinuate himself among them was to take one of their pamphlets and casually engage them in conversation.

Hama-no-machi and Nishihama-no-machi were the main thoroughfares in Nagasaki. Shops were jostled together on both sides of the streets, and the winter wind noisily ruffled the flag waving above a movie theater. Boxes of mandarin oranges were stacked outside the fruit stands, and from a record shop came the saccharine sound of a woman's voice singing the sentimental song, "If the Moon Were a Mirror." But there was something gloomy lurking beneath the city.

That gloomy mood pervaded Nagasaki. It came from a foreboding that Japan was falling into the bottom of a dark ravine.

Although the fighting had ceased in Manchuria, Japan had subsequently withdrawn from the League of Nations and become a foundling in the world. Domestically, during the past two or three years, right-wing fanatics had carried out the assassinations

---

1 A popular festival held each autumn in Nagasaki, blending Dutch and Chinese elements, that originated in the early seventeenth century.

of several cabinet members and laid plans to stage a coup d'état;
concurrently, the Communist Party was being methodically
suppressed and many of its members arrested. Though none of
the people could say anything concrete about what would become of Japan, there was a sense that everything was advancing in a direction that would lead to something deeply tragic,
and that sense planted a foreboding of gloom in the people's
hearts.

Winter winds stirring up dust at every street crossing. Flags
flapping loudly atop movie theaters. The masked face of the star
of Takarazuka Cinema, Ramon Mitsusaburō,[2] painted in gaudy
colors on billboards.

Today, too, the foreigners stood immovable against those
winds.

"Please read. It help you." The foreigners called out to passersby in shaky Japanese, but of late—perhaps because they no
longer had interest in what these foreigners had to offer—few
Japanese would stop to speak with them.

"Please read."

A middle-aged woman smiled feebly and shook her head at
one of the proffered pamphlets. The strongly built foreigner de-
jectedly pulled back his outstretched hand.

Ono stopped to speak to them and, with a solemn face, said,
"I read your pamphlet the other day. . . . And . . . I . . . I'd like to
hear what you have to say. Where can I come to talk with you?"

The faces of the foreigners beamed with joy.

"Please come our house."

"Where is it?"

"In Hongōchi. Where is reservoir."

---

2   Taking his theatrical name from popular Mexican silent film actor Ramón
    Navarro, Mitsusaburō (1901–1976) made nearly three hundred films—
    mostly chambara-style sword-fighting movies—between 1927 and his re-
    tirement in 1963.

Ono already knew this information. The location, the precise house in which they lived, and how many were living there together—this was all found in the investigative report prepared at police headquarters.

"When is a good time to visit you?"

"Yes, anytime. We there in afternoon."

As promised, Ono called at their home in Hongōchi the following day.

He got off the bus on the mountain road and walked a short distance. He looked at the reservoir that provided drinking water for the people of Nagasaki, brimming with bluish-black water and motionless as a swamp. On the slope of the mountain ahead of him stood a mortared building topped by a cross that caught the rays of the winter sun. This was where the Polish men lived.

When he pulled on the hanging rope that served as a doorbell, there was no response for a few moments until he heard the dull flapping of work shoes. A scruffy-faced brother poked his head through a small window in the door.

Hearing what Ono wanted, the brother opened the door and let him into the building. He was left waiting for a time in the humble parlor.

Eventually a priest wearing round spectacles came in and sat down across from Ono. The priest's complexion somehow suggested total exhaustion.

"You want to work here?" the priest unceremoniously asked. Caught off guard, Ono could only reply, "Am I allowed to work here?"

"Yes, please work here. Many people came here. Worked."

"Can I live here, too?"

"Yes. If you live same life as us, you can live here." The priest's Japanese couldn't be called fluent, but he was able to get his meaning across. Ono had difficulty weighing the true intentions of this man, who was willing to let a stranger live and work here without learning anything about him.

I wonder if he knows I'm a detective?

But there was no indication in the priest's eyes that he had any doubts about Ono.

This was more than Ono could have hoped for. And it was the priest who had proposed it all.

But don't get too comfortable with them. This might be part of their plan to camouflage what they're doing.

Ono recalled what he had been taught by a superior officer in the training he received when he was assigned to the Special Police unit. That particular officer had been able to infiltrate a cell of the Communist Party as a spy two years earlier.

It's most dangerous when they look as though they're letting their guard down. At times like that, you should just assume they're laying a trap for you.

Ono wondered whether the priest had casually agreed to let him live here in order to keep an eye on him.

"When should I plan on moving here?"

"Anytime."

"Then, tomorrow is okay?"

"Yes, anytime."

"What will I be doing here?"

"Work along with everyone. We have work in garden. We have printing of books."

The priest offered to show him around the building.

As they walked side by side, Ono abruptly asked, "If someone like me who you don't even know moved in here and turned out to be untrustworthy, what would you do?"

"There is nothing here. Thief be very disappointed."

"What's your name?"

"I'm Father Kolbe."

Several days passed. For a nonbeliever like Ono, everything was bewildering.

Nothing there could be called extravagant. Every single hour of the day was strictly scheduled so that no time would be wasted.

The wake-up bell sounded at 5:00 a.m. At 6:00 they left the building that served as their living quarters and went to attend mass in the church that occupied the same plot of land. At 7:00, breakfast. The meal consisted of only bread and coffee, without any butter or cheese or fruit.

The workday began at 7:30. Assignments to work in the garden or to do carpentry, sewing, printing, and office work were predetermined. They worked four hours in the morning, five in the afternoon. Time was also set aside for meditation and prayer.

Ono was granted his request to work in the office where the pamphlets were printed. He anticipated that, unlike gardening or sewing, if he worked in the printing office, he was much more likely to find out why they were printing and distributing the pamphlets.

As he sat in a handmade chair in the church, mimicking the actions of the others while observing the mass, Ono tried to memorize the names and faces of each man who lived there. Of the twenty-five men, four were Japanese and the remaining twenty-one were Polish. Ono wrote down the distinguishing characteristics of each man in his notebook.

He worked quietly in the printing office in an effort to gain the trust of the men. There was a thirty-minute break at 3:00 p.m. Some days, an appallingly nasty coffee was provided for them. It was Polish coffee made from barley.

One day, Ono asked a Polish brother who always poured the coffee for the men, "What did you do when you were young?" The brother was tall, with enormous hands and a body the very picture of hardiness.

"My father, a farmer. After primary school, I work in tailor shop," the brother replied, with some embarrassment.

Ono had the sense that this fellow wasn't alone, that the majority of the brothers had come from poor farming families in Poland. Perhaps that was why they all had robust bodies but seemed the very embodiment of simplicity.

"Why did you come to Japan?"

The man shrugged his shoulders. "Father Kolbe say we should come. So came to Japan." That was the sum total of his reply.

When Ono asked the other brothers, they all said that Kolbe had chosen them and that they had come to Japan via Siberia.

Father Kolbe, the man with the round spectacles and pale complexion, occasionally had a coughing spell, but he continued to pick out printer blocks alongside the other workers.

"Father Kolbe, not healthy," one of the brothers whispered to Ono.

"He does cough a lot, now that you mention it."

"Father Kolbe, even have fever, even tired, keep working."

"Why is he so reckless?"

The brother merely shrugged his shoulders.

✳ ✳ ✳

Ono came to understand that Father Kolbe was the key person at this monastery.

The men all belonged to the Franciscan Order, but it was Father Kolbe who had come up with the idea of doing missionary work in Japan. He had initially left Poland and traveled to this far eastern land, bringing four of the brothers with him.

Their primary work was publishing a pamphlet called *Knights of the Immaculata* and trying to persuade as many Japanese as possible to read it. Father Kolbe had devised this plan and was in charge of carrying it out.

Once he obtained this information, Ono began to keep a close eye on Father Kolbe, observing from a distance this nondescript, pale, skinny priest. He was convinced that if he could fathom this man's movements, he would be able to determine whether these foreigners were engaged in any hostile activities.

"Is he sick? He seems to cough a lot," he mentioned to a brother named Zeno.

"Father Kolbe, chest is bad. But, not sleep much. Not eat much." Zeno replied with a sad face.

Just as Zeno had said, Ono noticed Father Kolbe sometimes hacking dryly while he worked. It was obvious from the clouding of his eyes that he had a fever, but he seemed to be working through it.

"If he's that ill, why doesn't he eat well? Why doesn't he rest?"

"Father Kolbe always say: When we get to God's place, then we rest plenty."

"God's place?" An atheist himself, Ono could only grin sardonically at the incredible foolishness of such a notion.

Do these men honestly believe that there really is a God? Ono considered it the height of stupidity in these modern times to believe in anything like God. He was one of many Japanese who could only believe in those things he could discern with his eyes. To him, God and heaven were products of the human imagination, conjured up to escape the contradictions of the present day or the fear of death. Of course, as a detective with the Special Police unit, he despised Marxism, but he could concur with Marx's observation that religion is an opiate.

These men are wasting their entire lives for a make-believe God. Ono looked on with pity as the men labored in the garden or wrestled with the printing press. Here they were, separated from their homeland, traveling the great distance to Japan, and working themselves to the bone every day; these were meaningless lives.

You fools are being manipulated by something that doesn't even exist! he wanted to say to Father Kolbe and to Zeno and the other brothers. But he recognized that doing so was unrelated to his purpose there, so he didn't display even the slightest indication that he considered them delusional.

He was convinced that none of the men were aware of why he was there. But one day, as he was passing a Japanese brother named Yoshikawa in the hallway, the man said, "Mr. Ono, . . . you've practiced martial arts, haven't you?"

Ono caught his breath for a moment and peered at the man, but then he smiled and said, "Martial arts? Oh, I just did a little kendo back in the day."

"I knew it! I figured, the way the hair at your temples is thinning is because of the mask you wear. And you've practiced judo, too, haven't you? You walk a little bow-legged."

"I only dabbled in it, mostly just for fun. Is that way of walking I picked up still noticeable?" Ono was uneasy. How far had this brother seen into his ruse, and how much had he figured out? But the man's smile showed no suspicion.

"Well, . . . I did do a little training with the bamboo sword when I was in middle school," Yoshikawa replied. "To tell you the truth, when I first saw you, I thought maybe you were a policeman or some right-wing fanatic."

"A policeman? A right-winger?"

"Yes, we once had a right-wing extremist come snooping around our monastery. He claimed that all the 'Jesus types' were suspect because we believe in a foreign religion."

"So then," Ono swallowed and asked, "How did you deal with this guy?"

"Deal?" The brother acted as though it was perfectly obvious. "We let him dig around all he wanted. In the end we said nothing and acted as though he wasn't even here. There's nothing to find here, no matter how much digging a person does. Even though Father Kolbe and the Polish brothers knew who the man was, they didn't pry into his business and weren't bothered at all by his presence. Father Kolbe has taught us that our purpose in living is to learn to believe in others."

"Believe in others . . . ?"

"Yes. If we can't believe in others, we can't devote ourselves to helping them."

Believing in others. The words this brother had so innocently uttered sounded in Ono's ears as a painfully ironic indictment of himself. Ono was a man who had chosen a line of work that wasn't about believing in people at all, but about doubting them. His entire purpose in coming to this monastery was to sniff out and identify anything suspect occurring within its walls.

To believe in a phantom God, and to make the effort to trust unreliable human beings—Ono sensed these men were living in a completely different dimension from his own. They seemed far too removed from history and society and politics.

No matter how many fine words these men can conjure up . . . they're bound to be blown away by the storms of society and politics.

Ono felt something resembling either pity or contempt toward all the men living there.

That evening, on the pretext of taking care of an errand for the monastery, he went into town and met with Detective Kaneda at their usual yakitori shop.

"This is delicious." He rejoiced at being able to have some real human food for the first time in a while. "Those foreigners, they have to work with nothing but the worst slop to eat."

"And, what have you learned?" Detective Kaneda stared in amazement at his subordinate devouring his meal.

Ono wiped his mouth. "Mr. Kaneda, there really doesn't seem to be anything suspicious about them. But I'll keep trying a while longer to uncover something."

Just then, the window of a house across the road flew open and someone screamed, "They just said on the news that the prime minister has been assassinated!"

The incident sent shock waves throughout Japan.

Shortly before dawn that morning, as large snowflakes swirled in the air, fourteen hundred soldiers, led by some young officers, divided up into several regiments. One attacked the prime minister's residence at Nagata-chō while everyone still slept. Other regiments stormed the homes of the minister of finance, the lord keeper of the privy seal, the minister of the interior, and the inspector general of military education. The prime minister narrowly escaped with his life, but Finance Minister Takahashi, Interior Minister Saitō, and Inspector General Watanabe were all assassinated.[3]

In Nagasaki, at 7:00 p.m. on February 26, the radio news broadcast a report of the emergency situation, though details were scanty. At 8:15 p.m., it was reported that the prime minister was dead (a subsequent announcement clarified that the report of the prime minister's death was incorrect).

"This is terrible. We've got to get back to headquarters," Kaneda urged Ono, who was in something of a daze, and they hurried to the Nagasaki Police headquarters, fearing some disturbing incidents might occur in Nagasaki in response to the extraordinary events in Tokyo. The two detectives, along with all the other officers, were placed on alert throughout the night. To their relief the city of Nagasaki, swathed in the darkness of night, remained unperturbed through the dawn. But although it was quiet in Nagasaki, within that silence lurked indications that something ominous would be happening to Japan.

"What's going to become of Japan?" young Ono asked the senior detectives as he warmed his hands at the hibachi.

"Japan? We're going to become a powerful nation that can't be defeated by America or England. We have to. In times like

---

3   This is the notorious February 26 Incident of 1936. Despite the successful assassinations carried out by the rebels, the uprising was suppressed by imperial order, and many of the leaders were either tried and executed or committed suicide. Still, this major domestic disturbance led to the dissolution of the cabinet and the installation of a new cabinet that fell even more precariously under the control of the military.

these, it's no surprise that young army officers raised a rebellion when the government persists in being spineless." With no additional information coming in, Detective Kaneda made his vague forecast.

Ono felt gloomy as he returned to the monastery at Hongōchi the next morning. He was overcome with a sense of anxiety over Japan's future. Would his country become isolated in the world? Would more coup d'état attempts be made? But like Detective Kaneda, he too believed that Japan would overcome these trials and would have no choice but to become a powerful nation.

When he returned to the monastery that morning, the day's labors were proceeding as though nothing at all had occurred. Brother Gregorio was brandishing his hoe in the garden, and in the printing office, Brothers Severinus and Bartolomeo were silently at work at the press machine. Outside the kitchen, Brother Casiano was fetching water in a bucket.

"Do you men . . . do you know what happened in Tokyo yesterday?" Ono reproachfully asked one of the Japanese brothers.

"Yes. I heard that some soldiers had staged a rebellion . . ."

"And that means nothing to you?"

"Mr. Ono. That's something that happened out in the world. But we have no connection with the world here."

Ono wanted to tell the man that it made no difference whether they intended to have no connection with the world; soon enough they would be swept up in the violent storms of the world.

But, oblivious to Ono's reproaches, the foreign and Japanese brothers went into the chapel once they had completed their daily labors. There they knelt in prayer. Prayers that, to Ono's mind, were pointless, even foolish . . .

4

A MINOR SECRET

ON THE AFTERNOON of the third day after the February 26 Incident, which all of Japan had been following with keen interest, the uprising was somehow suppressed. But beneath the endlessly swirling white snow, the tramp of army boots and the repeat of rifles lingered in the ears of the people far longer than had any of the previous terrorist acts or assassinations of high-ranking officials. The tread of the army boots and the discharging of rifles were portents of a great war that was soon to come.

But Sachiko, still in elementary school, had no such presentiments of tragedy. In fact, after her first visit to the Walker home, she looked forward to the fun she would have at their house in late March every year: Van's birthday celebration was on March 27.[1]

The large cake made by Mrs. Walker had a candle for each year of his age. After the partygoers had counted "One, two, three!" Van blew out the flickering candle flames. The Japanese and foreign children at the party laughed boisterously at the ridiculous face he made as he puffed up his cheeks and blew with all his might.

---

1 March 27 happens to have been Endō's birthday.

They again played musical chairs. Everyone marched in a circle around the chairs while Mrs. Walker played the piano; as soon as she stopped, they scrambled to sit in the nearest chair. Because the number of chairs was one fewer than the number of participants, one person was always left standing. The child who captured the last seat at the end of the game was the winner.

Sachiko had played this same game on Christmas Day, so she had it down. She was also so fast that she had been chosen to be on the relay team at school, so none of the older boys were able to beat her.

Van lost out, followed by three Japanese boys and girls. Then Van's brother Jim was eliminated, leaving only Sachiko and a dark-skinned boy name Shūhei.

Shūhei seemed like a real scamp. He faced off against Sachiko, who looked a bit shy. That sheepish smile made Sachiko realize she had seen this boy somewhere before.

Mrs. Walker began playing the piano. The two children started circling the single remaining chair. The music sped up. Then it slowed again. The jittery children began to giggle. Suddenly the music stopped.

Sachiko and the boy collided with each other above the chair. With a swift motion, the boy grabbed Sachiko's bottom. Then, with a look of total innocence, he yielded the chair to her.

The partygoers, completely unaware of what had just happened, applauded loudly. Jim came to shake hands with the victor.

Sachiko had blushed bright red, but no one else was aware of how rude the boy had been. With a nonchalant face, he dug into a piece of cake.

Later, the children all went outside and played a game of capture the flag.[2]

---

2 The Japanese game, more literally "capture the battleship," was played with team members representing various military ships that guard the warship's commander from capture.

The yard looked down over Nagasaki Bay. They heard the steam whistle from a ship docked at the yard where Sachiko's father worked.

"Hey, what did you do that for?" Sachiko whispered to the boy, whose name was Kōda Shūhei. "I recognized you right away. I've seen you at Sunday mass at the church."

Shūhei was ruffled. "Don't know what you're talking about." He turned away from her.

For some reason, Sachiko couldn't bring herself to hate this boy, even though he had grabbed her bottom . . .

✳ ✳ ✳

Some days Sachiko would run into Shūhei or Jim. On Saturdays her mother sent her on errands to her aunt at the Ōura Church. Her aunt, a nun at the church, looked after the bishop and the priests.

Each time Sachiko headed for Ōura, she wondered whether she might see Shūhei or Jim. Even while she was conversing with her aunt, she would be listening to sounds from outside the window, trying to pick out the voices of the boys playing.

A ship comes into the offing,
A ship sets sail from Dejima.
The ships and the quays are decorated
With five colors of streamers.
A short haul from Kobe to Shanghai.

A boy was singing loudly as he rode in front of the church on a bicycle.

"Oh! I wonder if that's Jim!"

"Who is Jim?" her aunt asked in surprise. Sachiko told her that Jim was an American boy, the older brother of a boy she had helped one day.

"Really? His Japanese is certainly good for a foreigner. And he knows popular songs."

"Jim's Japanese is amazing. He's memorized all kinds of songs and even knows the 'Nagasaki Street Dance.'"

On the streets lately one often heard performances of "Nagasaki Street Dance," with lyrics by Saijō Yaso. Jim had performed the song in front of everyone at the birthday party.

Beloved girl from Dejima
In Nagasaki
Sa no arya sassa!
With a cross around her neck
Nan to sho no sho!

It was a little unusual to hear a chestnut-haired American sing "*Sa no arya sassa!,*" but it wasn't completely bizarre in a city with as many foreigners as Nagasaki had.

Sachiko left her aunt sitting where she was and ran to the front of the church, where Jim and Shūhei were practicing riding down the hill with both hands off the handlebars. Shūhei was clumsy, so seeing him trying to control his bike was like watching an ape doing acrobatics.

"Sat-chan!" Jim called out. "I knew you were here, so I sang in a loud voice to signal you!"

"I heard you."

"A bunch of us are going to explore a deserted house. Wanna come with us?" Like any other young American, Jim made none of the distinctions between boys and girls that Japanese children made. In fact, he went out of his way to invite girls.

"Deserted house?"

"Yeah, there's a big old house up the hill here. Shūhei and I have been talking about exploring it."

There remained several old wooden houses that had been occupied by foreigners living in Nagasaki during the Meiji era. In summer, weeds were left to grow rampant in the gardens, cicadas shrieked from the branches of giant camphor trees, and the houses felt somehow magical.

That day, Sachiko joined Jim and Shūhei and several other young children to explore one such house.

The rickety gate was tightly secured with rusty wire, but that presented no problem for these children. They went around to the back of the house and squeezed through the barbed-wire fence like a pack of brown rats.

"Sat-chan, take my hand." Jim grabbed Sachiko's hand from the other side of the fence.

In earlier days the garden must have had a beautiful lawn covering its sloping ground, but now it was thickly overgrown with withered grass and wild roses, making it more difficult to negotiate than the barbed-wire fence. Paint was peeling from the wood of the house and the window glass was broken out; only the French shutters were fastened tight. When Jim and his friends pushed against them, they opened with a creak.

"Wow!" the children cried. The floor of the octagonal-shaped room was littered with fragments of plaster that had fallen from the ceiling. Paint had flaked off the surrounding walls as though they had a skin disease, and the room was filled with a smell that was either plaster or cement mingled with the odors of mildew and dust.

"Jim, do you think maybe this could be a haunted house?" Shūhei asked with a quavering voice. His question was designed to frighten Sachiko and the other young children and make their exploration even more exciting. "Some evil person might have lived here. Everybody be on their guard!"

His words had the desired effect. Sachiko and the other children swallowed hard and walked nervously behind Jim and Shūhei down a hallway leading to the interior of the house.

A creaking sound from somewhere! Jim jerked in surprise and halted, then said, "That was just a sound from the shutters we pushed open."

The smells of plaster and paint filled the hallway. For some reason, cardboard boxes were strewn about the two rooms that flanked the hallway.

"Wait!" Shūhei signed to everyone. "Did you hear that strange voice off in the distance?"

Sachiko and the other children huddled around Jim and Shūhei and listened intently. They were so frightened they felt like crying, but it was too late to just leave, so they froze in place.

"It sounds like a baby crying."

A sound like soft weeping echoed from a room deep inside the abandoned house.

Sachiko couldn't bear it any longer. "Let's get out of here. I'm scared!"

"Don't worry. There's no such thing as ghosts," Jim reassured her.

"There are, too!" Shūhei responded, hoping to terrify Sachiko. "That voice . . . it just might be a ghost!"

Once again they clearly heard the softly weeping voice.

"Shū-chan, what are we going to do? Should we check it out?" Jim asked, determined to appear brave.

"Yeah, let's do it!" Cunningly, though, Shūhei made sure that Jim led the way down the hall, while he positioned himself so that he could flee at a moment's notice.

Spiderwebs covered the ceiling and the doors leading into the small rooms on either side of the hallway. The windows in the rooms were shut, so the webs tangled around the faces and hands of the children as they groped their way forward.

The crying had stopped. They began to think that perhaps they had merely imagined the faint sounds they had just heard.

When they stepped into the next room, they were suddenly surrounded with light. The shutter doors had fallen off, and the window glass was completely broken out, allowing the sunlight to pour into the room.

"See! There isn't any such thing as ghosts!" Jim shouted with relief.

Instantly courageous, Sachiko gleefully echoed Jim's words: "No ghosts! No ghosts!" Through the broken windows they could see the withered grass of the lawn, and beyond that, Nagasaki Bay sparkled a contented blue in the afternoon sun.

"Okay, that settles it. Starting today, this is going to be our secret hideout!" Shūhei proposed. Like a magician waving a wand to conjure up some great treasure, he had a gift for quickly coming up with suggestions for fun adventures.

"You mean we'd be coming here every day?" Sachiko looked flummoxed. "My house is too far away. I can't come every day."

"Just come when you can."

Thinking about this being their private hideout, kept secret even from their parents, Sachiko felt a mix of worry and elation. She had never before kept anything from her parents or her brother.

"Wait!" Jim suddenly shouted. From the next room they could hear the weeping voice even more distinctly.

While the others held their breath, Jim bravely turned the knob of the dusty door. The window in the next room was also broken out, letting the sunlight flood in. It must have been the kitchen years ago.

"Aha!" Jim peered into the room and then broke into a delighted laugh. "It's kittens, three of 'em. They look like they've just been born. I wonder where the mom has gone."

Surprised, Sachiko peered timidly between the shoulders of Jim and Shūhei at the three kittens, which crawled along the floor like toy animals.

The kittens were black or a mix of black and white.

"So cute!" she sighed, smiling.

"We thought their crying was ghosts. So they're really aren't any ghosts, just like Daddy said," Jim mumbled.

"What does 'Daddy' mean?"

"'Daddy' . . . it means Father."

"What should we do with these cats?"

"We should all take care of them," Shūhei volunteered. "If we take 'em home with us, we'll get scolded and they'll tell us to get rid of them. So we should all help take care of them."

Raising kittens at a secret hiding place that her parents and brother knew nothing about—a sense of adventure caused Sachiko's heart to pound with anxiety, but at the same time there was something invigorating about it.

Sachiko continued to think about that abandoned house during her classes at school. It had a view of the ocean, and its shutters with chipping paint rattled in the wind. The grass of the lawn was dead, and only wild cats lived there. The place looked abandoned, but she remembered when Shūhei had suddenly suggested that there could be dwarfs in red clothes and red hats singing and jumping around late at night in one of those rooms. That made Sachiko conclude that this might really be one of those enchanted houses she had read about in fairy tales.

She was still a young girl, so she wasn't allowed to go far from her home to play. She began using her aunt who worked as a nun at the church as an excuse to go to Ōura.

"Anything you need from auntie at Ōura?" she pestered her mother.

"You've certainly changed. You used to say you didn't like going to auntie's place." Her mother looked at Sachiko in disbelief, but she had no reason to forbid her daughter from going to her aunt's house to play.

She started visiting her aunt at the church for just a few minutes, then giving a quick dip of her head to the statue of Blessed
Mother Mary and running straight to the abandoned house. It
gave her a rush of pleasure to feed the kittens the dried sardines
she had snitched from her house.

"Hey, Sachiko's here." Jim and Shūhei had been playing catch
in the yard of the abandoned house but stopped and called out
to Sachiko as she hiked up her skirt, revealing her underpants
as she climbed through the barbed-wire fence at the rear.

"The kittens?"

"They're here. Inside the house."

But the two boys weren't as interested in the kittens as
Sachiko was. They hadn't discovered any monsters or pirates
living there, so there was nothing to fuel their excitement.
The abandoned house appeared to have become just another
ordinary location for them to play.

A black mother cat, her fur standing on end, howled menac-
ingly at Sachiko from behind the kittens. When Sachiko tossed
some dried sardines to the kittens, who gobbled them up, their
mother, though still somewhat sulky, stopped complaining.

"So cute!" Sachiko sighed, as Shūhei walked in.

"Hmph, they've got weird-looking faces, those kittens," he
baited Sachiko. "Is it true that your aunt is a nun at the church?"

"Uh-huh."

"Will you become a nun someday?"

"Not me!"

"Good. The nuns and priests are all so depressing. I don't like
'em."

Sachiko was startled. "You'll get struck down if you say things
like that!"

"Don't be stupid. If that's how God is, then I don't like Him
either!" Shūhei swaggered.

It would never have occurred to anyone in Sachiko's family to say anything bad about priests or nuns. Her parents had taught her that priests and nuns were to be respected by the faithful, since they devoted their entire lives to a higher cause.

Seeing the reproach in Sachiko's eyes, Shūhei apologized, "Yeah, you're probably right. . . . The other day, I saw a nun walking along with an umbrella after the rain had stopped, and she reminded me of a ninja."

"A ninja?"

"Yeah. The way they dress, they look like a poor excuse for a ninja."

When Sachiko got home that day, she told her mother about this conversation.

"Someday that boy is going to have to pay for talking like that," her mother said indignantly. But after thinking about it for a moment, she snickered, "But they really *do* look like ninjas!"

Jim and Shūhei were opposites in every conceivable way. Jim had pale skin and acted grown-up, as befits an oldest son, and was solicitous toward girls, while Shūhei was a dark-skinned rascal who had no qualms about calling girls "Hey, you!" or "Hey, squirt!" Whenever Shūhei thought up some prank to play, his eyes grew as round as acorns and a look of indescribable glee swept across his face. If his plan was particularly ruthless, it was Jim's role to hold him back, saying, "You can't do that! My daddy would kill me!"

One Sunday, Shūhei carried out an outrageous prank during mass at the Ōura Church.

Several masses were conducted at the church each Sunday. Sachiko and her parents and brother participated reverently in the mass, kneeling and sitting as directed. Sachiko glanced toward the statue of Santa Maria to the right of the altar. While the priest at the altar read from the Gospels in Latin, Sachiko indulged in daydreams about Kiku. Except for the occasional cough, it was silent during the mass, until suddenly a strange cry echoed through the sanctuary.

"MEOW! MEOW!"

The startled congregation turned to look toward the source of the howls. Without anyone noticing, someone had set three kittens loose in the chapel, and they mewed as they padded along.

Sachiko knew instantly who these cats were and who had brought them. She could scarcely breathe from fear and anxiety. A man quickly tossed the cats out and then ran outside, where he evidently apprehended the culprit.

"What do you think you're doing, you little scoundrel?! God will punish you for interrupting the mass!"

The man's voice rang loudly in the ears of the Christians in the sanctuary. For the remainder of the mass, Sachiko fretted about how Shūhei's face would look right now as he waited, held captive by the scruff of his neck.

The mass concluded. As the parishioners filed out in groups, they discussed what had just happened. "What kind of idiot would let cats loose in the chapel?" When they learned that the perpetrator was Shūhei, two or three of the adults sighed. "He's just hopeless. Whenever there's some sort of prank, you can always count on him being behind it."

Naturally, Shūhei was roundly scolded by the priests. Sachiko learned about this from her mother, who added, "You aren't to play with that boy anymore."

Sachiko could only reply, "Okay, I won't play with him." Regardless of her answer, her mind was caught up in thoughts of the abandoned house and the kittens. She wanted to play with Jim, and she knew with girlish instinct that Shūhei was not at heart a bad kid. And so, on the following Saturday, she again used the excuse of visiting her aunt at the monastery and set out for Ōura. As she chatted with her aunt, she strained her ears in an effort to hear the voice of Jim or Shūhei.

When she left the church, she caught sight of Shūhei climbing the slope directly ahead, holding something in his hand. He seemed down in the mouth. Maybe the scolding he had gotten from the adults had taken its toll.

Seeing his lonely, disheartened figure, Sachiko felt unbearably sorry for him and ran toward him.

"Shū-chan! Where are you going?"

"Nowhere."

For some reason he was caught off guard and tried to hide the paper-wrapped package he was holding in his hand. Sachiko immediately recognized that the pretty wrapping paper came from the Okamasa Department Store that had opened for business at Higashi Hama-machi two years earlier.

"Hey, let's go see the kittens!" Sachiko urged him, but Shūhei shook his head.

"I've got something to take care of here. You go by yourself."

Sachiko intuitively sensed something strange about his behavior. She pretended to have noticed nothing and walked ten steps before ducking behind a telephone pole to watch Shūhei. He placed the package on the stone steps leading to the church and then hid behind the fence, looking all around with wide eyes.

What in the world is Shūhei doing now?

Sachiko's heart began to pound. She couldn't see anyone nearby, and the afternoon sun glimmered as the season approached spring. Before long, a middle-aged woman came out of the chapel. As she stepped down the stone staircase, she caught sight of the paper-wrapped package.

With a look of suspicion, she picked up the parcel.

Inside the wrapping paper from the department store was a bundle covered in bamboo skin, of the sort used by butchers to wrap meat.

The woman's face twisted in revulsion the moment she opened up the bamboo-skin bundle. She screamed, "Disgusting!" and flung the bundle away. It contained several cat turds shaped like a human thumb.

She looked all around, her eyes filled with anger. Meanwhile, Shūhei tried to stay hidden, pressing his body tightly behind the gate of the church.

"Father! Father!!" She peered in Shūhei's direction and then turned around to call to the priest, who had just emerged from the chapel.

"Hashimoto-san. What's wrong?"

"Father, some little wretch has been spreading cat droppings here!"

"Cat droppings?"

"That's right. There was a nicely wrapped package from the Okamasa Store, with a bamboo-skin bundle inside. It was here on the steps, like somebody had dropped it. So I picked it up, thinking maybe I could find out who it belonged to, but when I opened it, these cat droppings fell out. I was so shocked!"

The aged priest walked down the stairs and looked where she was pointing. Several hard, gray objects were scattered around the bamboo parcel.

"Father, I know who pulled this prank."

The aged priest nodded. He realized that her finger was slowly moving until it pointed toward the rear of the gate. The tip of a dirty canvas sneaker belonging to the offender was poking out from behind it.

"Shūhei, come out of there," the priest snarled, but there was no response. "Even if you're hiding back there, Lord Jesus and the Blessed Virgin can see you. Wicked boy . . . !"

After a few moments Shūhei emerged from his hiding place, glancing sheepishly up at the priest and the woman.

"Why are you always doing these naughty things? First you let a cat in during mass. And then you defile the steps of the church with this filth . . ." The priest persisted with his sermon for a time, then meted out his punishment: "You're not to partake of the host for a month." Shūhei was banned from taking the tiny wafer that the priest offers during mass to the faithful, who believe it to be an emblem of the body of Christ.

After the priest and the woman were gone, Shūhei stood staring resentfully after them. Sachiko stepped out from behind the telephone pole but said nothing, merely watching him from a distance.

"Did you see all that?" When Shūhei saw her, he smiled in embarrassment.

"Shū-chan, tell me why you keep doing these awful things," she insisted with some amazement.

"Dunno. Don't know myself. When those naughty worms start wriggling inside me, I can't control them," he muttered pitifully.

Thanks to these two instances of mischief, the adults concluded that Shūhei was a good-for-nothing troublemaker, but Sachiko could never bring herself to dislike him because of what he had done.

The American boy Jim, who was the same age as Shūhei, was polite and clever, and he was popular among the Japanese children, who were always calling out "Jim-chan! Jim-chan!" But Sachiko felt more comfortable around Shūhei with his dark skin, his snub nose, and his mischievous ways than she did around Jim. An aroma like foreign-made soap seem to waft faintly from Jim's blond hair and his immaculately ironed shirts, while Shūhei always smelled of pickled daikon when she was with him. But best of all, she liked to look at Shūhei's face when he came up with some prank to play, because his eyes grew round as acorns and glimmered with animation.

One day, the children were playing hide-and-seek in the abandoned house. Jim was "it," and all the other children hid in various places around the house. Sachiko hid and tried to control her breathing in a pitch-dark little room that seemed to have once been used as a storage room. She heard footsteps, and then a shadowy figure approached her. But the figure didn't have Jim's refreshing aroma; instead it was a strange, sweaty smell that was very familiar to her.

"Shū-chan?" she whispered.

"What? It's you?"

They could hear Jim in the distance, searching one room after another. Sachiko felt a little frightened, and she pressed her body up against Shūhei's.

"Wow. You're really soft!" he muttered. Sachiko immediately fell silent with embarrassment.

"Do you know what a kiss is?" Shūhei asked her.

"I don't know any such thing."

"Dummy! Jim's mother and father are always kissing, aren't they?" He continued, "Sachiko, when we grow up, will you be my wife?" he asked in a half-serious voice.

"Uh-huh." She nodded.

He lowered his voice ever further and said, "Then will you try a kiss now?"

"If I did that, the priest and my mother would be mad."

"Then will you kiss me after we get married?"

"I will after we're married."

Sachiko sincerely felt that she would marry, as long as it was to Shūhei. She decided that she would defend him no matter what everyone might say when they were married.

After the game of hide-and-seek, the children raced down the stone stairs that paralleled the wall of the church. When they came to a flagstone path, they encountered a foreigner using an umbrella as a cane as he panted and painfully climbed the sloping road.

Sachiko nodded her head and said, "Father Kolbe, good day."

Startled, Father Kolbe stopped and peered through the lenses of his round-rimmed glasses at the children. "Ah, Sachiko. Are you well? Tomorrow I go back to Poland."

Shūhei, who was wary of priests, hid behind a telephone pole while the other children watched Sachiko and Father Kolbe from a safe distance.

Even when Sachiko heard the name "Poland," she could not recall where on the globe it was located. "Then, Father, when will you be coming back to Nagasaki?"

The priest lightly shrugged his shoulders and said, "I'd like to come back. But . . . I don't know. About coming back." As a member of his order, Father Kolbe was required to follow all directives from his superiors. His ability in Japanese was so elementary, he couldn't explain the situation to the young girl. "Miss Sachiko, please become a good child who will be loved by the Blessed Mother."

He took two or three steps to leave, but then, as though he had suddenly remembered something, he opened the breviary he held in his hand and took out a picture of the Blessed Mother that appeared to be a bookmark inserted between the pages. "Sachiko-san. This for you." He handed it to her.

The picture was the same as the one she had received some time ago from the priest, and which she had carefully placed in the chocolate box where she kept her treasures.

"Greater love than this no man hath, that a man lay down his life for his friends." The words from the Gospel of St. John were printed on the bookmark.

"Goodbye," Father Kolbe said, smiling eyes flashing through his round-rimmed glasses.

"Goodbye," replied Sachiko.

His shoulders lowered, the priest slowly climbed the stairs to the church. Viewed from behind, he looked utterly exhausted.

The following afternoon, he bid his brethren at the monastery what he hoped would be a temporary farewell, after which another Polish priest and two young Japanese brothers saw him off as far as the Ōhato harbor.

The *Nagasaki-Maru*, which years earlier had brought him to Japan, had already glided in to the quay at Dejima, black smoke swirling from its stack. Passengers on the deck and their well-wishers on the shore were shouting and tossing each other streamers of every color. A white seabird flew over the mast, and every so often the steam whistle blasted.

The priest shook hands with his three companions on the shore as they discussed what lay ahead. As they spoke, he caught sight of Ono, who was milling amid the crowd, carefully observing the priests.

"Mr. Ono!" When Father Kolbe called out to him, Ono had no choice but to walk toward them. "Thank you."

Ono was confounded by this expression of gratitude and could only mutter, "Not at all."

"Mr. Ono, this, for you." The priest held out the same kind of portrait of the Blessed Mother that he had given Sachiko the previous day. It, too, was imprinted with the words "Greater love than this no man hath, that a man lay down his life for his friends."

As the priest was about to board the boat, Ono suddenly called out "Father!" He shouted something as the priest turned toward him, but just at that moment the piercing steam whistle drowned out his words.

Much later, Ono recalled that scene with embarrassment, uncertain why he had thoughtlessly called out to Father Kolbe. He was even grateful that the sharp blast from the steam whistle had drowned out what he had said.

"Father!" he had called out. "Father, don't come back to Japan!"

Don't come back to Japan. Why had he said that?

I wonder how much I realized then what would be happening to Japan?

Ono was fully aware that Father Kolbe was not a dangerous character. Having insinuated himself into the monastery, Ono knew with certainty that there was nothing whatsoever suspect about the priest or his compatriots; in fact, far from being untrustworthy, these were men who had abandoned all attachments and desires in the world to labor for the Christian teachings they believed in.

But Ono instinctively sensed that the lives these men led were not likely to be permitted or accepted in Japan in the days ahead. A time was rapidly approaching in which Japan would be sucked into the vortex of a great crisis. In January of 1936, Japan had withdrawn from the London Naval Disarmament Conference; the following month had seen the February 26 Incident, in which army officers staged a coup-d'état; and in March Japanese troops clashed with Soviet forces at Changlingzi. Discord was fomenting among the Japanese military and the nationalists. Ono, as a member of the Special Police unit, had a premonition that any forces that attempted to block these developments would be brutally suppressed.

Father, don't come back to Japan.

What he had been trying to say was that, should the priest return to Japan, there was no way he would be warmly welcomed by the Japanese. Although a priest resided in a world unconnected to politics, there could be no question that the Japanese in coming days would look on foreign priests and Christians with suspicion and distrust.

Soon the departure gong was struck, the shouts of the well-wishers grew louder, and Father Kolbe hurriedly boarded the ship. With the many-colored streamers flapping in the wind like the tails of kites, the ship moved slowly from the quay.

Ono nodded to the foreign priest and the Japanese brothers who had accompanied Father Kolbe to the harbor and then left the wharf. As he walked, he glanced briefly at the small picture of the Blessed Mother that Father Kolbe had given him and then casually tossed it to the ground. The words printed beneath the picture—"Greater love than this no man hath, that a man lay down his life for his friends"—were ground under the wheels of a rickshaw that followed closely behind.

Father Kolbe watched motionlessly from the deck of the ship as the wharf and the city of Nagasaki beyond faded into the distance.

A letter he wrote that year from Shanghai to a compatriot in Nagasaki expressed what he felt as he departed: "As the ship moved farther and farther away from the quay, a thought popped into my mind. 'This is probably the last you'll see of this land.' And my eyes filled with tears."

5

DARK SURGING WAVES

A young woman dressed in the student uniform of Junshin[1] Women's Junior College was climbing the stone-paved slope.

Every house that had a view of Nagasaki Bay from the hillside either had its rain shutters closed or curtains drawn across its windows. Strict orders had come from the military and the police that no one was allowed to look in the direction of the Mitsubishi Shipyard.

"I hear they're building an enormous battleship at the shipyard." Despite strict scrutiny from the MPs and the Special Police, the residents of Nagasaki had a vague sense of what was being constructed at the yard.

According to the rumors that were cautiously circulating, the battleship was as gigantic as a fortress. It was an unsinkable battleship, surpassing the capabilities of any other nation in the world.

"Once that ship is finished, America has no hope of competing with us!" some claimed, their eyes twinkling as though they

---

1 Junshin, which means "Immaculate Heart"—in reference to the Blessed Mother Mary—in Japanese, is a leading Catholic school in Nagasaki, established as a girls' school in 1935.

had actually seen the ship. The very existence of such a battleship gave the citizens hope that it would signal a decisive end to the war between Japan and the United States.

Since the opening of hostilities, Japan had achieved one victory after another throughout the Pacific region. Following the surprise attack on Hawai'i on December 7 of the previous year, Japan had occupied Manila at the beginning of the year and toppled Singapore, and Dutch troops in Java had recently surrendered. Each victory was reported by a radio announcer's upbeat voice, while lantern-bearing students marched through the streets.

The young woman who had climbed up the slope entered through the gate to the church and pushed open the chapel door. It was deserted.

Apparently a frequent visitor, she sank down onto the kneelers near the statue of the Blessed Mother, closed her eyes, and began to pray.

When she left the chapel nearly twenty minutes later, a nun who had finished her chores in the rectory called out to her, "Sat-chan. You came yesterday too, didn't you. Is there something I can do for you?"

"No," Sachiko shook her head, "I just came to pray." She blushed, hoping it was not noticeable. The blush was related to her reason for coming to pray two days in a row.

Shūhei just finished his second day of testing . . .

Since childhood Sachiko had prayed at the foot of this statue, and today her petition was for the Blessed Mother to help Shūhei gain admission to the economics department at Keiō University.

It was a secret she could not mention to her parents or her classmates. She hadn't, she couldn't, confide that secret to anyone.

Shūhei had been in Tokyo for many months. Ever since his first failed attempt to pass the university entrance exams, he had been staying at a dormitory in a place called Yotsuya so that he could attend the Mathematics Academy located at Kanda.

Shūhei of course had no idea that Sachiko had been praying at the church for him to pass the exam. He had no clear-cut memories of having played with her at that old abandoned house.

Sachiko, on the other hand, remembered it very well. Six years had passed since that time, but she recalled what Shūhei had said to her in that room with the smell of plaster: "Will you be my wife?"

Of course Sachiko knew that those words were spoken in jest by a mischievous young man. In those days, similar promises were often made impulsively by her schoolmates and the neighborhood children.

But Sachiko had not forgotten what he said. Even now, as she was beginning to fill out the bodice of her Junshin uniform jacket, she kept warm within her heart fond memories of that abandoned house.

Those pleasant days as a young girl. Summer vacations, when everything around her seemed dyed in the same bright blue colors as the sky. All of her palpable memories of her days with Shūhei were linked to that abandoned house. It was the only time in her life when she could play capture the flag or shout and chase around freely with boys like Jim and Shūhei with no hesitation or embarrassment whatsoever.

But the time for play gradually decreased as she entered middle school and then the women's college. In part, this was because the young people had started to recognize some of their playmates as "the opposite sex," but even more so because the eyes and gossiping lips of the adults in a city such as Nagasaki were an annoyance. Shūhei abruptly began avoiding Sachiko, and she could no longer casually call out his name.

Yes, and then . . . Jim and Van went back to America . . .

It was the summer of 1939. Sachiko still remembered that there had been a severe drought in Nagasaki that summer, and the water levels at the Hongōchi reservoir that provided drinking water to its citizens had dropped precipitously.

In midsummer the Walker family had returned to the United States. Sachiko and Shūhei, along with many others, went to see them off at Nagasaki Station.

"Van-chan, take care of yourself! Jim-chan, take care!"

On that particular day, Jim and Van were neatly dressed in suits with ties, and their hair was smartly parted. Because of nerves, perhaps, even Van, who constantly scampered around, was strangely formal with Sachiko.

When the departure bell rang, Mrs. Walker quickly gave Sachiko a hug and whispered, "Goodbye, Sachiko-chan." Then she quickly added in English, "I won't forget you . . ."

The train inched forward; Jim and Van waved their hands energetically, and before long they had disappeared from view. The onlookers kept watching the train as it receded into the distance.

That experience marked the end of Sachiko's youth. With Jim gone, Sachiko and Shūhei grew apart from each other. In those days, middle school boys and young women from girls' schools were not allowed to play together as they can today.

Even so . . .

Even so, Sachiko could not forget about Shūhei. When she closed her eyes, she could always recollect his dark, chestnut-shaped face from their elementary school days. Shūhei, scolded for releasing cats in the church. Shūhei, tricking an adult by packaging up cat droppings in department-store wrapping paper. Shūhei, beaming with pride after he spelled out "S-H-U-H-E-I" in the snow with his own urine.

It didn't occur to seventeen-year-old Sachiko to question whether or not it was love she felt for him. Her feelings for him were more like those of a sister. Those sisterly feelings did not fade after she entered the Junshin Women's Junior College, even when the only opportunities she had to see him came in quick glances in the chapel on those occasions when he came to Sunday mass.

One Sunday ten days later—The customary mass was under way at the Ōura Church. Candles flickered at the altar, and the priest was reciting from the Gospels.

Her heart was already pounding when Sachiko looked over at Shūhei's close-cropped head, a head she hadn't seen in some time. It wasn't until she arrived at this mass that Sachiko learned that Shūhei had returned from Tokyo.

I wonder if he passed. . . . I think the first round of results must have been posted . . .

In all honesty, even as she droned the words of the prayers along with her mother, Sachiko's thoughts were elsewhere. Why can't the mass finish? But it was dragging along slower than usual. Then prayers for the imperial troops serving at the battlefront were added at the conclusion of the mass.

Finally liberated, Sachiko followed her mother and merged with the line of people exiting the chapel. Shūhei had already gone outside and was in conversation with several young men his age.

Sachiko couldn't bring herself to speak freely with Shūhei. This was a time when it took a great deal of courage for a young woman who had no particular business with a young man to speak directly with him. She played the nonchalant act and tried to listen in on what Shūhei was saying.

"For the Keiō University exam, you have to write all your answers in pen. Yeah. I forgot that they'd told us we couldn't use pencils. Damn, I thought! I was in real trouble, so I raised my hand and asked the young test proctor if I could borrow a fountain pen."

"You did?"

"It was a cheap pen, and I got ink all over my fingers. So I raised my hand again and asked if he had any toilet paper. He gave me the weirdest look!"

He was boasting to his friends about his own stupid mistakes. He hadn't changed at all.

Shūhei became aware of Sachiko's gaze on him, and he turned to look in her direction. He opened his eyes wide in surprise.

Sachiko instinctively looked away with girlish primness. She didn't want him thinking that she was paying any attention to him. For his part, Shūhei stared at her, his mouth agape (as it always was when he was surprised).

"Let's go," Sachiko urged her mother. Inwardly she couldn't imagine what in the world she thought she was doing, but outwardly she pretended she wasn't even aware of Shūhei's presence.

"You go on ahead," her mother responded. "I need to talk to your aunt about something. I'd like you to make breakfast."

"Okay."

Though in reality she wanted to look back at Shūhei, she adopted instead an icy pose and hurried down the stone steps. Her shapely legs moved nimbly beneath the skirt of her school uniform. She excelled in sports at school.

Why do a girl's feelings have to be so mixed up? What I think and what I do are totally unconnected!

She bitterly pondered her own contradictory actions. Just when she reached the house where once Father Kolbe and Brother Zeno had labored, someone unexpectedly leaped in front of her and shouted "Boo!" Sachiko froze in fright. It was Shūhei.

Her first impulse was to feign irritation, but her face broke into an unintended smile. She remembered how Shūhei had often hidden in the shadows and suddenly jumped out, delighted that he had frightened Sachiko and her girlfriends.

"Shū-chan, you really haven't changed at all, have you?"

"Well, you have, Sat-chan."

"What? How have I changed?"

"You've turned into a real young lady. When I went off to Tokyo, you were still a stinky, sweaty kid with bobbed hair. But when I saw you just now after mass . . . I was shocked. You're a young lady now."

Sachiko flushed at being called a "stinky, sweaty kid." But it didn't feel at all unpleasant to be told she had turned into a young lady.

Am I pretty? She actually wanted to ask, but she opted for "Shū-chan, did you pass the exams?"

"Actually, I . . . I didn't make it."

"What!?"

"So now . . . I get to wait another year before I can try again to get in to college." No longer cheerful, Shūhei averted his eyes. Sachiko, unsure how to console him, stopped walking and said, "I see." Suddenly Shūhei slapped her on the shoulder and laughingly said, "That would have been depressing, except this afternoon I got the results. I passed the first round of tests!"

"If you passed the first round, then you're going to be fine."

"I've got to. Half the applicants fail after the second round."

"What time will you find out the second-round results?"

"At three this afternoon. My buddies are gonna send me a telegram."

"Let me know if you pass."

"Sat-chan, could you come over this afternoon? I'm really lonely, and I want to go over to our old secret house to take my mind off things."

"Sure!" she nodded. She'd happily be there with him for a while if it would help soothe his anxious, lonely feelings.

"Then I'll be waiting in front of the house at 2:00."

"Okay."

She returned home and started preparing breakfast for her father and brother, who had finally woken up. Her father, who worked at the shipyard, increasingly had night work these days. It was a time when the slogan "Increased Production!" was posted in every section of the factory.

"Dad, if you don't hurry, you'll miss the 10 o'clock mass."

"Right."

Once she'd sent her father and brother off to mass, Sachiko was left alone to enjoy pleasant thoughts about Shūhei while she washed the dishes.

He's changed, too. Up till now, he'd pretend like he didn't even know me when we ran into each other.

Before Shūhei had gone off to the prep school in Tokyo, they had realized that others were watching them, and they had been hypersensitive to the fact that they were of opposite genders, so they could no longer play casually together. She was very happy that he had invited her to go walking with him for the first time in ages.

Sachiko never lied to her mother, but that afternoon, once she had finished cleaning up after lunch, for some reason she couldn't come right out and say, "I'm going to go meet Shūhei." She announced that she'd agreed to meet a friend and left the house, repeatedly justifying to herself that she hadn't actually lied to her mother.

But any feelings of remorse disappeared as she climbed the stone-paved slope and felt the joy of being able to spend time with Shūhei.

It was a warm day for early March. All was quiet in front of the church, much changed from the clamor after mass this morning. She paused there for a moment.

Mother Mary. I have a favor to ask, she pleaded inwardly. *Please help Shū-chan to pass. . . . If you help him pass. . . .* She paused to ponder. *I promise I won't argue with my brother for two whole months. And I won't answer back to my mother,* she murmured.

Since no one was watching, she hiked up her skirt and scrambled two steps at a time down the stone stairs that ran alongside the church building. It required no effort for the young athletic Sachiko.

The abandoned house, which she hadn't visited for a very long time, had deteriorated even more. The thick wire that kept the gate closed was caked with rust.

Shūhei was nowhere to be seen. She stood waiting for a while, but then heard a voice calling to her from inside the gate.

"Come around this way. You remember the rear gate we used back then, don't you?"

She went around back but hesitated as she started to straddle the barbed-wire fence. When she was a young girl, she'd blithely climbed over the fence, totally unconcerned that Jim and Shūhei could see her underpants.

"Shū-chan, turn your head away."

"Wha—?" He gaped at her, but he immediately recognized what she was referring to. He covered his face with both hands. "I'll do this. This'll be fine, won't it?"

But Sachiko shook her head. "No way!"

"Why not?"

"You're indecent. You're planning to peek between your fingers, aren't you? Just like you did in the old days."

He was forced to turn his back as she entered the garden.

"So, about another hour?"

"What is?"

"When the telegram comes."

"Oh, that." Shūhei smirked. Sachiko looked at him quizzically.

"What are you smiling at?"

"There's not going to be any telegram."

"What? No telegram?"

"Nope. I came back to Nagasaki because I've already been accepted at Keiō. Didn't you figure that out?"

"You passed?! Why did you lie to me? You're terrible!" She wanted to punch him in his back. Then, remembering the promise she had just made, in her heart she rapidly said a thank-you to Mother Mary.

"Well, if I'd said that, you wouldn't have come here, would you?" He flashed another cunning smile.

The desolate garden had not changed at all. She could remember the trees and the withered grasses that had been left to grow rampant. Each piece of vegetation brought back with almost painful vividness Sachiko's memories of the past. The only difference was the windows of the house from which the paint had peeled. The shutters and the window glass were gone, replaced by thick wooden boards nailed from the inside. The owner must have installed them to keep out intruders.

Other than that, everything was the same as it had been six years earlier. Sachiko almost felt as though she could hear the shouting voices of Jim and Van, and of Shūhei, still in elementary school then, as they tossed a ball back and forth.

"I wonder what Jim and Van are doing these days?"

"What are they up to?" Shūhei seemed to be having the same thoughts and nodded as he looked around the garden. "Jim's the same age as me, so he could be in college now. Van would still be in middle school. I never thought that Jim's country and my country would be at war with each other."

"That's true."

The two said nothing for a time.

"When I come here, I always think about cats."

"Cats?"

"You were naughty to bring those cats in during mass. The priest was so angry!"

"Oh, yeah? I don't remember it very well."

"Hey, you were really a bad kid back then. Why were you always playing pranks on people?"

With a droll smile Shūhei replied, "I have no idea."

"But now you're going to be a college student."

Abruptly Shūhei started chewing on his nails and muttered, "Well, I . . . I was accepted into the economics department at Keiō 'cause that's what my parents told me to do, but I really want to study literature."

"Literature?"

"Yeah. I want to write novels. So after I get to Keiō, I'm planning to sneak in and listen to some lectures in the literature department. Some of my favorite writers, like Satō Haruo and Nagai Kafū,[2] studied at Keiō. Have you read any of Satō's poetry?"

Sachiko blushed and shook her head. She had heard the name of the poet and novelist Satō Haruo, but the nuns at her girls' school did not approve of their students reading poetry or novels.

You and I sit facing each other,
You peering at the mountains to the west, the sun glaring in
    your eyes,
I staring entranced at the sea to the east,
Yet we both are here, relishing the same thoughts

Shūhei recited the poem in a soft voice.

"That's a poem by Satō Haruo?"

---

2 Satō (1892–1964) was acclaimed as both poet and a writer of fiction. Nagai (1879–1959), who spent time in both the United States and France, was best known for his stories of life among the women of the entertainment district.

"Yep. It's just like me and you right now. Sat-chan, would you like me to show you a book of his poems?"

"Please." Sachiko was very eager to read them.

Magician-like, Shūhei produced a tiny book out of his pocket. The words of the title, *Surrendering to Sentiment: A Poetry Collection*,[3] leapt powerfully into Sachiko's eyes.

Shūhei reverently opened the cover of the book, as though he were a priest holding a missal. Sachiko had never seen such an expression on his face.

"Why don't I read you some of the poems I like?"

"Sure."

Sometime later, Sachiko would come to think of this half hour as the most precious time she and Shūhei spent together. As she listened to Shūhei's voice, she forgot all about her home and school. As she studied his earnest profile, she was even able to forget the war and the times in which they lived.

Shūhei first read the charming "Days of Youth":

I go to the fields, I go to the mountains, I go to the shores,
I spread flowers on the hill at mid-day.
Thanks to your beautiful round eyes,
My grief exceeds the blueness of the sky.

Shūhei then recited some lines from the famous "Song of a Moonlit Night at the Water's Edge":

On days when I think of the one so far from me,
    so unattainable,
I learn what true love from the heart means.
It is a love that seeks nothing,

---

3 This collection, *Junrei shishū*, was published in 1921 as Satō's first book of poetry.

The feelings of a young girl of deep faith who,
Even on days when she has nothing for which she entreats,
Clasps her fingers together before the statue of the Blessed
    Mother Mary.

As he recited that stanza, Sachiko was entranced, her breath taken away to discover that words and feelings could come together to weave something so beautiful.

For some reason, in that moment she recalled what little her mother had told her about her grandmother's cousin, Kiku. It felt to her as though that verse was narrating the life story of Kiku, who had died at the base of the statue of the Blessed Mother because of her love for one particular man.

"Read that one more time," she implored Shūhei. When she again heard the words "It is a love that seeks nothing," the verse inscribed on the picture of the Blessed Mother that Father Kolbe had given her sprang back to her mind: "Greater love than this no man hath, that a man lay down his life for his friends."

"Sat-chan, you can understand from hearing these why I want to become a writer, can't you? I want to study hard, and maybe someday I'll be able to write a line this beautiful."

"You have to write it. You just have to . . ." Sachiko genuinely wanted that for Shūhei.

"But a year ago, when I told my dad and mom that I wanted to be a writer, they were furious with me. Both of them think that literature is only produced by decadent people. But I *am* going to become a writer, Sat-chan!"

The sun had begun to set, so the two stood up from their seats atop the rubble that had once been the veranda.

"I never knew . . . I never knew this about you, Shū-chan," Sachiko sighed.

They crawled over the barbed-wire fence and were about to leave just as a young soldier, evidently an enlisted man, wearing an armband that read "MP," was cycling past the house. Still clutching the handlebars of the bicycle, he glared piercingly at the two and began to interrogate them.

"Hey! You were just inside this vacant house, weren't you?"

"Yes."

"What business did you have going in there?"

The MP's face was browned by the sun. A steeled youthfulness almost seemed ready to burst from his muscular uniformed body.

"No business, really. We just went in while we were out walking." Shūhei remained immobile as he explained.

"Out walking?" The MP set down his bike and walked over to them. "So you two are out on a walk and it doesn't bother you at all to go inside a vacant house that belongs to somebody else? I'm sure you know that the houses in this neighborhood have blocked out their windows so they don't look out on Nagasaki Bay."

The MP was referring to the stern directive that had been sent out to all the houses in the Ōura area: in order to conceal the fact that a gigantic battleship was currently being built at the shipyard, they were not to carelessly leave their windows open.

"Yes."

"Then, if you knew that, why did you go in this abandoned house? What were you doing in there?" The MP, both fists pressed against his waist, glared at a blanching Shūhei, then peered at Sachiko with those same penetrating eyes.

"Yes, well . . . We were . . . reading poetry."

"Poetry?!"

"Yes. A book of poems by Satō Haruo."

"Satō? Let's see the book." Shūhei pulled *Surrendering to Sentiment* from his pocket. The MP took it and flipped through the pages as he asked, "Do you have any idea what sort of times we're living in right now?"

Shūhei did not respond.

"So you're out lollygagging with a girl and reading effeminate poems while soldiers of the Imperial Army are shedding their blood on the battlefield?"

"Poems aren't effeminate."

"What?!" The MP had assumed that Shūhei wouldn't talk back to him, so he stiffened, as though ready to pounce.

Shūhei retorted loudly, "What's wrong with reading poems?"

"Bastard! You answer back to me?!" The MP raised his right hand, still holding the book, and whacked Shūhei across the face. Shūhei staggered back two or three steps and stopped where he stood. The cover of *Surrendering to Sentiment* ripped off the book and fell to the ground. "I could easily take you into custody for trespassing in a vacant house in an off-limits defense zone. How about if you come with me to the military police headquarters."

"This is unfair! So unfair!" Weeping, Sachiko suddenly insinuated her body between Shūhei and the MP. "He hasn't done anything wrong!"

For an instant, the MP looked at Sachiko with a startled look on his face.

"Shū-chan has done nothing wrong!"

"Shū-chan? Brother and sister, are you?"

"No," Sachiko shook her head. "We're just friends."

"Friends? What sort of friends?"

"We go to the same church. We both belong to the Ōura Church."

A look of open contempt crossed his face. "Jesus-types, are you? So you're followers of the enemy religion, when Japan has its own religion?" He spat. "You believe in the same religion as the enemy soldiers from America and England. That alone is enough to call you unpatriotic."

He looked deprecatingly at Shūhei, who was licking his bloodied lips. "You couldn't even kill a soldier from America or

England, could you? 'Cause they believe in this Jesus guy too. I'm right, aren't I?"

He climbed back onto his bike, and without even a glance at the two, he pedaled off down the slope that began its descent at the church.

It was quiet. Shūhei still stood frozen, as though in a daze. Sachiko was crouched down, both hands covering her face, sobbing.

The two young people could not have anticipated what had just happened. It was like an unforeseen accident, but unlike an accident, they were both subjected to unmerited humiliation. They had been treated as though reading poetry or believing in Christianity were acts of treason against their homeland.

Still weeping, Sachiko picked up the book that had been discarded on the ground. The ripped cover and pages spilled open, and on one torn page, coincidentally enough, were the words of the poem that had so moved Sachiko:

I learned what true love from the heart means.
It is a love that seeks nothing.

"Stupid!" Shūhei's muttered voice was almost a groan. "Are we really living at a time when people can go around freely doing such stupid things?!"

But when Sachiko, her eyes brimming with tears, handed the poetry book to him, he forced a smile and said, "Ow! It's been a long time since I've been beaten that badly! When I was a kid, I got into all kinds of trouble and had beatings from the priests and from my mother, but I got used to those." He handed the poetry collection back to Sachiko.

"You keep this. You can put it back together with some glue. Keep it as a remembrance of the horrible things that were done to us today."

His words only magnified her impulse to weep, and again she covered her face with her hands.

She parted with Shūhei in front of the church. As she walked along the stone-paved street, she thought of the humiliation she had just experienced, and her chest tightened with anger and sorrow.

When she returned home, she meticulously repaired the cover of the poetry book. Then she used some waxed paper to hold the torn pages together.

Yet the tear on the cover remained, as though it were a wound that could not be healed. When she looked at the damage, memories of the shame she had just endured revived, searing and raw within her, as though she had been scorched by a hot iron.

"So you're followers of the enemy religion, when Japan has its own religion? You believe in the same religion as the enemy soldiers from America and England. That alone is enough to call you unpatriotic."

The soldier's swarthy face was darkly tanned from the sun. When he learned that Shūhei and Sachiko were both Christians, that swarthy face had displayed open disgust and suspicion.

"You couldn't even kill a soldier from America or England, could you? 'Cause they believe in this Jesus guy too."

His words surfaced one after another in her mind like bubbles rising in the water. She couldn't forget them no matter how hard she tried.

I wonder how Shū-chan is feeling right now?

She could vividly imagine the seething in his mind, moving from a Sunday morning filled with the joy of passing his exams to the undeserved violence that had been meted out to him. It was bitter, sad, and depressing for her.

Why couldn't they be allowed to read poetry? Was it wrong to savor something beautiful? Was being Japanese really so inconsistent with reading poems and being moved by beauty?

Is this the kind of world we're heading into with each new day?

With this uncertainty circling in her mind, she was unable to sleep much that night. Having kept from her parents the fact that she was going to meet Shūhei, there wasn't any way she could tell them about what had happened that day.

After only two or three days, she sent a feeler out to her father. "Somebody said something about us believing in the enemy's religion."

Her father had returned home unusually early that evening and was killing insects in their tiny vegetable garden. His eyes narrowed, "Who said such a thing?"

"A soldier. Not to me. To one of my friends . . ."

Her father sat on the veranda with a dispirited look on his face. "There are probably going to be more and more people in Japan who say things like that. But you mustn't forget that the blood of the Urakami people flows in your veins."

"What's this got to do with the blood of the Urakami people?"

"I must've told you about this before. The people of Urakami, no matter how much the rulers tortured them, would not give up their beliefs. They were forced out of their homes and exiled to places all over Japan, but no matter the tortures or the pains inflicted on them, they held on to their faith. That same Urakami blood flows in your veins, too."

"And so—?"

"And so, don't worry about the bad things people say to you. Tell them that we're allowed our religious freedom. Everyone ought to know that it's because of the sufferings of the Urakami people that Japan has freedom of religion today."

Even that strict injunction did nothing to lift Sachiko's gloom. All she could think about was the likelihood that the number of people who held ideas like those of that young, swarthy MP would only continue to increase in Japan.

6

THE PLACE OF DEATH

IT WAS A freight car used for transporting animals such as cattle or horses. But it was not cattle or horses jammed into the car; it was human beings, exhausted and covered with sweat and dust.

The train, each car crammed with eighty of the elderly, children, men and women, was slowly gliding through the wetlands near Kraków, the ancient capital of Poland. Night finally yielded to dawn, and the sky began to brighten.

The men and women in the freight cars, their bodies leaning against one another, their eyes closed, now sleeping and waking, waking and then sleeping, lifted their faces at the sharp sound of the locomotive's whistle.

One young man looked out the train car window, which was half concealed by piles of their belongings, at the increasingly bright scene outside.

Groves of birch and beech trees, and a small, dark swamp. Farms demarked by the tall trunks of poplar trees. Again today, morning was making its entry from the far reaches of the landscape, and the clouds were split apart by the golden light of the sun.

"Can you see the factory?" A man standing to his side asked despondently. The young man shook his head, also despondently.

They all believed that they were going to be pressed into forced labor at some Nazi munitions factory. Though they had no proof that this would be the case, they assumed that the many people who had been taken from places like the Jewish quarter in Warsaw and loaded into freight cars were being forced into harsh labor.

"See anything?"

"No." The young man focused his bloodshot, weary eyes on the horizon. Black forms appeared in the distance. The dark forms gradually took on the shape of row after row of military barracks-like buildings. The steam locomotive, as though announcing that they were approaching their destination, gave a whistle that sounded like a shrill scream.

"There's some smokestacks off in the distance," the young man told those around him. "Tall smokestacks."

Beside the barracks-like buildings, tall, slender chimneys rose into the brightening sky.

"Then those are the factories," a nearby man nodded, as though he now understood the situation. "The factories where we'll be put to work."

The others in the car stirred faintly at his words. Soon they would be able to get out of this cattle conveyance. Having stood on their feet for so many hours, their bodies had gone totally numb. They wanted to get out of the car as quickly as possible, stretch their bodies, drink some water, and urinate.

"Father," a nun called out to a man wearing round spectacles. "We'll be arriving soon."

"Thank you." The man identified as a priest, still in a shallow sleep, recalled the dream he had just seen.

In the dream, he had been walking along the stone-paved streets of faraway Nagasaki. He was on the sloping road leading to the Ōura Church. The little magazine press he and several compatriots operated was on that slope. From that position, they could look out over the tiny Japanese houses, the low mountains, and the beautiful bay.

"NA-GA-SA-KI," he muttered with fondness, as though calling out to something of great value. But he was not in NA-GA-SA-KI.

"This is Auschwitz!" the young man at the window shouted. "I can see a sign that says Auschwitz!"

At his shout, several people pushed the young man aside and pressed their faces against the window.

Auschwitz. . . . Every Jew and Pole had heard that name. They knew the name, but none knew with any certainty exactly what transpired there. Not one person had ever returned alive from there to tell them about the place.

Rumor had it that it was a place of forced labor. But that it was also a place where those who could not work, including the elderly and the sick and the children, were all herded together and slaughtered. No one knew how much of that was true.

But thanks to such rumors, the mere name of Auschwitz filled the Jews and the Poles with indescribable fear and uneasiness.

Something frightening goes on there. In that place . . .

And their train was about to arrive in Auschwitz.

The milky morning mist cleared away. Once it was light enough that they could clearly make out the trunks of the birch trees, they had no trouble spotting the double-ringed barbed-wire fence that cut through the grove and unfeelingly enclosed the compound. Further off in the distance were several rows of tile-roofed buildings that looked like military barracks. Did the tall smokestacks belong to the factories . . . ?

"There's people in there."

A cluster of people was crawling about like ants. All wore clown-like uniforms. Were they the ones interned here?

The train began to slow down.

"Oh dear God!" a weeping woman cried. "God, please help us! Please don't let them take us off the train here!"

She was not the only one with that wish. It was the hope of every man and woman jammed into that freight car.

Beneath their feet, however, they could hear the screech of the train passing over the siding. Through the window of the car, they saw a coal storehouse, and a coal car slowly passed by them. The train gave a panting whistle when it came to a stop at the tiny station.

The people in the cattle car cringed and held their breath. Then they heard the hoarse voice of a Nazi soldier, and when the door to the car was roughly slid open, the morning light came streaming in like a torrent. Several prisoners wearing those clown uniforms crawled up into the car and barked out orders.

"Leave your belongings. . . . Get out!"

Leaving their trunks, their rucksacks, and the bags that contained their only worldly possessions, they jumped down from the freight car.

The young man who had stood by the car's window joined the others in jumping onto the bare platform. This was the first ground they had stepped on for many hours, but that fact brought them no joy now.

Standing beside the young man, the priest was reaching up with both arms to help old grandmothers and plump women climb down from the car.

"Father, what will happen to us?" one woman asked, her face twisted in anxiety.

"I don't know. Be patient," he admonished her in a soft voice. "We are all suffering. You're not the only one."

They were forced to wait on the platform until afternoon. They were given no food. Exposed to the increasingly hot sunlight, some sat on the ground and tried to make up for the sleep they had mostly missed out on since the previous night.

At strategic positions all around them, Nazi SS soldiers with German shepherds on leashes kept a close eye on the group. Escape would be impossible; even if someone did try to flee, those barbed-wire fences would block their way.

Pretending to sleep, the young man stole glances at one of the red-roofed buildings across the way. The prisoners dressed in striped clown uniforms had disappeared, and it was eerily quiet all around them. Two stakes that appeared to be used for drying clothes had been erected between that building and the next, with three sets of newly washed prisoner uniforms dangling limply from them.

But as his weary eyes studied the stakes, he suddenly realized that he was not looking at prisoner uniforms. Those were, without any doubt, human beings drooping down like rags. They were the corpses of three humans that had suffered death by hanging.

His mouth frozen open with fear, the young man for a time could not tear his eyes away from the scene. He poked the priest, who stood beside him with his eyes closed, and whispered to him, no longer able to bear the horror of the sight by himself. "Father, look!"

The priest pushed his round glasses up on his nose and stared in the direction the young man was pointing.

"Tell no one," the priest hurriedly enjoined the young man. "There are women and children here. We mustn't alarm them for no reason."

"But . . . they'll eventually find out, won't they? This place is exactly what the rumors say it is. It's a place where everyone is murdered."

"But . . . there are many still alive here," the priest said in an effort to encourage the trembling youth. "We mustn't . . . mustn't lose hope."

"Father, aren't you afraid?" the young man asked, almost angrily.

"I'm . . . yes, I'm afraid." The priest nodded. "But I am a priest."

"Then pray to your God. Pray that I can stay alive. I want to keep on living. I'm still young!"

The priest placed his hand atop that of the young man. "I will pray for you," he promised in a whisper.

"What's your name, Father?"

"Kolbe."

"I'm Henryk Gajowniczek.[1] Please call me Henryk."

The gruff voice of a guard interrupted the initial conversation between these two men. One prisoner who accompanied the guard as translator ordered everyone to line up single file.

The men and women, old and young, formed a long queue and walked haltingly toward the assembly ground. An iron gate rose at the far side, and above the gate, the words ARBEIT MACHT FREI were written in decorative black letters. *Work Sets You Free.*

The line came to a stop.

Prisoners at the front of the queue were being divided up, some to the right and some to the left. A tall Nazi officer with shiny polished boots and a pistol in his belt directed them to proceed in one direction or the other.

"I hope I'm in the same group as you," the young man said softly to the priest.

They did not know what was in store after the line of prisoners had been divided up. Initially, women and men were assigned to separate groups, after which the elderly, children, those with physical infirmities, and those who complained of illness were

---

1 Endō has taken this surname from Franciszek Gajowniczek (1901–1995), a Polish army sergeant who spent almost five and a half years in the Auschwitz death camp, but Henryk is a fictional character unrelated to Franciszek.

pulled out from the two groups. This subdividing took a great deal of time, and it was nearly sunset when the apportioning was completed.

"So I did end up with you!" Young Henryk joined Father Kolbe's group and moved along beside him. They were led away by a kapo,[2] a prisoner wearing a striped uniform and wooden clogs.

As they marched away, they called out to the women and elderly and children they were leaving behind, "Be strong!"

Those who remained were the wives and fathers and children of the departing group. It was painful to be torn away from their family members, but no such grumbling was permitted in a concentration camp. They were separated for a time, but surely they would meet up again.

Passing beneath the gate proclaiming ARBEIT MACHT FREI, the men who were being led toward a barrack-like brick building suddenly swallowed in fear and stopped walking.

Two stakes stood in front of the building, where three prisoners hanging between them fluttered like pieces of laundry. But the three were not fluttering; these were the corpses of the men who had been hanged.

The group fell silent. All averted their rigid faces and stared at the ground.

"March!" The kapo said with a slight smile, "What are you surprised about? Did you think you were coming here to stay in a hotel? This is a concentration camp!"

They entered the brick building. Both sides of the long, narrow corridor were arrayed like honeycombs. An indescribably foul body stench and the smell of straw produced odors like those from an animal cage.

---

2   A Jewish prisoner given special privileges and minor administrative tasks in the camps. In *Man's Search for Meaning*, Viktor Frankl spells this "Capo."

The smells emanated from dilapidated three-level wooden beds arranged one beside another like silkworm shelves.

"Nine of you will sleep on each tier. That means twenty-seven of you on this one tier." Nine men were to lie down on a bare wooden shelf no more than two meters deep. It was unimaginable.

"There's no way. I couldn't possibly sleep like that," Henryk grumbled.

"You couldn't?" the kapo responded. "Fine, then you don't have to sleep there. Instead . . . here, come with me." He yanked roughly on Henryk's arm and stood him by the window. "If you don't like it here, maybe we should have you go over there."

Black smoke curled up against the gray, darkening sky from the tall chimneys that they had seen earlier through the window of the freight car. The smoke was undisturbed by any wind; a flock of birds returning to their nests drew a line against the evening sky.

"Go to a factory?"

"You think that's a factory, do you?" The kapo shrugged.

"Well, yes, there's smoke coming from the chimney," Henryk replied in bewilderment.

"Yes, there most definitely is smoke coming out. But what do you suppose is being burned to produce that smoke?" The kapo bared his yellowed teeth and grinned.

"I have no idea."

"It's smoke from the incinerated corpses of your comrades who were separated from you after you arrived. Would you care to join them?"

✳ ✳ ✳

His words were neither a threat nor a lie.

The elderly, the women, and the children who had been formed into a separate column beside the gate of the concentration camp only thirty minutes earlier had been left standing for a time, after which an affable Nazi officer greeted them. He was as gentle as a woman, and he spoke to them in fluent Polish.

"I'm sure you must be tired after your long journey. We want you to get a good sleep tonight and recover your strength. Those in need of a doctor will be examined later by a physician."

The women smiled in relief. None had expected to be given such consideration. Evidently the rumors circulating about Auschwitz were lies . . .

"First, though, our regulations require that you take showers. It's . . ." The officer seemed amused, "It's most impolite of me to say this to you, but it's in order to prevent an outbreak of lice."

Some in the group laughed out loud. The feelings of gloom that had oppressed them without relief were swept away, rebounding in the form of an unwarranted cheerfulness.

"March to the showers." At that command, the elderly and the women each took the hand of a child and started off in a direction opposite from that taken by their husbands and sons.

Without warning, music sounded from the direction of the chimneyed building. An orchestra made up of prisoners was playing a waltz, as if to welcome the new arrivals.

"March merrily to the merry music," the Nazi officer said kindheartedly, touching with his finger the cheek of an infant being carried by its mother at the front of the line.

As they neared the underground entrance, a Strauss waltz was played even more brightly and spiritedly. But the prisoner musicians performing the music, wearing their clown-striped uniforms, were careful not to glance toward the group. Their eyes seemed empty, as though utterly drained of emotion.

When they entered the underground passageway, which smelled of chemicals, the instincts of several of the women suggested danger to them. One of the women suddenly spun around and began racing toward the entrance.

"Stop!" the smiling officer shouted. His shout was immediately followed by the sharp report of a gunshot outside.

"That's what happens to those who disobey orders," the officer explained, exaggeratedly shrugging his shoulders. An indefinable, silent fear spread through the room.

The elderly and the women were herded into separate, large shower rooms. They removed their clothes and left them by the doorway. One of the mothers had concealed an infant beneath her clothing. The officer stepped up to her, clicked his tongue and shook his head. "Madam, this is not allowed."

When everyone had been moved into the shower rooms, the doors were shut with a great clatter. Then, at the order, "Give them something to eat," poisonous gas was released.

✳ ✳ ✳

It took only a few minutes before everything was over.

When the doors were reopened, naked corpses were piled atop one another in mountainous heaps.

✳ ✳ ✳

Trees in the forest far in the distance stretched their branches into the misty evening sky. Slowly, gently, smoke rose from the chimney.

There was no other movement inside the concentration camp. Just as on any peaceful evening, everything was quiet; it was the time when all silently awaited the arrival of night.

As though it were a herald of the coming of night, the smoke from the chimney lightly, unperturbably spread into the sky, where it turned a blueish purple. Flocks of birds etched hyperbolic curves as they flew back to their nests.

Young Henryk and the other men who had been crowded into their barrack stared at the scene as though in a trance. The women, the children, the aged, the ones they had been chatting with not long before, the ones whose weary faces they had looked into and encouraged to endure not so long before—among them their wives and sons and fathers—now had all been reduced to that black smoke.

It was not a bad dream. It was an indisputable fact.

That moment gave notice to the entire group that this truly was Auschwitz. Some still struggled desperately in their heads to deny what had just happened, but however they might try to negate it, the black smoke outside their window told the whole story.

"Do you understand?" The kapo who had led them to this room called loudly. "I'm sure you understand that this is not a hotel in the Alps . . . and there's no way to tell when you might be tossed underneath that smokestack."

Henryk looked toward Father Kolbe, hoping to find something he could cling to. The priest stood apart from the rest of the group, his eyes closed as he prayed. He was praying for the dead who had just now been consumed by the flames.

"You're not going to watch?" with a smirk, the kapo asked the priest. "What are you doing over there?"

"I am praying for those who have died."

"Praying?" The kapo twisted up his mouth and surveyed Father Kolbe with a mocking smile. "Are you . . . a priest?"

"Yes, I am."

"You were praying? Did everybody hear that? This son of a bitch says he was praying for the more than one hundred women and children who were burned to ash here. Why go to the trouble of praying to make everything all right? You can pray . . . but that will change nothing here. No matter how hard you pray, this being you call God will do nothing to save us!"

Pain filled Father Kolbe's eyes as he listened to those words.

"Listen, instead of praying, why don't you all line up and go to the dressing room. You'll have two minutes to take off all your clothes. Do you understand? Two minutes! Leave all of your possessions there. Don't even think about concealing anything."

The men, who had been standing dumbfounded, pulled themselves together and hurriedly formed rank.

"And one more thing." The tone of the kapo's voice changed. "I'm in charge in this room. And I'll be watching you every minute. I will tolerate no laziness or slacking off. Otherwise you'll be sent off to the gas chamber."

One hour later, they had been stripped naked. All their hair was shaved off. Not just the hair on their heads, but on their entire bodies. Besides their clothing, anything they had on their person—watches, lockets with photos of family members—was taken from them.

They were now utterly cut off from the lives they had been living. They were no longer allowed to feel pride or honor. In exchange, they were given striped prisoner uniforms and wooden clogs, which were also the signs of their subservience.

While they were being stripped naked, anyone who even slightly answered back, and any man who was the least bit slack in his movements was lashed severely with a whip kept in the room. The piercing cracks of the whip and barked orders would now set the rhythm for their daily lives.

When they had finished removing their clothes, they were given no further orders to work that night, and they were fed something resembling food for their evening meal.

✴ ✴ ✴

One bowl of watery soup—that was all. Their meals provided them with only four hundred calories of nutrition per day. The whip awaited any who grumbled. Any who resisted orders were either shot or tortured.

Following dinner, nine men lay down together on wooden planks only two meters wide, their bodies pressed against each other as they slept. No one spoke a word any longer. They had already learned that in order to survive in this place, they could not expend an ounce of meaningless energy.

Henryk squeezed his eyes shut and tried desperately to fall asleep. He could feel on his neck the breathing of the man pressed against his back. The shelves were saturated with body odors.

Someone was weeping. But no one asked him what was wrong.

"Oh God, please help us!" the weeping voice suddenly shouted.

"Shut up!" someone else bellowed. Thereafter the room was wrapped in the silence of death.

Prayers are of no use in this place, Henryk muttered to himself. *You can't depend on God. If you want to stay alive, you have only yourself to rely on.*

No matter what, I'm going to stay alive. I will not die here. That priest Kolbe with his round spectacles is welcome to pray if he wants to. You can't depend on God . . .

Henryk collapsed into a dead sleep.

Dawn came. It was still pitch dark when angry voices echoed through the room.

"Get up, you swine! Assemble in ranks outside in ten minutes."

Round holes had been cut into long wooden planks to make toilets. The men jostled to use them. The rims of the holes were caked with filth, but no one thought anything of it.

"Hurry and assemble. Swine!"

The whip cracked all throughout the room, and the panicked newcomers ran stumbling toward the courtyard, pulling up the pants on their prisoner uniforms as they went.

This was their first morning.

7

THE STUDENT DORMITORY

SACHIKO'S FEELINGS FOR Shūhei could be said to resemble those of a sister toward her older brother. Having no older brother of her own, Sachiko felt a closeness and a connection with this older male friend that she felt for no one else.

But it might also be said that this was Sachiko's first love. Not a single confession of the kind of romantic feelings exchanged between lovers had passed between these two. But after Shūhei returned to Tokyo, Sachiko began thinking about him in the deepest part of her consciousness.

Although a month had passed since Shūhei matriculated into Keiō University, not one message had come from him. He had promised to write her a letter as soon as he found lodgings. Had he totally forgotten his promise? Not a word from him.

I wonder if maybe a letter will come today? This thought filled her head throughout every class at school. The lectures from her teachers fell on deaf ears, while the tiny mailbox at her house rose up in her mind. She could almost see and hear as the letter from Shūhei landed with a thump in her mailbox.

"Mom, did I get any mail?" She casually inquired of her mother when she returned from school. She may have asked casually, but her heart felt as though it were going to begin pounding painfully.

"Let's see, no, nothing. Why?"

"No, that's fine." She could inquire no further, since her mother would begin to suspect something if she pressed too hard.

Accompanying her loneliness, resignation spread through her heart like ink dropped into water. *I guess Shū-chan has forgotten me after all. They say the young men at Keiō are popular with all the coeds.*

Yet along with her resignation, a sense of security welled within her when she decided that there was no reason a young woman should be infatuated with a fellow with such dusky skin and googly eyes. She had no idea how to resolve this irreconcilable mix of feelings.

Sachiko had never had an experience like this before. Since it was a first for her, she was at a total loss. She could neither confess nor discuss her feelings with her mother. It went without saying that she would be reprimanded were she to mention her dilemma to the nuns at Junshin Women's Junior College. The sisters believed that a female student of Sachiko's age was still too young to be agonizing over a young man, and some of the teachers at the school would regard her feelings as sinful.

I'm through with him, she decided. *He's the biggest irresponsible liar around. He makes me all worried about him over his entrance exams, and after that he acts like he doesn't even know me!*

Sachiko made every effort to forget Shūhei. She recalled every facial flaw and vilified each one.

Ridiculous. What's up with that forehead of his? He's a crabby old troublemaker! With a snub nose and goggle eyes!

Even so, during mass on Sundays, she would pray to the statue of the Blessed Mother that stood beside the altar.

Mother Mary, please help Shū-chan to send me at least one letter. If you'll do that, I'll never think about him again. Well, I'll make sure I forget him completely after maybe three months.

The Blessed Mother was gentler than the teachers at Junshin. She was quick to answer this charming young woman's request: a letter arrived from Shūhei the following day.

The characters Shūhei had written, which could only be described as a scrawl, leapt about on the white envelope. Sachiko could visualize his googly eyes behind each of his scribbled characters.

It's been a month since school started. I've been busy the whole month looking for a place to live and haven't had any time to write a letter. But I was finally accepted in the dorm for Christian students located at Shinano-machi in Tokyo.

It's a small dorm, with around twenty students from each of the main universities—Tokyo University, Waseda, Keiō, Sophia, and several others. We each have single rooms. The Tokyo University student in the room next to mine is named Sugii Yoshinori. He's in the agriculture department, but he likes literature, so I hang out in his room a lot. His bookcase is crammed with books I never even heard of.

Twice a week, a philosophy professor from Tokyo University, Yoshimitsu Yoshihiko,[1] visits our dorm. He's the housemaster here. He eats with us and leads lots of discussions with us, but to be honest, what he says is pretty deep, and it's hard for a lazy student like me to understand.

I was told that once you get accepted to Keiō, you're popular with all the women, but that turned out to be a total lie. No girl has ever looked at me or spoken to me. There's a weird fellow in my classes named Ōhashi Shin'ya. Like me, he

---

1 Yoshimitsu Yoshihiko (1904–1945) was a Japanese Catholic philosopher who studied in France under Jacques Maritain. While teaching at several universities in Tokyo, he was also housemaster at the Christian dormitory where Endō lived during his years at Keiō University.

wants to become a novelist, so we've become friends. The other
day he and I went walking at Meiji Gaien Park and ended
up following this one girl, but pretty soon she realized she was
being tailed, so she turned around and yelled "Morons!" The
women in Tokyo are really strong-willed, not at all like
Nagasaki women. But this will all count as part of my
training to be a novelist.

Sachiko read the letter twice—no, three or four times. It bothered her that Shūhei was out stalking girls.

"That's creepy. He really is no good." Sachiko shook her head when she read that chasing after girls was part of the training to become a novelist.

A second letter came three weeks later. Shūhei wrote about a minor incident that had occurred at his dormitory.

The other day, when all the students were out, a policeman
came to the dorm and searched every room without even
asking permission. He was looking for any books we might
have relating to communism.

As a result, Sugii was summoned to the police station. The
hilarious thing is that the detective found a book called An
Essay on the Principle of Population *in Sugii's room. The*
author's name in Japanese was written MARUSASU—
Malthius. He mistook that for MARUKUSU—Marx, and
made accusations against Sugii. The misunderstanding was
quickly cleared up. But it was an unsettling day.

Once again, this time lying in her bed, Sachiko read this letter over several times. It made her feel somehow happy.

Unconnected to her insignificant little emotions, however, around this time Japan began to lose the war against the

American forces. As always, the radio and newspapers announced a glorious victory in the naval battle at Midway, but in reality the Japanese Navy had suffered a lethal blow.

No matter how hard the government and the military command tried to manipulate the facts, the people were beginning to sniff out the reality that the war situation was dire. Rumors were being whispered around everywhere.

The streets of Tokyo were being increasingly laid waste, food was in short supply, and goods had disappeared from stores. Virtually every day along streets all over the city, young recruits with shaven heads leaving for the battlefield marched along, surrounded by apron-clad women and reservists waving paper flags.

"We may be drafted soon," the students in Shūhei's dorm began to discuss with trepidation. They had the privilege of a draft deferral because they were in school, but they were convinced that, with war conditions being what they were, that advantage would not be theirs forever.

"Does that mean we won't be able to go to school anymore?" Shūhei asked Sugii.

"Not go to school?! That's not the worst of it. We may die if we're sent to the Pacific." With a loud laugh, Sugii crushed Shūhei's naïve hopes. "Ah, you just barely got into school this semester, didn't you? That must make this extra painful for you." A look of sympathy crossed his face.

Still, Shūhei could not actually grasp the possibility that he might be sent to the battlefield, or that his student deferment might be eliminated. But although he couldn't sense it as a reality, a dark apprehension seized his heart.

To escape his anxiety, when Shūhei returned to his dorm after classes, he read poetry. He thumbed through other works of literature. He was attempting to flee the bleakness of the present situation by immersing himself in the world of poetry.

One day when he returned from school, his books of literature and poetry were scattered on his floor, and there were indications that his drawers had been opened.

The police have come sniffing around again, he instantly realized. An older woman who did cleaning and cooking at the dorm had fear on her face when she told the students, "There were two of them today, and they stayed a long time." Hesitantly she reported, "They said they're especially keeping an eye on Christians."

"What do they think we're going to do?!" bellowed one of the students, unable to restrain himself. "Just because we're Christians doesn't mean we're going to become spies!"

"But that's not what the police think," Sugii shook his head. "You may not know this, but Protestants are strictly antiwar."

"Antiwar?"

"Yes. There's obviously a contradiction between the Christian teaching 'Thou shalt not kill' and acts of war. Protestants with enough courage have been saying that, and they've been arrested by the police for it."

Shūhei had never heard anything like this. Sugii, even though he was studying agriculture, was well-versed in literature and had taught Shūhei a lot, but he evidently kept to himself many things that none of the others knew about.

Sugii tossed cold water on the credulous optimism of the younger Shūhei.

"Everything was fine as long as we were winning the war. But now that the situation has taken a turn for the worse, the government and the police are tightening their grip on the people by sniffing out anybody who is the least suspicious. There's no question that one of the groups that looks suspicious to them is us Christians. In the eyes of the police, we're traitors who believe in an enemy religion."

"Enemy religion"—those words called up in Shūhei's mind that day when a military policeman he encountered on the sloping road at Ōura had spat out those same words. The humiliation of that moment, combined with the pain when the officer had slapped him, rose up in his mind with suffocating reality.

"They're keeping it a secret, but several of the Protestants who are opposed to this war have been hauled away by the police."

"How come you know all this, Sugii?" Shūhei asked in amazement.

"I have a classmate from middle school who works for the Home Ministry. He told me."

"What about Catholics?"

"Catholics?" A look of scorn showed up on Sugii's face even though he himself was Catholic. "The Catholics don't have as much courage as the Protestants. Haven't you heard that people at the Watchtower Press and members of the Wesleyan Holiness Church were tied up and taken away?"

"I had no idea."

"Of course you didn't. Just this past March, Father Toda[2] of Sapporo was the one Catholic who was indicted."

"Why?"

"He told his congregation that this war was ill-advised, and that Japanese troops were enforcing occupation policies in the South Seas that ignored the feelings of the native people."

This was all news to Shūhei. Sugii repeated his warning, half threateningly, that because they were Christians they could be summoned before the police at any time.

---

2 Father Toda Tatewaki (1898–1945) was a Catholic priest who ministered in Sapporo and Yokohama. He was arrested but released for lack of evidence. Just three days after Japan's surrender on August 15, 1945, he was assassinated by an unknown assailant.

However, for the time being police officers stopped coming to the dormitory. Fortunately, at Shūhei's school, Keiō University, there were many easygoing students but no narrow-minded nationalists.

Even when Shūhei revealed to Ōhashi and some of his other classmates that he was a Christian, no one felt any antipathy toward him, and in fact one even said, "Really? How fashionable!"

To evade the dark feelings of anxiety swirling deep in his mind, Shūhei began devouring works of literature at his school's library.

Sugii gave him the names of various writers and books. He had collected the writings of authors such as the Japan Romantic School writers, Hofmannsthal, Rilke, and Carossa, and he loaned copies to Shūhei.

Shūhei made an attempt to persuade Sachiko that he himself had become a first-rate poet by sending her some verses he had written. He was certain that even sentimental poems that were mocked by the older Sugii would deeply impress Sachiko.

Basically, she doesn't really understand anything. He looked down on Sachiko the same way an older brother condescends toward his younger sister.

Sachiko kept each one of Shūhei's sporadic letters, along with the poems he enclosed with them, in the box that had once contained chocolates. It was the same box where she had placed the picture of the Blessed Mother she had received from Father Kolbe.

She couldn't really tell whether Shūhei's poems were good or abysmal. But they were precious to Sachiko because Shūhei had written them.

Nightfall in autumn
A sad look on the dog's face

As he takes a dump.
Watching the shitting mongrel,
I felt I was seeing Life.

This was one of Shūhei's verses from around that time. Sachiko thought it was foul and lacking in grace compared with the beautiful, moving poems of Satō Haruo, and when she wrote that matter-of-fact reaction to Shūhei, she seemed to have struck a nerve. In his angry response, he wrote, "Why should I waste any more time with someone like you who doesn't understand art?" But scarcely ten days passed before he sent another verse. After all, this self-styled poetic genius had no readers other than Sachiko to whom he could show his work.

In addition to his poems, he sent her a short story titled "I Am a Dog." Taking that sorrowful dog who had been defecating in autumn as its protagonist, this "masterwork" (as Shūhei himself called it) parodied the times they lived in, but Sachiko couldn't find anything interesting in it. For one thing, it was obvious that he had taken his title from Natsume Sōseki's novel, *I Am a Cat*.

Still, Sachiko knew that she was the only person Shūhei was sending his poems and stories to. More than anything she was comforted to know that he had chosen her as his one and only reader.

I am snot. Because snot does mankind no good
I am snot to today's world.
I am a snot-like human being.
Those who pursue literature in today's world are snot.

In private Sachiko showed this typically odd verse to her mother. But her mother failed to appreciate Shūhei's literary talent. She merely twisted up her face and muttered, "Well, that's nasty. He's a little funny in the head, isn't he?"

July came. The streets of Nagasaki began to fill with the cries of cicadas. From inside the temple precincts in the Tera-machi district, the grating chorus of large brown cicadas startled the passersby who were wiping sweat from their brows.

At Sachiko's school, when the first semester tests were concluded, the one-week summer break was canceled out by labor assignments foisted on the students. They worked as a "Patriotic Team" at the Mitsubishi Shipyard.

Sachiko worked there, bathed in sweat and dressed in women's work trousers. She and the other young women were assigned to wash the work clothes of the factory employees.

Shūhei will be coming home soon.

That thought made it easy for her to do the work that all the other young women privately complained about. Her classmates all seemed like children to her, doubling over in laughter the way they did and understanding nothing about love.

On the day a ceremony was held to celebrate the completion of their work assignment, summer clouds, whiter even than newly laundered handkerchiefs, billowed in the offing at Nagasaki Bay.

On the dais, a soldier who had been brought in from who knows where was giving a hackneyed speech: "At this time of critical importance in the war situation, we citizens must incorporate a belief in absolute victory into our daily lives, and though this be your summer vacation, you must not allow yourselves to slack off."

Still, when he finished talking, it was indeed summer vacation. The students gleefully passed through the factory gate and raced to their homes.

"Hey, Sat-chan!" Takeda Mieko, one of her classmates, came running after Sachiko. She was slender, with a narrow back. "Do you have any plans for vacation?"

"Nope, no plans."

"Well then, do you want to come with us on an overnight trip to Shimabara? If the war gets any worse, I doubt we'll be able to take trips like this anymore. And this is our last summer vacation."

"An overnighter?" Sachiko thought it over, and decided it was something her mother would approve of.

"When?"

"Next Monday. I'm working out the details with Misato."

Sachiko agreed to go, hoping that it wouldn't be the day that Shūhei returned home. His last letter had said he'd be coming back from Tokyo at the end of this week or the start of next.

When she arrived at home, her mother, who was eating a tomato grown in their tiny vegetable garden, said nervously, "Sat-chan, be sure to wash your hands really well. They say that dengue fever is coming to Nagasaki."

During that summer vacation, oppressively hot days passed one after another. Food was difficult to obtain, but Sachiko filled each day swimming with her brother at the beach at Mogi or helping her mother. Every week seemed interminable, and she always wished Sundays would come faster. If Shūhei had returned home, she might run into him at Sunday mass.

During mass the following Sunday, she scanned through all the men and women kneeling in prayer, but Shūhei was not among them.

As she left the church in disappointment, the congregants gathered outside the chapel, discussing the dengue epidemic and the names of Christians who had been drafted into the military.

"I hear that Brother Ide and Brother Uchiyama have been called up." The number of Christians being drafted was growing as the war turned more savage.

That afternoon, Takeda Mieko stopped by to discuss the trip planned for the next day. They were to meet in front of Nagasaki

Station at 1:00 p.m. From there they planned to proceed to Isahaya by bus, then change buses and travel to Shimabara.

It was a trip they were all looking forward to, but at the same time Sachiko felt a certain indefinable sense of emptiness about it. She realized for the first time how important Shūhei was to her.

Could I actually be in love with Shū-chan? She cross-examined herself over and over, tossing and turning through a sleepless night.

The following day, Sachiko and Mieko waited for Misato in the scorching heat at the bus stand in front of Nagasaki Station.

"It's so hot!" Sachiko already looked exhausted as she wiped the sweat from her brow. "What's happened to her? Misato usually isn't this late."

"You're in a nasty mood, aren't you?" Mieko grinned.

"Sorry! It was so hot last night I had a hard time sleeping." She glanced indifferently toward the station. Suddenly her face lit up like a forest illuminated by sunlight after a rain shower.

She was looking directly at the exit where train passengers would emerge. Among those passengers, wearing a white shirt and carrying a steamer trunk, was Shūhei.

Indifferently, Shūhei glanced out. When he saw Sachiko waiting by the bus stand, his mouth dropped open in surprise. His mouth always seemed to gape open when he was surprised.

Jumping to conclusions, he asked, "What are you doing here? You came to welcome me home? But how did you know when I'd be arriving?"

"We're on our way to Shimabara," Sachiko hurriedly explained.

Shūhei's face showed obvious disappointment. "Right now?" he mumbled.

Just then Misato arrived. Mieko and Misato watched Sachiko and Shūhei from a distance.

"Who are those two?"

"Some friends from Junshin."

"Hmm. Pretty nice-looking girls. Why don't you introduce me?"

Sachiko introduced her two friends. With friendly curiosity, Shūhei asked them about their travel plans.

"I've been to that area maybe three times. You need to visit Hara Castle. You can see the ruins of Hara Castle, where the Shimabara Rebellion[3] took place. Let's see—you should take the Shimabara Rail Line." He gave them his recommendations even though they hadn't requested any.

The bus to Isahaya arrived.

"I'll be back in Nagasaki in two days," Sachiko whispered to Shūhei, but he was staring open-mouthed at the beautiful profile of Mieko. "You heard me, didn't you? Shū-chan, are you listening to me?"

"Of course I am."

The bus set out. Shūhei again shouldered his trunk and watched the bus depart, his mouth still flopping open.

Sachiko and her friends arrived at Shimabara that evening and stayed with some of Mieko's relatives.

Water seemed to be everywhere in Shimabara. The sounds of water flowing through the town were clearly audible.

Mieko's relatives were very kind. Taking into consideration the difficulty of obtaining sufficient food in Nagasaki, they cut back on their own rations of rice and served up fresh fish and prawns, the likes of which couldn't be found in Nagasaki these days.

The following morning, one member of their host's family took them to see some samurai mansions that were still preserved

---

3 Detailed later in this chapter, the rebellion, which lasted from December 1637 to April 1638, is considered the dying gasp of Christianity in feudal Japan.

in one section of the town and guided them to the Imamura execution grounds. The town was silent except for the sounds of the water that flowed in every direction from cool, clear streams. Even along streets lined on both sides by well-maintained samurai residences, the water in the irrigation ditches flowed clean and translucent.

Near midday, they got on a train and went to see the ruins of Hara Castle, the remains of the castle where Christians from Shimabara and Amakusa fought against the armies of the Tokugawa shogunate and were annihilated.

A bracing wind scented with seawater blew through the open windows of the train. The ocean stretched far into the distance beyond Shimabara, and Kumamoto Prefecture and the Amakusa Islands looked green against the horizon. In the opposite direction, the mountains at Unzen towered against a backdrop of white summer clouds.

There were none of the smells of war in this sky or this ocean. The three schoolgirls softly sang some ballads, inhaled deeply the warm breeze, and joyfully stepped off the train. In the afternoon sun, cicadas blared forth their own torrent of song.

Hara Castle was also known as Haru Castle—the "castle of spring." Suffering under the suppression of Christianity and the crushing tax burden, the peasants of Amakusa had crossed the bay and set up temporary fortifications in this abandoned castle. The government attacked the castle, even calling on assistance from Holland, eventually storming the castle after the loss of many of their own soldiers. Even the women and children who had taken refuge in the castle were slaughtered.

That same castle, which had been engulfed in a vortex of war cries and the echo of gunfire, was now buried beneath potato fields. Moss-covered stones from the castle walls were scattered across the ground, and weeds thrived atop the shelter that had shielded the women and children from the rains and dews during the siege—the stillness of the area was amplified amid the cries of the cicadas.

Mieko read an explanatory plaque: "It says that thirty thousand people were killed here."

"Thirty thousand!"

Thirty thousand was a number dozens of times larger than the total student population at Junshin Women's Junior College. And every one of those men and women had been slaughtered. Sachiko could almost smell their blood in the cries of the cicadas, sounds she felt were reverberating from the lowest of hells.

Could something like this happen again in Japan? Sachiko suddenly wondered. But she said nothing.

Someone was crouching down in the potato fields. She thought it was a farmer, but the man was dressed in a white shirt and casual slacks. He looked their way and grinned.

It was Shūhei.

"Whaaa?!" Mieko cried. Misato's eyes opened wide. Mieko turned a suspicious look toward Sachiko. "Did you invite him here?" she asked accusingly.

Sachiko quickly shook her head. "I know nothing about this. I mean, he's . . ."

Mieko was not yet persuaded. "You must have known he'd come here."

As though he hadn't even noticed Sachiko's embarrassment, Shūhei approached them with a friendly air. "I got here about an hour ago. I took the first morning bus from Nagasaki. I know it's summer vacation, but it's boring to just stay at home." He coolly explained himself. When he realized the three young women were saying nothing, he asked with concern, "Am I intruding here?"

"You're not intruding, but . . ." Sachiko tried to be sensitive to both sides. "We're just surprised to see you."

Shūhei explained to the young women that the spot where they were standing in the potato fields had been the outer rim of the castle, and that farther on was the inner citadel where Amakusa Shirō[4] had made his stand. He went on to tell them that Amakusa Shirō had been supreme commander here, even though he had still been a young man, and that his older sister and mother had been taken as hostages by the enemy.

"Amakusa Shirō was killed, too?"

"Of course. The Mound of Heads on Nishizaka slope in Nagasaki is the place where they buried the heads of all the people killed here. War back then and even now is a miserable business. They ran out of food here at the castle, and when the government forces cut open the bellies of captured prisoners, they say they found kombu pulled from the ocean."

"You know a lot about this, Shū-chan."

"Yeah, I do. Last night and this morning I sweated my way through some history books so I could impress you with my knowledge."

Mieko and Misato burst into laughter at Shūhei's all-too-frank confession, which finally seemed to break the ice and put them in a good mood.

"Say, from the lookout point a little farther ahead, the ocean is beautiful."

Following Shūhei's suggestion, they walked to the edge of the cliff that rose perpendicular from the ocean. The ocean breezes blew against their cheeks. The ultramarine ocean stretched out below, and directly beneath them the water was clear and cold, so clear they could even identify strands of seaweed. Two or three fishing boats floated in the offing.

---

4 Shirō was executed in 1638, at the age of seventeen, by the victorious government army.

"So beautiful!" Misato sighed. "If only there wasn't this war," she muttered to herself.

Sachiko wondered why only humans had to spill each other's blood when the realm of nature was so beautiful. It was heart-rending to see how beautiful the ocean and mountains and sky were today at these ruins where such copious amounts of blood had been shed.

"Wow!" Shūhei suddenly shouted in excitement from across the potato field.

"What is it?" Sachiko called from the distance.

"Pottery! I found some broken pieces of pottery!" his voice quavered as he held up a fragment of some object. "Sat-chan, this is from around the time of the Shimabara Rebellion. It could be from a water jug that Amakusa Shirō's army used."

The young women approached and peered at the object Shūhei held. It was a shard of pottery that still retained some dark blue coloration.

"This is an amazing discovery! I've got to show this to the newspapers," Shūhei announced in a shrill voice.

"I wonder what will happen?" Mieko and Misato, who had until now kept their distance from Shūhei, were amazed at this discovery. "Do you think we'll be in the papers?" Mieko asked with eager expectation.

"They'll publish a photo of us for sure. 'Miraculous Discovery by Keiō University Student Kōda Shūhei and Three Students from Junshin Women's Junior College.' That'll be the headline in big letters. . . . Say, we should keep digging here. There may be other fragments."

Using tree branches and sharply pointed rocks, the four began digging feverishly into places in the dry ground that Shūhei pointed out to them. Before long, several large mud-covered fragments emerged. The young women shouted joyously.

Horseflies swarmed around their faces as they dug, but Shūhei was so caught up staring with sparkling eyes at these three-hundred-year-old pottery fragments he didn't even think to swat them away. His profile that day was the same as the day he had read poems by Satō Haruo to Sachiko.

"Aha!" Heaving a deep sigh, Shūhei muttered to himself. "This jar, . . . it witnessed all the great brutality of the battle at Shimabara. O jar, tell us those tales from history, those ghastly tales of history . . ."

"Is something wrong with him? What's he babbling to himself about?" Misato whispered to Sachiko.

"He's a poet. He's creating a poem right now," Sachiko explained.

"Oh. . . . A poet. I see." Misato nodded, but she still looked doubtful.

"This jar is a storyteller!" Shūhei shouted.

"Storyteller?"

"That's right. Relating the stories from three hundred years ago, of the battles where thirty thousand men and women were slaughtered."

Moved by Shūhei's words, the young women gazed as though hypnotized at the dark blue shards of pottery. It almost felt as though they could hear the cries of battle and the pounding of horses' hooves coming from the broken fragments.

✳ ✳ ✳

"What are you doing?" Someone called from behind them.

They turned around to find an old woman in rustic clothes standing, gazing at them suspiciously.

"Us? Madam, we've just made a great discovery. We're pretty sure that these came from the time of the Shimabara Rebellion," Shūhei energetically announced. "Madam, has anything like this ever been found around here before? If they have, then it'll prove that they're most likely from waterpots kept in the castle."

The old woman clasped her hands behind her back and closely examined the fragment Shūhei held out to her. . . . Then she gave a bitter smile of regret and said, "This is . . . this is actually from a manure pot that we use all the time."

"Manure pot?"

"Right. It's an old used pot we put manure in. You were planning to take those pieces home with you, were you?"

An indescribable expression spread across Shūhei's face. It was a motley blend of astonishment, consternation, and humiliation.

"Bbzzzzzz . . ." A sound something like the cry of a mosquito escaped from his mouth. Mieko and Misato turned their heads away, trying desperately not to laugh. Poor sad Shūhei . . . Sachiko's face flared with embarrassment as acute as Shūhei's.

8

A CONVERSATION ABOUT LOVE

HENRYK REALIZED THAT, over the course of fewer than three days, two men had vanished from their room. The kapo in charge of their barrack had come to summon the men, and they had never returned.

"What happened to them?" someone asked the kapo.

"They weren't suited to the work. . . . So they disappeared."

"Disappeared?"

"Disappeared like smoke in a furnace."

The room fell silent. There was only one thought in each of the men's minds.

There may come a day when the same thing happens to me.

Those unable to work, those who appeared to have weak physical constitutions, those with pasty complexions—they were in the greatest jeopardy. There was no way to tell when the Nazis might send them off to the gas chamber.

The kapo's wooden club fell mercilessly, like torrents of rain on men who answered back and men who displayed any attitude of resistance. Those who failed in an escape attempt were hanged to death in front of the entire group of prisoners during morning roll call as a warning to every man.

Escape: initially, many considered it. But when they learned that those who fled and were recaptured were sent to torture chambers and then hanged, they gradually lost the courage to attempt it. And, upon hearing that this prison camp was surrounded by swamps and forests, and that they would have to figure out how to get through several high-voltage barbed-wire fences, virtually everyone abandoned the thought of escape.

Furthermore, the daily starvation rations were weakening the body and mind of each prisoner. The energy and courage to escape drained from their withering bodies.

Every day, the tall chimneys of the gas chambers and the incinerators spewed out black smoke. Two or three times a day, train cars crammed full of Jews or Poles arrived at Auschwitz. Infants, the ailing, and the elderly were taken from those cars directly to the gas chambers. Beneath the chimneys belching black smoke, as many as two thousand souls a day were engulfed in flames and exterminated.

I want to live! I want to survive!

To survive this hell—that was Henryk's sole, all-encompassing desire. He was not alone in this.

In order to stay alive, he must not fall ill. In order to stay alive, he could not lose the physical ability to work. Were either of those calamities to befall him, all he could look forward to was the gas chamber.

To survive, he must care nothing about others. If one of his comrades was being beaten, he could not help him out. Were he to attempt to help, he too would be beaten. If a man became ill, all Henryk could do was shut his eyes to the man's misfortune. The sorts of "concern" and "compassion" he had felt in the world of humanity were strictly forbidden to him here. Otherwise, he would never survive.

The egoism of each individual man was mercilessly laid bare here.

"God, you say? You can take your God and shove him!" That became Henryk's constant refrain. Henryk felt only anger each time he saw Father Kolbe close his eyes in prayer during work breaks and before meals.

There had never been a God in this world. Before anyone needed a God, they first needed a scrap of bread, even if it was caked in mud.

Why should there be a God? He's no good to anyone, can't be depended on.

As Henryk came to these realizations, he sensed that he was gradually losing all human sympathy. No matter the degree to which another man was suffering, Henryk no longer felt anything toward him.

Early each morning, still under the shroud of darkness, the prisoners formed ranks in front of their barracks and set off in teams to perform their labor assignments.

"March, two, three, four . . . two, three, four. Salute!"

Searchlights from the watchtowers shone down on the teams of prisoners who tramped out the prison gates at gruffly shouted orders from the kapos. If a man fell the slightest bit out of rank because of weakness, the kapo viciously pummeled him. Even if Henryk witnessed it, however, he felt no empathy or compassion.

On occasion a prisoner was subjected to severe discipline in front of all the other men. Even when some of his comrades collapsed from exhaustion as they worked and were brutally kicked by the guards, Henryk and the others watched with apathetic eyes.

This was the first step toward acquiring the ability to adapt to hell. It was asking too much to feel sympathy toward each and every other man's suffering. One could not go on living by weeping at each man's death. Perhaps this is what instinctively provided them with the survival technique of heartlessness.

Eventually they felt nothing at all when they saw the black smoke rising from the gas chambers . . .

In the interest of survival, Henryk stayed on the good side of his kapo and worked assiduously when he was being watched by Nazi soldiers. But to avoid sapping all his strength, he relaxed a little in his work when he wasn't under observation. Yet even in such circumstances, some prisoners never developed a knack for self-preservation. Father Kolbe was one of them.

The work team that included Father Kolbe and Henryk was assigned to reclaim the wetlands that surrounded the Auschwitz camp. Additional land for new barracks and other buildings was needed to accommodate the prisoners that were being sent in ever-increasing numbers. Throughout the day, the prisoners hauled earth in lorries and carried tree branches on their shoulders, laboring amid the shouted orders of the kapos and the German soldiers with their cudgels. On rainy days they were forced to crawl through the mud and across the marshy ground.

Father Kolbe was not adept at this sort of work. He never tried to slack off in his work, though he often coughed and staggered. But when his movements bogged down because of his weak body, he was beaten without mercy by the German soldiers.

"You swine of a priest!" The soldiers had a habit of calling all the priests, not just Father Kolbe, "swine of a priest." Each time Father Kolbe was struck and tumbled into the muddy water, his round glasses invariably went flying. But no one offered to pick them up for him. They knew that any man who picked them up would be in for his own share of brutality.

One evening, Henryk chanced to end up riding in the same lorry with Father Kolbe as they returned work tools to their sheds. One of the earpieces on the priest's glasses had broken off, so Father Kolbe had hung them from his ears with string. He sat with his eyes closed, breathing heavily.

"Father . . ." Another prisoner riding in the same lorry asked, painfully, "Do you really believe there's a God? If He's there . . . please show me that He is. When I . . . when I first saw that black smoke, I stopped believing in things like God and love."

Henryk listened quietly to the question. He shared this man's feelings.

The question sparked a brief debate among the other prisoners, so Henryk could not recall precisely how Father Kolbe had responded.

"The black smoke is a manifestation of the sins the Nazis are committing," one prisoner insisted.

"That black smoke has nothing to do with God," another prisoner interjected. "It's a mistake to put the blame for all the suffering in this camp on God and then say you can't believe in Him," he asserted.

"Then why does God ignore the black smoke in silence? Why doesn't He put a stop to it?" retorted the man who had asked Father Kolbe the original question. "If God is someone who closes His eyes to that black smoke as it consumes women and babies, I refuse to believe in Him."

He turned to face the priest. "Father, why aren't you answering?"

A look of pain fluttered behind the lenses of Father Kolbe's thick glasses.

"I . . . I can well understand . . . how you feel," he feebly responded to the man. "And yet . . . it seems to me that God has given to man something that can triumph over the black smoke from the gas chambers."

"Given us something that can triumph over the black smoke? . . . And what would that be?"

"The . . . the will to love."

Looks of unutterable contempt twisted the lips of the prisoners, and they turned their heads away. Their expressions clearly displayed their sense that there was no longer any point in talking with this hard-headed cleric . . .

Love: it was a word that men used in times of peace. The word had meaning only on evenings when the lights of the city gleamed; when babies giggled in their mothers' arms; when young women sat by windows, their heads resting on the shoulders of young men as they gazed at the rose-colored sunset; and when families all gathered around tables for pleasant dinners together.

Love: a word that set people's teeth on edge when priests and pastors pronounced it from their pulpits as the congregants sat listening, wearing their only good suits during masses at the church. God is love, men must love one another. Those are the sorts of things priests and pastors taught, weren't they . . . ?

In this place, though, something like love had no more value than a bounced check. In this world, infants were torn from their mothers' arms and tossed into the gas chamber. In this world, at night, instead of the gleaming lights of the city, searchlight beacons from the guard towers illuminated every corner of the camp, surrounded by barbed-wire fences. In this world, rather than the cheerful, laughing voices from a family gathering, screams of torture filled the air without warning. In this world, any who believed in love were slaughtered, and none who tried to love others could be allowed to live.

"So you think . . . you think there's love here, Father?" the prisoner gave a convulsive laugh. "Do you really believe that?"

"If there is no love here, . . ." the priest said hoarsely, "then we must create love ourselves . . ."

"Ridiculous! I've had enough of this."

The lorry came to a stop with a creak, and the prisoners quickly leaped to the ground at the angry shouts of the soldiers waiting outside the warehouse.

That night there was a beautiful sunset. Even if love was utterly lacking, the evening sun dyed the sky the same rosy color as it did in times of peace.

✳ ✳ ✳

One rain-splattered morning, Henryk and the other prisoners were awakened earlier than normal by the startling sound of barking dogs.

The Nazi guards kept a pack of German shepherds at the prison camp. Some of the guards would purposely set one loose to attack a prisoner and then laugh in mad glee. The dog would leap on the weak, scraggly prisoner and begin to gnaw on his arms and legs.

"Swine! Get up!" The kapo rattled the edges of their beds with his club, shouting angrily at them.

"Today . . . we have something wonderful for you to see."

Howling shepherd dogs, the clattering boots of the Nazi soldiers . . . these were sufficient for the prisoners to imagine what was going on. In some unit, a man had planned his escape and been captured.

Auschwitz was surrounded by swampland. A man would have to make his way through a succession of barbed-wire fences in order to cross through the swamp and make it to a village. The runaway would most certainly be caught by the pack of German shepherds as he slowly trudged through the swamp.

All the prisoners wordlessly lined up beneath the rainclouds outside their barracks. The black clouds cracked apart and a milky sky peeked out. Facing the ranks of prisoners, three men stood with their hands lashed with wire behind their backs, guarded by Nazi soldiers.

"1586, 2147, 2710," a Nazi officer in glisteningly shined boots read out three numbers from a piece of paper. The numbers were used in place of the three men's names.

Just like farm animals, the prisoners here were called by their numbers. Just like farm animals, within a very few days after their arrival in this camp, the prisoners had their individual numbers tattooed into their forearms.

"These three will now be hanged."

The officer turned toward the assembled prisoners to provide them with a short lecture. "In the future, should there be any runaways, for each escapee we will take twenty men from his barrack and they will be starved to death."

His order and his lecture were all too short and over all too soon. But short and abrupt though they were, his words were more than sufficiently terrifying.

The soldiers had a vague notion that the basement of Block 13 contained an asphyxiation chamber and a starvation chamber. Men taken to Block 13 never returned. According to rumors, the block was provided with torture devices; firing squads did their work behind the building, while the two rooms in the basement were used for the cruelest tortures of all.

Large numbers of prisoners were jammed into the small asphyxiation chamber, where oxygen was evacuated and the captives were confined until they stopped breathing. In the starvation chamber, no water or food was provided, and the prisoners were left until they died of starvation.

Those were only rumors, until the brief comments of the officer confirmed for Henryk and his comrades that they were true. Fear ripped through their bodies from their feet to the crowns of their heads.

The German shepherds barked while the three men dangled from the gallows like limp rags. But the remaining prisoners could only stare at the executions and the corpses with emotionless eyes. It was as though this scene had nothing to do with them but rather was some event in a far-distant world; what sent them into shudders was knowing of the existence of a starvation chamber. Rain began to fall on their quaking bodies.

Yet even for the prisoners in this camp, once every two weeks they had a day when they had no work to do. These were Sundays, when the Nazi officers and guards rested from their labors.

These were the only days when no cargo trains carrying new prisoners arrived at the Auschwitz station. No black smoke swirled from the tall chimneys. The commandant of the camp and his staff enjoyed the day in their own homes with their wives and children, and in the officers hall there were gatherings to listen to the music of Mozart.

On such days, the prisoners walked like somnambulists along the perimeter of the barbed-wire fence or crouched on the ground to massage their spindly legs.

All emotion had been swept from the faces of the prisoners, Henryk included. The flesh on their cheeks had sloughed off, making it impossible to tell from their demented looks what they were thinking in their hearts. But the prisoners were all thinking about just one thing.

Does anyone in the world out there know what is happening to us in here?

They no longer knew anything about the outside world, which felt shrouded in mist. What were the movements on the war front? Were the Allied forces winning? Were the Germans rallying? They had no way of knowing. All they knew for certain was that, at some point, this war would end.

If Germany wins . . .

It was a horrifying thought. Were Germany to win, even if they survived, they would never be released from this camp. They would be locked away here and forced to continue their work.

Such frightful imaginings inspired a fierce yearning, like a last-gasp hope, for escape. The dark purple forest and the horizon they could see beyond the barbed wire that vibrated from the high-voltage electrical current. Freedom existed out there. And life . . .

But these impulses were momentary, and immediately hopelessness again dominated their minds. Escape from this place was all but impossibly difficult. *All but impossible* . . . but what if, that one all-but-impossible possibility . . .

On one of those Sunday days of rest, Henryk stood at the barbed-wire fence and pondered this possibility. Another prisoner came and stood next to him, also looking out at the forest and the horizon.

It was the same prisoner from the lorry who had told Father Kolbe he could not believe in God.

"How old are you?" he asked Henryk. When Henryk responded that he was nineteen, the prisoner muttered sympathetically, "You're still so young. . . ." When Henryk did not reply, he suddenly asked, "Why don't you think about escaping from here?"

Henryk shrugged his shoulders. He was concerned that this man might be an informant charged with reporting the movements of the prisoners to the kapo.

"You needn't be uneasy about me," he said, as though he had read Henryk's thoughts.

"There's no way to escape," Henryk answered irritably, but the man shook his head.

"There might be a way. If you and I work together, or maybe if a group of us cooperated together."

"But . . . they told us that if anyone escaped, twenty men for each runaway would be put in the starvation chambers."

"So what?" The man spat out the words. "That's not our problem. Look, if you start thinking about anybody else here . . . you can't stay alive. This isn't the normal human world. There's not a soul in that normal world who has the right to blame us if we steal another man's bread, or if we stand by and watch somebody else be butchered!" He angrily pressed on. "Any moralist worth his salt, if he looked at Auschwitz, would say that we had no other choices, no matter what it was we had done. What other choice do we have, unless it's just to stand by and watch while someone else is murdered?"

Henryk nodded. Just then, for whatever reason, the face and the words of Father Kolbe, wearing his thick, round-rimmed glasses, popped up in his mind. "If there is no love here, then we must create love ourselves. . . ." Henryk spat on the ground, filling the spittle with a curse: *Love is bullshit. Love can do nothing to rescue a man from starvation . . .*

"Do you want to escape with me? What do you think?" The man pressed for an answer. "If we stay here like this, even if we don't end up getting sent to the gas chamber, we'll weaken and die for sure. You realize your body's losing strength every single day, don't you?"

The man was right. One slice of bread and some watery soup each day—that was all the sustenance they were given. When he should eat that single slice of bread was a daily concern for each man; that one meager slice of bread wasn't merely the source of all his energy for the day, it governed every aspect of his mind. At this rate, they would grow emaciated, and malnutrition would cause their bellies to swell until they were dead.

"But right now, you still have some body strength left. If you don't do it now, you'll never have another chance to escape."

The man was an expert at persuasion. But Henryk lowered his eyes and said, "I can't do it." He was still worried that the man might be a Nazi spy.

"You can't?" Surprisingly, the man began laughing. "Well, of course not. Everything I've been saying has just been a joke. I was only toying with you. It's easy to do with someone young like you."

The man quickly moved away from Henryk, as though nothing had transpired between them, and staggered toward his barrack.

Henryk sat on the ground, clutching his fleshless thighs, and watched the man disappear.

He had the feeling the man must have been a spy after all. A spy who struck up conversations with one prisoner at a time, searching out any who might be intending to escape and reporting them to the kapo or a Nazi officer. That was how the man assured the safety of his own life.

This place is a living hell.

Each man had to lay bare every ounce of his egoism, deceive all the others, and do whatever vile act was necessary to survive. Henryk recognized that this man just now was an example of that egoism.

Henryk suddenly wanted to see Father Kolbe. He wanted to see the face of the priest in the round-rimmed glasses, a man he had mocked up until now. He had the feeling that the priest was the only man in this naked hell who was trying to remain a human being.

A dozen or so prisoners were lined up at the water faucet in the courtyard. They caught the thinly flowing water in their palms and tried to wash their grime-caked necks and legs. The prisoners were given the leisure to do this only on a Sunday once every two weeks.

Henryk spotted the priest in that group. When his turn came, the priest washed his slender arms and legs with the water that trickled from the faucet. He saw Henryk and gave him a feeble smile from behind his glasses. He called out "I . . . I've been keeping my promise to you."

"A promise with me?"

"That first day, when we arrived at the station here, you asked me a favor while we waited on the platform. That I would pray you could survive. I pray for you every day."

Henryk didn't have the faintest hope that such a prayer would have any effect. It was true, though, that as they had stood at the station beneath the afternoon sun, he had asked Father Kolbe to do that for him. To pray for him . . .

"Do you think we're going to survive?" He sat on the ground beside the priest. "I'm . . . I'm still young. I don't want to die in a place like this."

"You'll make it all right. That's what I've been praying to God for you." The priest offered words of encouragement as he stared off far into the distance. From the tone of his voice, it sounded as though he somehow knew that Henryk would survive.

"And what about you? You feel the same way, don't you?" Henryk asked. "You don't want to be thrown in the gas chamber, do you?"

"I am a priest . . . I surrender myself to whatever fate God has in mind for me."

"That's just a kind of despair!"

"It's not despair. It's how I've felt throughout my life. Even when I went to the Orient."

"You've been to the Orient?"

"To Japan. A city called Nagasaki."

Henryk was aware that there was a country called Japan in the Far East, but he'd never heard of a place called Nagasaki.

"It's a charming little town. It's like a town built of toy models. Even during my time here, I've sometimes dreamt of Nagasaki."

Henryk grew irritable. Father Kolbe had started reminiscing about things that made him seem as though he wasn't even one of the prisoners panting for life in this concentration camp.

"Lots of hills. . . . You can see the bay from up on the hills, and the Japanese people—"

"To hell with Nagasaki!" Henryk's outburst was filled with hatred. "You're a splendid one, aren't you! Don't talk in this place like you're the only one who knows everything. Oh, I get it. It's because you're a priest. Well, I'm not a priest. I'm just a common man. Just like everybody else, all I think about is satisfying my hunger and staying alive. I want to live, even if it means I have to push other people out of my way. I suppose you've never hurt another person."

Father Kolbe listened silently to Henryk's rant. Then he said, "Please forgive me if I've offended you. I have wounded other people in the past."

"I have wounded other people in the past." Hatefully, Henryk mimicked the priest's voice and words. "I can't stand your self-important tone."

"No, it's true. Even in Nagasaki, I can remember hurting the feelings of several of my comrades. It's because I was too strict with them . . ."

Although on a sudden impulse Henryk had wanted to meet up with Father Kolbe, now that they were together all he could feel was something midway between hatred and anger.

There was just too much of a gap between this priest's voice and speech and the realities of life in the prison camp. Hearing "love" preached in a world where wraithlike clusters of prisoners scrambled and fought for a single slice of bread only made Henryk want to vomit. There was not a single reason to believe a sermon on God's love in a place where innocent babies were hurled into gas chambers and destroyed.

"Father, I don't believe in heaven. But I do believe in hell. This camp is hell."

"This is not yet hell. Hell is . . . Henryk, hell is a place where love has utterly died out. But love hasn't perished here yet."

"Not perished?" Henryk shouted indignantly. "How can you say that?!"

"Yesterday I saw a prisoner share half his ration of bread with another prisoner whose body was failing him. The bread he could only get one piece of in a day."

"I don't believe you," Henryk shook his head. "That couldn't have happened in this camp."

"No, it happened. I saw it, and it made me feel that I could still believe in humanity. I realized that men still have their freedom at all times, and I felt ashamed of myself. That particular man could have gobbled down every last bit of his own bread right in front of the feeble man. But instead he shared it with him. No matter how terrible the circumstances or the situation . . . men can still perform acts of love. That's what I realized."

"Why me? . . . Why talk to me about this?" Henryk glared at the priest as he began to back away. "You're welcome to believe in people. But in a place like this, I can't believe in others. If I tried to put my faith in anybody, I'd never know when he might turn on me. If you're going to look at what that man did and then turn around and give your own bread to some dying bastard, that's your choice. But you won't impress anyone. They'll just call you a hypocrite, a sentimental soft old fool. Love's no big deal. I've told who knows how many women that I loved them."

"But, Henryk, it's not that easy to love." Sorrow flickered in Father Kolbe's eyes.

"Go to hell!"

Father Kolbe watched, as Henryk retreated with a curse on his lips. Then he closed his eyes. When he closed his eyes, he could see scenes of Nagasaki projected on his eyelids. The sloping road leading up to Ōura after the rain. A rainbow reflected in a puddle of water. The view of the bay from the hills at Ōura. So many ships. The sound of the Japanese walking along in their wooden clogs. It had all looked so strange to him when he first arrived in Japan. And there was the press building where he and several younger comrades had worked.

Love is never that easy. He demanded a strict monastic way of life from his younger comrades in Japan, but his good intentions had ended up producing the opposite effect and wounding several of the young monks. He realized that what he had done then out of love had instead deeply, painfully hurt others.

The priest had some of the same thoughts as his fellow prisoners. *I wonder . . . I wonder whether the Japanese in Nagasaki know that I'm in a place like this?*

9

ANGUISH

SHŪHEI'S DORMITORY WAS right next to Shinano-machi Station on the government railway line. The dorm building was constructed of wood, which had been painted a persimmon color, and around twenty students from several different universities lived there. Because all the students were Christian, the building also contained a tiny chapel and a library room.

As Shūhei wrote in one of his letters to Sachiko, Yoshimitsu Yoshihiko, a professor at Tokyo University, stayed two nights a week as the dormitory dean for these students.

Yoshimitsu was a philosopher, a man of fiery faith and scholarly curiosity. He had studied in France under the remarkable tutelage of Jacques Maritain, exploring Christian philosophy, and then had returned to Japan. He was conversant not only in philosophy but also in literature and the arts, and when he dined with the dorm students, he spoke passionately with them about life and religion.

Seated at the foot of the table where the senior students ate, Shūhei listened to all these discussions, but in his state of ignorance, this philosopher's remarks were too difficult for him. The names of foreign philosophers Shūhei had never read—Descartes, Pascal, Kierkegaard—popped up with great frequency in the discussion, and unfamiliar terms such as "existential" and "the order of existence" only muddled his mind.

Many evenings after dinner, Shūhei visited the room of his valued friend Sugii.

"Professor Yoshimitsu's comments are too hard, and I really don't know what's going on."

"I don't understand them, either," Sugii laughed loudly. "But there's some pretty easy stuff in his books, so I'll loan you a few."

In addition to articles on philosophy, Yoshimitsu had published essays about Rilke and Dostoevsky. Those were the "easy" writings that Sugii was talking about.

Gazing out the window, Shūhei said forlornly, "Hey, Sugii. Things aren't looking good for Japan right now, are they?" From the window he could look down at the platform of Shinano-machi Station, bathed in the evening light of autumn. There on the platform stood men dressed in the mandatory civilian uniforms, with puttees wrapped around their lower legs, and women wearing the compulsory cotton work trousers, all of them waiting patiently for a train that seemed greatly delayed.

"I heard that Japan's combined fleet has been badly damaged. The dad of one of my friends, who's in the navy, told that in confidence to his family."

"Really? No surprise, I guess," Sugii muttered, a look of sadness filling the intelligent eyes behind his glasses.

"I guess we'll be called up pretty soon."

"Do you really think we'll be drafted?"

"Of course we will. We've been able to avoid the draft thanks to our student deferments, but with the situation like it is now, we have no idea when we'll be called up. You better resign yourself to it."

Shūhei peered at the various books of literature lining Sugii's shelves and wondered how much longer they would be allowed to read books.

"Sugii!"

"What is it?"

"I'm not sure what I should think."

"About what?"

"We Christians are taught to respect human life. We've been told 'Thou shalt not kill.' But if I'm drafted as a soldier . . . I'll have to kill the enemy. And I don't know what the church thinks about that."

The water in the kettle on the stove whistled. Sugii stared at the floor and said nothing.

This innocent question formed by his younger friend, whom he regarded as a younger brother, was the same question Sugii had. In fact, every student in this dorm, even though they never uttered it aloud, must have harbored the same concern in their hearts.

The church has taught us that it's a sin to kill another person. But we're going to be sent off to fight in a war where you kill people. How do we deal with this contradiction?

Still saying nothing, Sugii pulled out a canister of black tea and two teacups. Sugar was in short supply, so he used none, but he set out on a plate some broken pieces of glucose he had taken from a school laboratory. This was all Sugii had to offer his friends at a time when food was in such short supply.

"We need to stop thinking about these difficult questions," he said sympathetically. "Thinking's not going to resolve anything."

"Does that mean you don't have the kinds of worries that I do, Sugii?"

"Of course I have them. But the only possible solution is to refuse to enlist. It takes real courage to do that. When I ask myself whether I have that kind of courage or not, I realize it's all out of my hands."

"Refuse to enlist. Hmm." Shūhei heaved a sigh.

Refuse to enlist. It wasn't difficult to say the words. But Shūhei had heard about the kinds of severe punishments that awaited a man who refused to become a soldier after he had received his draft notice.

"I heard about one guy who evaded the draft and hid out somewhere, but when they caught him, he was shot to death by the military police right in front of his mother."

"That's probably just a rumor. But you'd certainly end up in court, charged as a traitor to country."

"Can a state really control and restrict a man's freedom so much? What does the Christian Church think about this war?"

In response to Shūhei's question, Sugii cited a European theologian who propounded the theory of a "holy war." His premise was that fighting a war can be sanctioned when its goal is to defend God and righteousness upon the earth.

"If that's the case, is Japan's war right now being called a righteous war?"

"How can there be either righteousness or unrighteousness in a war?"

The two talked on and on, sipping on the unsweetened black tea. But the conversation just kept going around in circles, leading to no resolution of the core issue.

"I'm sorry I stayed so long." It had gotten late, and Shūhei stood up to leave. Sugii slapped him on the shoulder with a smile and said, "Don't think too hard about these unsolvable problems."

Shūhei stretched out on the futon that he never bothered folding up and thought about what Sugii had said.

"It takes courage to actually refuse to enlist. When I ask myself whether I have that kind of courage or not, I realize it's all out of my hands."

The voice of the announcer at Shinano-machi Station sounded forlorn as he notified people waiting on the platform that a train was about to arrive. Shūhei picked up the poetry collection lying next to his pillow. Reading poetry and thinking about

Sachiko—these were the only means he had to block out the thundering sound of footsteps closing in on him.

✳ ✳ ✳

The following day, Shūhei was sitting on the grass on the school grounds, talking with his friend Ōhashi Shin'ya.

"Tell me, do you think this war is a righteous war?" he asked with an anguished look on his face.

Ōhashi was from Kobe. His face exactly resembled that of a raccoon that has just crawled out of its hole. He was shy and scared of other people, and he seldom fit in with the students in his class, but he hit it off with Shūhei, and the two often hung out together.

"A righteous war? Where did that question come from?"

In retrospect it seems incredible, but neither Shūhei nor Ōhashi had received Marxist baptism the way those of the previous generation had. In addition, because they had been kept ignorant of the realities in the outside world, they had no way to examine objectively or even think about the war with China or the Pacific War. They had no frame of reference with which to apply the phrase "war of aggression" to the current war.

Shūhei told Ōhashi about the phrase "holy war" and the discussion he and Sugii had had about it the previous day.

"What about antiwar? I guess there's that way of looking at it, too." Ōhashi opened his eyes wide, in profound surprise. "I've never even considered whether this war was right or wrong."

"I was the same way. I asked your opinion just now because I'd never thought about it."

Their whispered conversation was conducted by one in Kansai dialect, by the other in Nagasaki dialect. With the meager knowledge available to them, neither had the ability to judge the situation in the world or the meaning of the present war.

"Listen . . ." Shūhei made sure that no one in the vicinity was listening in before he lowered his voice even further to ask, "Tell me honestly. Do you feel patriotic? I mean, do you love the way Japan is today?"

"Japan today?" Ōhashi muttered in embarrassment. "Japan today . . . I hate it. Soldiers are the only ones who can push everybody else around."

"Then . . . do you really want to become a soldier and die for Japan the way it is today?"

"Of course I don't."

"I don't, either."

Shūhei found a pebble in the grass and tossed it. The pebble drew a parabola and landed on the school grounds, which were illuminated by the autumn sun. From the grounds they could hear the voices of some students dressed in drill uniforms as they practiced marksmanship.

"Could you kill someone in a war? Aren't you afraid to kill another person?"

"Sure I'm afraid. But if I found myself in that situation, I'd probably go mad just like the other guy, and then I might be able to kill him."

"I couldn't do it. When you kill another human being, you're wiping out every part of that man's life. Once you've read literature, there's no way you can cancel out another man's life."

"That's all well and good, but what alternatives do you and I have?"

Just as when Shūhei had discussed this with Sugii, he found all Ōhashi could do was feebly mutter, "What alternatives do we have? . . . If it's going to happen, it'll happen. Until it does, why can't you just forget about all these depressing things?"

Shūhei nodded in agreement with Ōhashi.

The footsteps of fate that were closing in on them—they must do something in order to forget that inevitability. Very little time was left to them. Ōhashi and Shūhei felt the keen urgency of their situation.

The two young men had scarcely dipped their feet into the sea of youth. They'd never had any serious relationships with young women. They'd never tasted the delights of love.

They became preoccupied with youth and love for the first time thanks to stories that a young teacher in their German class related to them about the German writer Hermann Hesse.

The teacher seemed to be a genuine Hesse devotee, and she relished the opportunity to show her class a book containing watercolor illustrations by Hesse himself. Beyond a stand of tall poplar trees rose a bluish-tinted mountain range. Above the mountains gently floated cirrus clouds the color of sheep's wool. As she showed this picture to her students, the teacher told them about one of Hesse's short stories, in which the young protagonist heaved a rucksack onto his back and went hiking every day in bluish mountains just like those in the illustration.

"The journey is life, and the bluish mountain range is the longings of youth," the young teacher explained. "There are many stories in German literature with protagonists who are young people on journeys."

Shūhei and Ōhashi were deeply moved by Hesse's stories, and after class they borrowed some translations of Hesse's works and began reading them.

"What story are you reading in your book?" Shūhei asked. Digging boogers from his nose, Ōhashi replied, "Mine's about a young man who goes out hiking in the mist, searching for the house of a young woman that he knew many years before who came from a distant village. He discovers that the young woman has married a boring old man . . ." He lowered his voice. "And then here's what Hesse writes: 'Once she had let him kiss her chestnut-colored nipples.'"

"Kiss her chestnut-colored nipples!?" Shūhei felt a strange dizziness in his head when he heard those words. He and Ōhashi had definitely never done anything remotely close to kissing a girl's chestnut-colored nipples; they'd never even seen a girl's white breasts.

"So, do you think the two of us will die in this war . . . without ever kissing chestnut-colored nipples like those?"

"Yamazaki Yōkichi said there's places in Shinjuku where you can see naked women . . ."

"Idiot! No matter how down on my luck I am, I'm still a Christian! I'm not like that oversexed loser. You really feel like it would be okay for us to go to a place like that? Think about it!"

The two each heaved a sigh, then Ōhashi cried out as though a bright idea had suddenly occurred to him. "I know—let's pretend we're Hesse heroes and set out on a reckless journey!"

"Journey?"

"Yes! Don't you remember our teacher said that the journey is life, and those blue mountains are our longings? Let's go to the mountains. We'll stay one night . . . and if we're lucky, we might have the same kind of experiences as Kawabata's hero in 'The Dancing Girl of Izu.'"[1]

"So we'll go to Izu?"

"Yeah. There's a place my dad knows about at Atagawa on the Izu Peninsula. . . . They might let us stay for free."

They might be able to have some experience on this journey that would embellish the drab years of their youth even more than bluish mountains would. That thought cheered the hearts of Shūhei and Ōhashi.

---

1   An early story by Kawabata Yasunari (1899–1972), the first Japanese author to win the Nobel Prize for Literature. The story traces the journey of a college student who falls in with a lower-class troupe of traveling players. It is extremely popular and considered very romantic by many young Japanese.

"Okay, but there's one condition," Ōhashi said hesitantly.

"What kind of condition?"

"If we stay at their place, will you tell them you're a pre-med student?"

"Pre-med? . . . Why would I have to tell them I'm going to become a doctor?"

"Well, . . . there's two daughters in the family. . . . Both of them are ugly as sin. Still, their late father was a village doctor in Atagawa, and so they want a budding doctor as a son-in-law." Ōhashi's raccoon-like eyes flashed cunningly. "So if you'll pretend to be in the pre-med program . . . they'll give us a warm welcome. And they'll probably let us stay for free."

Shūhei snorted, but the idea of staying at a hot-springs resort town on the Izu Peninsula was very appealing. Even better, on their hiking journey to Atagawa, they just might have romantic experiences like the hero in "The Dancing Girl of Izu."

The skies were clear on Saturday morning. He was to meet up with Ōhashi at Shinjuku Station. On his way out of the dorm, he told Sugii about the journey.

"Do you really think that things will end up so pleasant in this world of ours?" The older Sugii gave Shūhei a look of pity.

Unlike today, the trains on the Odakyū Line were rickety, partly because of the war situation. After the trains crossed the Tama River, they stopped at every provincial station while the number of passengers dwindled.

"Hey, just like you promised, right?" As they passed the Sagami Ōno Station, Ōhashi grew a bit anxious. "You've got to behave like a pre-med student."

"It's fine for you to say 'behave like,' but what is it I'm supposed to do?"

"You just have to put on airs like a med student. You know, have an intelligent look on your face, and every once in a while toss a German word into the conversation."

"Just toss in a German word?"

Shūhei folded his arms and pondered. His German language class was challenging for him, no matter how hard he tried, so he had no confidence in his abilities.

They arrived at Odawara in the early afternoon. There they changed trains to the Tōkaidō Line. Their plan was to disembark at Itō, and from there walk along the coastal road until they reached Atagawa.

When they got off the train at Itō Station, there were stores selling turbo snails cooked in the shell, an unusual sight in those days. Because of the food shortages, rice wasn't served as an accompaniment, only the turbos. After the two young men ate three turbos each, they trotted off on a road on the outskirts of town.

Mandarin orange plantations ran along both sides of the road, the fields encircled by ropes so the oranges wouldn't be stolen. The fruit was still small and green.

From time to time a bus whipped past them, blanketing them in dust. But the heroes in Hesse stories never rode buses. Their rucksacks on their backs, they fixed their eyes on their longed-for "bluish mountains" and continued their journey on foot.

"Phew, I'm exhausted!" They had walked for only an hour when Ōhashi cried out, "My feet are killing me . . . and my throat is so dry! These romantic journeys really wear you out, don't they?"

"We've walked quite a ways, and we haven't seen a single Mädchen, not one blessed girl!"

The gray road, surrounded on both sides by mandarin orange plantations, stretched far off into the distance. They couldn't see the ocean from there, and not a single young woman, the sort who would show up in "The Dancing Girl of Izu," materialized on the path.

Before long, Shūhei and Ōhashi began to quarrel over this tremendous discrepancy between their dream and reality. The initial mistake made by these foolish young men lay in their belief that the same kind of romantic story that appears in "The Dancing Girl of Izu" would happen to them as well.

"Ōhashi, I'm so thirsty I could die!"

They clambered up a hill where orange fields covered the slope and tore off a couple of the still-green fruits. Within moments, however, their faces puckered up and they hurled the oranges to the ground.

"Blech! Sour! Those are totally inedible!"

"What it comes down to is that I fell for your smooth talk."

"What do you mean? It's too late to back out now. You're the one who said you didn't want to be called up to fight without ever kissing chestnut-colored nipples!"

Trading insults in Kansai and Nagasaki dialects, the two were exhausted as evening approached, and, dragging their blistered feet along, they finally arrived at the coastal village. The soiled, blackened roofs of the hot-springs resorts faced the ocean, lined up as though piled on top of one another. White steam swirled in the twilit sky, but by now nothing seemed even vaguely romantic to these two weary young men. They were hungry and wanted to collapse onto the floor mats at the earliest possible moment.

They quickly located the Miyabe home that had belonged to the acquaintance of Ōhashi's father. The deceased owner had been the village doctor, so most of the villagers knew where he lived.

"Good evening?" Ōhashi timidly called out from the entryway of the ancient-looking traditional-style house. Shūhei stood behind him, his legs so fatigued it took all his endurance to keep from collapsing on the spot.

The door to the entryway opened, and an old woman emerged, suspicion clearly written on her face. Ōhashi bowed obsequiously, repeating over and over, "My father and mother send their regards." Finally left with no choice, the old woman with some annoyance let them into her house.

From the run-down parlor they could see a run-down pond. It all felt very much like a doctor's home in a hot-springs resort area.

"Ma'am, my friend here is studying to become a doctor." Holding his teacup politely in both hands, Ōhashi introduced Shūhei. A short time later, a young, dark-skinned woman who appeared to be a daughter of the family brought in a tray holding three or four steamed potatoes.

"Times being what they are, we have nothing to offer you to go along with the tea," the old woman mumbled, obviously flummoxed by these unexpected guests.

"Ma'am, these are really delicious potatoes," Ōhashi, his mouth stuffed with the steamed potatoes, anxiously groped for the right words of compliment. "Surely you must have some kind of secret recipe for steaming these potatoes."

"Secret recipe? All I did was steam them."

"Really? But I've never tasted steamed potatoes this delicious in my life. . . ." His legs began to go numb as he continued to sit on his heels in formal posture.

It was obvious that the old lady was hoping that Ōhashi and Shūhei would leave quickly. At this rate, she might even have to feed them dinner. But if she tossed them out, they'd have no choice other than to sleep outside.

"Ma'am, my friend here is going to be a doctor . . ." Ōhashi repeated the same thing several times, hoping to win her over. The desperate workings of Ōhashi's mind were so obvious to Shūhei that it was almost suffocating.

But the old woman and her dark-skinned daughter merely gave half-hearted responses—"Uh-huh"—each time Ōhashi mentioned Shūhei's "medical" studies, and the conversation went nowhere.

Unable to bear it any longer, Ōhashi turned to Shūhei and asked, "Hey, how do you say 'The potatoes are delicious' in German?"

"Da . . . dasu, poteto . . . ist . . . goodo." Shūhei lowered his eyes and said softly. He used "poteto" because he had no idea how to say "potato" in German.

In an instant the dark-skinned daughter put her hand over her mouth to control her laughter, and she all but tumbled out of the room.

"What are you doing! That was rude! Keiko!" The old woman directed an apologetic look toward the two young men, who were staring at her daughter dumbfounded. "I'm so sorry. She may be grown up physically . . . but she's still a child."

"Is the young lady still in high school?" Ōhashi nodded and asked.

The old woman shook her head. "No, she's attending Tokyo Women's Medical University. She's studying to become a doctor."

Ōhashi's raccoon-like face contorted in pain as he looked at Shūhei. Shūhei was staring at the floor, looking as though he was about to cry. For a time, the three said nothing.

"Umm, . . ." Ōhashi finally said, in a strained voice, "Ma'am, I think it's about time we were going."

"Oh?" The old woman nodded, obviously relieved. These two students had shown up close to dinnertime, and she was hoping they would leave as soon as possible.

The two young men went out. Nightfall had already enshrouded the hot-springs town, and the sea was dark as its waves broke against the shore. The hot steam had a grimy smell to it. If this had been a time of peace, they probably would have heard the sounds of samisens playing, but times being what they were, every inn and restaurant felt deserted.

"I'm sorry! This wasn't how it was supposed to be. I never thought we'd end up like this, honest!"

There was no reason to complain. Their dreams of "The Dancing Girl of Izu" had come to naught. The two exhausted young men walked to the bus stop. They planned to take the bus back to Itō, but the last bus of the day wasn't leaving for another hour.

Thus ended the pathetic journey to the Izu Peninsula of this duo, who returned to Tokyo with faces that closely resembled those of scrawny stray cats. As for Hesse's hero, he was able to meet up again with the young woman from his past who had let him kiss her chestnut-colored nipples, and the young man in "The Dancing Girl of Izu" also had a chance meeting with a charming young woman in the course of his journey. But all Shūhei and Ōhashi had acquired on their journey were blisters on their feet and empty stomachs.

Still, on the following day Shūhei managed to write a letter to Sachiko:

> *The journey that Ōhashi and I took down the Izu Peninsula was a series of dreamlike episodes, and we walked the roads of Izu with a collection of Hesse's poetry in our pockets.*
>
> *On both sides of the roads were mandarin orange groves with delicious-looking fruit. Beyond the hills of orange plantations, we could see the ocean at Izu. I remembered the ocean at Shimabara that we saw when I went there with you and Takeda-san and Takahashi-san.*
>
> *We were welcomed into the home of a doctor, an acquaintance of Ōhashi, in a hot-springs resort town called Atagawa. I got to know the young lady of the house. The following day, threadlike rain fell, and in the rain we could hear the playing of samisens, and we felt as though we had fully immersed ourselves in the sentimental atmosphere of a hot-springs town . . .*

Foolishly enough, Sachiko believed every word of the nonsense in his letter, and she was worried about the young woman Shūhei had gotten to know.

But he wrote this with such honesty, I'm sure they ended up as nothing more than friends.

She tried to calm her troubled heart with that thought.

✳ ✳ ✳

The students were well aware that every aspect of the war situation had turned sharply against the Axis powers of Japan, Germany, and Italy.

The mortal struggle over Guadalcanal between the naval forces of Japan and the United States continued relentlessly, but the prospects for a Japanese victory looked abysmal. In Europe, the Soviet Army had launched a fierce counteroffensive against Germany at Stalingrad. The Allied forces, which had been in a disadvantageous position until then, had rallied.

The more likely it seemed that Japan was plunging to the bottom of a dark valley, and the louder sounded the distant footsteps portending the drafting of college students, the harder Shūhei and Ōhashi struggled to forget what was happening all around them. They strove to ignore it all.

"Hey, isn't Kafū[2] amazing?! Wow, that Kafū!" Around this time, Ōhashi was totally absorbed in the poetic sensibilities and lifestyle of Nagai Kafū. He was naturally drawn to early works such as *Tales of France* and *American Stories*, but he was also in the throes of ecstasy when it came to *Fair-Weather Geta* and

---

2   Nagai Kafū (1879–1959) was a famed bohemian writer who exemplified the desire to separate oneself from the unpleasantness of contemporary society and politics. He was one of the few leading writers who was able to ignore government pressure to write pro-war propaganda. Despite his nonconformist ways, Kafū did teach at Keiō University from 1910 to 1916 and founded the school's prominent literary journal, *Mita Bungaku.*

Quiet Rain, and with a peculiar look on his face, he announced to Shūhei, "I'm going to live the Shitamachi[3] life from now on."

Shūhei borrowed some of Kafū's writings from Ōhashi and was swiftly caught up in the Kafū mystique.

"It's really too bad we weren't attending Keiō when Kafū Sensei was teaching there." He sounded truly disappointed as they talked in the schoolyard, where a cold wind was blowing.

"That's the truth! If I'd been able to learn French from Kafū Sensei, even someone like me could have studied Gide in the original," Ōhashi muttered.

The two young men made a pledge that they would live the Edo cultural life, the better to follow the teachings of Kafū Sensei. That said, they couldn't imitate every aspect of Kafū's life: they weren't about to apprentice themselves to a traditional comic storyteller, or learn to play the samisen, or steep themselves in debauchery in the pleasure quarters. About all they could do was wander the hilly roads at Azabu and Roppongi on Sundays, just as Kafū described his own activities in *Fair-Weather Geta*.

"Listen, yours truly is thinking at the very least that I should find an apartment in Shitamachi." One day, Ōhashi, looking as though he had thought long and hard about it, confessed his determination to Shūhei. Ōhashi had started to refer to himself as "yours truly" as part of his effort to put on Edo airs, but everything that followed it was in his usual Kansai dialect, which made his classmates burst out laughing.

"In Shitamachi?"

---

3 Shitamachi is the name of the older, more traditional merchant district of Edo, the center of the entertainment arts in the seventeenth through nineteenth centuries, and maintained some of that aura in the twentieth century. It was the ideal place for nonconformists such as Kafū to escape the unpleasant realities of life in wartime Japan.

"Yep. Let's say that there's a place where a woman teaches the samisen near the Sumida River. Yours truly could rent out a room on the second floor. I could stare at the flow of the river from my window every single day. And I could listen to my landlady playing the samisen!"

"Wow." Shūhei was emotionally stirred as he listened to Ōhashi talk.

"And maybe . . . Say, wouldn't it be exciting if my teacher fell for me! Every day yours truly would doze off as I watched from my second-floor window as the river flowed by."

"Dozing off, huh?"

"Yeah. How elegant is that!"

"Ōhashi," Shūhei asked, a bit plaintively, "The picture you paint is a little different from Kafū Sensei's life. It seems more like something out of *The Casebook of Inspector Hanshichi*."[4]

But Ōhashi was actually able to turn his determination into reality. He rented a room in Shitamachi.

The room Ōhashi found was in a neighborhood near the Tomioka Hachiman Shrine, on the opposite side of the Eitaibashi Bridge. It must have been the influence of Kafū Sensei's novella, *A Strange Tale from East of the River*,[5] that led Ōhashi to seek out a place on the opposite shores of the Sumida River.

In his imagination, of course, his landlord was supposed to be a female samisen teacher, but because of a variety of circumstances, he turned out to be an old man who ran a tobacco shop.

---

4 Another wildly popular series of stories about a Sherlock Holmesian detective. The author, Okamoto Kidō (1872–1939), published sixty-nine stories about Inspector Hanshichi between 1916 and 1937.

5 Published in 1932, this is perhaps the best-known of Kafū's discursive, semiautobiographical writings. Here, an elderly writer pursues an affair with a prostitute who lives "east of the river." In its depiction of nostalgia for Edo culture and the ways in which the subtle movements of nature reflect the meandering of human emotions, it is a masterpiece.

Once his lodgings had been decided, Ōhashi boasted to Shūhei, "Just a week from now, and yours truly will be living in the Shitamachi of Edo days. It won't be like you, living in a cheap student apartment in Shinano-machi. There's people who call the area where I'll be living 'The Penis of Tokyo.'"

"Penis? What does that mean?"

"You haven't heard of Penis? It's the name of the City of Water in Italy. That's because a bunch of canals flow through the city, transporting logs from lumberyards. Just like in Penis."

"I see. So that whole area is called the Penis of Tokyo?" Shūhei was deeply moved by the romantic connotations of that name. He of course had no idea that Ōhashi had mistaken Venice for Penis,[6] and he had no clue what the real meaning of the English word "penis" was.

On the day Ōhashi moved to the Penis of Tokyo, Shūhei went to help out. The biggest challenge was finding a truck they could move his belongings in, but they finally entreated the owner of a small factory in the neighborhood to let them use his tiny truck to transport Ōhashi's bedding and bookcases and his treasured books. After crossing Eitaibashi Bridge and leaving the Sumida River behind them, the truck began driving between rows of gloomy-looking houses.

"I can't hear anybody playing the samisen," a disillusioned Shūhei muttered. All they could hear were banging noises coming from the neighborhood factory that was just next door.

A room with new tatami mats on the floor, a fragrant breeze blowing through the window, and the view of the river below—that was the kind of Edo-atmosphere room Shūhei had imagined. Instead it was a second-floor room with brown discolored tat-

---

6 Ōhashi's blunder works nicely in Japanese; "penis" in katakana is written ペニス, while the transcription for "Venice" differs only in the tiny mark placed above the first character: ベニス.

ami and an indescribably foul smell. He was again astonished at the enormous gap between dream and reality. But the fact that Ōhashi had moved to Shitamachi was in itself exciting.

"I'm going to do just what Kafū Sensei wrote about in *Fair-Weather Geta*, as he strolled around Azabu. There's a temple there called Chōmeiji—the Temple of Long Life. And the Mimeguri Shrine. And then there's the Tomioka Hachiman Shrine. They've all been there since the Edo period. And I'm going to write my first story, and I'll call it 'Fair-Weather Shoes.'"

"That's it! 'Fair-Weather Shoes'! That's a perfect title!" Shūhei looked at Ōhashi's ecstatically euphoric face, and for some inexplicable reason he felt a faint anxiety. Dreams and reality are so different. There's such a gap between plans and reality. He had come to understand that clearly on their Izu trip. And he worried that the same sort of thing might happen to his friend this time around.

It took little time for his anxiety to be proved correct. The following day, after spending his first night in Shitamachi, a look of regret was written across Ōhashi's raccoon-like face, and he was scratching incessantly around his neck.

"I couldn't sleep at all. The room is filled with bedbugs."

"Bedbugs? Really?"

"Yeah. It wasn't supposed to be like this. . . . I'm telling you, it's no easy thing to live like Kafū Sensei!"

This was another matter that Shūhei kept secret from Sachiko. Sachiko was the one person he was determined would believe that every day for him and Ōhashi was a literary and poetic experience:

> *From the window of Ōhashi's room you can see the Sumida River flowing past. And in the evenings, geisha ride alongside the river in rickshaws.*

Once again his report to Sachiko was utter nonsense.

10

ESCAPE

THE PRISONER THOUGHT through his plan of escape. He watched for an opportunity. At this point he regretted his own stupidity in asking that spineless Henryk if he would become his accomplice.

That bastard . . . he might tell the kapo what I'm planning.

If that happened, his only option would be to play innocent to the bitter end. *But I'd likely end up on the blacklist of the kapo and the Nazi officers.*

He kept a close watch on Henryk every day to determine what moves he might make. Realizing after a week, then ten days, had passed that there was no particular change in the kapo's attitude toward him, he finally breathed a sigh of relief.

The man had been a history teacher at a high school in Kraków, near Auschwitz. When Germany occupied Poland in the fall of 1939, he immediately joined an underground unit in Kraków and began to function as a member of the Nazi resistance. None of his colleagues or students at the high school knew that he was an anti-Nazi resistance fighter.

But at the beginning of 1941, the Nazi Gestapo arrested one of his comrades, and through torture and intimidation they were able to extract from him the names of several members of the movement. His was one of those names.

One day in February on his way home from school, two men wearing black felt hats and gray overcoats called out to him on Kraków's medieval public square. A powdery snow was falling in Kraków that day, and he was escorted away as the delicate flakes fell around him. He could still vividly remember what had happened at each moment on that dark evening.

For some reason, he was a believer in his own good fortune. Despite intense questioning by the Gestapo, he was able to explain away his activities and convince them that he was of no importance in the resistance organization. As a result he avoided the firing squad and was sent to this concentration camp.

My luck is good. I'm sure I'll succeed at escaping.

To maintain this faith in himself and to stir up his courage, he inwardly intoned these words as though they were some magic charm; even when he had been stuffed into the cargo train alongside other Poles and Jews being sent to this camp, and even after he had been shoved into this barrack, he set escape as his one and only goal. There was no servile act he declined to perform so that he might be able to seize the opportunity when it came. The chance to escape might unexpectedly present itself at any time, so he must ensure the trust of the kapo and the Nazi soldiers. In order to be trusted, he made sure to perform his menial tasks and flatter the soldiers.

He stayed close to the kapo, complimented him, and worked hard whenever the kapo was watching. Initially, he was not assigned outdoor labor but was instead ordered to dispose of the corpses of those that had been killed in the gas chamber or incinerated in the ovens.

The greatest disposal problem at Auschwitz was the fact that they had run out of places to bury the massive numbers of human bodies that were exterminated each day in the gas chambers. The solution reached by the camp commandant, Rudolf Höss, was to smash the bones of those incinerated in the ovens and then scatter the ashes.

The task that the man was ordered to perform was to smash the bones into dust. Each day he sat down among the mountains of bones and crushed them with a wooden mallet. He assiduously carried out his distressing work. Over time, he gradually gained the trust of the kapo and the Nazi soldiers.

Perhaps because he had been recognized for his diligent work habits, he was assigned to a labor team that worked outside. His team had the harsh job of filling in the swamps that surrounded the Auschwitz camp. And though it was grueling work, he was grateful for it. It could provide him with an opportunity for escape.

No better than worms!

His eyes were filled with scorn as he watched the other prisoners shouldering heavy basketloads and brandishing pickaxes, scurrying around like ants at each angry shout from the kapo.

Worms. . . . The prisoners had already been emasculated. Whether beaten or kicked, they behaved like donkeys, obediently, servilely following orders. They had given up all hope. There was not a speck of will left to escape from this camp or to fight against the Nazis.

The man held their impotence in contempt. He continually reminded himself that to be a human being meant to fight against your fate, and that those who had lost that will to fight were cowards, no longer qualified to be called human.

If I'm able to escape, twenty of these lowlifes will be executed.

The man recalled the announcement made by the Nazi SS officer on that rainy day when all the prisoners had stood in ranks outside.

Twenty prisoners executed because of me. . . . Why should I care?

He could almost visualize twenty of the prisoners being hauled away and driven into the starvation chamber by rifle-carrying Nazi soldiers. No doubt the crestfallen prisoners would be filled with hatred and curse his name for consigning them to such a terrifying death. Had he not escaped, they would not have been "chosen" for such a fate.

He felt not the slightest ache in his heart. So twenty prisoners die because of him . . . that's just the way it goes.

Even if they stayed alive another year in this place, sooner or later they would die before the war ended. These worms serve as a labor force for the Nazis, but they benefit the cause of justice not one whit. Those who contribute nothing to the cause of justice are no better than dirt. I have no need to suffer just because the dirt is blown away by the wind.

As a history teacher at the Kraków high school, he believed in the progress of mankind and of history, but he also knew that a great many people had died and would continue to die in order for that progress to occur. Yes, there are those who contribute to the progress of history, but there are countless numbers of those who are utterly useless, devoid of all value whatsoever. History calmly casts off those who are useless, who have no worth. That was perfectly natural. In addition—

This business of morality—it changes depending on the circumstances men are placed in.

It was only in times of peace, in a peaceable world, that the execution of twenty innocent people because of the actions of one man could be called evil. Here in Auschwitz, the moral principles of Auschwitz held sway. The killing of twenty prisoners who provided labor for the Nazis because one man fighting against the Nazis had escaped—it couldn't be helped. It was not something that should be disparaged. That was how this man thought.

Standing side by side with the worms, the man dug up soil, panting fiercely as he pushed the trolley, all the while making plans for his escape and watching for the right opportunity.

Fortunately for him, having been raised in Kraków, he was very familiar with the layout of the surrounding areas. Dozens of times he had come to this swampy area to hunt. The vast majority of prisoners were convinced that it would be virtually impossible to escape through the swamps around Auschwitz, but in his view, the area would actually make it difficult for his pursuers to track his escape route.

One day the prisoners were working under the watchful eyes of the German soldiers, just as on every other day.

Next to the forest, one group of prisoners was carrying and dragging logs from a felled tree to deposit in the wetlands. Another group was pushing a trolley filled with soil that would be dumped into the marshes.

This task, repeated daily, continued until evening, with the exception of a brief break at midday. Those weak in body labored sluggishly, but when the kapo caught them slacking off, he beat them mercilessly with his club.

One of the prisoners who was pushing a trolley suddenly gasped for breath and collapsed on the road. The kapo came rushing over and kicked the man, shouting, "Lazy pig!" But the prisoner no longer had the strength to get up. He could only lay there and take the kicking. The German guards smirked as they watched from a distance.

"Drag this bastard off the roadway!" At this command from the kapo, two prisoners who had been helping push the trolley began dragging their motionless comrade to the side of the road.

"The bastard . . . he's no good to us now," the kapo called to the German soldiers. "He's *kaput.*"

"Kaput," of course, was the word the prisoners used to describe a comrade who was no longer of any use.

Two German soldiers came running over. When they determined that the prisoner was already dead, they quickly left their posts to report to the commander.

All the prisoners in the area joined the kapo to gather around the corpse.

The man took advantage of this singular moment. In an instant, he sped into the forest.

He did a quick calculation in his head as he sprinted between the trunks of the larch trees. *Five minutes until the Nazi soldiers return with the commander. Another two minutes before that son-of-a-bitch kapo realizes I'm gone. I've got to be far out of the sight of my pursuers before that seven minutes passes!*

Thereafter his mind went blank. He had no time to think about anything.

A small dark swamp lay ahead of him. He was surrounded by wetlands; if he headed toward the swamp, his pursuers would have no difficulty locating his footprints. He purposely left toe prints along the path leading into the waters of the swamp, then planted his feet on top of those prints, going back in the direction he had come from and then heading into the forest. Using every ounce of his strength, he leapt and grabbed onto a high tree branch and pulled himself up to sit on the branch, then climbed to the top of the tree. At that very moment, from somewhere in the forest he heard the shouting voices of armed soldiers.

Luckily for him, the soldiers had not brought their search dogs with them. The dogs would easily have sniffed out the man's scent from the tree and immediately located him.

Very close by he heard the sound of two soldiers' feet tramping on the ground. He held his breath and hid between the branches of the tree. Sweat pouring from his face dropped straight to the ground. His scent attracted winged insects.

The soldiers were standing directly beneath him. One of the two for no particular reason looked upward. A drop of the man's sweat fell directly onto the soldier's face.

Feeling something cool strike his face, the German soldier instinctively brought his right hand up to his cheek, but just then the other soldier discovered the fugitive's footprints on the edge of the swamp and shouted in a shrill voice.

That shrill cry miraculously saved the fugitive. The two soldiers stood in the black mire, pointing and conferring together, then headed back to report what they had discovered.

The man hurriedly slid down the tree. No doubt those two soldiers would come back with others and bring the search dogs as well.

Fortunately, thanks to the many hunting trips he had taken here during high school vacations, he knew the area well. He calculated that it would take forty to fifty minutes for a new group of pursuers to arrive here with their search dogs.

Again he set out in a frantic run. His feet by now were covered in blood. He stopped and sat on the ground, tearing off patches of his prisoner uniform and using them as bandages to bind his feet. He was afraid the search dogs would smell the blood.

Sooner than he had estimated he heard the barking of dogs in the distance.

The dogs seemed to be following his escape route with great precision. The distance between him and their yapping voices was gradually narrowing. Doubtless the Nazi soldiers had removed the chains that restrained the search dogs and had ordered them to kill the fugitive.

He ran to another small swampy bog, where he made a quick decision and dove into the water. It was the only way he could think of to wipe out traces of his scent.

He slowly went under the water, gradually approaching the opposite shore. Carefully he submerged his body until only his head poked out, then hid his face behind the eucalyptus leaves that drooped down from the bank.

Soon he heard the barking of the dogs at one end of the bog. Three German shepherds had clustered at the edge of the water into which he had dived and were barking in his direction. But the dogs apparently lacked the courage to jump into the water.

When four or five German soldiers appeared from the thicket, he plunged his face beneath the water. From time to time he would poke only his eyes and nose out of the water to see what the soldiers were doing.

The German soldiers showed no sign of abandoning the search. They took the long way around the shore and began advancing in his direction. If they reached the spot where he was hiding, there was no escape route.

Once again he buried himself in the water and slowly made his way to the spot where he had jumped into the swamp. If the German soldiers walking along the shore were to discover him just as his face poked above the surface of the water, it would all be over. But this was the only means of survival left to him, and he had to wager everything on this movement.

He crawled up onto the shore and decided to go back along the road he had taken to arrive here. Even if the search dogs picked up his scent there, the soldiers wouldn't be convinced that he had returned to the same spot.

His only threads of hope were that nightfall would hide him, and that when it became dark the soldiers would abandon their pursuit and return to the camp.

In his mind he pictured himself captured and dangling like a dust rag from the gallows in front of all the prisoners. Thoughts of the twenty men who would be sent to the starvation chamber because of him did not cross his mind.

✳ ✳ ✳

The following morning, during roll call for the prisoners in Barrack 14, which included Henryk and Father Kolbe, the SS officer announced that the fugitive had not yet been located.

"We therefore demand that you remember the agreement each of you made. The agreement was that in the case of one escapee, twenty of you will be chosen at random and executed.

Those who are selected will of course be placed in the starvation chamber."

It was a refreshing June morning, and the voice of the officer, who wore a sharply pressed uniform, sounded youthful in the bracing air. He wore a baton on his right hip, a black stick which eventually would be randomly pointed at one prisoner after another as he selected those who were to be executed with a simple: "You . . . and you . . ."

The blood drained from the prisoners' faces as they listened to the officer's words. They did not move a muscle, their bodies stiffened in fear.

The officer stared one by one at the prisoners' faces. He seemed to enjoy the looks of panic that appeared on each of them.

Soldiers carrying assault rifles were lined up to the rear. The search dogs crouched at their feet, watching the prisoners with moist, black, innocent eyes.

"However, . . ." the officer continued, a thin smile on his lips, "through the good offices of the Führer, we will be delaying this selection until 6:00 p.m. today. When fugitive prisoner 7251 is apprehended, you will all be released. If he is not captured, then without delay twenty of you will be required to take responsibility for his escape."

The shoulders of the prisoners trembled slightly. At least the terrifying ordeal had been delayed until 6:00 p.m.

"None of you is to take a single step from this place until 6:00. And you will have neither water nor food until 6:00. You will keep in mind that this suffering has been brought upon you by the fugitive prisoner."

The officer deftly raised one arm. "Heil Hitler!" His speech to the prisoners was finished. He left with the two soldiers at his side.

Standing in the refreshing morning air, the prisoners were able to experience a fleeting sense of relief at the possibility that they might go on living, but the feeling passed quickly. As they stood at attention for two, three, then four hours, a heavy leaden pain settled into their legs and spines. If they shifted their feet or tried to move their bodies, they were clobbered by the sticks of the soldiers and the kapo.

At the end of one of the ranks, a man crumpled to the ground. When the kapo kicked him, the man tried desperately to get back on his feet, but again he fell. He had lost consciousness.

During the five-hour waiting period, nearly twenty men fainted. They were dragged out of formation and stacked atop one another like inanimate objects.

"These bastards . . . they're on their way to the gas chamber," one soldier pointed and taunted.

It's his fault. It's all . . . it's all that man's fault.

Not one of the prisoners envied the fugitive. Henryk, too, hated the man who had forced him into this situation. It was the man who had tried to lure him into escaping with him.

Hurry and catch him! To hell with him!

That was Henryk's earnest wish.

Look at us. Thanks to you . . . we're going to be killed!

At around 4:00 p.m., the same officer returned and whispered something to one of the guards. His orders were to give the prisoners a thirty-minute rest.

"Stand at ease!" The moment that order was shouted by the kapo, the entire group of men slumped to the ground as though collapsing from exhaustion. All suffered from anemia. Some vomited as soon as they crouched down. Henryk was one of those.

"Go get some soup!"

At those words, Henryk suddenly remembered that he had eaten nothing since morning. But he was so exhausted he didn't even feel like eating.

They may have called it "soup," but it was more like hot water. As the men slurped it from a wooden bowl with a wooden spoon, the order came, "Stand!"

For the next two hours, Henryk lost his vision. He heard dull thuds one after another to his right and to his left. They were the sounds of prisoners who were collapsing after losing all their strength.

"You swine!"

Henryk heard the kapo's angry shout as though it were coming from another world. He lost all sensation throughout his body. All he could feel was anxiety—"I hope that fateful hour of 6:00 never comes, I hope that 6:00 never comes . . ."

But the sky at the horizon line, oblivious to Henryk's entreaty, gradually changed from its orange tint to the blazing red glow of evening. Henryk and the other prisoners sensed from the color of the sky that the appointed hour was upon them. The officer, again accompanied by two soldiers, slowly approached. Just as he had that morning, he carried a baton on his right hip. He stopped in front of the prisoners and stared intently at them.

He cast a scornful glance toward the men who had already fainted and been dragged out of formation, where they were piled on top of one another, and then, with a creak of his boots, he stood before the assembled prisoners.

"It is 6:00 p.m." He spoke with a smile—a fake smile, amiable, even gentle, that was in stark contrast to the cruel pronouncement he was about to make. "I'm sure you remember . . . what I said I would do at 6:00. That's right. Nazis always keep their promises. Twenty of you must die thanks to the one runaway."

His baton clutched in his hand, he began to walk slowly from one end of the front row of prisoners to the opposite end. His well-polished boots creaked as he walked, and a faint aroma of eau de cologne wafted from his neatly pressed uniform.

"Those I point to will step outside the ranks."

The prisoners were silent, emitting not even a cough. With their eyes opened wide, they steeled themselves during this moment frozen in time.

Just then, a soldier came running up to the commander and whispered something to him. In the distance they could hear the howls of the search dogs.

He's been captured! The fugitive has been captured!

O God! Henryk called out to a God he did not even believe in.

The smell of urine pierced their noses. Released from the tension of the moment, several of the men had unwittingly wet themselves.

With the search dogs in the lead, the pursuers who had apprehended the fugitive slowly approached the camp.

The fugitive was naked to the waist, but his torso and feet were bathed in blood. No doubt he had resisted capture, and as he had struggled the search dogs had pounced on him and torn at his flesh with their fangs.

Dragging his feet, the fugitive walked past the prisoners, who gasped as they watched him go by. German soldiers with rifles followed behind him, their faces tense.

The captured fugitive gave the men who until yesterday had been his comrades a look of defiance. His eyes clearly displayed his contempt.

Don't any of you have the courage to escape? His eyes were saying. *Are you just going to follow whatever the Nazis tell you to do like sheep?*

For their part, the prisoners subjected to his scornful gaze stared back at the traitor's face with revulsion.

Because of this man, they had suffered deathlike torment for the entire day.

Because of this man, twenty of them might have been executed.

A fierce anger and loathing came to a boil in Henryk's heart, as well as in those of many of the other prisoners; they looked forward to experiencing the exhilaration of revenge when, in just a few moments, they would get to watch the man be hanged.

I hope he dies in torment!

For a fleeting moment, Henryk had the sense that if the Nazi soldiers didn't wrap a rope around the man's neck, they might kill him with their own hands.

The SS officer seemed to have sufficient sensitivity that he understood both of these mentalities, and he took his time maliciously enjoying the psychological clashes occurring among the prisoners. Planting a smile on his cheeks, he asked the group, "Do you wish to have this man set free? Think it over. Thanks to this man's actions, today we and you are totally worn out. I'm quite sure none of you wish to have another day as painful as today has been." He paused, making sure that the prisoners all had an opportunity to see his smile.

"I am planning to hang this man, but if any of you wish to object to that . . ."

Every man was silent.

Even if they had objected to the decision, there was no way the officer would pay them any heed. At a signal from one of the German soldiers, the kapo placed a rope around the man's neck.

Far beyond the camp, the evening sun that had glowed a rosy pink was gradually transitioning to a dark blue, but an afterglow still illuminated the earth.

"You can all go to hell!" the fugitive cried in a loud voice. Those were the last words he uttered in mortality. His dangling body, catching the pale light of the setting sun, spun almost imperceptibly.

"Dismissed!"

Finally allowed to disperse, the prisoners returned to their barracks with heads bowed. A world void of love. A world where, instead of love, men hated one another and yearned only for vengeance.

If the world is lacking in love, we must create love . . .

Father Kolbe's words streamed faintly across Henryk's brain like a wisp of smoke. And hovering over those words was the cry of the executed man:

You can all go to hell!

11

GIRLISH INNOCENCE

ON SUNDAY MORNINGS at the Christian dormitory, the students who weren't satisfied with the dorm's tiny chapel set out for mass at a church. Often they would go to the church at Sophia University, located just one train station away at Yotsuya.

Shūhei, on the other hand . . .

Being a late riser, Sunday mornings were like every other morning for him. He burrowed under his covers and lay there sound asleep, and even when Sugii called out, "Hey! Get up! Get up!!" he would respond drowsily—"Yeah, yeah, I know"—and often would fall right back asleep. Particular in the winter, when it was especially hard to get out of bed, he would pretend to be in a deep sleep even when Sugii tried to rouse him.

"You're hopeless. You think you deserve to be called a Christian?" Sugii would shake his head and then leave with the other students. Right around the time Shūhei sluggishly got up, the students who had gone to church were just returning to the dorm.

On the first Sunday in December, Sugii tore the futon off Shūhei's bed, and they set out for mass at the chapel called Kultur Heim[1] on the Sophia University campus.

---

1 Originally built in 1897, at one point it was part of the Tokyo residence of General Takashima Tomonosuke. A Jesuit group bought the building in 1912.

The Kultur Heim was a small building on the Sophia campus, the site of lectures on culture, and mass was celebrated daily there in the second-floor chapel.

Once inside the chapel, even Shūhei became docile, and he knelt along with Sugii and the other students.

A foreign priest was celebrating the mass. Through the chapel windows the students could see a poorly tended garden and a large black crow perched on the branch of a tree in the garden.

With his hands folded in prayer, Shūhei glanced casually around the chapel and noticed a young woman also kneeling three pews in front of them; he recognized her as a student at Futaba Women's College.

She had a beautiful profile. It was the sort of face one might see in a Raphael painting.

Shūhei stared at the young woman as though drawn magnetically toward her. When he realized how imprudent he was being, he quickly shifted his attention to the altar.

Throughout the mass, he was aware only of her. He knew he was being disrespectful to God, but during the mass he was drawn far more to her than he was to God.

"Stop it!" God said to Shūhei. "Why exactly did you come here?"

"I'm sorry." Shūhei tried very hard to think about God. But fewer than three minutes had passed before his mind, just like water flowing downhill, turned again toward the slender back of this young woman.

"You're a pretty hopeless young fellow, you know," God muttered, thoroughly disgusted with Shūhei. "Who is more important—Me, or this young woman?"

When the mass ended, Shūhei followed the young woman out of the church. She exited together with a refined woman he assumed was her mother.

"Sugii!" On the train back to their dorm, Shūhei grinned and said, "I think I ought to be going to church every Sunday."

"Yes, you should. You get a good feeling there, don't you?"

"It's a good feeling, but there are other good things about being there. Today for the first time I understood what the grace of God means."

Sugii gave his younger classmate a suspicious look.

The next day, Shūhei told Ōhashi about the young woman. "She could be the younger sister of Hara Setsuko.[2] In fact, she looks just like Setsuko."

Shūhei gave his impassioned report, complete with dramatic gestures with hands and body. A look of jealousy flashed on Ōhashi's badger-like face, and he asked, "Am I allowed to go to mass?"

"You? Why would someone like you, who's not even a Christian, go to a church mass? The mass is sacred and inspiring. It's not something you come to just to gape at young women!"

"But, didn't you say you were totally charmed by her throughout the mass?"

Jesus whispered in Shūhei's ear: "Let Ōhashi come to church. Even if he comes just to see the young woman, who can say whether that might not be the impetus for his heart to change?"

Shūhei muttered under his breath, "But, Lord Jesus, his motivation is so blatantly obvious."

"Come now, you're a badger in the same hole, aren't you? There are many paths that lead to the top of the mountain."

---

2 Hara (1920–2015) was one of the most popular film actresses in Japan for decades. She appeared in six films directed by Ozu Yasujirō, including *Tokyo Story*, considered by many critics the pinnacle of Japanese cinema. She also worked with directors Kurosawa Akira, Kinoshita Keisuke, and Naruse Mikio. Endō wrote in one of his essays about seeing her in a film: "We would sigh or let out a great breath from the depths of our hearts, for what we felt was precisely this: Can it be possible that such a woman exists in this world?"

Shūhei decided he would go along with Lord Jesus's shrewd encouragement, and the following Sunday he took Ōhashi with him to the church at Sophia University.

Sugii and the other students at the dormitory watched with suspicion that Sunday morning when Shūhei leapt out of bed without any prodding, slipped on the shoes he had polished the previous day, and made all the other preparations to attend church.

"A friend of mine from Keiō is waiting for me at Yotsuya Station. He's been pestering me to let him see a mass," Shūhei explained with an nonchalant expression on his face.

A sleepy-looking Ōhashi stood waiting at Yotsuya Station. With drowsy eyes he grumbled that it had taken him an hour to get here from Shitamachi.

"Now, just be patient. It won't be long before I show you something that'll rouse you from your sleep. One look at this young woman and your exhaustion will vanish."

There was a kind of exotic air about the Sophia University campus. In particular, the Kultur Heim was swathed in an atmosphere of solemnity. Just as the two young men stepped into the building, a piece by Bach began to play in the chapel, announcing the start of the mass.

Ōhashi gazed curiously around the chapel and said, "Pretty stylish! You'd think there wasn't even a war going on."

"Okay, listen," Shūhei explained. "During the mass, all you have to do is sit there. We'll be busy standing up and kneeling and going up to the altar. You just sit still."

Despite the fact that it was wartime, the church this Sunday was packed. The worshippers were not just Japanese; some foreigners sat among them.

After a few minutes, Shūhei sat up straight and told Ōhashi, who sat beside him, "That's her . . ."

"Which girl is it? I can't see anything but people's backs."

"Shh! In just a few minutes . . . you'll have a clear view of her. During the Eucharist."

"What's a Euchar?"

A foreigner sitting behind them clicked his tongue at their annoying chatter.

Describing this later to Sachiko, Shūhei's imagination, as it so often did, embellished his encounter with this young woman at mass and added some touches of color to the story.

Foolishly, he was totally insensitive to the irritation his letter would cause Sachiko and what her reaction would be. In Shūhei's mind, Sachiko was like a younger sister.

Sachiko took everything he said as the absolute truth, respected him as having the makings of a future poet, and read the poems and essays he occasionally sent her with flashing eyes (. . . or so Shūhei thought).

For Shūhei, Sachiko was the only person to whom he could reveal his talent—since it appeared that his parents and Sugii, and even Ōhashi, didn't have a very high opinion of his skills—and therefore the one person who could assure him that his unspoken pride in his gifts was justified.

She doesn't understand anything. She's just a girl.

Hidden somewhere in Shūhei's heart was a condescending attitude toward Sachiko, the way an older brother looks down on his younger sister. In his letter to Sachiko, he wrote,

> *This young woman somehow seems to get along with me better than she does with Ōhashi. When I spoke to her after mass, she was smiling when she answered.*

This wasn't exactly a fabrication on Shūhei's part. When he left the second-floor chapel and started down the stairs with the other members of the congregation, Shūhei had summoned up his courage and spoken to the young woman.

"Excuse me. What time is it right now?"

As she descended the stairs, the young woman looked at her watch, smiled, and said, "It's 10:30."

That was the sum total of their conversation; it was clear that she displayed no more interest in Shūhei and his friends than she would to a rock on the roadside.

Next Sunday we might go boating with her on the Tama River.

That was undoubtedly what Ōhashi and Shūhei hoped would happen. But it was only these two young men who harbored this vain hope, and there was more than enough room to doubt that it would be realized.

When Sachiko read Shūhei's letter, she felt somehow sad. And worried.

Shūhei and Sachiko were certainly not engaged to each other, nor were they even girlfriend and boyfriend. But from a young age Sachiko had held special feelings for Shūhei. Even now, as a young woman, her feelings for a young man who could be called neither a brother nor a friend had not faded.

She reread the letter, composed in Shūhei's sloppy writing that looked like a swarm of ants scurrying around the page.

I wonder what kind of girl she is? He says she's as pretty as Hara Setsuko, but I wonder whether that's true.

Sachiko was aware that in situations such as this one, ridiculous exaggerations often made their way into what Shūhei wrote, but that portion of his letter gnawed at her.

Sachiko regarded the young women of Tokyo as dazzling and enviable, and the thought that this particular young woman was as good-looking as Hara Setsuko made Sachiko self-conscious about her own dark complexion.

But most galling of all was the fact that Sachiko couldn't fathom what was going through Shūhei's mind when he cluelessly decided to write her such a letter.

I wonder what he thinks about me.

She was convinced that she understood Shūhei better than anyone else did. His mother could remember each of the many mischievous acts of Shūhei's youth. Members of the church congregation were still convinced that he was beyond help. But Sachiko was confident that she served as a bulwark to protect him from the backbiting and insults of these people.

In addition, she had the arrogance to believe that she was the one and only admirer of Shūhei's poems and short stories. Though she knew nothing about composition, she wrote to Shūhei that she was treasuring everything he wrote.

Shūhei, however, understood nothing about Sachiko's feelings.

Insensitively and thoughtlessly, he had written to her about the young woman he had met in Tokyo.

As she thought it over, by degrees Sachiko's anger mounted.

I'm not going to have anything more to do with him. I'm totally done with him. She repeated this to bolster her courage.

That evening, she tore a page out of her notebook and wrote,

1. *I'm not writing him any more letters*
2. *I'm not going to see him again*

After itemizing her resolve in a mere two lines, she hid the piece of paper in the chocolate box where she kept everything that was valuable to her. It was the same chocolate box where she kept the postcard she had received from Father Kolbe, the one that included the verse, "Greater love than this no man hath, that a man lay down his life for his friends."

"Mom, I'm thinking I might move to the women's quarters," she suddenly announced that day.

"Women's quarters" referred to the female religious order that the women of Urakami village—who might be called Sachiko's relatives—had established. The women who joined this order spent their lives unmarried, maintaining their faith and aiding the sick.

"I'll go to the women's quarters and become a virgin sister."

"Oh, you will?" Her mother laughed and refused to believe Sachiko would actually do it, but Sachiko was half serious.

Having made this tragically heroic decision, Sachiko stopped writing letters to Shūhei.

Strangely enough—

As though he had somehow sensed what she had decided, letters from Shūhei also abruptly stopped coming.

Even in wartime, a bustling atmosphere filled the streets of Nagasaki as evening approached. Since goods of all kinds had virtually disappeared from their shelves, the shopping districts were miserably deserted, but people walked around as though they were quite preoccupied.

When Sachiko returned home from school, the first thing she did was look in the mailbox. Her greatest uncertainty revolved around whether a letter had arrived from Tokyo.

The fact that there were no more communications increased Sachiko's feelings of suffocation.

So, has he gotten closer to that person in Tokyo and forgotten all about me?

The imagination knows no limits or bounds. Sachiko conjured up a picture of Shūhei strolling the bustling districts of Tokyo with that Hara-Setsuko-look-alike woman, and it made her sad. She could almost see Shūhei helping her into a boat on the Tama River, with he and Ōhashi taking turns rowing, and that pained her.

What does he really mean to me? Sachiko asked herself apprehensively. *I'm not engaged to him. He's not my boyfriend. He's just somebody I played with when I was little.*

She had plenty of childhood friends beside Shūhei. Over and over again she told herself that it was ridiculous to suffer this much just because she wasn't receiving letters from a young man who was neither fiancé nor lover.

Once she had experienced these feelings, Sachiko, like all young women who have fallen in love, tried everything she could think of to disavow him. She reminded herself of each of his flaws—his sloppiness, his willful personality—and tried her best to dislike such an egotistical coward.

But ultimately her struggle was in vain. The struggle was no more than a struggle. Just as a person writhing in a mud swamp ends up sinking deeper, Shūhei ended up on Sachiko's mind from morning till night.

I'm a terrible woman.

Every time thoughts of that Hara Setsuko look-alike flitted across her mind, Sachiko managed to convince herself that she was a bad woman.

Ever since childhood, she had disliked people who were jealous of others or who despised others. Now that she herself was caught up in a maelstrom of hateful feelings, she concluded that she must be a terrible woman.

O Blessed Mother Mary! Please help me! At Sunday mass in the Ōura Church, this was Sachiko's prayer to the statue of the Blessed Mother. This was the same statue of the Blessed Mother before which Kiku, the cousin of her grandmother Mitsu, had stood, venting her anger and complaints when she had fallen in love with a man for the first time.

Many long years had passed since then. Kiku had died, and the man she had loved, Seikichi, was no longer among the living; only this statue of the Immaculata still responded as she always had: gazing steadily with eyes of purity at those who came to pray before her. And just as she had listened to Kiku's impassioned pronouncements of love, so too she listened to Sachiko's girlish explanation of her troubles . . .

As Christmas approached, Sachiko felt somehow stifled.

Part of it was because there were no letters from Shūhei, but in addition, she knew that he was planning to return to Nagasaki just before Christmas.

Once he came back, they would certainly run into each other at church.

When she saw him, would her resolve collapse with a single blow? If he spoke to her, would she immediately reply?

She had made up her mind simply out of obstinacy to remain aloof from Shūhei, but she was worried that her resolve would easily be snapped.

Please, don't ever let me see him again for the rest of my life!

That was her prayer to the Blessed Mother, but abruptly she felt agitated—what was she to do if the Blessed Mother heard her prayer and sent Shūhei far away?

She quickly modified the prayer she had so earnestly offered. *But, please let me see him for just a short time!*

But it was for a different reason that her heart was heavy as Christmas approached.

It is the custom for Catholics, just before Christmas, in a practice called the Sacrament of Penance, to confess all their sins to the priest, who sits in the confessional in a corner of the chapel.

If she went to the confessional, she would have to confess secretly to the priest all about herself and Shūhei. She would have to tell him how jealous she felt toward the woman in Tokyo that Shūhei had written about in his letters.

The thought depressed her, and even though Christmas drew nearer day by day, she had lost all desire to go to church.

"Sachiko, you haven't gone to confess yet," her mother noticed and chided her. "Your aunt wants to know why you haven't come yet."

Her aunt was a nun who helped out at the Ōura rectory, so she must have told Sachiko's mother that her daughter hadn't yet shown up to confess.

Her mother's hounding was so insistent that she finally had no choice but to act. Christmas was only two days away.

She felt apprehensive as she climbed the slope where Father Kolbe and Brother Zeno had lived. Her apprehension was the result of female intuition, which convinced her that Shūhei was already back in Nagasaki and would be at the church.

With that thought, her feet felt heavy.

When she reached the top of the slope, she stopped and took a deep breath.

Just as her premonition had warned her, Shūhei was coming down the stone steps of the church wearing his round Keiō University cap.

Shūhei paused on the stairs. And with a totally carefree, happy-go-lucky look, he shouted, "Hey!" Sachiko was silent and turned her head away. He did not even notice.

"I just got back yesterday. I stopped by to say hello to the priests."

Still Sachiko said nothing, her feelings a complex mix of happiness and annoyance.

"Did you come to see your aunt? If you're not in a hurry, let's take a walk."

"I have something to do. I can't." Sachiko ignored him and responded in a cold, overly formal fashion.

"Something to do? What is it?"

"I've come to the church to do my confession."

Shūhei shook his head. "Ah, well if that's the case, it'd be better not to go right now. There's only one priest in the church, and there's a lot of people waiting to confess. You should come later." Then he added, "Smart people kill a half an hour before they go to confess. And besides, Sat-chan . . . I've brought you a gift." He pointed to something that was poking out of his pocket.

"I don't need any gifts."

"Why not? . . . It's a fountain pen that I took extra special care to bring to you. I hear you can't get fountain pens even in Tokyo these days. . . . I got you one designed especially for women."

"A fountain pen?"

"That's right."

The annoyance and sadness she had been feeling evaporated in an instant. Her mood improved when she realized that Shūhei had not forgotten her.

"Show me!"

"Don't be in such a rush! I'll present it to you at my leisure in the garden at the vacant house." Shūhei set off walking, like a person luring a pet by waving treats in front of its nose.

Sachiko followed him and said, "Where can you buy a fountain pen these days?"

"It was on the train coming home. The guy sitting next to me looked like he might be a factory worker. He told me he'd lost his job when the factory that makes pens burned down. They gave him some fountain pens in place of his salary, and he said he'd sell me one cheap and asked me to buy one. . . . And I thought, yeah, I'll buy one for Sat-chan."

"Gosh!" Joy came surging up unbidden inside her and she smiled broadly, but she said nothing further.

The abandoned Western-style home was still unoccupied, and there was no indication that any repairs had been done to it.

The two stood in the garden and looked out over Nagasaki Bay, which spread out beneath a leaden sky. It had been strictly forbidden for anyone to look toward the bay while an enormous battleship was being constructed at the Mitsubishi Shipyard. But that summer, the giant battleship disappeared from the bay, and according to rumors, it had been towed to the Kure Naval Base at Hiroshima.

"I wonder what Jim and Van are doing these days?"

Coming to this abandoned house, it was inevitable that they would remember Jim and Van, with whom they had played here many years ago. In fact, they almost felt they could see the two boys chasing around the garden right now.

Inside some newspaper wrapping that Shūhei pulled from his pocket were two pink fountain pens designed for women.

"One of these is for you, Sat-chan. The other . . . it's for my other friend." Because Shūhei thought of Sachiko like a younger sister, he had never imagined that she would be feeling anything out of the ordinary for him.

That insensitivity led him without a second thought to show both of the pens to Sachiko.

"The color of these pens makes them seem a little like they were made for younger girls, and I worried whether you would like it. . . . What do you think? Do you dislike the color?"

"Unh-unh," she replied in a lifeless voice.

"Honest? That's great. I wonder if my friend in Tokyo will like it too? After New Year's when I go back to Tokyo I'm thinking maybe I'll give it to her after mass on Sunday."

Sachiko said nothing.

Although she stared toward the bay with sorrowful eyes, Shūhei as always talked on and on, totally absorbed only in himself.

"Of course I can't tell her that this came out of the wreckage from a factory fire, so I'm going to have it wrapped at a department store in Nagasaki and then give it to her. But somehow I feel like I'm hoodwinking her."

Again Sachiko said nothing.

"I'd really like you to meet her. I think you'd become really good friends."

Tears began to glisten in Sachiko's eyes. Trying hard not to listen to Shūhei's tactless jabbering, she thought back on the days of her childhood when they had played together in this abandoned house.

She wondered what Jim and Van were doing now. What did they think about this brutal war that their country was fighting with Japan? Had they developed a hatred for Japanese people like Sachiko and Shūhei . . . ?

She tried to force herself to think about such things, but Shūhei's voice mercilessly penetrated into her ears.

"To tell the truth, since me and Ōhashi always see her on Sundays at Sophia University, weirdly enough for me, these days I never skip mass."

"Shū-chan . . . do you really love her that much?" With her eyes lowered, she asked in a soft voice.

"Love her? Well, if I didn't *like* her I wouldn't have bought her a fountain pen."

"But . . . you bought one for me too."

"You've been my friend since we were little kids, Sat-chan." Before he could say anything further, Shūhei realized that Sachiko's shoulders were quivering faintly. Her tiny fists were clenched tightly on her lap, as though she were suffering some terrible pain.

"Sat-chan, what's wrong?"

Suddenly, Sachiko began to wail loudly. She began to pound Shūhei's chest wildly with her clenched fists.

"Idiot! Idiot!! You're such an idiot!!"

Shūhei was stunned and widened his eyes until they were as round as acorns. Although initially he had understood nothing, even with his own limited imagination he finally realized what was happening. No, that's impossible. Impossible . . . She . . .

In that instant, a jumbled mixture of feelings swept across his face. Bewilderment, confusion, and a smile of delight . . .

✳ ✳ ✳

Christmas that year was celebrated quietly, with a nighttime mass at the Ōura Church so that the police and the citizens who detested Christians would not be provoked against them.

The bell to announce the mass was not rung. The volume of the organ was also kept low. Still, near midnight the Christians climbed the icy stone steps up the slope and silently thronged into the chapel. It almost felt that it could have been one of the gatherings during the age of persecution when the first Japanese Christians met secretly in the catacombs.

There was no choir and no music was played. The light of the candles flickered at the altar, and the veils of the women who knelt in the chapel fluttered; here and there, an elderly parishioner coughed. An infant would suddenly burst out crying. This was the dreary atmosphere in which the mass was conducted. The priest gave the following homily:

"I believe that all of you are familiar with the history of this Ōura Church. And I'm certain that you have heard about the famous discovery of the hidden Christians that took place at this church. It's probably been a long time since you were reminded of the extraordinary faith of the Urakami Christians who were the first to see this statue of the Blessed Mother beside this altar."

The parishioners thought it strange that the priest suddenly began relating the story of the discovery of the Urakami Christians by Father Petitjean, when this was supposed to be the Christmas mass. The priest ignored their puzzled looks.

"I ask you to recall one more time the story of the sufferings of those Urakami Christians. They were all illiterate peasants. But no matter what force or coercion was applied to them, they never caved in. Ironically, their faith has turned out to the benefit of Japan. Thanks to them, the Japanese of today have obtained freedom of belief and of religion."

This homily by the priest, so obviously inappropriate to the occasion, seemed to be aimed at making some point by telling the story of the Urakami Christians. But what was he trying to say?

Seated in the fifth row from the front, Shūhei listened attentively to what the priest was suggesting in his homily. He understood the priest's courageous, heartfelt message . . .

The priest calmly returned the topic of his homily to Christmas:

"Our Lord was born in Bethlehem almost two thousand years ago. Our Lord was born in a stable. In a filthy animal shed. Even so, on that night, just as tonight, the stars glittered in the heavens and surely the skies were clear. Through the birth of Our Lord, the stars shone brightly and the skies cleared. Our Lord favored the world with a night of peace."

At these words, Shūhei's knees began to quiver. It was painfully clear to him what the priest was trying to say.

The parishioners faced forward, saying not a word. There was no way to tell whether all of them reacted to this homily in the same way that Shūhei had. No matter how much time passed, Shūhei would not forget this priest's homily on this night.

12

A SUMMER ABLAZE

ON A SUNDAY morning Heinrich Martin, adjutant of the Auschwitz concentration camp, finished drinking the hot, aromatic coffee his wife Olga had made for him and immediately headed out into his garden to tend his flowerbeds.

The season being early summer, many varieties of flowers, damp from the morning dew, were blooming in the flowerbeds. Martin gazed with satisfaction at each of the flowers, then went into the shed to change into his work clothes.

He had loved flowers since childhood. It had started with his surprise when the single tiny seed his mother had given him sent up a delightful bud from beneath the ground.

In his own childish way he felt he had sensed the indescribable mystery of life in that soft, tiny bud. Eventually the bud became a stalk and sprouted leaves, and when it blossomed into a large yellow flower he was able to relish a joy he had never felt before.

This is my flower. This sunflower belongs only to me.

Thereafter he planted many different kinds of flowers.

Anemones, hyacinths, zinnias.

"You're such a sweet child," his grandmother had said as she watched him with his flowers. "A person who loves flowers so much could never do anything bad."

Martin's flowers were a source of pride for his mother and grandmother. Martin himself enjoyed presenting them with birthday gifts of the flowers on which he had lavished such care.

One day, the dahlia he had worked so hard to grow was covered with something black. It was a swarm of harmful insects.

When he discovered the pests, an inexpressible chill and fury raced down Martin's spine. Up until now, he had squished any caterpillars he found on his flowers and then stomped on them with his shoes, but this was the first time he had seen such a huge swarm of tiny bugs lined up in ranks on his flowers.

He decided that he would drop the insects one by one onto a piece of paper and then set fire to them. The paper was instantly charred brown, and when the tongues of flame began to move, the insects trapped in the fire tried to scamper away but were burned to death. How delightful that was!

"You're such a sweet child," his grandmother repeated when she saw his dahlias.

Forty years had passed since then. He still enjoyed cultivating flowers.

Only on those days of rest twice each month was he able to forget the darkness of the work he did, as he dug in the soil in his garden. Only then did he have a slight release from his busy schedule each day.

The busy schedule of each day. His work was hectic, but that was not due to any formal orders; rather it was the result of confidential directions given to him by Heinrich Himmler, the Reichsführer of the Schutzstaffel, who had come to inspect the camp in March.

At a meal following the inspection, Himmler said to Kommandant Rudolf Höss, and to Martin, "We wish to expand Auschwitz to accommodate twenty thousand prisoners. After all, the purpose of the concentration camps is to exterminate the Jews from the earth."

Official orders would probably be sent down in the fall, but Martin consulted with Höss daily to lay plans for the camp's expansion.

At the same time, however, expansion obviously meant that a great many more prisoners would have to be eliminated each day. How exactly were they to dispose of so many corpses?

For almost an hour Martin spent a rewarding, peaceful time amid the fragrance of his flowers. Drawn to that fragrance, a black butterfly slowly came to rest on one of the flowers.

The children came rushing out of the house.

"Lotte!" The boy, carrying a shovel, called out to the older girl. Lotte looked back at her father and smiled, forming rose-colored dimples in her cheeks.

"Lotte and Wilhelm, come over here. A big black butterfly has landed on one of the flowers."

The brother and sister hurried over to his side and crouched down to peer with wide eyes at the large black butterfly.

As he looked at their blond hair and innocent faces, he suddenly remembered that on the previous day he has seen several children about the same age as his own children lined up in front of the gas chamber.

Each child had held its mother's hand; unaware, unknowing, they innocently proceeded one step at a time into the large ashen-colored building. Evidently the mothers and their children had no idea that death, its mouth gaping blackly open for them, waited inside this ashen-colored building.

Martin had stopped for a moment to survey the scene and stared at one of his men, who was leading the entire group with an uncommon gentleness.

His men took seriously the roles they had been assigned in this drama, in accordance with their orders, which stated: "You will treat the prisoners headed for the gas chambers with particular kindness to avoid arousing unnecessary fear, useless confusion, and the wasting of time."

A number of children, walking toward the gas chamber as they clung to their mothers' hands, had no idea they were about to be slaughtered.

Those children would be about the same age as his own children, Lotte and Wilhelm, who stood beside him gazing at the butterfly.

For a fleeting moment the thought sent dark melancholy racing through his chest. But it was only a fleeting moment, and immediately Martin was able to shift his thoughts, just as a magician swaps the cards in his deck.

Once again he rehearsed in his mind the firm principles that he reminded himself of on a constant basis. *That place and my home here are completely separate worlds. I must never bring any of what transpires there into my home.*

That place and my home here are completely separate worlds. Consequently, he had never told his wife Olga about anything that happened in the concentration camp. He had never told her about the great numbers of Polish people and Jews who were packed like sardines into cargo trains and transported to the camp each day, or about the elderly incapable of work who, along with the women and children, were immediately "eliminated" in the gas chambers. Nor had he told her about the great numbers of Poles and Jews, and any Germans who held beliefs hostile to the nation, who were forced to work there like domesticated animals. Because these were all part of a separate world, he did not tell his wife about the screams of those being tortured, or of the medical experiments that were being conducted.

But he was not alone in this. The camp kommandant, Lieutenant Colonel Höss, had told him that he too kept everything a secret from his family.

"If my wife found out . . . I'm sure she would leave me," Höss had said with a grim look on his face.

Höss was scheduled to come to Martin's house to discuss several matters that evening.

That same afternoon after lunch, Martin went with his wife Olga and his children to play beside a nearby stream.

His children had a delightful time. As they splashed in the water and shouted while they frolicked and raced about, Martin and his wife spread a blanket on the grass and lay down next to each another, listening to the sound of the wind drifting above the branches of the trees.

"Dear," Olga said with great hesitation, "there's something I'd like to ask you about."

"What is it?" Martin stuck a blade of grass between his teeth and turned to face his wife.

"Since we came here to Auschwitz—once in a while there are times when I really don't understand what is going on with you."

"With me?"

"Yes. Sometimes there's a dark expression in your eyes that makes me feel like I'm looking at a different person. I never saw that darkness in your eyes before we came here. What is going on?"

Martin had always feared that the time would come when his wife's intuition would penetrate his secrets. *Does she have some vague idea what is going on? Of what we are doing at the concentration camp . . . ?*

"Is your work going badly?"

"No, everything is going just fine."

"Well then . . ."

"Nothing is going on. Maybe I'm just exhausted from working too hard."

He stroked Olga's hair, trying very hard to cover his trembling. To conceal what was going on, what his hellish work was all about . . .

"If that's the case, all right, but . . ." Olga muttered, and she asked no further questions. Or perhaps it was more a case of being hesitant to ask anything more.

"Tonight after dinner, the kommandant will be coming over."

"Kommandant Höss is coming over . . . ?"

"We have some business to discuss. He said he was going to bring you a record of some Mozart music."

Kommandant Höss knew that Olga loved music, especially the music of Mozart. He had told Martin that he would bring Olga a recording of the *Requiem* that he had just acquired.

It was about time for the children to stop playing in the water. As they were getting ready to return home Lotte suddenly said something unexpected. "I just saw a strange man running through the forest. He was wearing zebra pajamas."

"Zebra pajamas? What are you talking about?" Olga scolded her daughter and explained to her husband, "She's been looking at too many picture books. The picture book I just bought her had a drawing of a zebra."

Zebra-like pajamas—that was the kind of uniform worn by prisoners in the concentration camp. But surely there couldn't be a prisoner in these woods.

"Let's go home," Martin urged his family. There was a chance he might receive a phone call notifying him that someone had escaped from the concentration camp.

That evening, around the time the family finished their dinner, they heard the sound of an automobile outside. Kommandant Höss had ordered his men to be strictly on time, and he too was a man who never arrived late for an appointment.

He was a short man. As he entered the house, he greeted Olga politely by kissing her hand. One of the unique characteristics of this kommandant was the courteous, well-mannered attitude he always displayed to the wives of his men. He affectionately picked up Lotte and Wilhelm and kissed them on their cheeks.

After sending the children off to bed, the Martins and Höss sat in the parlor and listened to the Mozart *Requiem*. A fellow Nazi living in occupied Paris had sent the recording to Höss.

"So beautiful . . ." Olga whispered after listening to the second movement through the conclusion of the Kyrie. Höss too had his eyes closed. Martin studied the man's profile and felt his body shaking. He himself did not know why he was trembling.

The three discussed a variety of topics as they drank an apple liqueur. Olga inquired about Höss's wife and children and then left the two men in the parlor and went upstairs to her bedroom.

After Olga had gone, Höss asked in a hushed voice about matters of greatest concern to them. "Your wife seems to suspect nothing."

"Yes, I think that's true."

"My wife knows nothing either."

"Kommandant, how much longer do you think we can go on living this double life?" Martin asked with a look of concern. "I am a completely different man when I am here at home and when I am working at the camp. We take on different personalities depending on where we are. Up until now everything has gone smoothly. But whether we can keep this up . . . ?"

"We must keep it up," Höss muttered, his eyes closed and the glass of liqueur pressed against his lips. It was as though he was not speaking to Martin but to himself. "It is our duty."

"I understand that. But . . . has there been anyone in the history of the world until now who has killed as many people as we have?"

"I wonder how many prisoners we have killed," Höss spoke as though he were dreaming.

"About . . . two million."

"Two million, is it? But we have been ordered by Commander Himmler to exterminate another two million here. We haven't yet achieved . . . even half that."

"When do you think the war will end?"

"I have no idea."

"Do you believe that there is a God?"

At this question from Martin, Höss opened his eyes and stared piercingly at his subordinate.

"Why . . . why would you . . . why would you ask such a thing?"

"I don't believe there's a God," Martin said in a hoarse voice. "But sometimes I wonder . . . once you and I die . . . will we be punished for what we have done?"

The two men fell silent as they sipped their liqueur. This was the first time they had allowed another human being even a glimpse into some of their true feelings.

Ordinarily, those who were employed at the concentration camp never attempted to talk about their feelings with each another. They never knew where an informant might be lurking. It was clear to them what would happen were an informant to send a letter denouncing them to their superiors in Berlin.

"In any case, I learned after coming to this camp that a person can grow accustomed to any situation whatsoever. I feel as though that's especially true when I look at the prisoners who are disposing of corpses from the gas chambers . . ." Höss muttered as though speaking to himself.

Prisoners who disposed of corpses would transport the bodies to the incinerators in trolleys and then pound the charred bones into powder. There was no other way dispose of the dead, who could number as many as a thousand or even fifteen hundred in a single day.

"I once saw a prisoner who was sifting through the mountain of corpses heaped up in the gas chamber when he discovered something that had belonged to his own wife. How do you suppose he reacted? His body shook for just a moment, but then he quietly carried on with his work."

Martin had no response. They heard a faint noise from the second floor—Olga's footsteps.

"It's simply a matter of getting used to it. It's all about adaptability. That man, just like all the other prisoners, is no longer moved by anything that takes place at the camp. Even if he discovered the corpse of his own wife sprawled out in the gas chamber, it could no longer hold any surprise for him. In the same way, we adapt ourselves to this life over time. I don't think it bothers us in the least to be leading double lives. During wartime you live as a person of war; when peace comes you live as a person of peace. And you'll likely forget the past. At least that's what I have concluded."

"Is it possible to forget it all?"

"There are great depths in the heart of man. So deep as to be bottomless."

Just then the phone rang. Both Höss and Martin's faces jerked upward; it was unusual for the phone to ring this late at night.

Picking up the receiver, Martin's expression suddenly darkened as he listened to the voice on the other end.

"I understand. I will let the kommandant know. The search must be carried out meticulously."

With that order, he hung up the phone. "This afternoon another prisoner escaped. They are searching for him right now, but they have not yet located him." He heaved a deep sigh and sat back down.

"This makes three since last month, including the one we hanged after our dogs tracked him down in the swamp. I can't shake the feeling that Polish farmers are assisting the fugitives."

"We must send out a notice that we will punish anyone who aids escapees or hides them."

Martin suddenly remembered what Lotte had said this afternoon as they were playing by the stream: a man wearing zebra pajamas had run past.

That was him! That was when it happened.

"Kommandant, in the event that we are unable to capture the escaped prisoner, will you then execute twenty prisoners as a warning to all?"

"We have no choice," Höss nodded sullenly. "There is nothing else to be done."

After briefly discussing some other business with Martin, Höss departed.

Martin saw his superior to the front door, but even after Höss's car had disappeared in the distance he stood motionless in his garden for a time.

The air, filled with the smells of grass and soil blended with the night dew, felt cold against his skin. Insects cried out from all directions.

Beyond his garden the forest where he had taken his children today to play in the stream stretched out blackly. This forest extended voicelessly to the outskirts of Kraków.

I wonder if the escaped prisoner is still lurking like an animal in that forest?

It was when a prisoner escaped that Martin became conscious of the fact that a fugitive was in fact a human being like himself. Those who wandered aimlessly about the camp were nothing more than a mass of bodies all dressed in the same prisoner uniforms. Nothing about that mass changed when another one or two of them was killed or sent off to the gas chamber.

Thanks to you, twenty lives will be lost, in his mind he called out toward the forest. *That doesn't bother you in the slightest, does it? I'm sure all you care about is saving yourself. You're all just a mass of egoists.*

He carefully wiped the mud from his shoes, locked the front door, and went upstairs to his bedroom.

"Has the kommandant gone?" Olga called out sleepily from the bed.

"Uh-huh," he replied as he brushed his teeth at the sink.

"I thought I heard the phone ringing a little while ago."

"It was nothing." Martin changed into his pajamas, turned off the light, and crawled into bed next to his wife's warm body. His mind hazily wandered back over tonight's conversation.

He and Höss had already murdered more people than anyone else in history. Not even Napoleon had wiped out almost two million lives. Besides, those Napoleon killed were his opponents in war, but every day he and Höss had killed the elderly and women and children who offered no resistance, who could not resist.

Yet, for some reason he felt no pain in his heart. He felt such tranquility that it seemed uncanny. There were times when a dark feeling, an empty feeling swept over him like a seizure, but even that was fleeting, and after it passed all was peaceful again. Never once had he experienced the sort of pain that would feel as though his heart was being gouged out.

I wonder if I have changed?

But he didn't seem to be the only one who had changed. To all appearances, neither Kommandant Höss nor any of the other workers at the camp were suffering in any way. At first the work was unpleasant, but now he could go to the dining hall and enjoy a delicious steak immediately after inspecting corpses in the gas chambers. All the other workers seemed equally capable of relishing the steaks they stuffed into their mouths. From the window of the dining hall, they could see smoke billowing into the sky as the corpses of murdered women and children were incinerated.

Have I just gotten used to it? Have I merely grown accustomed to it?

Martin recalled what Höss had said: "There are great depths in the heart of man."

"Dear, the children . . ." Olga muttered faintly in her sleep. Martin gently stroked her body to help her sleep soundly.

Early the following morning when he arrived at the camp, most of the prisoners had departed for their work assignments, but those from Block 14 were standing by themselves in the courtyard. Until a fugitive was brought back to the camp, all who were in the same block were held collectively responsible.

"Has he been found?" Martin asked the SS soldier who saluted him.

"No. Not yet, Herr Adjutant." The soldier clicked his heels loudly and saluted.

Martin went into his office with a bitter look on his face. The tapping as the typists struck the keys on their machines sounded like the firing of machine guns. These female typists spent every day creating cards with the names of those who had been brought to the camp, along with a list of names of those who had been exterminated.

Dr. Hoffman was waiting patiently for Martin.

"We would like to request that three children from among the Jews arriving today be provided to us for experimental use. This is Dr. Kaufman's request."

"What are the new experiments?"

"Experiments with pulmonary tuberculosis."

At this camp a number of prisoners were selected to be used by the doctors in place of guinea pigs in medical experiments. This time, the bacteria causing pulmonary tuberculosis would be implanted in the three children.

"That's fine."

As he filled out the permission form, for just a brief moment he thought of his own two children. Right now Lotte and Wilhelm were likely playing in the flower bed in his garden. Raising their voices in bright laughter . . .

Today, however, three children about the same age as his own were going to be injected with *Mycobacterium tuberculosis* for no other reason than the fact they were Jewish. As subjects for experimentation . . .

He signed the permission form. It was simply a matter of growing accustomed to these things. It was a matter of adapting to the situation. Even so, a heavy dark stone fell with a dull splash into the well of his heart . . .

If there is a God . . . I suppose I will be punished by that God.

His thoughts had drifted elsewhere as he absentmindedly listened to Dr. Hoffman's explanation of something or other.

No, there can't be a God. And what is God anyway? No such being exists.

Today was not particularly different from any other day.

The sky was clear, and the temperature gradually climbed. Near midday a cargo train crammed with Jews and Poles arrived at the Auschwitz station as it always did with a screeching of its wheels. Exhausted people waited motionless on the platform for the selection process to be carried out. Knowing nothing, sensing nothing . . .

Three hours later the doors to the gas chambers would close. Soon, black smoke would rise from the chimneys. It was their daily ritual.

In the afternoon the prisoners from Block 14 were still being forced to stand in ranks. One prisoner after another would collapse from the heat.

"Still not caught?" Martin sullenly asked a soldier.

"Not yet, Herr Adjutant." The soldier loudly clicked his heels and saluted.

The afternoon passed and evening approached. When Martin peered out his office window, the prisoners being disciplined were still standing in place. The fugitive had not yet been caught.

The tapping of the typewriter keys, which had been going on all day, suddenly stopped, and the women who worked there began preparing to leave. They nodded and bid farewell to each other and went out of the room.

Left alone in the building, Martin rubbed his tired eyes and sat motionless at his desk. As adjutant, he could scarcely return home until this fugitive incident was resolved.

At 5:30 an SS officer named Müller came in seeking instructions. With one arm raised in salute he said, "In another thirty minutes it will be 6 o'clock. I would like to execute twenty of the prisoners as I promised if the escaped prisoner is not captured by then."

No matter what the issue, this man was as precise as the hands on a clock. He was like a mechanized man who strictly followed every rule.

"Müller, don't you think twenty . . . is a bit too many?" Martin waved his hand. "How about making it five?"

"But, Herr Adjutant, I have already announced to these prisoners that twenty will be required. If we do not honor our demands, they will no longer take us seriously."

"I understand that, but . . . This is the first time that such a requirement will be enforced, so why not execute perhaps five of them this time and then increase the number to be killed if there are any further escapees?"

An obvious look of dissatisfaction and contempt appeared on Müller's face.

"But, Herr Adjutant, with all due deference . . ."

Martin and Müller finally agreed to reduce the number to be killed from twenty to ten.

"Will you be coming with me?" the officer asked.

"Yes."

The time was nearing 6:00 p.m. There was as yet no wireless communication from the pursuers.

Martin followed Müller out of the building.

It was twilight. The western skies over the concentration camp blazed like a flame. The evening sky glowed crimson with a rose-colored tint extending all the way to the ground. This was the most beautiful hour of the day, when nature granted its blessings to the earth. At that most beautiful of hours, the most painful of punishments was about to be carried out.

Müller's boots squeaked as he walked. He took great pride in being an SS officer and seemed to think that one who would be an officer could not exhibit the slightest unkemptness in his uniform. His boots were always polished, and the fragrance of eau de cologne drifted faintly from his jacket.

Seeing his superior officer and the adjutant approaching, the soldier who stood guard in front of the prisoners snapped to attention.

The prisoners stood erect as rods. Here and there prisoners who had fainted from anemia because of the heat and exhaustion lay on the ground.

"All right, everyone—it's 6 o'clock!" Müller said gleefully. "However, unfortunately for myself, and also for all of you, the fugitive has not been captured."

Müller was silent for a time, perhaps searching out a reaction to his words on the faces of each of the prisoners.

"As I promised you earlier, we are going to have twenty of you die. Consider this a parting gift left for each of you by the fugitive. If you must hate someone, you should hate the fugitive. We did warn you that this would happen."

As Müller strolled leisurely in front of the prisoners, he gave the same speech as the one he had given just after the prisoner escaped. For his part, Martin stood beside the military guard and closely observed the ceremony.

"Well then, those I point to are to line up here in front."

When Müller finished speaking, the bodies of the prisoners, which seemed as though they had been frozen in place, twitched visibly. The moment for the selection of the sacrificial victims had finally come.

Those who were chosen would be taken from here to the starvation chambers. They would remain there from tonight until they were dead.

Müller slowly turned and began walking between the ranks of men. He would stop, peer deeply into a prisoner's face, and then, enjoying the shudders of fear on the sweat-soaked face, he would set off walking again. Every second seemed to the prisoners to last an eternity.

Henryk put up a brave front as the sound of Miller's boots slowly approached him.

O God . . .

Staring at a spot in space, Henryk struggled desperately to assume an expression that would attract no attention. He knew of no way to protect himself other than to avoid stirring up waves in Müller's mind.

The footsteps suddenly stopped. A low voice said "You." The first sacrificial victim had been chosen.

The prisoners tried not to move a single muscle. They clung tenaciously to the hope that Müller would finish this task quickly.

The man who had been selected seemed not to possess the strength to step out of rank; he did not move. When the kapo jabbed him in the back, the sacrificial victim staggered to the front.

"You . . . and you . . ."

Henryk realized that Müller had speeded up the selection process. His footsteps gradually drew near. Henryk inhaled the faint aroma of eau de cologne.

In just a moment he would hear the squeaking boots right next to him.

Hurry! . . . Walk past me. Hurry!

Henryk struggled with all his might to hold himself motionless even as it felt that his body might collapse. If he were to fall over right now, Müller's gaze would undoubtedly be drawn toward him.

Müller stopped directly in front of him. He peered into Henryk's face, then slowly compared Henryk with the man standing next to him. A thin smile crossed Müller's lips.

That faint smile. Evident in that indistinct smile was the thrill of being able to control the life or death of one man by means of nothing more than his own whim.

"You."

Müller's finger was at first aimed toward Henryk, but then it moved to point to the man beside him. It wasn't Henryk, but the man next to him . . . he was the one who was chosen.

In that moment, Henryk felt the intense joy of having been "saved." He felt not the slightest sympathy for those who were selected.

His neighbor who had been selected began to cry. Hearing the man's weeping voice elicited no pain whatsoever in Henryk's heart. *I'm going to be all right. In any case there is the possibility that I will continue to live at least until another man escapes.*

"This time, we are going to stop with these ten," Müller said to the prisoners. "That is our special favor to you. But next time, expect no lenient treatment. We will show no mercy in executing twenty of you for one escapee."

The ten men who were selected were lined up facing the rest of the prisoners. The blood had already drained from their faces, which were starkly white. Death was about to claim these ten.

Henryk realized for the first time that the prisoner who had been next to him was short in stature. Facing the other prisoners, he wept like a child, his shoulders shaking. The other nine men were either struggling to withstand the shock they had received or were completely overwhelmed by the situation.

The prisoners who had been spared, facing the condemned men, were forced to stare directly at the looks of anguish on the faces of these ten. Yet those who had been spared were still consumed by the joy of their escape from death.

What it comes down to is that you . . . your luck was bad.

It's not my fault . . . not my fault that you have to die. In his mind Henryk spoke these words to the weeping man, even as he continued to relish his own elation. *It's not my fault! It's not my fault!*

✳ ✳ ✳

Müller saluted Adjutant Martin and said, "We have selected the ten men. Is there anything you want to say to them?"

"No, nothing," Martin replied ill-humoredly and averted his eyes.

"All right, then, you ten, remove your wooden clogs." This was the common practice at the camp for those about to be executed. "Left face, left!"

The starvation chamber they were about to be thrust into was in the basement of Block 13, which could be seen off to the left. On the first floor was an interrogation room and a torture chamber; in the basement were the starvation chamber and the asphyxiation chamber.

These last two rooms were where the cruelest deaths took place. They were rooms of extermination from which the only escape was to die, either of starvation or from lack of air.

"My wife . . . I want to see my wife . . . and my children!"

The man who had dissolved into sobs suddenly wailed loudly. It sounded as though all his internal organs were being squeezed out of him.

Müller gave a signal to the soldiers to take the man to Block 13.

Then it happened. One of the prisoners from the group whose lives had been spared broke rank and slowly stepped forward. Perhaps because he had been made to stand in place for so long, his gait was sluggish, resembling that of a child's toy doll. He dragged his feet as though they were made of lead.

His body was emaciated, and he wore round glasses.

In a weary voice, he said, "I . . . please allow me to take the place of this weeping man."

After making his request, the prisoner whose round glasses were perched on a weary face stood clumsily at attention in front of Müller.

It was a posture of complete submissiveness, like that of a monk listening to orders from the abbot at a monastery.

"What did you say?" The tone of Müller's voice was almost eerily gentle.

"Would you . . . would you please let me die in place of this prisoner," the man softly repeated his request.

A look of astonishment resembling consternation flashed across Müller's face—in fact, also across the faces of the soldiers standing behind him.

"What are you saying?"

"He has a wife and children. . . . I am a priest and have no wife or child to mourn my death. And I am an old man."

Müller stared at the prisoner's face in blank amazement. Finally he asked, "What is your name and number?"

"Maximilian Kolbe. Number 16670."

For a time, Müller said nothing. He looked back at Adjutant Martin in search of some assistance. But Martin's face had become rigid in response to this unfathomable situation.

"Do you realize what will happen to you?"

"I do."

For some reason, Müller averted his eyes. Without looking up, he said to the weeping prisoner he had initially selected, "You . . . return to ranks. The rest of you who have been selected . . . march!"

Listlessly, with their shoulders drooping, the nine sacrificial victims began walking. Father Kolbe, separated somewhat from the group, followed at the rear, his head hanging. He looked for all the world like an old, pathetic donkey. But for the first time the soldiers and the kapo did not raise their voices in derision. The remaining prisoners watched in amazement as the ten men marched away.

In the background, the evening sun painted the sky crimson as the black shadows of the ten men dragged their legs in procession. The scene resembled a final dazzling farewell as the summer day closed in that moment just before day summoned forth the night.

Meanwhile, the ten wretched men who were being forced to say their farewells to the world were being driven, staggering and colliding with one another, toward Block 13.

"Dismissed!" the kapo ordered, his voice scratchy from the dryness of his throat. Several of the prisoners did not move. Henryk was among those who continued to watch as the figures of the victims grew smaller in the distance.

Suddenly, he heard a loud whimpering voice directly beside him. It was the man whose life had been spared by Father Kolbe.

"I . . ." Wiping the tears from his face with his hand, he muttered something. But no one could make out what he said.

The evening sun continued to bathe the sky the color of blood.

Adjutant Martin walked alongside Father Kolbe. At close proximity, he noticed that one of the arms on the priest's glasses had been torn off and been replaced by a string that dangled from his ear.

"Father Kolbe." Taking care that neither the soldiers nor Müller could hear him, Martin whispered to the priest, "I am . . . I am going to hell, aren't I?"

13

THE DEATH OF KOLBE

MARTIN HAD NOT made this comment out of a desire to mock the man in the round broken glasses. Nor had he said it as a confession of the pain in his own heart.

He had merely been curious to know what this priest thought about a man like himself—a man whose daily job was to send blameless women, children, and elderly people to the gas chamber.

The priest raised his head in surprise at Martin's abrupt question, which the adjutant repeated: "I am . . . I am going to hell, aren't I?"

"Why . . . why are you asking me that?"

"I'm sure you know why without even having to ask."

"Do you . . . are the things that you are doing causing you pain?"

With a somewhat rueful smile, Martin shook his head. "If that were the case, I wouldn't be asking the question. Ironically enough, I feel nothing at all, despite how many people I have killed. I'm not just putting on a brave face. To be honest, my heart is at peace to an almost revolting degree. Of course, once in a while I'll have a flare-up of depression. A wave of melancholy will wash over me. But it never lasts long, and then when I look at the corpses of the prisoners . . . I feel nothing. You are going to be dying soon, and I'm sure I'll see your dead body, too . . . but I doubt I'll feel anything then, either. It's a bit unsettling to realize that's how I am. That's why I asked you that question."

The priest closed his eyes, rather like an ascetic bearing up under intense suffering.

Müller watched the two men with a quizzical look on his face. He couldn't understand why his adjutant was talking with the cleric as though he was speaking with a friend.

"Why did you do that?" Martin asked the priest.

"Do what?"

"Substitute your own life for that of another prisoner."

"He has a wife and children. But . . ."

"I already heard that. What I want to know . . . this action you have chosen to carry out . . . did you do it to gratify your own ego? Perhaps out of vanity? You'll admit there is such a thing as performing a righteous act out of conceit or smugness."

His eyes still shut, Father Kolbe did not respond to this inquiry. Just as the Jesus in whom he believed was silent in response to Herod's taunts.

Then, in a soft voice, the priest said, "Until I am dead, I shall be praying for that man and for you. For you as well."

"Praying for me? Praying what?"

"That you will not lose hope in yourself."

Martin shrugged his shoulders and smiled woefully.

The condemned men were approaching Block 13. It was a rectangular red brick building, like all the other block buildings.

"Farewell," the priest lowered his head and said in a raspy voice.

"Auf wiedersehen," Martin replied. "I hope that your suffering will not last long." Turning on his heels, he returned by himself to the building where his office was located.

The flame of the evening sun had died out. The wide purple night cooled the soil that still retained heat from the daylight.

How quiet it is. My heart feels no pain. It's almost eerily silent.

How different the Martin when he was at home from the Martin when he was here. At the camp, he was devoid of emotion no matter what he witnessed—whether evil or good. *It's all about growing accustomed to it*, he muttered to himself.

✳ ✳ ✳

That evening, a number of prisoners gathered at the window of their barrack and, without speaking a word, stared unblinking at Block 13.

Although they did not exchange a single word aloud, their thoughts were one.

I wonder what is happening to Father Kolbe right now? Has he already been put into the asphyxiation bunker?

But Block 13, already beginning to be shrouded in the deep purple evening mist, revealed only the gray outlines of a military barrack. Lights were glowing in several of the windows in the building, but all of the other windows were dark.

None of the screams that accompany torture issued from the building.

They heard no gunshots.

It was utterly silent, giving the prisoners no hint of what was happening inside the building.

Maybe they're still in the interrogation room while their paperwork is being processed, a middle-aged prisoner standing at the window wondered.

He had once been sent to Block 13 to deliver a message. So he knew the kinds of rooms the building contained.

The layout of the building was essentially the same as all the other barracks. One difference was the room directly to the right of the entrance, which functioned as an interrogation room. Prisoners brought there were initially subjected to cruel questioning.

Next were two rooms where prisoners condemned to death were detained until their execution, and, like the prisoners' rooms in the other barracks, they had beds that resembled silkworm trays.

Directly across the hallway opposite that room was the torture chamber. Its various instruments and racks of torture were reminiscent of those used in medieval times. Prisoners brought here screamed and groaned until they were splattered with blood and fainted away.

At the top of the stairs leading to the basement was a dressing room where the prisoners stripped off all their clothing. One of the three basement rooms was a break room for the prison officers. A second was the starvation bunker, and next to it was the asphyxiation bunker.

There were no windows in the two execution rooms. The four walls were of thick concrete, with only a small round opening in the iron door. Through that hole, the officers could peer inside the rooms each morning and determine how many had starved to death or how many had suffocated from lack of air.

Once the interrogation finishes, the ten men will have their clothes taken from them at the top of the stairs and have to stand there stark naked, the middle-aged prisoner standing at the window of his barrack muttered to himself. *Then they'll file down the stairs of death, walk along the hallway of death, and be put into the rooms of death. The thick doors will be shut.*

He imagined what Father Kolbe would look like, what expression he would wear on his face as he descended those death stairs along with the other nine men. The middle-aged man had exchanged a few conversations with Father Kolbe. Would the priest still be wearing his round, broken glasses? And what would be going through his mind? Would he be thinking of the

sufferings of Jesus, who died for love, and try to bear his own
pains by comparing Jesus's last moments with his own?

*O God, if it be thy will, please take this cup of death from me.
Nevertheless, if it be thy will that I die . . .*

Even Jesus had suffered the fear of death to that extremity.

Twilight had completely enveloped Block 13. The lights in
three windows were the only evidence of its existence.

The other prisoners who had gathered at the barrack window
pondered the scene they had witnessed only one hour earlier.

Father Kolbe staggering to the front of the line. His round
glasses with a missing arm that had been repaired with a piece
of string hung over his ear. "Please allow me to take the place of
this man . . ." The prisoners could still remember the priest's
weary voice. Henryk, too, remembered. Seated on the floor he
turned it over in his mind.

Why did the priest do that?

Like Adjutant Martin, Henryk tried to detect any sort of
religious pride in the heart of the priest that might be aimed
at displaying himself as worthy of praise, or from the self-
satisfaction that comes from having performed a noble act. In
the final analysis, the human heart cannot avoid such egoism.

No matter how hard he tried to view the motivation for Father
Kolbe's actions as mere pride or self-satisfaction, Henryk had to
admit that there was something more to it. Certainly no one was
so foolish that they would choose a brutal, painful, wretched
death in the starvation bunker simply out of pride. No one was
idiotic enough to die in the most miserable manner as a result
of nothing greater than self-satisfaction.

Then why did he do it?

Henryk pressed his forehead against the wall. He actually
knew the answer to that question. But he did not want to admit it.

*A man can't go on living in a place like this . . . merely on the basis
of love. The most important thing . . . more important than love or*

anything else . . . is to stay alive here. It's far more vital to stay alive until this war ends, no matter what happens.

That is what half of Henryk's heart was telling him. But the other half had taken hold of Henryk's mind and was trying to encourage him to ponder more deeply what Father Kolbe had done.

"Here's your soup." The prisoner on kitchen duty distributed bowls of soup for dinner. Soup. It was soup in name alone; in reality it was nothing more than muddy hot water. That and half a slice of bread left over from lunch. That was all the prisoners had for their evening meal. Henryk lined up with his wooden bowl and his wooden spoon. The customary battles over places in line began.

They all wanted more than a single ladle's worth of soup. To that end, they all vied to be at the head of the line. The struggle over a single ladle of soup led these men, who had once held such positions in society as store managers or company officials, to contend in this unseemly fashion.

Sipping their soup and stuffing the half slice of bread into their mouths—after taking as much time as they could to stretch out the opportunity to enjoy their food—the only task remaining for them was to lie down, nine per bed, and go to sleep.

Night fastened itself on the window. Searchlights from the watchtowers swept by from time to time. Then, only darkness. Eternal darkness . . . darkness devoid of love.

If there is no love in the world, we must create it . . .

Henryk suddenly recalled Father Kolbe's declaration.

At that same moment, the starvation bunker in which the priest and the other nine prisoners were confined was plunged into darkness.

✳ ✳ ✳

One day passed since Father Kolbe and the others had been locked in the starvation bunker, then two days.

Both of those days were radiant summer days, so beautiful that they gave the impression that everything had been dyed in the blue of the sky. In Martin's garden, the morning chill seemed permeated by the aroma of the flowers blooming in the beds he had so diligently maintained.

After drinking a glass of cold milk that morning, Martin drove himself to the concentration camp. In the evening, when the horizon to the west was bathed the same rosy color it had been two days earlier, he drove back to his home, escorted by soldiers on motorcycles.

"Did you have a good day today?" his wife Olga would ask him every evening when he returned.

"I got some good work done," he would answer, purposely whistling to put on a show of cheeriness. For an instant, something flashed across his vision. It was the face of Father Kolbe, wearing his round glasses and gazing in his direction.

To drive the priest's face away, he hurriedly asked his wife, "And how was your day?"

"It was a little busy. I went to the dentist's office to pay my bill to Dr. Gessel,[1] and the children . . ."

Martin told his wife nothing about the camp. One prisoner had escaped, and ten men were put into the starvation bunker—he of course did not mention any of that, or the fact that among them was a priest who had voluntarily taken the place of another man.

Within the confines of his home, he was first and last a good husband and a good father.

✳ ✳ ✳

---

1   See chapter 2, note 5.

The third day came.

When he arrived at the camp that morning, he phoned Block 13 from his office. Müller answered.

"How are they doing?"

"Three days, and not one of them has died. Yes, that's right. We continue to watch them. I'm sure two or three will be gone within another week," Müller responded in a monotone voice.

✳ ✳ ✳

"Strictly speaking, what will do them in is not so much starvation as not drinking a single drop of water."

"And the Father . . . ?"

"The father? Oh, you mean the priest? He's . . . he's still alive." Martin hung up the phone and covered his face with both hands.

He could not understand why he was so bothered by Father Kolbe.

He should be completely inured to the daily deaths of prisoners. One of his responsibilities was to sign the roster with the numbers of prisoners that were being sent to the gas chambers. At his signature alone, a thousand, even two thousand Jews and Poles disappeared daily.

Then why was he so disturbed by that one wretched man . . . ?

At nightfall, the sky through his window seemed to glow like a flame. Then came the night. Nature recapitulated its daily rhythms, seemingly indifferent to the many audible groans and screams coming from the camp.

Martin straightened his desk in preparation to returning home and went outside. A soldier saluted him as he climbed into his car. His motorcycle escorts set out ahead of him.

As he gripped the steering wheel, he slipped on the face of good husband and good father for the benefit of Olga and his children. And in his mind he muttered, "I'll grow accustomed to it soon, and I'll forget . . ."

✳ ✳ ✳

Six days passed.

Martin had stopped asking the soldiers, "How are they doing?"

It was not because he had become apathetic. To the contrary, it was because the fates of the ten men confined in the starvation bunker—especially the priest in the round glasses—had settled like a ponderous, heavy weight in Martin's heart.

Day by day, images of the priest assumed distinct shape in his heart. Every word of the conversation he had exchanged with the priest as they walked toward Block 13 came back into his heart so vividly that it caused him pain.

Why? He's not the only one being executed. Martin repeated these words over and over to himself as he sat at his office desk. *What is wrong with you?*

He knew considerably more about the current situation in the starvation bunker than did the SS soldiers, since as adjutant he received reports on the conditions.

A prisoner was ordered to inspect the starvation bunker daily; even the thought of trying to enter was distasteful to the SS soldiers. Should the prisoner discover someone who had died of starvation, he was to drag the corpse outside the bunker and clean out the exterminated prisoner's chamber pot.

Each morning, when the designated prisoner, whose name was Borgowiec, opened the door to the starvation bunker, he heard faint voices singing. The condemned men, their conspicuously emaciated nude bodies propped up against the bare walls of the cell, were singing a hymn. Father Kolbe was among them.

They peered back at Borgowiec with large, sunken, blackly veiled eyes. Not a single word of resentment or hatred spill from their lips. On rare occasions one prisoner might plead, "Water . . . won't you please give me some water?"

The others continued to sing hymns in feeble, lifeless voices. Father Kolbe sang along with them . . .

Eventually the singing voices faded and were heard less frequently. From that point forward, just as one locates the carcass of a dead insect inside a cage each day, Borgowiec began to discover corpses in different corners of the room. Father Kolbe, however, was still among the several survivors.

The condition of the prisoners was communicated every day to Adjutant Martin. After receiving the reports by phone from Müller (who related the situation with strict accuracy, as though he were relaying statistics), Martin kept his eyes closed for a long while. The unbroken sounds of the female workers tapping on their typewriter keys could be heard from the room next to his office.

Evening came, and Martin straightened his desk and prepared to return home.

Glancing out the window, he saw that the afterglow of the sunset was still aflame.

He climbed into his car and donned his mask of good husband and good father. Kicking up dust, the escort motorcycles set off ahead of his car.

In his garden the summer dahlias were now in full bloom, just as they were every summer. Once summer ended, however, they would wither away. His wife Olga told him that today she had read Goethe's poem, "Marienbad Elegy."

✳ ✳ ✳

More than a week had passed since they had been cast into the starvation bunker. All of the prisoners in Block 14 were aware that, of the ten men, five had already died and been carted away.

They learned this directly from Borgowiec, thanks to his assignment at the starvation bunker.

Despite all that was happening, the daily lives of the prisoners did not change. The egoism of the men in Block 14 was still openly on display as they verbally abused one another, skirmished with one another, and pushed others out of their way.

But though their outward lives were the same, the prisoners were not indifferent to the fate of the ten men in the starvation bunker. As they labored, news was passed by word of mouth that yesterday one man, today one more man, had died, and each of them stopped digging with their shovels and for just a moment stood erect, while some closed their eyes and muttered to themselves the words of a prayer. At such times, not even the kapo shouted at them.

That in itself was an unusual scene, at this camp where everyone had grown utterly inured to death. This was a rarity among prisoners who had descended into apathy over the suffering of others.

In addition—

Although no one spoke it aloud, they all carried two questions in their minds each day: "What is happening with Father Kolbe? Is he still alive?"

It was unusual that no one gave voice to these questions. For some reason they seemed afraid to ask. Perhaps they felt that if they spoke the words their fears would be realized.

The daytime heat continued intense, torturous.

It's been six days.

It's been seven days.

Each day Henryk, as though he were looking upon something fearsome, cast quick glances at the red brick building where Father Kolbe and the others were being starved to death.

The windows of the building reflected the stark sunlight. The intensity of the reflected light seemed to convey with unquestionable clarity the sufferings of the men who had been tossed into the building and given neither a crumb of bread nor a single drop of water.

It's not my fault! Henryk quickly averted his eyes. And yet a bitter feeling, like the acrid taste of gastric fluids, welled up in his chest. Credit for all that went to Father Kolbe and his broken round glasses.

Henryk recalled his first meeting with the priest on the train platform and the conversation he had had with him that Sunday at the water fountain. The fact that the priest had stirred up his anger also revived among his memories.

What had made Henryk furious at the priest was Kolbe's assertion that even though they lived in such a wretched world, he still believed in the nonsensical notion that there is a God. When the priest proclaimed his beliefs, Henryk thought, *God can go to hell!* He cared nothing for a God who would abandon this wretched world . . .

Yet at this very moment the priest was in the starvation bunker as one of five surviving men. Even though seven days had already passed. He had not yet died.

✳ ✳ ✳

Eventually ten days had passed. Martin knew from Müller's report that, of the ten condemned men, six were dead and only four were still alive, among them Father Kolbe.

"I don't think it will be any more than five days before we have them all cleaned up." Müller used the phrase "cleaned up" to describe the deaths of the prisoners. For Müller the death of prisoners seemed no different from doing a clean sweep of his house to get rid of unnecessary trash.

The eleventh day.

The telephone report from Müller: "As we have anticipated, the weakening of the four prisoners is acute, and they are no longer able to speak. I think we can get this all taken care of tomorrow or the following day."

The twelfth day.

"Unfortunately the situation today is the same as it was yesterday. The four prisoners are still alive. Adjutant Martin, do you wish to leave them as they are, or do you wish to try another method?"

The thirteenth day.

"As of this morning, the four have still not died. I don't think there is a need to keep them alive any longer. Consequently, we are of the opinion that if they continue to live until tomorrow, we would like to put an end to it."

"Put an end to it? By what means?" Martin asked, sensing that his own voice had become scratchy.

"Injections of carbolic acid."

Today too was exceedingly hot, and as he spoke on the telephone the sound of typewriter keys being struck in the next room was unbearable. From the window, sunlight that seemed hot enough to melt tin streamed onto the floor.

"I'll think about it."

Placing the receiver back on its cradle, it was almost agonizing for Martin to wipe the sweat from his forehead. Once again the face of Father Kolbe in his round broken glasses appeared before him. The sorrowful eyes looking toward him from behind those glasses. That face that seemed to be withstanding something. For some reason these images sent sharp pains through Martin's chest.

That pain increased in intensity with each passing day. In order to escape from that pain, from that face, he must put an end to Father Kolbe. Once he was rid of the priest, he could return to being accustomed to this place. He would again be able to wear two faces of his own, one here in the camp and one at home.

He lifted up the receiver and dialed 1-3. It was the number to reach Müller.

"About your proposal to kill the prisoners tomorrow with the injections. . . . I approve."

"I understand, Herr Adjutant. I will at once select a doctor to perform the injections. Could I ask you to contact the kommandant?"

He sensed a degree of excitement in Müller's voice. He too wanted to finish this matter off.

I'll forget, Miller forcefully told himself. *I'll be able to forget that face, that face with the round glasses.*

✳ ✳ ✳

August 14.

It was already hot by morning. At breakfast, Martin uncharacteristically scolded his son Wilhelm for drinking his milk slowly.

"What is wrong with you today?" a startled Olga asked. Martin did not reply. He was well aware of why he was on edge.

When he reached the camp, he immediately phoned Müller and was told that the four men were still alive.

"Then I will contact the medical office right now. Yes, we will dispose of them with the injections. Will you be there, Herr Adjutant?"

Martin declined, saying he had work to do. He tried to look over the paperwork sent his way. But his mind was elsewhere. Impatiently he left his office and went out into the hallway.

The red brick building containing the starvation bunker and the asphyxiation bunker were visible from the window of the bathroom at the end of the hallway. Pretending to wash his hands, he peered at the building through the branches of the poplar tree whose leaves had wilted in the heat.

Soon he saw a doctor in a white smock heading toward the building, accompanied by a single soldier. The doctor held a wooden box containing the injection syringe. It was the same timorous doctor who had previously come to relay orders from his superiors for Martin to send over some children to replace the guinea pigs used in live experiments with *Mycobacterium tuberculosis*.

If this doctor had not been assigned to a concentration camp, he'd be running a tiny clinic in some country village. He would probably have been a respectable doctor loved by all the villagers and always invited to the weddings of all the young women.

But fate had delivered him here, and fate had made him a party to the killing of Father Kolbe.

Five minutes passed from the time the doctor disappeared into the building.

Martin stared with vacant eyes at the wall beside the bathroom window. A spider clung to the stone casing surrounding the window, its body glistening as though it had been smeared with oil. The spider seemed to be basking comfortably in the sunlight.

Seven minutes passed. Ten minutes passed. Somewhere nearby he could hear the flapping of the wings of bees. The air again today was clear.

The white-frocked doctor emerged, walking hesitantly through the doorway of the building. With bent back and the wooden box clutched in his hands, he headed toward the courtyard.

It was finished. Everything was over. The surviving four had been disposed of. The life of Father Kolbe of the broken round glasses had been terminated.

Nothing had changed. The spider still clung to the stone window casing, basking in the sunlight, the bees still noisily flapped their wings, and the sky was still blue.

The sky was still blue. Had no one known this camp existed or what had just occurred, this would be an altogether beautiful summer morning where all was serene . . .

✳ ✳ ✳

At that same hour, Henryk and the other prisoners in Block 14 were being herded outside to work at reclaiming the swamp area.

They felled the elms, the larch trees, and the white birches in the forest. The trunks of the fallen trees were carried to a swampy region and tossed into the bogs as materials for the construction of drainage ditches. Dried-out soil was used to gradually fill in the wetlands.

The groups of men dressed in prison uniforms worked like swarms of ants in the areas apportioned to them. Beneath the hot rays of the sun, the kapos shouted, kicking those who were idle or any who had crouched down out of exhaustion, all under the watchful eyes of the Nazi SS guards, who found it all amusing.

Finally the prisoners were given a break at midday. After thirty minutes of rest, they returned to the same labors as before. Prisoners who had collapsed onto the ground as though they were dead slowly staggered to their feet, grabbed their shovels, and again began pushing the trolleys.

It was just then that word of the deaths of the four men, including Father Kolbe, reached the prisoners from Block 14.

They did not know who had delivered the news. But unlike other events, happenings at the camp were relayed to the prisoners with unusual speed and promptness.

"Father Kolbe and the others . . . have died."

"Father Kolbe and the others . . . have died."

The news was conveyed from those felling trees to those pushing trolleys, from those pushing trolleys to those working in the swampy areas.

For a moment—and it was only a brief moment—a profound silence and a cessation of all movement spread like ripples to encompass them all. Some shut their eyes tightly, while others muttered under their breath. But it was just for a moment, after which they returned to their labors as though nothing at all had happened.

As they resumed their work, each man in turn felt something passing through the deepest regions of his heart. The news of Father Kolbe's death, like the shadow from the wings of a large bird swooping across a mountain slope, left something, imparted something deep within the hearts of those pushing the trolleys, those wielding their hoes, and those digging with their shovels, after which it vanished.

Not one of them could say what that "something" was. It was not anything that could be expressed in words. The prisoners of Block 14 who had experienced it fell silent, saying very little to one another as they continued their work.

Nightfall came.

Again today the horizon to the west was painted a rosy hue. Whistles signaling the end of work sounded here and there, and the men lined up for roll call. The flaming skies and the clouds that reminded them of castles in the evening sun spread before their eyes. As the prisoners shouted out their numbers, the evening sun, looking like a moist glass bead, gradually set.

"Ah!" one prisoner muttered, "This world is truly . . . beautiful!"

No one said anything in response. Ah, this world is truly beautiful! Until yesterday this world was void of all love and all joy. It was a world that had nothing to offer but fear, sorrow, torture, and death. Today that world was truly beautiful.

They all knew what had changed this world. The man who had created love in this loveless world . . .

Thereafter, for a long while—

In the concentration camp, from deep within Henryk's memory, the image of Father Kolbe, wearing his broken, round glasses, frequently appeared.

Naturally, he wasn't constantly aware of the Father each moment of every wretched day.

In fact, quite to the contrary, just as before Henryk continued to carry within himself an impulse that drove him to want to stay alive, to not die. To that end, just like the other prisoners, he wore his egoism on the surface, shoved weaklings aside so that he could snatch up more than his share of soup, and when it came time to work, chose tasks that would allow him to cut corners.

But once in a while—

Yes, once in a while, without any warning—for instance, when he saw the afterglow of the sunset in the sky as a row of prisoners trudged back to the camp along the muddy road, pushing a trolley ahead of them—suddenly the face of Father Kolbe, wearing his damaged round glasses, popped up in his mind.

The expression on the father's face when it appeared before him always seemed filled with sorrow. He looked out through his thick glasses sadly at Henryk and the other prisoners. It was with grief that he watched the prisoners again today being driven like animals, their backs lashed by the kapo's whip. While he was still alive the priest was often beaten, kicked, and knocked to the ground by the kapos at his workplace, and it was always this expression of sorrow on his face when he got back on his feet.

But that face did not constantly linger before Henryk's eyes. He quickly forgot it or made a conscious effort to drive it away. It bothered him because it seemed to Henryk that the face was always saying to him: "If there is no love here, we must create love."

Each time he heard that voice, Henryk became enraged and retorted,

I'm not you! I'm not a priest! I'm just a common, ordinary man. There is no way I could do what you did, take the place of someone else and wind up starving to death.

You're strong! I'm weak, I'm a weak man. Just leave me alone! he shouted silently at the face of Father Kolbe.

Although it wasn't something that he necessarily wished for, he would suddenly recall one or two conversations he had exchanged with Father Kolbe.

"I'm praying for you. I have not forgotten the promise I made to you at the train station."

That promise was made on the day they arrived at this corner of hell. It was while they were all squatting on the train platform, knowing nothing of the kind of place this was. The Father had also told him he had once lived in a town called Nagasaki in Japan.

"It's a small town, with beautiful mountains and a beautiful ocean. And there are so many hills! The Japanese people tie strings to wooden planks and put them on their feet, and they are able to walk with amazing dexterity. You can hear the clatter of their clogs everywhere on those hills . . ."

NA-GA-SA-KI. That was the first time Henryk had heard the name of such a village in a country called Japan, a place he would never have anything to do with throughout his life.

Several months passed.

During that time, one after another, prisoners in Block 14 died of debilitation.

Even those with minor illnesses were unable to survive the relentless forced labor and the scant food they were given.

There was no shortage of men to take the place of those who had died. Almost every day people were sent to this concentration camp from various Nazi-occupied lands.

The new arrivals were sorted out like animals; those who couldn't contribute to the labor force were "disposed of," while the remainder were thrown into barracks where there was space.

These new arrivals, ignorant of what would be happening to them, had their hair shaved off and even the hairs on their bodies shorn; then they were doused with chemicals to ward off fleas, dressed in striped prisoner uniforms, and finally the chimneys spouting black smoke were pointed out to them through the windows of their barracks.

"What are they . . . ? I wonder what they are burning there." Just like Henryk and the others when they first arrived, these newcomers asked simply and ignorantly.

"That? That's smoke from the corpses of your comrades you were just separated from."

With feelings of exhilaration Henryk hurled these words into the faces of the newcomers. That exhilaration included in part the joy of dragging these men into the same hell he and the others were experiencing. It's okay to be shocked. Go ahead and suffer. We've been living this hellish life day after day . . .

Still, Henryk had survived. Employing his own egoism and survival skills, he had remained alive even as others died of enervation. He was like an insect whose life force allows it to continue moving even while most other insects perish in the autumn . . .

No matter what happens, I will not die here! He repeated these words to himself every day in an effort to keep his own energy aflame.

Around the same time, one man who shared his sleeping platform was noticeably declining. Something that looked like a white powder erupted on his face and his skin dried up; oddly, his belly was the only part of his body that swelled up. Henryk knew that the man was only one step away from death from malnutrition.

Ultimately, one day while the man was working he staggered and collapsed from anemia. A kapo beat and kicked him and forced him to stand on his feet. As he dug with his shovel, Henryk watched the pathetic scene.

Why don't you give him your bread? Suddenly an unexpected voice echoed in his ears. He had heard that soft, whisper-like voice before. It was the voice of Father Kolbe. *He may die. Won't you give him your bread?*

Henryk shook his head. If he gave away this single slice of bread provided to him today, he would be the one who collapsed.

I don't want to!

He may die. Before he dies, I at least want him to experience love. Kolbe's voice was pleading. Henryk recalled the hunched shoulders of the priest as he staggered forward from the ranks that evening in August so that he could take the place of a man marked for death.

Henryk handed his bread to the man. His eyes filled with tears, the man simply muttered, "Ah, I cannot believe it." This was the sole act of love that Henryk was able to perform. Still, he had carried out an act of love.

14

STEP BY STEP

A NEW YEAR began: 1943. Starting in January, every aspect of life in Japan changed drastically. Both Japan and Germany were losing the war. The Japanese government made every effort to keep reality hidden from the people, but German forces had been annihilated at Stalingrad, and the hues of defeat were deepening for Japan.

In May, Shūhei, as he often did, set out with Ōhashi from Hiyoshi on a Tōyoko Line train and got off at Shibuya Station.

Even though it was late spring, the plaza and the buildings at Shibuya all seemed very quiet. A dust devil spun and swirled up bits of garbage and scraps of paper that had collected on the street and frolicked with them like a child.

Most of the stores had virtually no goods left to sell. In the window of a coffee shop, a cardboard sign read "Kelp Tea Available," and in various locations hung posters imploring, "Keep Up the Fight!" But the streets were all as gloomy and taciturn as elderly men.

"Would you like to go look at a used bookstore at Miyamasu-zaka?" Ōhashi asked Shūhei. "I hear they've got two books by Izumi Kyōka."[1] In the aftermath of the bedbug incident, Ōhashi

---

1 Izumi Kyōka (1873–1939) stands out among writers of his time for the gothically grotesque, occasionally supernatural nature of his stories and plays.

had gradually distanced himself from the tastes of the Edo period and from the writer Nagai Kafū, and these days whenever he opened his mouth he invariably talked about no one except "Izumi Kyōka, Izumi Kyōka."

"What's so good about Izumi Kyōka?" Shūhei had once asked Ōhashi. His friend encouraged him to read the story "The Holy Man of Mount Kōya," and Shūhei was astounded by the whimsical beauty of the work, but after he finished reading it, a sudden feeling of emptiness swept over him.

"Do you think maybe Kyōka's writings are . . . too beautiful for the times we live in? He creates such a distant, unattainable world."

"Exactly! Isn't it great?"

"But Kyōka doesn't offer any answers to the suffering of those of us who are knocked around by the war."

"Can anybody give us answers? When I'm reading Kyōka, I can forget about everything that's depressing."

The two young men exchanged their adolescent theories of literature as they climbed the hill at Miyamasu-zaka, in the direction of the streetcar depot.

Even though Shūhei purposely disagreed with a lot of what Ōhashi had to say, in reality he was agonizingly aware of the feelings of this friend who always put on an easygoing air.

At some point they would have to go to war. They might die in battle. These conjectures laid a suffocating burden of pressure on the daily lives of Shūhei and Ōhashi. Whether they were at school, in their dorms, or walking down the street, sometimes without any warning this realization would pierce their chests like a sharp blade.

"The Holy Man of Mount Kōya," written in 1900, is a fascinating mix of mythical characters and eroticism composed in traditional storytelling style.

Even if I study . . . If I'm going to die in war, what's the point?
Shūhei sensed this question always welling up inside him. And
Ōhashi felt the same way, even though he never put it into words.

And so—

Shūhei knew full well that Ōhashi was struggling to escape
his feelings of suppression by fleeing into the fantasy world of
Izumi Kyōka. They stopped by the used bookstore, but someone had already purchased the Kyōka books. It was a time when
even trifling books quickly vanished from the shelves. Everyone
was starved for the printed word. Words that told the truth . . .

At Shūhei's invitation, Ōhashi went with him to his student
dorm in Shinano-machi. He had virtually nothing to eat in his
room, but he boiled some water and thought maybe he could
fry up some dried potatoes that had been sent to him from
Nagasaki.

When they entered the dorm building, they ran into Sugii.
Seeing Shūhei, his eyes clouded over and he said, "Hey, apparently they've decided."

"Decided what?"

"To abolish our draft deferments, to make us become
soldiers . . ."

"Is that for sure?"

"Yeah. This time it appears to be for sure." Sugii folded his
arms. "I know a guy who's already graduated and works as an
official at the Ministry of Education. He told me on the sly. He
said that very soon there would be a discussion of the proposal
to do away with student draft deferments. . . ." With that, Sugii
hurriedly put on his shoes and ran out.

"What are we going to do?" Ōhashi muttered, his face uncharacteristically pale.

"How should I . . . how should I know?" Miffed, Shūhei took
off his shoes and climbed the stairs of his dormitory. His room
was on the second floor. Ōhashi followed him up.

After they entered the room, they sat down and said nothing for a while.

During that period of silence, their emotions somehow calmed.

Outside the window it was a somber evening in late spring. From time to time they could hear the sound of trains gliding into the Shinano-machi Station and the voice of the announcer.

"Nothing we can do. This is . . . I guess this is just the fate of our generation. 'How kind of you to allow me to become a soldier.'" Ōhashi lay on his back, facing the ceiling.

"Do you . . . do you think you'd be able to kill someone?" Shūhei asked.

"There's no guarantee that, even if we're drafted, we'll be sent to the battlefield. I'm not sure we have to start thinking right away, like you're doing, about having to kill people if we become soldiers."

"No matter how many fancy words they use to describe it, no matter whether they present it as a just cause, ultimately war is about killing people. And we become complicit in that."

Ōhashi, still lying on his back, cast a probing look at Shūhei. And then he said, "You really are a Christian, aren't you."

"Why do you say that?"

"Nobody else is really hung up on killing the enemy, on killing other people. In your case, though, it seems like you've become totally neurotic about this. That means you really are a Christian, doesn't it?"

Shūhei did not reply, but he essentially felt that what Ōhashi had said was true. It could be that other students who ended up on the battlefield wouldn't worry to such a degree about shooting an enemy.

But for him—

Having been born and raised in Nagasaki, each time he attended mass at the Ōura Church, since childhood he had been coached into reciting one of God's Ten Commandments, which declared, "Thou shalt not kill." It terrified him to imagine taking the life of another person, even if it was the enemy.

Even the enemy was a human being. He was a human being who had his own daily existence, the life he had led up to the present time. That life would be eliminated in a split second. It was frightening no matter how he thought about it.

Just then, the ringing of a bell and the voice of a man shouting, "Extra! Extra!" pierced through the late autumn night.

"Another extra edition?" Ōhashi slowly got to his feet.

The voice of a student in the dormitory cried out, "Admiral Yamamoto[2] has . . . has been killed in battle!"

A door to one of the rooms flew open and a different voice asked, "Is that true?"

"It's true! It says here, 'Heroic Death in Battle over South Pacific.'"

All fell eerily silent.

Shūhei and Ōhashi, straining their ears from the second floor to hear this exchange, knew how deep a loss it was to have Commander-in-Chief Yamamoto die in battle.

"Seems more and more like we're going to lose, doesn't it?" Ōhashi said as he sipped his tea and fried some dried potatoes on the hibachi. "But there's no point in doing nothing but complain. Since I'm going to be a soldier, I'll do what I have to do."

"Do? Do what?"

---

2 Marshal Admiral Yamamoto Isoroku (1884–1943) was commander-in-chief of Japan's combined fleet and primary architect of the attack on Pearl Harbor, even though he had serious reservations about Japan's ability to defeat the United States in a protracted war. He also formulated the Midway operation, which led to a decisive defeat for Japanese naval forces and turned the tide of the war. Yamamoto died when the plane that was carrying him on an inspection tour in the South Pacific was shot down by US Air Force planes on April 18, 1943.

"I'll fight, of course. And I may end up doing that thing you hate—killing people. As long as it's for our country of Japan."

"Country? What is a country?" Shūhei countered, his face turning red. "Do you actually love our country? This Japan? This Japan that beats up people who produce literature, this Japan that despises people who admire beautiful things—do you actually love her from the bottom of your heart? Myself, I'm gradually . . . I'm gradually coming to dislike Japan. A Japan that senselessly boasts about nothing but its soldiers . . ."

Contrary to his nature, Ōhashi grew serious and retorted, "I hate that Japan, too. What I want to protect. . . . No, what I . . . what I will go to the battlefield and try to protect is . . ."

"Go ahead and say it. What is it?"

"It's my mother. . . . and my sister. And there's another person that I want to protect . . ."

Shūhei looked at Ōhashi in surprise. "Her? Are you still in love with her?"

Ōhashi turned his head away in embarrassment and shoved a dry potato into his mouth.

The young woman they had met at mass in Kultur Heim at Sophia University. A young woman named Chūjō Hideko.

Shūhei had completely forgotten about her. For a brief time he had been on the verge of falling for her, but ever since the previous Christmas in Nagasaki, when he saw the tears on Sachiko's face, all traces of Hideko had evaporated into thin air.

And because that was the case with him, he had blithely assumed that Ōhashi had completely forgotten about Hideko, too.

Now Ōhashi was maintaining that he would go to war for his mother, his sister, and for Hideko.

"For me, Japan means my mom, and my sister, and her. I'll become a soldier to protect those women."

Shūhei understood how Ōhashi felt.

He could never bring himself to go willingly to the battle-field unless he thought and felt the same way about his nation as Ōhashi did. Even Shūhei, with the same fate awaiting him, could agree with the manner in which Ōhashi had arrived at this painfully earnest admission.

"So, are you saying you could give up your life for her?"

"By 'her' . . . you mean Hideko?"

"Right."

"If it was to protect her, I feel like I could die."

Shūhei hugged his knees and thought of Sachiko. Could he die in order to protect her?

Each day thereafter, their hearts pounded every time they picked up a newspaper, worried they would see the words, "Student Deferments Cancelled." But May came, and then even when the rainy season arrived in June, such a headline had not appeared.

"Hey, Sugii, are you sure what your friend told you is true?" Shūhei asked, having grown a bit skeptical.

"I really think it's true. My friend isn't the kind of person to spread false rumors. The government must be waiting for the right time to do it," Sugii replied confidently.

Even though "Student Deferments Cancelled" hadn't yet been announced, the news in the papers implied nothing but defeat for Japan. After Admiral Yamamoto was killed over the ocean surrounding the Solomon Islands, twenty-five hundred Japanese soldiers had suffered honorable deaths[3] in the Battle of Attu.

---

3 "Gyokusai," the term I have translated as "honorable death," can also refer to the practice of Japanese soldiers who, facing inevitable defeat or capture, commit suicide with grenades or the like. In the case of the Attu battle, those Japanese soldiers who were not killed in the fighting committed

The outlook for Germany, the other leading Axis power, was also ominous, and following the defeat of German forces at Stalingrad in February, a Soviet counteroffensive was launched. Italy, too, was being routed in many locations.

In June, at Keiō University, the length of classes was shortened and military drills for the students were stepped up. A decision was made that students would assist until summer vacation in the production of munitions at a factory near Hiyoshi.

For Ōhashi and Shūhei, it was the first experience of working in a factory. At the plant they were given work uniforms, and they wrapped their legs in puttees before they set out for work.

They were not told what was being produced in the factory, but it became immediately obvious that they were building airplanes. As they worked, all the young factory workers and the additional laborers who had been pressed into service wore headbands that read, "Absolute Victory." A poster on the wall said, in large lettering, "Maintain the Spirit of Attu!"

Amid the noises from thunderous cranes and lathes, Ōhashi and Shūhei were first taught how to operate the lathes. It was not difficult. Those in poor health were sent to do office work; they produced graphs and organized attendance records.

But as he looked at what was going on around him, Shūhei felt as though the citizens and students forced into labor were actually engaged in pointless, meaningless work.

Dear Sat-chan:

The reason I haven't written you a letter in a while is because I come back from the factory totally exhausted and I don't have the energy to do anything else.

---

suicide. Only thirty of the original twenty-five hundred survived and were taken prisoner.

I go to the factory three days a week, and on the other three days I have classes. Even though we're students, we only have three days to study.

Besides that, we have to sacrifice our Sundays to receive military training. So we get no time to rest our bodies.

The toughest thing about student life in Tokyo is that we have very little food to eat. All we get at the dorm is a bit of rationed rice. There's nothing more than a handful of rice on our plates, so we take a long time chewing on it. Somebody told us that if we did that, we could trick our empty stomachs into thinking they were satisfied.

They've started selling this weird powder at the stores in Tokyo. When you put the powder in and boil up a small amount of rice, it strangely makes it look as though there's more rice than there actually is.

At our dorm, the old lady who cooks for us uses the powder when she boils rice. The rice puffs up a little so that it looks like there's more than the actual amount. But that's only how it looks. In reality nothing has changed.

At the factory at three in the afternoon, we're given a bowl of rice cereal with a few vegetables. They give us one small aluminum cup containing something that looks like it must be white water with no more than three or four grains of rice in it.

Thanks to all this, there's not a single day we're not thinking about food. When I mentioned to Ōhashi and some of my other friends about eating sweet bean rice cakes, they listened with sparkling eyes and hungrily swallowed down their saliva.

"Those rice cakes, so white and so soft against my teeth, and the way the sweet, sweet bean jam inside squeezes out onto your tongue"—I describe it for them in great detail.

Lately they've started coming to me and asking me to tell them about the rice cakes again.

Ah, whatever happened to those days when I could eat those rice cakes and rice balls covered with sweet red beans to my heart's content?

I want to eat some Nagasaki udon. I want some ikkokko.[4]
I want to eat Nagasaki fish until I'm stuffed.

I think about that every day. Why are we humans so pathetic?

The other day I had a dream about something other than food.

You remember a long time ago you were talking with a foreign priest on the slope in front of the Ōura Church, don't you? I think his name was Father Kolbe.

Father Kolbe appeared in my dream. He had such a gentle face, and he told us how much he missed Nagasaki.

When I responded that he and I were in Nagasaki, Father Kolbe shook his head.

I wonder why I had a dream like that?

There's rumors flying around that we're going to be forced to work during summer vacation too.

The rainy season ended, and the hot, humid summer arrived all at once.

Every open space in Tokyo was buried, sweltering, beneath the leaves of tomato and potato and pumpkin plants. Since none of the vegetable or fish stores had any products to sell, people began growing vegetables with their own hands.

Ordinarily this would be the time for summer break, but the students were forced to work at the factory through the end of July. Ōhashi and Shūhei had to perform pointless odd jobs every

---

4 A specialty confection of Nagasaki, these steamed buns are filled with black sugar, sesame seeds, and sweeteners.

day in the dusty building while the machinery continued to make a tremendous racket.

"I'm starting to think that all that talk about ending student deferments was just a phony rumor," Ōhashi, standing in line with Shūhei and holding an aluminum cup, said during their 3:00 p.m. distribution of rice cereal.

"No, Sugii insists it's absolutely going to happen."

"Are you sure Sugii didn't just hear wrong?"

"I seriously doubt it. He's not a liar, and he swears it's true."

"Really . . . ?" Deep in thought, Ōhashi looked up and said, "Have you been going to mass at Sophia lately?"

"I haven't." Shūhei looked at the floor. "Not lately."

"I wonder if she's doing okay. . . ." Shūhei recalled what Ōhashi had said about going to war in order to protect his mother and sister and Hideko and suggested, "If you're that worried about her, why don't you just go to mass at Sophia yourself?"

"How is a non-Christian like me supposed to go to a place like that? But you're the Christian—why aren't you going to mass?"

Shūhei was stumped for an answer.

Truth be told, lately he had started to lose the desire to go to church. For some time now he had been plagued by a single concern—the Japanese church itself had long urged its followers to recite the commandment "Thou shalt not kill," but he couldn't help feeling that after Japan went to war, the church closed its eyes to everything and pretended to know nothing.

Gradually he had come to hate this "don't rock the boat" philosophy of the Japanese church. What happened to the church's belief in the commandment "Thou shalt not kill"? The church in Japan lacked the power to provide any answers to young people like Shūhei who harbored such concerns.

Shūhei lost the desire to attend mass when he read the newspaper on July 19. The paper reported that American planes had bombed Rome itself, the capital of Italy, which was one of Japan's Axis allies. In response, a Japanese priest had commented, "This was an inhumane act, proving that the enemy will employ any means to achieve their goal," but this statement was denounced by many, including a renowned legal scholar who was himself a Catholic.

Cowards! That was Shūhei's heartfelt thought as he read the newspaper story. This was clearly a statement reeking of self-preservation and conciliation.

"Sugii, look at what the Japanese church has done."

Sugii read the newspaper that Shūhei thrust out to him, then looked up from the story and took his friend to task. "Well, suppose that this priest had made some sort of antiwar statement, what do you think would have happened? It would cause terrible problems for us as Christians."

Shūhei was not fully satisfied with Sugii's views.

He understood the sort of trouble that could come upon Christians if a priest or someone else in a position to speak for believers made a declaration based on the admonition against killing, since it could be interpreted as opposition to the war effort and to national policy. The police as well as the common populace would doubtless begin treating the Christians as unpatriotic citizens.

However—

However, there was still something in Shūhei's heart that continued to rankle. He couldn't help but feel that this attitude of the Japanese church was a betrayal of their solemn responsibility to heed the commandment not to kill.

Consequently—

Over time, going to mass on Sundays became distasteful to him. No matter how many sublime statements and scriptures the priest referenced in the mass, somewhere in Shūhei's heart rose the urge to cry out, *This is deception!* He felt they were all cowards, all cowards!

When he confessed these feelings to Ōhashi during break time at the plant, Ōhashi got a peculiar look on his face and simply said, "Hmm." Shūhei couldn't tell whether his friend understood his feelings or not. But Ōhashi laughed and said, "You Christians sure have a wide variety of complicated troubles."

"Well, what kinds of troubles do you have?"

"Me? . . . Right now? I'd really like to see Hideko one more time before I get drafted. That's all. Will you take me with you to Sophia this coming Sunday?" His voice was unusually strained.

Seeing a look like that of an abandoned puppy on his friend's face, Shūhei suddenly felt sorry for him and reluctantly replied, "Okay."

On the appointed Sunday, Shūhei went to Kultur Heim on the Sophia campus for the first time in a while.

Mass was conducted modestly, perhaps out of deference to society and the police. The organ was not played and no homily was given. The flames of several candles at the altar flickered drearily.

The number of men and women kneeling during the mass was not all that different from in the past; the biggest change was that the men were wearing the national uniform and had their legs wrapped in puttees, while the women wore the compulsory work pants.

Shūhei sat near the rear window and tried to locate Hideko without attracting notice.

She was kneeling beside her mother in the fifth row from the front. She was wearing the uniform of her school, Futaba, and wore black pants in place of work pants.

Ōhashi poked Shūhei with his elbow and cheerfully whispered, "She's here!"

Halfway through the mass, they heard loud shouting from the main floor.

The voice was clearly audible in the second-floor chapel.

A man shouted, "You bastards who believe in the enemy's religion are traitors to your country!"

Someone in a low voice tried to pacify him, but that seemed only to agitate him more.

"So what do you people think about the current state of things and our holy war? At a time when we must become one hundred million fireballs and annihilate the savage British and Americans, you believe in the religion of England and America and you worship the God that our enemies worship. Don't you people feel any shame toward our soldiers on the front lines?"

His voice grew increasingly loud, and those in the chapel upstairs could hear every word.

At the altar the foreign priest continued with the mass as though he could hear nothing.

The shouting voice finally stopped. When Shūhei heard the shouts, he was reminded of the time outside the deserted house at Ōura when he had been insulted and beaten by a military policeman.

There was a great deal of similarity between the abusive voice of the military policeman and the voice of the man downstairs. Even the words and the logic of their invectives were somehow identical.

The homily-free mass ended in less than an hour. The people stood up from their kneelers, and Shūhei and Ōhashi exited the chapel, leaving two or three people in between themselves and Hideko.

From the landing of the stairs, members of the congregation saw a man at the entrance to Kultur Heim wearing a national uniform with puttees wrapped around his legs.

The eyes of the man were filled with hatred as he glared at the Christians coming down the stairs. "You there! You call yourselves Japanese?!" He was shouting again. "It may be Sunday, but in the factories and workplaces are production warriors who have sacrificed their day off in order to labor for victory in this holy war. Yet you people associate with foreigners and participate in the enemy's religious rituals alongside foreigners!"

The Christians seemed unable to move for a few moments, but then they headed outside, ignoring the man.

This sent him into a rage. "Are you . . . are you mocking me?!"

The man blocked the doorway and stood in front of Hideko, who was trying to go outside with her mother.

"So you . . . you're a college girl, are you? Did you know that there are some college girls so eager to build fighter planes that they write out their requests in blood . . . ?"

"Why don't you mind your own business!" The voice came from someone standing next to Shūhei; Ōhashi, playing the innocent, had responded in place of Hideko.

"What?!"

"Take a look at these people here. They're Japanese, aren't they? What makes these Japanese here unpatriotic? I work every day at a munitions factory. Even though today is Sunday, I'm heading off now for military training. You don't know what the hell you're talking about. For starters, you're the one who hasn't been to the factory this morning—you've just come here and screamed your head off."

"What's that you're saying?!"

"If you've got enough free time to do this, why don't you be on your way and help with the building of airplanes?"

No one could have imagined that Ōhashi, who was always so easygoing and foolhardy, had this much courage.

"Or are you maybe the police?"

The man did not reply.

"It doesn't figure that you're a policeman. If you were the police, you would have known that the constitution for many years has recognized the people's right to freedom of religion. I'm right, aren't I?"

The man said nothing for a moment. Clearly he was thrown off by Ōhashi's unexpected counterattack. "Freedom of religion? That's for peacetime. In wartime the Japanese have to have a Japanese mind-set," he retorted in frustration, but he must have sensed that his position had weakened. "I just want you people to have that frame of mind. You can understand that, can't you?"

With that as his parting line, the man squared his shoulders and left the Kultur Heim.

The Christians stood where they were, dumbfounded.

Finally an elderly man approached Ōhashi and held out his hand. "Well spoken, young man!"

Ōhashi blinked his eyes as though he had just come to his senses. "Uh-huh." In embarrassment, he brushed his hand against the man's hand and then disappeared as though fleeing. Shūhei followed him.

"That was a surprise! I never thought you were such a great speech maker."

"I . . . what did I . . . what did I say?" Ōhashi was sweating and his face was pale.

"What? You mean you don't know what you said?"

"I was kind of in a daze. The man was condemning us, so I just started yelling back at him without really knowing what I was saying."

Ōhashi sat down on the bank of the canal that ran alongside the Sophia campus and heaved a sigh that might have been an expression of either concern or relief.

"Ōhashi," Shūhei peered into his friend's face and said, "Do you really . . . do you really love her that much?"

"Yeah, but even if I love her, nothing will come of it."

"Why not?"

"We . . . we'll be heading off to war before long, won't we?" Ōhashi muttered these words with deep emotion.

"Let's get out of here."

The two young men stood up and brushed the dirt from their pants.

Just then Shūhei happened to glance up and realized that Hideko and her mother were standing nearby, watching them.

"Ōhashi, it's her."

Ōhashi's face and body stiffened like a rod.

Hideko's mother nodded politely to Shūhei and Ōhashi and said, "What you did just now . . . thank you so much. It was kind of you to take our part when we didn't know what we should do."

The two young men were flustered, and all they could do was mutter inaudibly, "No, really . . ."

"I have no idea what we would have done if we had been there by ourselves."

"Right."

The young men's only thought was to give a quick bow and hurry off, but Hideko's mother continued, "I was wondering . . . have you two already had breakfast? If you haven't . . . the times being what they are, we really don't have much but, . . . would you like to come to our home?"

Shūhei could tell that Ōhashi, standing next to him, was shaking almost imperceptibly. Hideko, standing behind her mother, smiled and nodded.

"Thank you. But that would be a little presumptuous of us." Shūhei tried to decline the invitation in a high-pitched voice, but Ōhashi, breathing heavily, broke in. "No, we'll . . . we'll come. Yes, we'll come."

Perhaps because she found his hurried remark amusing, Hideko lowered her eyes and tried to stifle her laughter.

Led by Hideko and her mother, they arrived at a neighbor-hood of wealthy residences at Kōji-machi in front of Yotsuya Station. As they walked along the deserted streets of Kōji-machi, Hideko's mother tried to make the two young men feel at ease by asking them about topics that would be of interest to them, such as school.

A luxurious house, surrounded by a garden lushly planted with trees and bushes. A Western-style home, so British in design it almost seemed as though a Westminster clock would chime at any moment from a room at the end the hallway.

They went into the ivory-covered house. A plate outside the door identified the homeowner as "Chūjō Kōji." It felt like a name they had seen somewhere before.

They were directed into a sunroom with glass on three sides. Many pots of orchids had been arranged along the floor. From the room they had a view of the well-kept garden, which wasn't all that large, and they saw a man in work clothes trimming branches with scissors.

"We really have nothing to offer you." Hideko and her mother took turns bringing in some homemade bread, teacups with black tea, and tomatoes arranged on a plate.

Hideko opened a window and called to the man in work clothes, "Papa!"

"Yes!" The man turned toward the window and then slowly came inside. After he heard from Hideko what had happened at the church, he said, "I understand you have been very kind to my family. . . ." He sat down in a wicker chair beside the two young men. "I've heard that recently these kinds of encounters are increasing, and it really concerns me. These types seem to think that they are the only true patriots."

Mr. Chūjō also encouraged the two young men to have some breakfast. "I'm not a believer in Christianity myself, but my wife and daughter have been going to church for a long time now," he added. "I'm very displeased with the narrow-minded attitude of some people who immediately assume that Christians are un-patriotic. That attitude is no different from that of stupid people who think that those who purport to be Japanese must not read books or newspapers written in English because it's the language of the enemy, or that it's contemptible for people to study English. I've heard in fact, quite to the contrary, that there are some young people in the United States who are being asked to study Japanese so they can understand the situation in Japan . . ."

Shūhei and Ōhashi listened respectfully to what Mr. Chūjō said. In the present situation, this felt like the first time they had met anyone who would speak with such frankness.

"Recently, apron-wearing women from the National Defense Women's Association have been handing out leaflets on street corners. The leaflets say that extravagance is our enemy. People like that don't understand that it's far more extravagant to be wasting precious time by doing what they're doing while a war is going on. One woman from that group grabbed hold of a young lady who had had her hair done up in a permanent and warned her that she must stop this kind of hair styling because it was too much like the Americans and the British. . . . Everything has gone mad."

"Papa, that's enough!" Hideko's mother interjected, a bit worried. "You're alarming these two young men. I'm sorry, my husband resigned from the Ministry of Foreign Affairs because he comes right out and bluntly says what he's thinking."

"So . . . you are a diplomat?" Ōhashi asked gingerly.

"Yes. Even a man like the one you see here. I was ambassador to a country in South America, but when I came back to Japan I clashed with the military leaders and ended up resigning. I had advised them that if we were going to fight a war against the United States, we had to learn a great deal more about the United States."

With a chuckle, Hideko explained, "And that's why, as you just saw, he's pretending to be a gardener."

Her father's face was unsmiling when he said, "But those tomatoes you boys are eating right now. Those were grown from seeds I worked very hard to cultivate. Delicious, aren't they?"

"Oh yes, they are delicious."

"Hmm, you're from Kyushu, are you? I can tell from the way you speak. Which part of Kyushu are you from?"

"From Nagasaki."

"I love that town. It's rare for towns in Japan to have food that delicious."

It thrilled Shūhei almost to the point of quivering to hear Nagasaki praised in this manner.

Everything in this home was delightful. Mr. Chūjō's habit of freely speaking his mind was exhilarating for the two young men.

When they stood up in preparation to leave, Mr. Chūjō peered at them and said softly, "You be sure to get your bodies in shape." At their quizzical look, he muttered something that seemed to hint at his meaning, "You never know when you'll be drafted."

Once they were outside, Ōhashi was utterly dizzy with excitement. It had been an unprecedented afternoon for him, as he got to know Hideko and was even allowed in her house.

For his part, however, Shūhei pondered the puzzling words Mr. Chūjō had just said. Was he perhaps intimating to them that very soon students would be called into the military?

Perhaps it was just as Sugii had said. Very soon the student draft deferment would be eliminated . . .

Shūhei guessed this from the intimations in Mr. Chūjō's comment and the expression on his face. Had he told them this secretively out of gratitude to them for helping his daughter?

"Really? I didn't totally understand what he was saying." Ōhashi, who was still in ecstasy, inclined his head doubtfully, but Shūhei felt something akin to certainty about it.

Strangely, he felt composed. Because he had been able to anticipate that this might happen, he didn't receive the sort of shock, like being whacked over the head with a pole, that he would have if this had been the first he had heard of it.

Instead, Shūhei was left to deal with the torment that was buried deep within his feelings of composure.

So in the end . . . I'll be going into the military without any kind of relief from my anguish.

His youthfulness wouldn't allow him to manage his own sufferings as adults seemed able to do, however vaguely and half-heartedly. It was discomforting to see that even the church in which he had been raised was caught up in the billowing waves and forced to go along helplessly with the war. That disgusted him.

Summer vacation finally came in August. He had been forced to work in the factory throughout the month of July and spent all the rest of his time in military training.

He returned exhausted to Kyushu, having sat in the aisle between seats on a crowded train.

Even after he got back home, Shūhei did not go right away to the Ōura Church to pay his respects as he usually did. On the first Sunday, he also concocted an excuse and did not attend mass. His mother was worried about him, seeing shadows of depression on a face that had normally been that of a jester.

"What in the world has happened to you?"

"Nothing has happened. Just leave it alone." With an angry look he left his house and walked up the slope leading to Ōura.

It seemed the only thing that could provide any repose for him right now was the garden at the old deserted house.

When he passed in front of the church, he bumped into a nun, Sachiko's aunt. She called out to Shūhei, who had averted his eyes. "Ah, so you're back home are you?"

"Yes, I'm back." He bowed quickly and climbed up the slope until he was standing in front of the deserted house.

The garden was overgrown with summer grasses. Katydids cried noisily.

He sat down on a rock and pulled a book of poetry by Satō Haruo from his pocket. Immersing himself in poetry—that was the only way he could escape from his present mood.

I was able to learn the meaning of true love from the heart,
It is a love that seeks nothing

Someone came sneaking up from behind Shūhei.

He looked up; it was Sachiko.

In the half year that he hadn't seen her, Sachiko had changed so much that Shūhei had to catch his breath. She was no longer a schoolgirl. She was a young woman. He could see it in her face, and in the roundness that her body had taken on . . .

"If you were back, why didn't you tell me?" Sachiko glared angrily at Shūhei. "I was stunned just now when my aunt told me she had seen you."

Shūhei did not reply but merely stared at the ocean.

"But I figured you would probably come here, so I ran over. You've lost a little weight, haven't you?"

"There's really nothing worth eating in Tokyo."

"When did you get back?"

"Four days ago," Shūhei answered honestly.

"Then why didn't you come to mass on Sunday?"

Staring at the ground, Shūhei was momentarily lost in thought, and then muttered, "Sat-chan . . . we students are going to be drafted soon."

"What?" With wide-open eyes, Sachiko peered at Shūhei. To her his words were a bolt out of the blue. "Is that true?"

"It's true. The government hasn't announced it yet, but it looks like the student draft deferment is going to be eliminated very soon. If that happens . . . I'll have to go to war."

Sachiko could say nothing.

"Sat-chan, the reason I didn't come to mass on Sunday . . . and I didn't go when I was in Tokyo . . . is because I can't believe in the church's stance."

Sachiko was still unable speak.

"Ever since we were little, the Japanese church has repeated over and over that we must not kill. But now that the war started, they feign ignorance and won't even discuss it."

"But, it's not just the Japanese church. The churches in America and England are just the same, aren't they?"

"Yes, but little by little I've stopped believing in the Christian church."

A look of distress flashed visibly across Sachiko's face. She had no idea how to respond to Shūhei. But an indescribable sorrow billowed within her chest.

"No, I can't bear that." She spoke softly. But pain pervaded that soft voice.

"Can't bear what?"

"I can't bear you abandoning God."

"But I can't help it. . . . I just can't accept it." Seeing Sachiko growing uneasy before his eyes, Shūhei regretted saying as much as he had. "I'm sorry. I shouldn't have said any of this to you. But ever since we were young, I've always told you everything."

"Uh-huh." Sachiko nodded, and for the first time felt a faint joy expanding in her heart. It pleased her that Shūhei could tell her about the anguish in his heart without hiding anything. "Have you told the priest about this?"

"About what?"

"About the feelings you just told me about."

"What would be the point of telling him? It's obvious that if I said anything bad about the church, I'd just get reprimanded. And besides . . . the priests don't have answers. If they had any sort of response, they would've talked to us a long time ago."

Sachiko had nothing to say.

"All right, fine. It can only cause pain to say things like this to you. So don't worry about it. I promise I'll find answers on my own."

Sachiko hesitantly asked something that had begun worrying her. "Are you sure . . . that students are going to be drafted soon?"

"I'm sure. I think it's almost certain."

"But even if you are drafted . . . that doesn't necessarily mean you'll be sent to the battlefield, right?" She didn't say this so much to Shūhei as to quell her own anxiety.

"You really are naïve, aren't you, Sat-chan? Japan is losing so badly now they're having to recruit students. I'll bet students will be sent to the battlefront now before everybody else." Shūhei stuck a blade of grass between his teeth and said, "Sat-chan, promise me you won't say anything about this to anybody?"

"What?"

"If you promise me you won't mention this to anybody, I'll tell you something that just occurred to me."

"What is it?"

"You and I had religious training that taught us that we couldn't kill another person, that it was wrong to kill. That means I can't be part of a military that orders murder. So even if orders to enlist come, I'll be fine as long as I don't enlist."

Sachiko stared blankly into Shūhei's face. She wasn't sure what he was trying to say.

"To avoid being enlisted, a person would have to fail the conscription physical. And to fail . . . you'd have to be a person with a serious illness or have some sort of physical impairment."

Sachiko had no response.

"So everything will be all right if I decide to go that route. Say, for example, if I cut off two or three fingers on my right hand, I wouldn't be able to pull the trigger on a rifle. They wouldn't be able to draft me then, right?"

Sachiko listened to Shūhei, her eyes filled with alarm. At first she wondered whether he was saying this just to frighten her, but she carefully studied the expression on his face, and he seemed to be serious.

"You've got to promise me you won't tell anyone about this," he repeated.

✳ ✳ ✳

With the number of remaining days curtailed, that summer vacation felt to Shūhei as though it would be his last.

The war had turned the city of Nagasaki into an absolutely wretched wasteland. There were no more goods left to sell in the stores in the shopping district at Hama-no-machi, and the blistering sunlight beat down on streets that were nearly devoid of passersby. At houses here and there tall tomato plants grew in the open spaces and katydids cried out. Since there was no food to be had, every household had its own kitchen garden.

All the festivals that the citizens of Nagasaki once took delight in had been canceled. There were no more of the famous kite competitions or the Peron boat-rowing festivals that the young people were wildly enthusiastic about. Rumor had it that military police were patrolling around Mount Kazagashira, making sure that no one was looking down from the mountain into the bay, which now had military fortifications.

Despite the restrictions, the Urabon festival[5] was performed, though modestly and secretively. Families who had lost a loved one in battle placed homegrown vegetables in front of portraits

---

5 A Buddhist festival held in summer to honor the spirits of ancestors.

of deceased men dressed in their military uniforms; incense was offered, and a sultry smoke rose from the incense sticks.

Even the release of the floating lanterns was no longer performed as enthusiastically as in the past. Only a few families gathered by the seashore at Ōhato.

Hoping to be able to forget even for a brief moment about the war, Shūhei went to look at the ocean. There were days when he wanted to go swimming just to drive everything from his consciousness.

At the swimming area on Nezumi Island, some elementary school students were being taught how to swim, and Shūhei could hear the small children making a racket.

As he listened to the voices of the children and heard the sound of breaking waves, he couldn't help but recall the days of his youth when everything had been so fun. As a youth, he too had learned to swim here at Nezumi Island. His swimming teacher, Mr. Tanaka, owned a shop that sold Western-style clothing at Hama-no-machi. He had now gone off to war.

While he was swimming, at a place a bit removed from the schoolchildren, Shūhei noticed two young women nearby, swimming the breaststroke.

When he stepped onto the beach, they also came out of the water, and he was surprised to discover that it was Sachiko and her friend Takeda Mieko, whom he had met on their trip to Shimabara.

"Hey, so you're here swimming too." He gave a quick greeting and averted his eyes. He was embarrassed to see how completely Sachiko's body had become that of a grown woman. It felt like he was meeting this woman in a black swimsuit for the first time since the days of his youth.

"Right now Mieko is working along with some students from the Nagasaki Technical School at the Mitsubishi ordnance plant. The students at that school have all given up their summer vacation and been placed in a patriotic corps to work at the factory."

"It's the same in Tokyo."

"Mieko is in love with one of those students."

"I'm not in love with him . . . ! He's only a friend. Just a friend."

"Liar. You told me before that you're in love with him."

Sachiko and Mieko taunted one another and laughed together.

Closing his eyes, Shūhei listened to those laughing voices as though they came from a far, far distant place. The ocean breezes. The happy laughter of the young women. Would he soon be bidding farewell to all of that, never to hear it again . . . ?

15

THAT DAY

SACHIKO AND SHŪHEI met up several times through the end of the summer vacation, but neither of them again brought up the subject of Shūhei's religious doubts.

His doubts—

They were causing torment in his heart, which he had expressed to Sachiko with an anguished look that day in the deserted house at Ōura. He had told her that he couldn't accept the stance of the church, and that with the way he was feeling right now, he could not bring himself to want to go to war. He told her that it was cowardly of the church he had once believed in to adopt a position contrary to what it had always taught. And he had confessed to her that this was his reason for withdrawing from the church.

Each of his concerns seemed as though it would crush Sachiko's heart.

She had no idea how to respond to Shūhei's anguish. All she could do was peer into his face, on the brink of tears herself.

When Shūhei had announced to her that he intended to leave the church, Sachiko felt pain and sorrow piercing through her entire body. The blood of many generations of Kirishitans who had practiced their faith in secret flowed through her veins. Her father, her mother, and her grandfather had all been Christian from their childhoods. The church and her family were tightly bonded together, like the flesh and shell of a snail. And now Shūhei was leaving that same church.

It terrified her.

Because it terrified her, for the remainder of the summer she avoided even thinking about his concerns. However, at mass every Sunday she earnestly prayed to the Blessed Mother, "Holy Mother Mary, Shū-chan hasn't come to mass again today. Please help him to come. . . . I can't do anything to help him with his struggles. . . . But when I imagine all the frightening things that he thinks about, I don't feel like he's the same Shū-chan I've always known . . ."

The Blessed Mother gazed down at Sachiko with a look of wonderment on her face. The same look she had on her face many years ago in this same location when a woman named Kiku had gone on at great length about her concerns . . .

Shūhei had sternly forbidden her to speak with others about these things, so she had not been able to consult her mother or the priests at Ōura about any of it. Besides, if she had told her mother, it was a given that her mother would think her strange and ask, "Why are you so worried about a fellow like this?"

In the latter part of August, Shūhei promptly returned to Tokyo. He had labor service to perform at the factory.

None of the students in Nagasaki had been able to enjoy their break from school either. Those from the technical school in Nagasaki and from the medical school, like those in Tokyo, were put to work during the hot closing days of August at the shipbuilding and steel manufacturing plants operated by Mitsubishi and Kawanami. Sachiko had graduated from the women's junior college and was helping around the house, but acting on advice from neighbors, she was sent to do office work at the rice rationing bureau. Without that responsibility, she might have been commandeered to work at Sasebo.

"He's got a bad reputation, you know." One day after she had visited her aunt at the church and returned home, Sachiko's mother had denounced Shūhei. "I'm told he's been saying negative things about the church. He doesn't come to mass, and the priests are upset with him."

It incensed Sachiko to hear her mother criticize Shūhei, and she fought back like a sister defending her older brother. "People all have their own problems. There's no such thing as good or evil when it comes to problems. What's so bad about talking openly about things that bother you?"

Her mother was surprised at Sachiko's sudden flare-up, and with an exasperated look she said, "Why do you always side with him?"

"We've been friends since we were children."

"But . . . oh, don't tell me that you actually—" her mother started to say, but then worriedly caught herself.

That evening, after Sachiko had gone to bed, her parents conversed in hushed voices.

✳ ✳ ✳

"We've got to get you married off before you get too attached to this loser. Your father says the same thing."

The following day, after her husband had left for work at the Mitsubishi Shipyard, Sachiko's mother half in jest told her daughter that she disapproved of her relationship with Shūhei.

"What do you mean by 'loser'?"

"Nothing. I was just kidding."

And yet, three days later, relatives from Urakami had recommended three possible marriage partners.

"Right now, the one in this photo has been called up and is in the navy, but since he's an accountant he won't be sent to the battlefield. He's working at the naval arsenal at Sasebo . . ."

In the photograph, a young man sat up straight in a chair, his hair neatly parted in a style unusual in wartime, dressed not in his military uniform but in the national uniform he had worn prior to induction.

With no more than a passing glance at the photograph, Sachiko shook her head contemptuously and said, "I don't like him. Not this kind of person."

"What don't you like about him?"

"Looks like he's pasted his hair down with oil. It's creepy."

"Well, he's a soldier now, so he's had his head shaved."

"In any case, I don't like him."

It made no difference to Sachiko what the reason was. Whether the man had grown his hair out or had his head shaved, either became a pretext for her to refuse him.

Once she had turned down the three marriage possibilities that the Urakami relatives had thoughtfully provided, it was now her mother's turn to get angry. Her father opened up the evening paper and said nothing.

"So just what are your intentions?"

"I don't intend to get married yet."

"Please don't tell me that you're in love with that Shūhei." Her mother did not miss noticing that Sachiko's face turned red. "Just what kind of relationship do you have with that young man?"

"Don't go suggesting anything improper. We're childhood friends. You should know that."

"And there's nothing more to it, right?"

Why did they think it was wrong of her to like Shūhei? Was it because Shūhei had stopped attending mass? If that was it, then the priests needed to help him resolve the agony in his heart. That was all Sachiko could think about in her bed that night.

In response to her mother's questions, she continued to insist that she and Shūhei were nothing more than childhood friends,

but the more she thought about it, the more she was convinced
that there was something stronger in her feelings for him.

During summer break, Shūhei had not said anything to Sachiko resembling what a boyfriend would say. It was true that
she had waited and waited for him to utter just one phrase, something along the lines of "I like you" or "I love you," but even
though he talked incessantly, even willfully, about his own struggles, he had never once revealed anything about the most cru-
cial matter of all—any feelings he might have for her.

I wonder what he really thinks about me. This concern ebbed and
flowed incessantly in Sachiko's heart, just like the waves at Ōhato
that receded and then rolled in, rolled in and then receded.

She knew that Shūhei felt close to her the way a brother feels
close to his sister. But perhaps because they had behaved until
now like siblings, awkwardness and embarrassment had become
a hindrance to displaying any deeper feelings. That seemed like
a reasonable explanation to Sachiko.

But that made her feel incredibly forlorn.

"I . . . I really like you . . ." She wanted him to say that just
once, and it wouldn't upset her even if he was just joking.

Out of her loneliness and impatience, Sachiko wrote in one
of her letters to Shūhei that her mother was encouraging her to
consider meeting with potential marriage partners. Maybe
Shūhei would panic when he read it. He might get jealous.
Maybe he would realize that if he dawdled, she might end up
married to some other young man.

Such calculations were unconsciously at work in the letter she
wrote. She could hardly bear the wait to find out how Shūhei
would reply.

But no reply came. Even though a week, then ten days, passed
after she mailed her letter, there was no response from Shūhei.

She felt as though it meant nothing to Shūhei that she would
be meeting with possible marriage partners.

"Mother," Sachiko said one day, "I'm going to meet with one of those marriage candidates."

Having her daughter be the one to make the decision caused a look on Sachiko's mother's face like that of a pigeon nicked by a peashooter. "Are you serious?"

"I brought it up myself, didn't I? Of course I'm serious."

"You're such a strange child."

Her mother could not understand the tremendous swings in Sachiko's thought processes.

The man she would be meeting was yet another one recommended by her Urakami relatives, a young man who worked at the railway office. He had not yet been drafted because he had contracted a temporary pleural infection, but according to the report from the go-between, he was now completely healthy.

Evidently his parents, unsure when he might be drafted, wanted to get him married as soon as possible.

Shū-chan, you're such an idiot! Inwardly Sachiko berated Shūhei on the day her mother, with Sachiko's consent for a meeting with the young man, headed to Urakami to notify the relatives. *I'm going to wind up someone else's bride.*

Because this meeting to consider the possibility of marriage was being held in wartime, it was going to be conducted in a very simple manner at the home of the man's older sister. The sister and her husband lived in Hongōchi, beside a reservoir that provided water for the city.

On the appointed day, Sachiko boarded the bus for Hongōchi, accompanied by her mother and one of their relatives from Urakami. At her mother's insistence, she had applied a bit of makeup. But with even that small amount of touch-up, her face took on a remarkable resemblance to her grandmother Mitsu.

It did not take long for Sachiko to regret her rash decision as she rode in the bus, which rattled and shook as it hurried along the uneven road. She had agreed to this meeting not because she wanted to get to know this young man, but in order to provoke Shūhei.

The heat of late summer was still extreme, and the cries of the cicadas were relentless; looking out at the scenery, Sachiko had to admit, and not for the first time, that her heart was inclined toward Shūhei.

She caught a glimpse of a crucifix. A monastery stood at the top of the hill. She tugged on her mother's sleeve and said, "Look, that's the monastery of the Knights of the Immaculata. . . . That's the monastery where Brother Zeno and Father Kolbe worked. Do you remember them?"

"Of course I remember them."

"Father Kolbe has gone back to his country. I wonder what he's doing now?"

Her mother said disinterestedly, "Hmm, I wonder if he's still passing out his pamphlets in Poland."

Sachiko remembered that when she had been a young girl, Brother Zeno and the others had handed out some pamphlets that they had printed themselves to passersby on the busy streets of downtown Nagasaki. Father Kolbe, with those round glasses and an always exhausted look on his face. That picture with the scripture, "Greater love than this no man hath, that a man lay down his life for his friends." She had learned in school that Poland was a large agricultural country with many farms, and she wondered whether the priest these days had gotten healthier by drinking a lot of milk . . .

The young man she met that day was a Christian, the very epitome of solemnity.

"So, are you fond of cigarettes and saké?" Sachiko's relative asked.

The older sister responded for her brother, "He doesn't smoke or drink. He gives his ration of cigarettes to the priests at the church. Some of the priests at the church like to smoke."

Through the whole thing, Sachiko sat listening in silence. Everything about the young man was so different from Shūhei that she had to stifle a laugh. She had the feeling that Shūhei would say of a young fellow who didn't smoke or drink, "What a moron!"

On their way back home, Sachiko's mother, hoping to influence Sachiko's attitude toward the young man, said, "He's a solid young man. I'm sure you could feel at ease with a man like that."

"He's . . . not my type. He's so serious . . ."

Having come all this way, Sachiko decided she wanted to stop in at the Knights of the Immaculata monastery. She had the feeling that perhaps Father Kolbe and Brother Zeno might be there.

They still had forty or fifty minutes until the bus to Nagasaki arrived. Buses ran less frequently during the war.

As they climbed the sloping path to the monastery, Sachiko's mother grumbled, "If you persist in being so selfish, nobody will marry you."

"But if I don't like the man I don't like him."

"Well then, just what kind of man do you like? And don't tell me it would be a man like Shūhei."

Sachiko did not answer, and scurrying past her mother, who had an uneasy expression on her face, she raced energetically up the hill.

A strong afternoon sun beat down on the cabbage and corn growing in the fields. The building she could see beyond the fields, perhaps the printing office on the monastery grounds, was the place where the monks worked. Mingling among several Japanese friars were a few foreigners busily working and wearing the same kind of clothing that Brother Zeno and Father Kolbe had worn.

When Sachiko and her mother reached the edge of the property and looked toward the church and the three-story monastery, a foreign monk at the entrance to the monastery noticed them and called out, "It's very hot there. Why don't you come over here?"

Sachiko and her mother hesitated briefly but then accepted the monk's invitation and headed toward the monastery building. There must have been a cowshed nearby: the smell of damp fodder blew into their faces.

"You two are Christians?" the monk asked amiably as he took potatoes from a bucket and peeled the skins off.

"Yes," Sachiko nodded. "Does Brother Zeno happen to be here?"

"Brother Zeno, not here. In Tokyo. You know Brother Zeno?"

Sachiko's mother answered for her. "Yes, when he came to Japan we saw him frequently at Ōura. . . . My daughter here was very young at the time, and Brother Zeno was very partial to her."

"And Father Kolbe . . . has he not come back from Poland yet?" Sachiko asked, rather proud of herself. She wanted to make it clear to this foreign monk that she was aware that the Father had returned to his homeland for a time.

"Father Kolbe?" The hand peeling the skin from the potatoes suddenly froze. Sachiko saw the monk's face stiffen. From the change in his expression, she had a premonition that something had happened to the priest.

"Father Kolbe . . . has died." The monk answered in a soft voice. "Father Kolbe murdered by German soldiers." The monk seemed frustrated by his inability to explain in detail with his clumsy Japanese.

"He was murdered?!" Sachiko's mother was stunned. "You mean that priest was murdered?"

"Yes."

✳ ✳ ✳

A dispirited Sachiko and her mother waited at the bus stop for a charcoal bus that seemed as though it might never come. All around them they could hear the chirping of the evening cicadas, their voices sounding forlorn.

"Those cicadas are so annoying . . . !" Sachiko said, almost angrily. "Dad is working overtime today, so we've got to make sure we remember to heat up the bath . . ." Her mother wiped the perspiration from her face and said nothing. Sachiko wasn't sure how to process what she had just heard, so she kept bringing up unrelated subjects. "I wonder if Mitsuo is taking good care of the house while we're away. He's such a problem. He hates going to pick up our rations."

Despite her efforts to talk about trivial things, one scene had leapt up before her eyes. Father Kolbe had come to the church to say goodbye as he was preparing to leave Japan right at the time when she and Shūhei had been playing together in front of the Ōura Church.

As always, utter exhaustion had been written all over the priest's face. His complexion had never been good, and compared to Brother Zeno he was conspicuously taciturn. His Japanese was not all that good. An image of his face with those round glasses came back into Sachiko's mind with great clarity.

Why would a priest like Father Kolbe be murdered?

She didn't know any of the details, because of the limited Japanese of the monk who had given them the news. All she did learn was that Father Kolbe had died in the summer two years earlier. Not from disease or an accident, but according to the monk's report, he had been killed by the Germans. The monk had told them nothing about where he had been murdered. When she asked why he had been killed, the monk shrugged his shoulders with a mournful look. Sachiko wasn't sure whether he had shrugged because he didn't know the reason, or because he didn't wish to talk about it.

I wonder if he was killed . . . because he believed in Christianity? She pondered as she stared in the direction from which the bus would be arriving. But weren't the Germans also believers in

Christianity? It seemed impossible that the Father had been slaughtered because of his faith in Christ.

Rattling along the rough road, the bus finally arrived. It was a rustic bus, battered from many years of use. The passengers appeared to have come from shopping trips in Ōmura and Obama and had placed their baskets and rucksacks on the floor of the bus.

"Do you think Father Kolbe . . . was killed in the fighting?" Sachiko whispered to her mother.

"I doubt a priest can become a soldier," her mother shook her head. "So I can't think of any reason for a Father to be murdered. . . . Sachiko, you have to be sure to take good care of the picture he gave you," she muttered.

They could see the lights of Nagasaki at the base of the hill. The sky had already turned a pale gray. Father Kolbe no longer lived in this world. The thought made Sachiko feel strangely sad.

Deep within her heart, she hated war. For someone like Father Kolbe to be killed, and for Shūhei to be in such agony . . .

Over the course of days, these feelings gouged with unexpected sharpness into Sachiko's consciousness.

When she gazed out the window of her house at Nagasaki Bay in the evening, or turned her eyes toward the luxuriant hills of Ōura to her left, or again in the daytime, when she worked at the rationing bureau, the reality that Father Kolbe had been murdered and was no longer part of this world caused a suffocating tightness in her chest.

At the same time she sensed Father Kolbe's face looking toward her.

Father, why did they kill you? When she posed the question to that shadowy image of his face, the priest did not reply, merely blinking his eyes sadly behind his round glasses. He was mournfully silent, as though he could not explain in words why he had been murdered.

When she returned home from the rationing bureau, she took out the chocolate box that she had treasured since childhood. Inside the box were items that even now were precious to her, such as letters she had received from Shūhei. The picture from Father Kolbe was also there.

"A man dies for his friends. There is no greater love." The picture of the Blessed Mother, imprinted with words to that effect from the Bible—it was the only keepsake she had from Father Kolbe.

"There is no greater love . . ."

But what is love? It felt as though Shūhei was asking her that question, but perhaps the love described in the words on this picture was of a different nature.

The chocolate box also contained a sheet of paper with the words of that poem she liked, taken from the collection of verses by Satō Haruo that Shūhei had given her:

I was able to learn the meaning of true love from the heart,
It is a love that seeks nothing

What is love exactly? She had always been taught by the priests that love meant to make another person happy. One can even give up one's own life in order to make a friend happy. "No greater love" was written on the picture she had received from Father Kolbe. And it said in Satō Haruo's poem that "true love . . . seeks nothing."

Maybe . . . maybe Father Kolbe was killed in order to bring happiness to someone else.

It seemed odd to Sachiko that her mind was so preoccupied with thoughts of Father Kolbe. She had not known the priest all that well. The person who had always spoken to her at the printing office beside the church had been Brother Zeno . . .

And yet, for several days now Sachiko's thoughts had been centered on Father Kolbe.

Even after September had passed, no letters had arrived from Shūhei. Then one morning what she had most feared was written in bold black lettering on the front page of the morning newspaper:

OFFICIAL ANNOUNCEMENT REGARDING DRAFT DEFERMENTS FOR CURRENT STUDENTS

The headline to the accompanying article read,

STUDENT DRAFT DEFERMENTS CANCELED

The following morning—
Sachiko slipped from her bed, but the sounds she made in the washroom awakened her mother.

"Are you awake already? That's unusual for you."

"I'm going to mass."

"To mass? Why in the world . . . ?"

"No special reason."

She finished getting ready and went out onto the street where the chill of night lingered. The street was deserted except for one collarless stray dog that sniffed around the base of a telephone pole and then disappeared down a side street. She descended the slope and headed toward Ōhato. A group of young men naked to the waist were practicing bayonet drills in the park.

Sachiko walked from Dejima to Ōura. Then she climbed the slope leading to the church, just as Kiku had done many years before. In Kiku's day, where once both sides of the path were bordered by terraced fields, now several houses were arrayed in rows. Long ago, the printing office where Father Kolbe and Brother Zeno worked had also stood along that path.

She climbed the stone steps and quietly opened the door to the chapel. Two lighted candles at the altar fluttered like moths; the mass had just begun. Besides the priest who was performing the mass, the chapel was deserted except for two nuns and an older woman who did cleaning for the church.

The two nuns noticed Sachiko and looked at her in surprise. They had not expected this young woman, whom they had known since her childhood, to come to this early morning mass.

Sachiko crossed herself and knit her hands in prayer. And just as Kiku had done many years before when she entered this chapel, she directed her eyes to the right of the altar. There stood the statue of the Immaculata, looking unblinkingly in Sachiko's direction.

"Blessed Mother, please do something to help Shūhei. If you help him, I will come to mass every morning for a month."

She wasn't sure how to explain her feelings to the statue of the Blessed Mother. She was expressing her personal anguish, so perhaps it was not a prayer in the usual sense of the word. No—it really was a prayer. The sort of prayer in which a child tells her mother everything.

"He says he's not going to come to church anymore. He says the church has deceived him. He's angry that the church that preaches against killing can't do anything or say anything to help Christians who are sent to war. I don't know anything I can say to Shūhei. I don't have any idea how to comfort him."

The nuns looked curiously at Sachiko as she muttered the words with her face buried in the palms of her hands.

"Shūhei says he can't bear the idea of going to war unless he's satisfied with the answers to his concerns. He says he'll do anything to avoid becoming a soldier. He's serious about it, so he's really struggling. Blessed Mother, please do something for him."

Unlike Sundays, there was no homily during mass on weekdays, so the services ended in half an hour.

"Sat-chan, what a surprise to see you here! What in the world is going on with you?" One of the nuns teased Sachiko outside the chapel.

An innocent look on her face, Sachiko responded, "No particular reason. I was just out walking and decided I'd come to mass."

16

A DECISION

THAT DAY . . .

After finishing their meager dinner, several students from the dorm gathered in the cafeteria and talked quietly together.

"I really can't get excited about my studies anymore. I mean, we're going to be drafted soon." When a student made that comment, one of the more serious students retorted almost angrily, "That's why we should be studying while we still can."

A student in the law department stared at the floor and muttered regretfully, "Things being what they are, I wish I had gotten into the science program." Some of the other students nodded in agreement. A decision had been made to draft only the students in the humanities division, while those in the law and science programs remained exempt.

Under ordinary circumstances, Shūhei would have been the first to join in with the group, spouting off whatever foolish thoughts came into his head, but today he promptly returned to his room after dinner.

This morning, when he saw the headlines in the morning paper—

It struck him as odd that he was not more shocked. He merely felt that what was going to come had finally come.

Perhaps it was because Shūhei had already been warned that this was going to happen by Sugii, and he had had time to gradually get used to the idea.

Although he was not shocked, starting that morning a painful something, like bitter gastric juices, repeatedly gushed up in his chest. His pain was unrelated to the fact that he would have to abandon his studies and be drafted.

The pain came from elsewhere. It came from his inability to handle the question of what he should do if he were sent to war and had to kill another person.

Part of that problem stemmed from the fact that he was a Christian . . .

The other part had to do with being a human being who had studied literature and poetry . . .

As a Christian, no matter how he looked at it, he couldn't help but feel a contradiction between what the church had long taught and the realities of this war. In addition, as one who had come to know novels and poems, he could not bring himself to label a world righteous when it approved of one human being killing another human he had never met.

Killing. It was not merely stealing away the creaturely existence of another person; it meant stealing away from those who loved him another man's entire life, his daily pursuits, even his past. For Shūhei, who had studied literature, that was the most frightening of all possibilities, the one thing he must absolutely avoid doing.

And yet, everything around him was advancing in support of such acts. Even the church was mute on the subject. Ōhashi and Sugii and the rest of the Christian students in this dormitory struggled to avoid the issue altogether.

"No matter how hard you think about it, there's nothing you can do about it," Ōhashi chided him with a look of mockery in his eyes.

Perhaps it was as Ōhashi said. But still a pain like bitter acid kept pumping into his chest.

At the same time—

Shūhei realized what a coward he was. He was fully aware that he lacked the strength to hold fast to his own beliefs no matter the consequences.

It was likely that eventually he, just like the Japanese church, would acquiesce to the popular beliefs of society, finally to be engulfed by them as he headed off to war.

He opened the drawer to his desk and pulled out the knife that he had recently bought at a stationary shop. It was an inexpensive knife, but if he put all of his strength into it, it should be sharp enough to cut off one finger.

He could still remember the words of the soldier in charge of military training at the school who had snarled with disdain, "No bastard without an index finger can fire a gun."

The blade of the knife glistened sharply beneath the electric lights.

If he was truly determined not to go to war, all he had to do was cut off his index finger with this knife.

"And if thine eye scandalize thee, pluck it out." He seemed to recall reading chilling words to this effect in the Bible. If it meant defending his beliefs, just one finger amounted to nothing at all.

Shūhei picked up the knife and clutched it in his left hand. He spread the fingers of his right hand wide and placed the hand on top of his desk.

Now just do it! A voice close to his ears ordered him.

Shūhei shut his eyes.

Just . . . just go ahead and cut it off!

Perspiration bathed his forehead. He set the knife down on his desk and groaned, *I can't do it! I guess . . . I am a coward after all.*

Shūhei gazed around his room, which was illuminated by a weak light. The futon that he never put away. The books in his bookcase. And his agonized profile, reflected in the window glass.

He was having trouble breathing. He might remain motionless in this room, but that would obviously provide no resolution to his problem.

Still, it would have been pointless to join in that evening's debate with the other dorm students. On those occasions when he had insisted that the church could offer no answers to his anguish and his doubts, most of the other students had looked at him with suspicion. Evidently they considered his words blasphemy against the church.

Older students such as Sugii had cautioned him, "Just don't think about things." "Even if you think about it, nothing will come of it."

It was already pitch black outside, and the familiar melancholy voice blared on the platform of Shinano-machi Station, "A train is arriving. A train is arriving."

Shūhei grabbed his cap and left his room. Lately he had acquired the habit of going walking at times like this, with no fixed destination in mind.

When he turned out the light to his room, he caught a glimpse of the knife that he had just tossed down on his desk. The blade flashed, once again filling him with feelings of humiliation and defeat.

He walked from Shinano-machi to Shio-chō in Yotsuya. Because there was nothing at all left to sell, scarcely a single shop between his dorm and Shio-chō was open; the only stores that still had their lights on were general stores, some of them displaying dreary signs that read, "We Have Cleanser," and one coffee shop that sold kelp tea instead of coffee.

He was walking with no goal in mind. Not knowing how to deal with the fog that had gathered in his mind, Shūhei was merely moving his feet aimlessly along the nighttime streets toward Shinjuku.

The road at night from Shio-chō to Shinjuku was deserted. From time to time a streetcar passed by with a grinding shriek.

Shūhei continued walking, staring straight ahead, when suddenly he realized how ridiculous it was to be doing what he was doing. The mere act of walking offered no solution to his problems. Once again he recalled the blade of the knife that he had left on his desk.

Feeling weary, Shūhei decided to return to his dorm. He took a backstreet that ran parallel to the road he had first taken.

This neighborhood was lined with quiet homes of the wealthy, similar to those at Kōji-machi where the Chūjō family lived. Because it was wartime, dim gate lamps provided the only light, and no sound emerged from within the houses.

Sandwiched in between two of those houses was a tiny church. It was a Protestant church, so Shūhei and his dorm mates had never come here, but he knew from earlier walks that there was a church here.

As he passed by, he noticed that the front door of the church was open and suddenly wondered, *Should I go inside?*

His legs were tired, so he decided he would go in for a short rest.

When he went inside, faint lighting illuminated only the walls of the chapel; there was a preacher's pulpit and pews where the members would sit. Unlike Catholic churches, the space was empty and void of decoration.

He sat down in one of the pews and looked around the chapel, which reminded him of a warehouse. Lacking an altar or rows of candles like those one would find in Catholic churches, this church made Shūhei feel uneasy.

When he had settled down he noticed a paper banner hanging to the side of the pulpit; on it was written the words "GOD IS LOVE."

Most likely the minister here had given a sermon to his flock on that topic this past Sunday.

Staring at the words on the banner made his teeth stand on edge. Shūhei began to feel an indescribable irritation. Feelings even of anger surged inside him.

It was unbearably discomforting that a pastor who would give such a sermon to others could close his eyes to the war in which people were being killed. It was all so irreconcilable.

They're all lying! All liars!

Shūhei impulsively rose to his feet and started to leave the deserted church. Just then a middle-aged man with sunken cheeks came into the chapel, his keys rattling. Seeing Shūhei, a look of suspicion swept across his face, but he said, "Please, you're welcome to stay." Apparently he was the pastor here. "Is this your first time here?"

"Yes."

"Did you wish to hear about Christianity?" The man asked in a nasal voice. The insistent voice and the feminine gestures were a feature common among Japanese priests and pastors.

I'm a Christian. I'm not a Protestant, but . . . Shūhei started to say, but suddenly he was overwhelmed by an urge to try to wound the feelings of this all-too-pastor-like pastor.

"Yes."

"Then why don't I give you a pamphlet to introduce you to Christianity. I'm afraid it's only a mimeographed copy."

"Could I ask you a question?"

The pastor smiled momentarily at Shūhei's Nagasaki dialect, but again in his nasal voice he replied, "Why, yes, of course."

"Up there it says 'GOD IS LOVE.' Is that really true?"

"Yes, that's what we believe."

"If that's the case, does this God who is love . . . this God who is love approve of wars where people hate each other and kill each other?"

A guarded look swept across the pastor's face, as though it had been smoothed out by a brush. Shūhei was very familiar with this look of wariness so characteristic of Christians . . .

The pastor fixed his eyes on Shūhei. He seemed to be worried that Shūhei might be with the police. He had heard that detectives would often use questions like this to trap and ferret out anyone with antiwar sentiments.

"I'm not a police detective," Shūhei hurriedly shook his head. "Please don't worry."

"I don't actually think you're a detective but . . . exactly what is it you want to ask?" The pastor's voice changed from its earlier feminine tone to one evincing a prickly, high-strung disposition.

"I don't understand why Christianity approves of war. That's my question to you."

"War is . . . war is not an act of God. It is an act of man," the pastor answered, somewhat perplexed. "It is a desperate act of humanity."

"So are you saying that that's why the church condones war? A war of mutual hatred, mutual murder . . . ?"

"No, the church doesn't condone it, but . . ."

"But the Christian countries of the world send out military chaplains, don't they? They bless the soldiers who are going to war, don't they? Even in Japan, the church hasn't said that it's opposed to war, has it?"

"Are you . . . a Red?"

"What do you mean by calling me a Red—do you mean a communist?"

"No, that's not what I meant. It's just that the church lies outside the realm of politics. The church is a place where all we concern ourselves with is the souls of men."

The more the man's voice rose into higher octaves, the more Shūhei sensed a lack of confidence in this pastor.

"You say the church has no connection with politics, but . . ." Shūhei retorted. "Let's say a Christian received a draft notice— what would you say to him?"

The pastor seemed unable to grasp Shūhei's true motives. "How would I respond . . . ? But every person's situation is different, isn't it?"

"Then if that man ended up having to kill someone on the battlefield, is it all right for him to kill? How would you respond if I asked you that?"

The pastor averted his eyes and said nothing.

"I am . . ." Shūhei muttered. "I will be going into the military soon. That's why I'm asking you. I've thought it over myself, but I still can't come up with an answer. I've asked others, but they don't know, either."

Silence enveloped the two men. The pastor raised his head and in a lifeless voice replied, "I don't know how to answer you."

He glanced up at Shūhei's face. The earlier superciliousness had disappeared from the pastor's own face.

"I thought eventually I would be getting questions like that from young people like you. I have no confidence in how I should answer . . ."

Shūhei suddenly felt an incredible sadness. But he felt no resentment toward this pastor.

"We Christian believers in Japan. . . . If only each of us had the courage to say that killing others goes against the teachings of God. . . . But I don't have that kind of courage myself."

Shūhei said nothing in reply.

"I'm very sorry. . . . Please forgive me."

Shūhei nodded almost imperceptibly. This man, too, was only human. Even he was weak. A man with a certain degree of cowardice. It was clear to Shūhei that he had no right to condemn this man.

"Thank you. . . . Thank you very much," Shūhei said. As he started to leave the church, the pastor stopped him.

"Young man . . . please, if you can, do your best to come back alive."

It was totally black outside. From somewhere, he could smell the odor of dead leaves.

When he returned to his dormitory at Shinano-machi, he found a letter from Sachiko in his mail slot.

He opened the envelope as he climbed the stairs. In the letter she had written that she had met with a potential marriage candidate, and that Father Kolbe had died.

So you've met with a possible husband?

He stopped and with heavy feelings reread those lines in the letter.

Shūhei was of course shaken by Sachiko's news that she had met with a potential marriage candidate. He thought of her as a younger sister but also as the only person who was impressed by his poetry and his stories. They had played together when they were children. She was a childhood friend who always did exactly what he told her to do.

But now she had suddenly become a grown woman, and he felt as though she was drifting away from him forever. Now she might be marrying another man.

The one phrase that escaped his throat after he read Sachiko's letter was, "Don't get married!"

But—

As a man who would soon be going to war, he had no authority to stop her. A man who might very well die on the battlefield had no right to exert control over the lives of young women.

Understanding that, Shūhei did not know how to reply to Sachiko's letter. He put off writing her day after day until finally he left her letter unanswered.

I'm sure she thinks I'm a coward.

Holding in his hands the letter that notified him of her marriage interview and the death of father Kolbe, Shūhei appeared to be smiling through his tears.

He had few memories of Father Kolbe. Even at the news that the priest had been murdered, he felt no particularly deep emotion. Instead, what flickered like a flame inside his head was his recent conversation with the pastor.

At least he is still honest. But the church in Japan . . .

Once again he noticed the knife sitting on his desk. The blade of the knife glimmered under his electric lamp.

If only I had been able to find a good way to avoid going into the military. . . . I've got to come up with a good plan right now.

"There has to be a way! There just has to be a way!"

Shūhei recklessly shouted the words, then quickly covered his mouth with his hand. But what kind of method could there be?

Shūhei had heard of a man who purposely maltreated his own body and was thereby able to avoid the draft. Similar stories often made the rounds at his school these days. Someone heard of a case where a young man failed his physical by drinking an enormous amount of soy sauce on the day of his exam so that he could pretend to have heart problems.[1]

But Shūhei had a difficult time believing that such tactics could be successful. The sharp eyes of Japanese recruitment officers would easily see through such deceptions.

He also heard about a man who ran away on the day he was called up and returned to his family's home. Rumor had it that immediately thereafter, the military police surrounded his home and the man was shot to death before his mother's eyes. Shūhei didn't know whether the rumor was true. But there might still be a way to avoid the draft that no one had yet thought of.

---

1   This was reportedly attempted by a number of young men, based on the belief that the ingestion of a large amount of sodium-laden soy sauce would raise their blood pressure to dangerous levels.

That night in bed, he pressed his face against his pillow and muttered, "There just has to be. There just has to be a way!"

✳ ✳ ✳

The leaves on the trees at the outer gardens of the Meiji Shrine near the dormitory gradually began to change color.

When Shūhei arrived at school the next day, a student was circulating among his friends waving a piece of paper and asking, "Have you gotten one of these?" He had already received orders for his draft physical.

Initially it was only one or two young men a day, but before long more than half of the students had received the same kind of white notice. The letter instructed them to return to their hometowns, proceed to the locations where the physicals were being administered, and receive their exam on the designated date.

One day Shūhei received an envelope containing the same white paper, sent special delivery from Nagasaki. Black lettering on the paper instructed him to receive his draft physical on October 14 at his hometown of Kuroishi-machi in Nagasaki Prefecture.

The classrooms became increasingly vacant, as though teeth were being yanked out. Students were returning one after another to their hometowns. Occasionally during class the teacher would look up and glance around at the empty seats, moved by deep emotion.

Some teachers ended their classes by saying, as though only to themselves, such things as, "Wars aren't just about people having to die. Staying alive is also of great importance to the nation."

Shūhei boarded the night train and left Tokyo. Here and there in the jam-packed train car he could see the uniforms of students who, like himself, were going to undergo their draft physicals. The realization that his time had finally come stabbed sharply into his chest.

The day after his return to Nagasaki, he made it a point to meet up with Sachiko's aunt at the Ōura Church to notify her that he was back.

✳ ✳ ✳

Shūhei met Sachiko in the garden of the deserted house that was their own private rendezvous spot. "My exam is day after tomorrow, so tomorrow night I have to go to Kuroishi. I'm in good shape physically, so no matter how you look at it, I'll probably pass with a classification of Grade A or B+."[2]

"If you pass, do you have to enlist right away?"

"Not right away. I imagine I'll be enlisting at the end of this year or early next year."

"Really . . . ?" Sachiko felt as though the waves of an enormous, irresistible dark fate were crashing in on them. Running away now was impossible. Where would these great dark waves carry Sachiko and Shūhei? Those waves had already borne Father Kolbe to his death.

Sachiko turned her head away and softly asked, "You're no longer thinking . . . about doing that frightening thing, right?"

"What frightening thing?"

"What you said the last time we were here that made me cry."

"Oh, that? I've forgotten all about that."

---

2 Roughly paralleling the US draft classifications of 1-A through 4-F, the Japanese draft system designated potential draftees on an A through E scale, with those in the A category declared fit to serve, while those I am calling B+ were in a category for men somewhat less physically fit but desiring to serve, or who had been chosen through a lottery system.

Sachiko peered suspiciously into Shūhei's face and sensed that he was lying. His torment had not yet been resolved.

Shūhei stared at Nagasaki Bay. He looked so forlorn that Sachiko felt as though the life was being squeezed out of her chest.

✳ ✳ ✳

The day of the draft physical.

Young men from surrounding villages assembled at the elementary school in Kuroishi-machi, and after receiving instructions from the enlistment officer, they divided into rows, removed their clothing, and stood naked except for their loincloths.

The bodies of Shūhei and the other students were easily distinguished from the impressive physiques of the young men who had built up their bodies by laboring as fishermen and farmers.

In individual classrooms, their weight, height, vision, color-blindness, and other factors were tested, and blood was drawn from their arms to check the sedimentation rate of their blood cells.

"Remove your loincloths and get on all fours." In the last classroom, a military doctor wearing a white frock coat made Shūhei and the others crouch like dogs to examine them for venereal disease and hemorrhoids.

After their examinations were completed, the young men waited for a time, then lined up once again in front of the examining officer, where they shouted out their test numbers and surname and were informed of the results.

"Grade B+, Pass." The officer announced to Shūhei, who stood at attention.

"In a few days an enlistment notification will be sent to you. Until then, work at being mentally prepared."

"Yes, sir. I shall work at being mentally prepared until I receive my enlistment notification." Like the other young men had done, Shūhei repeated the words of his orders in parrot-like fashion. As he did, he felt as though he had just taken the first step into a very unfamiliar world.

After the students had listened to some words of admonition, they were allowed to leave. Shūhei joined a group of students who were walking across the elementary school playground toward the bus stop.

The town lay along the coast, where leaden waves came lapping at the black beach.

At least thirty young men had already lined up at the bus stop, while others streamed toward the station where they would board a train.

As Shūhei watched the line of young men in their black school uniforms he thought, *I wonder how many of these guys will be killed in the war?*

He headed for the beach to wait for the queue to disperse. He sat down on a rock and watched as the waves broke against the shore in the blowing wind. The waves smashed against crags, then fell, shooting up a spray of water. One after another, dark waves surged in from the offing.

A twig at the water's edge caught his attention. His eyes were drawn to one tip of the twig frantically clinging to the shore, fighting with all its might to resist the incoming waves.

Before he realized what he was doing, Shūhei was calling out encouragement to the twig: *Come on! Don't let the waves sweep you away!* He felt as though the twig was himself, struggling against the waves of war.

But the waves repeatedly engulfed the twig, then in an instant wiped out its existence. He couldn't even spot the twig as it was caught up and carried away by the waves.

Shūhei stood up and trudged back to the bus stop.

Once again he told himself, *There has to be a way. There just has to be. There's got to be a way to avoid killing another person*—at least, that's what he wanted to think.

When he reached the bus stop, the light of the sun had started to fade, and all of the young men who had come for their examinations were gone. A middle-aged man with piercing eyes wearing a national uniform sat on a weathered bench, smoking a cigarette. Sitting next to him, a local elderly woman held a large furoshiki containing vegetables.

While he waited for the bus to come, Shūhei took a paperback book from his pocket and began reading. Each time he casually glanced up, the man in the national uniform was always staring at him.

The bus arrived. The elderly woman boarded, followed by the man in the national uniform, and finally Shūhei climbed on.

When he sat down on the torn seat, the vibrations from the rural road shook his buttocks. As though he somehow couldn't bear the vibrating, the man in the national uniform got up from his seat and sat down next to Shūhei.

"So how did your draft physical turn out?" the man asked, smiling.

"Pardon?" Shūhei looked up suspiciously, but he felt compelled to answer. "Grade B+."

"Well now, the grandson of a fisherman from around here got an average rating, so a B+ grade is really impressive. You should be proud and definitely report the result to your family." He paused and then said, "You are a Christian, are you?"

Surprised, Shūhei asked, "Why would you know something like that?"

"Well, the police station is very good about investigating each individual. Since a number of young Christian men were receiving their draft physicals today, I came here to observe the examinations."

"So are you . . . a police detective?" Shūhei asked in a hoarse voice.

The man nodded. "Indeed I am. My name is Ono, from the Nagasaki police station. Thanks to my work, I know about many

Christians and priests and pastors. My responsibility is, well, to observe whether Christians are slacking off from their duties as citizens. Although it's certainly not true of all of you, once in a while we do find a Christian who has some strange ideas."

Shūhei had no reply.

"For instance, we sometimes encounter untrustworthy fellows who say that this war is a mistake, or that our policies in the South Pacific have gone too far. One Christian refused to enlist even though he had already received his draft notice. Of course, he was a Protestant. . . . Catholics right now are quite docile." The man grinned. But his eyes were not smiling. "Recently we had a Christian of that sort show up in Fukuoka. He claimed that Christianity and Japan's policies were not in harmony, so he was arrested by the military police. Even though he had graduated from the Imperial University, because he refused to appear for the inspection of reservists, we had no choice but to arrest him. Of course you went right ahead and had your draft physical today, so you're all right."

From time to time the bus shook violently. Shūhei listened in silence to the words of this detective, spoken softly and nonchalantly. But he sensed his knees faintly quivering. It was as though the detective had seen through his own feelings.

"I'm sure you don't have the same views as a man like that, now do you?" The detective directed his piercing gaze toward the quivering of Shūhei's knees.

"No, I don't."

"Well then, that's good. Still, we had a report that you said something unusual to another Christian at the Ōura Church."

"What are they claiming I said?"

"Did you say that the church is helpless to do anything about this war?"

"I did not." Shūhei sensed that his own voice was strained. "I never said any such thing!"

"Now, there's no need to become so upset. You just need to understand that the police have a responsibility to investigate every report we receive."

Compounding Shūhei's fears, the sensation that he was falling into a deep swamp filled the inside of his head.

The bus descended along the mountain path and finally entered the town. The ocean was now far away.

"You have been to the Knights of the Immaculata monastery, haven't you?"

"No, I haven't."

"I actually worked there seven or eight years ago." Detective Ono peered at Shūhei, who had fallen silent. "My station ordered me to investigate the place. There wasn't anything suspicious about the monks. But we felt at the time that their way of life wasn't in keeping with the aims of the Japanese government. There was a priest there by the name of Kolbe. Now, he was impressive."

Shūhei still said nothing.

"Did you ever meet Father Kolbe?"

"I did."

"What did you think of him?"

"I don't remember much about him. But I heard that he died."

The sound that came from Ono's mouth sounded somehow like the hooting of an owl. The detective thought for a few moments and then said, as though to himself, "It might be better for a man like that not to go on living."

The bus entered Nagasaki, and the detective got off at Hotarujaya. As he disembarked he said deliberately, "Thank you for your help." A somehow unpleasant feeling lodged in Shūhei's chest. It wasn't because of what the detective had just said. It was because he recalled the sound of his own voice and the expressions on his face when the detective's comments unnerved him.

I suppose I'll end up doing nothing and become a soldier. He mocked himself as he looked out at the streets lined with low gray roofs. He felt as though he had come to understand who he really was.

He didn't go straight home, but climbed the hill toward Ōura. It pained him to think of having to misrepresent his own intolerable feelings to his family.

When he unconsciously found himself standing in front of the Ōura Church, he started to head toward the deserted house but stopped himself. He saw a young woman going through the door to the church, and from behind it looked like it might be Sachiko.

He hesitated for a moment, then climbed the stone steps and approached the door. He quietly looked inside.

To his right, Sachiko was kneeling beneath the statue of the Blessed Mother. Her hands clasped, she was pouring out her heart in prayer.

Taking care that she would not notice him, Shūhei sat down at the rear of the chapel and stared at Sachiko's back. They were the only two people in the chapel. The evening sun streamed through the windows.

Looking at Sachiko from behind, for some reason Shūhei felt on the verge of tears. He had the strong impression that the number of days remaining to him were few.

The remaining days were few. He would die having only lived one-third of a normal lifetime. He would die without knowing the meaning of life, or the meaning of love—without knowing romance, without knowing a woman.

Against the back of his eyelids he could see the twig that was clinging desperately to the wave-swept shore. But the twig had ultimately been swept away by the breaking waves. And the same would soon be happening to the twig that was his own life.

Sachiko finished her prayer and stood up. She turned around, noticed Shūhei, and stopped, her eyes wide. Shūhei nodded and went outside ahead of her.

"Why are you here?" he asked her.

"Why . . . ?" She blushed as though embarrassed. "Lately I've been coming here every day."

"Okay, but why do you come here?"

"Because I promised I would come every day and pray for you."

Shūhei looked into her face with surprise. "Every day? You come here every day for me?"

"Yes . . . as a woman . . . there isn't anything I can do for you except to pray . . ."

Shūhei had known nothing about this, and he had perceived nothing. Sachiko had not said anything to him about it.

Like a strong wind slapping against his cheeks, the love of this one woman shook his heart.

"You've been doing that . . . ?" He looked away awkwardly and repeated, "You've been doing that . . . ?"

"And . . . how did your examination go?"

"I passed with Grade B+." He deliberately pasted a cheerful look on his face. "Now that it's finally decided, I'm feeling quite relieved. 'Be not therefore solicitous for tomorrow.' That's what it says in the Bible."

17

AS THOUGH THERE WERE
NO WAR

"BE NOT THEREFORE solicitous for tomorrow. . . . Sufficient for the day is the evil thereof."

Sachiko ached at the realization that Shūhei was working painstakingly to live every day in high spirits until he had to return to Tokyo.

Few days remained for them. They were determined to devour and relish each and every second of those few remaining days, and to make those days a final testament of life. To both Shūhei and Sachiko—indeed, to every individual who spent their youth in the midst of this war—this seemed the only possible way to live.

Almost every day, the two met up in front of the Ōura Church and spent those few fleeting moments together in the garden of the deserted house. For Sachiko, who had her work at the rationing bureau and chores to do for her family, having even only an hour of free time was enough for her, and those scarce hours together were irreplaceably precious to both of them.

Clumsy at being in love, they simply sat down side by side while Shūhei read her some of the poems and stories that he loved:

As though there were no war,
let us bask in the sun and frolic in the wind.
As though there were no war,
Let us read poems and savor the written word.

Had it been a different poem, Sachiko would have asked, "Who wrote that?" But this came after he had read her a famous poem by Baudelaire titled "Autumn Song":

Farewell, summer light that was too briefly radiant

So when he read her this new poem, she didn't ask who had written it. Even without asking, she knew at once that Shūhei had written the graceless verse.

Despite the artlessness of the poem, Shūhei's feelings were abundantly communicated to Sachiko's heart.

"As though there were no war, let us bask in the sun and frolic in the wind."

As always Shūhei was completely intoxicated by his own poem and said, "Sat-chan, let's go hike to a place where we can bask in the sun and frolic in the wind!"

"Where would we go?"

"Let's just hop on a bus and go wherever it takes us. We'll come back the same day."

"Okay."

"But if we do this, we have to ignore the fact that there's a war going on. Let's behave as though no such thing existed. I won't be enlisting! Let's pretend that's true and just go have fun."

The sun had already started to set, the sky to the west was tinted red, and Nagasaki Bay too was turning a vibrant rose color. It was time for Sachiko to go home.

The two promised each other that they would go hiking together the following Saturday.

"As though there were no war, . . ." Shūhei happily repeated the same words. "Since we'll be ignoring the war, we'll act as though I won't be enlisting."

Sachiko closed her eyes. . . . His feelings were transmitted to her almost palpably.

Saturday—

Shūhei and Sachiko caught an early morning bus and headed toward the Shimabara Peninsula. After discussing several different plans, they decided they would return to the Shimabara beach where they had once enjoyed the day with Takeda Mieko and Takahashi Misato.

To that end, Sachiko told her mother the first lie she had told in her life. Even though it was only a day trip, if she had told them that she was traveling alone with Shūhei, her Catholic parents would undoubtedly have been horrified.

"Who's going with you?" her mother asked.

"Mieko and Misato." She turned her face to the side and her heart was pounding as she answered, but even her mother, who was usually sharply perceptive, merely said, "All right," and showed no signs of suspicion.

Strangely Sachiko felt no pangs of conscience, no stabbing at her chest. Although this was the first significant lie she had ever told her mother, she did not have the slightest sense that she had done something wrong.

She even felt as though she could proudly say to the Blessed Mother,

Holy Mother Mary, you're a woman too, so I think you understand how I'm feeling.

Deep within her heart she was confident that she could do anything as long as it was for Shūhei, the man she loved.

✳ ✳ ✳

When they boarded the bus that Saturday, Shūhei whispered in Sachiko's ear, "All right, this entire day we're going to totally ignore anything related to the war."

"Right." She nodded broadly. Even if ultimately they could not resist the great dark power, unsympathetic to their hopes and wishes, that was pressing down on them, for just this one day they were going to ignore all of that. They were going to behave as though such things did not even exist . . .

"Pretty amazing that your mother gave you permission to go with me," Shūhei abruptly commented as the bus headed toward Obama.

With a smile, Sachiko replied, "Actually, I lied to her."

"You did?!" He stared fondly at Sachiko. It was the first time he had ever looked at her in that way.

They passed through the village of Tachibana, then continued on through Chijiwa, which was the hometown of one of the members of the Tenshō Boys Mission.[1] It was 11:00 a.m. when they arrived at Obama-chō, where white steam spurted from the hot springs.

Military policemen were posted at various spots in this village as well, but the two young people ignored them. They transferred to a different bus, acting as though they hadn't even noticed the officers.

As if to make up for the bumpiness of the road, the ocean they could see on both sides of the bus was so clear and beautiful one could almost be brought to tears. Glittering so brilliantly, as though the entire surface of the water had been strewn with needles, the ocean, the wind, the sunlight—all of nature, heedless of the war, stretched out before their eyes a verdant blue, radiant and calm.

I want to make this one day with Sachiko perfect, Shūhei told himself.

---

1 In 1582, three warlords who had been converted to Christianity helped arrange a delegation of four teenage Christians to visit Europe; the boy mentioned here was known as Chijiwa Miguel. They visited Macau, Goa, Lisbon, and Rome, meeting along the way King Philip II of Spain, Pope Gregory XIII (who died two days after their audience), and his successor, Pope Sixtus V. They returned to Japan in 1590.

I want to make this one day with Shūhei perfect, Sachiko told herself.

The fishing harbor of Kuchinotsu was not far from the expansive pine forest at Kazusa. When they reached Kazusa, something made the two young people feel like getting off the bus. The inlet, enfolded by a cape, was wondrously beautiful and serene.

Midday—

Noontime at the fishing harbor in autumn was silent as the grave. Several fishing boats were tied up at the tiny dock, but there was no sign of people. The only movement resembling that of a living thing was the reflection of the waves that the sunlight projected onto the boat decks.

"Do you think they're all napping?" No sound came from the village, eliciting a peculiar look from Shūhei as he surveyed their surroundings. The narrow road stretched out whitely, with the roofs of the houses packed so closely together they looked like people with their foreheads pressed together. A rooster crowed lazily far off in the distance.

The two walked aimlessly along the road.

"I feel as though I once walked through a village like this in my dreams," Shūhei suddenly announced, as though he had just recalled it. "And I'm sure it felt like nobody was in the village then, either."

Sachiko had been thinking that she had had the same sort of dream as Shūhei. The only difference was that, in her dream, the deserted village had felt foreboding, but she got none of that feeling here in Kuchinotsu.

They saw a temple at the top of a set of stone steps, where a giant camphor tree spread its branches like a mother cradling her child. They stood beneath the enormous tree and looked out at the sleepy harbor and the sleepy ocean that lay beyond the black roofs that seemed stacked atop one another. A faint breeze blew in from the ocean.

There is no war. There is no such thing as time, Shūhei thought.

"Sat-chan, I'm really glad we came here."

Beneath the camphor tree, Sachiko set out the bento boxes that she had prepared. Their lunch consisted only of rice balls wrapped in seaweed and some pickled vegetables, but Shūhei ate so heartily that, after he was finished, he licked off each of his fingers.

Gazing at the ocean here, he was reminded of the ocean that he had seen at the Kuroishi beach on the day he underwent his draft physical. That day, the water was rough in the offing, and a succession of waves came pressing in on the shore, washing away the twig that had clung to the beach.

But today, the inlet here at Kuchinotsu was calm and peaceful. It was so quiet that it stirred no reminders of the fate that awaited Shūhei and many other young men; beyond the cape the beach glimmered whitely.

"Sat-chan. Why don't we head over to that white beach and gather some shells?" He made the suggestion while Sachiko was cleaning up after they finished eating.

They climbed down the steps from the temple. The smell of fish was pungent when they entered the back streets of the village, where fishing nets had been hung out to dry. But not a single sound emerged from the houses, making them wonder if anyone was actually in them.

Taking the back roads, they reached the harbor and started walking toward the white beach.

"Oh, it's so beautiful!" Sachiko exclaimed. The egg-white-colored beach stretched out before their eyes.

They removed their shoes and raced along the beach like little children. Beneath the afternoon sun, the white sand sheathed their bare feet with just the right amount of warmth. Shells whose silver and pink colors brightly reflected the sun were scattered through the white sand. Collecting some of the beautiful shells, Sachiko wrapped them in a handkerchief.

"Come over here. This feels great!" Shūhei had rolled his pants up to his knees and was soaking his feet in the froth from the waves at the water's edge. They could see all the way to the bottom of the sea, which left them wondering whether an ocean could really be this clear.

"It's just like an aquarium. So many little fish swimming in a row. Sat-chan, do you have a towel? We might be able to scoop some of them up with a towel."

Sachiko hiked up her skirt and stepped into the water. They tried to startle the little fish swimming in a school, and they caught crabs that were scrambling between the seaweed that adhered to rocks. As though there were no war. Frolicking with the ocean, frolicking with the sunlight, frolicking with the wind . . .

"Look! A ship is heading out."

From Kuchinotsu harbor, which had been so quiet it seemed asleep, they saw a single fishing boat, its engine churning with precision, heading toward the offing.

"It must be going to Kumamoto Prefecture. Sat-chan, you know about this, right? Even though this is a desolate fishing village now, a long time ago ships from Portugal and Spain visited here. Chinese people lived here, too, and there were churches and schools that helped turn it into a prosperous international port. And I read in a book that in the Meiji period, there were some young women from poor families here who were sold to other countries. But now the face of the harbor is peaceful, and every sign of those events and where they took place in this village has been wiped out." Shūhei paused for a moment and then continued, "Sat-chan, even tiny villages like this one have their own unique faces. I felt that just now. Someone once wrote that every person's individual face is a compilation of many different expressions, stretching far back into the past, and I think that a village like this has collected all kinds of expressions too—sad expressions, happy expressions—to create its current face. The quiet here at Kuchinotsu is not simply quiet. It's a quiet that has seen much."

As Sachiko listened to Shūhei, he suddenly seemed to be more of an adult than she was. The Shūhei who looked like an adult. The childish Shūhei. The Shūhei who spoke in a mature manner. The Shūhei making an impish face. The Shūhei who displayed many different faces, like a kaleidoscope—Sachiko loved that Shūhei. Without question, he was very different from that other man she had met as a potential suitor, that man who was the very image of sobriety.

They suddenly realized that the sun that had been shining down on the ocean had weakened with the passing of time. The sands on the beach that had felt pleasantly warm on their feet until just a short time ago were now streaked with shadows redolent of evening. It was time for them to head back home. The one day in which they had behaved as though there was no war was drawing to a close.

"Sat-chan, it's time we caught the bus." His eyes still fixed on the ocean, he urged Sachiko to prepare for their return. Seen from behind, his figure looked intensely forlorn.

"No!" Sachiko shook her head.

Stymied, Shūhei replied, "But if we miss this bus, we'll have to wait four hours for the next one."

"I don't care if we take the last bus." Sachiko sat down on the sand, hugged her knees with both arms, and said resentfully, "I want to stay like this forever. . . . Do you want to leave?"

"I'd like to stay with you forever, too. But we couldn't get away with that. You know how angry your mother would be with you, don't you?"

It felt to Shūhei as though he was seeing for the first time an intensity that had been hidden away inside this young woman. Something intense—it was a fierceness in the blood that connected Sachiko with the blood that had flowed in the veins of Kiku from Urakami. Kiku, who had sacrificed everything for the man she loved; Kiku, who had given even her life for him.

"I've already told my mother a lie so that I could come here." Shūhei felt that he was on the verge of giving in to Sachiko, who was behaving like a spoiled child, but in a forceful voice aimed at combatting her stubbornness, he said, "Absolutely not! What are you saying?"

He must not allow himself to be pulled in any further by Sachiko's emotions. He was one of many men who would soon be enlisting in the military. He was one who might possibly be sent to the battlefield.

These two young people were restrained by shackles that kept them from feeling any further love for another person. Shūhei had been thinking about those shackles ever since he received word that Sachiko was meeting with a potential marriage partner, and he felt he had no authority to ruin any happiness she might attain in her life.

We have to behave as though we were brother and sister. We mustn't let it become anything more than that, Shūhei once again reminded himself.

"Don't be so bull-headed! I'm leaving, but if you want to stay here you can stay by yourself."

He took four or five steps without looking back. From behind him, Sachiko bellowed, "Coward!"

"That's right, I'm a coward. But we are Christians, aren't we? And so the choice between good and bad ultimately lies with us."

He headed toward the bus stop alone, but before long he heard footsteps chasing after him.

"Coward!" Bitterly she repeated the same insult. But her voice was not as forceful as it had been.

"I didn't realize you were so stubborn."

"I don't know what you're talking about."

The sun was already setting and fading over the port at Kuchinotsu. They began to hear the noises of human activity here and there in the village that, until just now, had seemed asleep. A girl with a baby strapped to her back was playing jump rope with her friends on a narrow road, while an old woman grilled fish on a charcoal brazier. These smells of humanity—Shūhei felt as though it would not be long before he could no longer inhale them.

It was a little after 7:00 when they returned to Nagasaki.

"It's a good thing we didn't get back too late," Shūhei patted Sachiko's shoulder. "Well, I'll see you later."

He disappeared around a dark corner. Sachiko watched until she could no longer see him, then cut through Hama-chō on her way home. From a radio in some shop, a voice was singing, "The young blood of the naval air force cadets . . ."

How sad . . . ! The image of Shūhei's retreating figure still lingered in the pupils of her eyes. When she had angrily called him a coward, Sachiko had felt only sorrow for Shūhei, who, though half flustered, was struggling mightily to keep himself under control. She knew to a painful degree how he felt. She also understood what was going through his mind, and why he had been so eager to return home so quickly . . .

When she got home, her father was still not there. At the entryway, her mother greeted her with a grim expression on her face.

"I'm home!" Afraid that something had gone wrong, Sachiko held out a package of dried fish she had bought at Kuchinotsu and said, "This is for you," but her mother made no move to take it from her.

"You're a liar. Why would you go so far as to lie to your mother? Who did you go off with for the entire day? Tell me the truth!"

Sachiko did not reply.

"Today I happened to run into Misato at the city office. I asked her if she'd ended up not going hiking with you, and what do you know? She said she'd never even discussed it with you. I was so embarrassed. Now don't tell me you went off somewhere with that Shūhei!"

Sachiko still could not respond.

"Why aren't you saying anything? Give me a straight answer!"

Sachiko turned her sulking face to the side and said, "All right, I went to Kuchinotsu with Shūhei. What's wrong with that? We're not doing any of the nasty things you think we are. Why is it wrong for a man and a woman to like each other?"

When she had finished speaking, she felt exhilarated, now that she had finally spewed out some of the things that had been piling up in her heart for a long while.

Horrified, her mother said, "Sachiko, you say such disturbing things. When a young man and a young woman who aren't married to each other wander around together, people from the church and our friends might say all kinds of insulting things. I should think you would understand at least that much."

"Insults and mean gossip don't mean a thing. The people from the church are quick to hurl insults and filthy gossip without knowing anything about the kind of person Shūhei is. That's because they think they're the only ones who are really Christians. But we aren't doing a single thing that we would be ashamed of before God."

Seeing her daughter become so confidently defiant, her mother seemed somewhat relieved. "So there really hasn't been anything like that between you two?"

"Nothing at all. But if something had happened, why would that be so bad? I don't think something like that is a sin. Don't you think that the Blessed Mother would agree with me?"

Sachiko's father, hearing later that day about his wife's conversation with their daughter, folded his arms and muttered, "She really does have Kiku's blood flowing through her veins, doesn't she?"

The following day, Shūhei returned to Tokyo.

18

LETTERS FROM SHŪHEI

Sat-chan, thank you for seeing me off at Nagasaki station. The train was jam-packed, but I was finally able to get a seat at Moji. I'm back in Tokyo, but nobody can settle down at school or at the dormitory, either. One after another, all the guys are returning from having their draft physicals. Almost everybody is classified as Grade B+, just like me.

"I'm Grade B+, and you're Grade A." "The Japanese military's physical standards have really dropped, haven't they!"

Those are the kinds of conversations I have with Ōhashi.

We hear there's going to be a rally soon where people can show their support for the students who are departing for the front lines. It'll be sponsored by the Ministry of Education and held at the playing field in the outer gardens of Meiji Shrine. I think probably before that, they'll decide which branch of the military I'll be enlisted in and the unit I'll be signed up with, either in the army or the navy.

That one day I spent with you was truly precious to me. It hurt when you called me a coward, but now that I've thought about it, I'm okay with it. I don't have any right to control your life. Last night I had a debate about this with Ōhashi in

*the dorm. He's still hung up on that young woman. You know
who I'm talking about: Chūjō Hideko.*

*"I just want to get one last look at her. And I'd like to talk
to her one more time before I wind up in the barracks." Ōhashi
looks embarrassed when he says things like that. "In our
situation we can't hope for anything more than that."*

*I agree with him about that. Maybe this is a bit of an
overstatement, but we're forbidden to fall in love, to be in love
with a young woman. How can anyone say "I love you" to
men who might die in the war? And is it possible that a man
who takes the life of someone, even if it's the enemy, has the
right to father her child? Those are some of the things we
talked about among ourselves yesterday.*

*Sugii says, "Just don't think about it. Thinking about it
won't do you any good. Thinking about it will just cause you
to suffer."*

*But evidently I am a man who has a serious side in me
somewhere.*

*Sat-chan, what sort of generation did we end up being
born in? We're not allowed to feel anything like love; we were
born so that we could abandon all possibility of living.*

*Recently I started thinking a lot about how the church isn't
absolute, that the church, just like us, is weak and messy and
cowardly, just like a twig on the beach that's about to be
washed away by the gigantic waves of war.*

*The church, too, has its weaknesses. If I didn't believe that,
then I couldn't tolerate the attitude of the church that averts
its eyes from what is happening and secludes itself, trying to
escape from it all.*

*When I get home from school, I always open the mailbox at
the dormitory and check to see whether there's any mail
addressed to me. That's how we're notified of where we'll be*

enlisting and what units we'll be joining. Before I go off to war I want things settled in my mind. I want to achieve some degree of understanding before I actually become a soldier.

Another letter—

Sat-chan, maybe you already know this from talking with people at church, but my enlistment notice has arrived. I'll be joining the Second Division of the navy at Sasebo. I had convinced myself that I'd be drafted into the army, so I hadn't even considered the possibility that I'd end up in the navy. I'm kind of relieved, since I'll be near Nagasaki.

How am I feeling right now? I can't really describe it. It's an odd feeling, like somehow all the things I've been agonizing over for such a long time have been settled by something from outside myself. I could cry or I could laugh, but the trolley that we've been loaded into has been set on the tracks and is racing now toward a predetermined destination. It's impossible to go against it. One solitary individual can't begin to defy the power of a great nation. That sense of resignation is part of what I'm feeling. But my feeling that this is all beyond my comprehension hasn't been whisked away. The questions that I've spoken with you about—Why would a church that preaches love assent to this war? Is it right for a Christian to become a soldier? Is it right to kill another person even if that person is the enemy?—those questions are like live coals that've been planted in the ashes of a hibachi, where they continue to smolder at the base of my consciousness . . .

It's been several days since I wrote the above. Ōhashi has finally received his enlistment notice. He'll be enlisting in an army division at Osaka.

"It has the reputation of being a division that's not so strict about tradition, so they won't squash me too hard, don't you think?" Ōhashi always talks optimistically to cover for the trembling in his heart.

Lately I've been thinking a lot about Jim and Van. I know you'll remember them as the childhood friends we played with at that abandoned house in Ōura. Back then it never occurred to us to think "Because you're an American . . ." or "Because we're Japanese. . . ." If we were to run into them even now, I'm sure we'd be delighted to see them. I'll never forget my memories of playing musical chairs at Jim's house or of racing around the beach together on our bicycles.

But it's possible that Jim is a soldier now off in training somewhere. Maybe Jim or Van and I might meet up again on the battlefield with the goal of killing each other. Would I have to kill them even if I felt no animosity or hatred toward them? Would they have to kill me? Why does a nation have the right to force people to do that? And why does the church approve of such things . . . ?

Sat-chan, after you read this letter, please burn it. I don't want it causing trouble for you.

Now one romantic tale.

Ōhashi finally got up his courage and wrote her a letter. He said there wasn't any way he could send it himself, so I went and posted it for him. He may talk big, but he's still such a baby. He stood behind me and heaved a deep sigh when he heard the faint thump of the letter as it hit the bottom of the mailbox.

"I wonder if she'll answer me?"

Her answer came yesterday. He found out that her father, who had resigned from the Ministry of Foreign Affairs, after trying to find a way to cope with the food shortages, recently

moved his family to a cottage in Karuizawa where there is
plenty of land. So Hideko had written in a charming hand,
"Since we're in Karuizawa, I might be able to see you, but I
shouldn't be thinking only of myself, right?"

With excitement on his face, Ōhashi shouted, "I don't care
whether it's Karuizawa or hell, I'm going to go see her!"

✳ ✳ ✳

Even though Shūhei had asked her to burn the letter, Sachiko
had no wish to do so. She was keeping his letters, which lately
had been coming more frequently, in her chocolate box. Ever
since childhood she had always put important items in that
chocolate box. It was the same box into which she had placed
the picture that Father Kolbe had given her with the words
"Greater love than this no man hath, that a man lay down his
life for his friends."

Recently she had seen a newsreel at the movie theater showing a rally where citizens demonstrated their support for the students who were heading off to war:

Scenes from the rally
Emotion gripping every heart
Shouts echoing through the forest

Following these captions, the camera captured the faces of
students marching in ranks, trampling on wet leaves as rain fell
on the playground in the outer gardens of Meiji Shrine.

"This morning at 8 a.m., student conscripts from 77 schools in
Tokyo, Chiba, Kanagawa, and Saitama Prefectures gathered at
their appointed locations. More than sixty-five thousand specta-
tors filled the seats to capacity, representing 107 schools that are

sending students off to fight." The announcer's voice sprang from the screen, and the faces of the marching students and the people seeing them off flashed one after another on the screen.

Sachiko searched in vain among those many faces to see if she could locate Shūhei.

Another letter from Shūhei—

> *I finally gave in to Ōhashi's whims, and we decided we'd go to Karuizawa. These days, with droves of students coming back from military service plus those heading out to serve, it was next to impossible to get train tickets, so Ōhashi stayed over in my room, and in the dark hours of the early morning, we took turns standing in line at the Shinano-machi Station and finally were able to get tickets.*
>
> *The next morning when we arrived at Ueno Station, students had formed circles on every train platform. Those who were going back to their hometowns to enlist were surrounded by friends who had come to see them off, all singing their school songs or their dorm songs. The circles expanded and contracted, and sometimes their singing voices would change into ferocious shouts. Ōhashi and I watched the scene with some amazement.*
>
> *As we watched, a kind of sad feeling rose up inside me. As you know very well, it's likely I'll still have unresolved feelings when I join the navy, but these fellows, too, seem unsure how to come to grips with the cruel fate that has suddenly enveloped them. That was very clear from the expressions on each of their faces and the desperation in their singing voices.*
>
> *"Ōhashi, do you think you'll be leaving Tokyo like that?"*
>
> *Ōhashi ducked his head and muttered, "Gee, I won't know until the time comes."*

Looking out at the platform after we boarded the train,
the eddies of well-wishers that had expanded into storms
continued to swell in numbers. But one student who settled
himself on his seat in a train wore a lonely look on his face, in
total contrast to the wild horseplay he had just been a part of.
When the train began to move, he suddenly pressed his face
against the window and stared intently at the black ware-
houses, black homes, and black Tokyo. I knew with painful
empathy how he was feeling.

I may not return to Tokyo ever again. I may never again
be able to study in Tokyo. *I'm sure that's how he was feeling.*

Each time the train stopped, whether in Akabane or
Ōmiya, I saw the same eddies of students. Student conscripts,
wearing armbands displaying the Rising Sun flag, always
stood at the center of those swirling eddies.

The students scrambled onto the train, as though herded in
by the ringing of the departure bell, but once the train began
to move and their well-wishers had disappeared from view,
the loneliness and worry that arose on their faces wasn't hard
to understand.

The sky, which had been overcast since morning, finally
cleared as we approached Takasaki. Signs proclaiming
"CONGRATULATIONS ON YOUR ENLISTMENT!"
or "THE IMPERIAL FORCES WILL SURELY BE
VICTORIOUS!" had been set up in rice fields along the
tracks, but the forests and rivers and the green mountains that
we could see in the distance carried no scent of the war; it felt
as though nature offered the only comfort for our hearts.

To our left we could see the enchanted Mount Myōgi,[1] and
before long, after we passed through a series of tunnels,

---

1 "Enchanted" because the mountain is ranked as one of the three most rug-
gedly beautiful sights in Japan.

suddenly a bright light shone into the train cars. We had
reached Karuizawa. Sat-chan, you've probably climbed
Mount Aso; the plateaus here are a lot smaller than the ones
surrounding Aso, but they give you the impression that you're
in a foreign country. Fields of withered pampas grass spread
out in all directions, and here and there forests of white birch
and larch trees stretch into the distance.

"Look! That's Mount Osama!" His eyes wide, Ōhashi
pointed toward a tall mountain that was languidly belching
out yellowish smoke. "So that's an active volcano. I've never
seen one before."

He seemed very moved.

When we got off at Karuizawa Station, it was as cold as
midwinter in Tokyo, but the sight of a woman with bright red
cheeks standing on the platform holding a basket of apples
made a strong impression on me. It's hard to even find apples
in Tokyo anymore.

We came out of the station, but we had no idea how to
get to Hideko's cottage, so Ōhashi and I wandered lost for a
while. Finally, with directions from a station employee, we
climbed onto a dilapidated old train with trolley-like cars on
the Kusakaru Line and got off at the Old Karuizawa
Station.

Even then we had to walk around for some time before we
found her house. Most of the summer cottages, which were
surrounded by groves of tall trees, had their doors shut, and it
felt as though no one lived there. From a clump of trees whose
leaves had fallen we heard the sharp cries of shrikes.

"It smells weird around here, doesn't it," Ōhashi said. To
me it smelled like something was burning. When we finally
found her cottage, Ōhashi was incredibly flustered, and like a
frightened dog he made no move to go inside. Suppressing my
own embarrassment, I ventured into the large garden, where

I could smell burning charcoal that gave off the odor I had just smelled. Apparently someone was burning wood behind the cottage. When I called out, Hideko's mother, dressed in work trousers, came around to the front in response.

I was surprised how much she had changed since we were invited into her home in Kōji-machi. Her cheeks were flushed, like those of the woman selling apples that we saw at the station, and it seemed like the flesh on those cheeks had sunken a bit. She reminded me of a farmer's wife.

"So you really came, did you? I wasn't sure you would, but where's Mr. Ōhashi?"

Ōhashi was still hiding at the front gate. She called his name. When she heard that, Hideko came running out.

She looked very different than when we had met her at mass in the Kultur Heim. She was dressed just like a country girl, in a sweater with work trousers made of dark blue cloth with white splashes—but she was, when all was said and done, her.

When she came out, a shamefaced Ōhashi finally appeared. "We've both found out where we go to enlist."

"Really?" Hideko's mother spoke in a rather disheartened voice. To dispel that mood, she put on a cheerful face and said, "Hideko and I have just been roasting chestnuts. Won't you come this way?" She invited us to come around to the rear of the cottage. A deep forest with many varieties of trees spread out behind the cottage; flames flickered and smoke rose into the air. Two large bags placed beside the open fires were filled with mountain chestnuts.

"Where did you gather these?" Ōhashi tried to put on airs by speaking in the Tokyo dialect.

"In the forest over there. Come September, the groves all around are filled with mountain chestnuts that have fallen

from the trees. If you had arrived a bit earlier, you could have gone gathering chestnuts with us," Sachiko's mother told them. "You can even gather walnuts in these woods."

"I learned for the first time in my life that the meat of the walnuts that we've been eating is what gets planted to produce walnut trees."

Amid the flickering flames and the smoke, the mountain chestnuts burst open. For the fun of it, we tossed dead branches one after another into the fire.

"Papa should be coming home right about now."

"Where has he gone?"

"He went to Komuro to buy some oil cake fertilizer. For the fields . . ."

In the early afternoon, Mr. Chūjō came home, a rucksack on his back. His tanned face looked less like that of a foreign diplomat and more like that of a gentleman farmer.

"Hello, thank you for coming!" he smiled at us.

They served us lunch. Mrs. Chūjō steamed a huge mound of potatoes and salted them—it was really delicious!

"I gather that you two will be soldiers soon." After lunch, Mr. Chūjō pulled out a bottle of his prized whiskey. "I've been saving this just for this day. Drink up!"

The first whiskey I'd ever tasted in my life burned like fire as it went down my throat, and Ōhashi's throat, too. I suddenly thought, I'll never be drinking like this again in my entire life.

"There's something I want to say to you. I don't know how you feel about this, but you mustn't forget that coming back from the war alive is also to the benefit of Japan. I don't know how the war will end, but once it's over, it will be your job to heal the wounds Japan has suffered. Returning alive, even if you have to grit your teeth to do it, is also a form of patriotism."

"How, exactly, would you define a 'country'? At this point in my life, I don't know what a 'country' or a 'nation' really is." I inquired of Mr. Chūjō like a child questioning its father.

"In my own way, I think I understand . . . understand the feelings that drive you to ask that question. . . ." From the look in his eyes, it seemed to me that he had a clear understanding of my dilemma. "I would probably have thought about the same sorts of things if I were you."

We watched through the window as shrikes flew into the grove and leaped from one tree branch to another. Ōhashi and I nervously studied Mr. Chūjō's face.

"I think of the nation and the country as two different things. If I were you, I wouldn't take up arms with the attitude that I was fighting for a nation whose political policies felt nebulous and in direct opposition to my own views. I would rather feel inside that I was fighting for my country."

"And what exactly is the kind of country that you're talking about?"

"For me, a country is a gathering together of many people who don't know how to relate this war to their own lives. I think you two actually belong in that category. I wonder if maybe that's the case not just for you, but also for all of the students who are enlisting now and being registered with their units. Young people, whether we're talking about those from yesterday or today or tomorrow, ultimately go to war suffering and agonizing over the same problems. Some of you will force yourselves to embrace the ideals of 'the great eternal cause' or 'all eight corners of the world under one roof'[2] that are spouted by intellectuals who are nothing more than

---

2   Both of these were popular propaganda slogans used by the Japanese military government; the second suggests that all of Asia needs to unite under Japan's protective "roof" in order to drive out the Western imperialists.

mouthpieces for the government. But nobody can truly accept those ideals deep down inside, even if they've forced them down their own throats. They're only doing it to justify themselves."

As he spoke, Mr. Chūjō poured even more of his prized whiskey into our cups and downed another glass himself.

"Listen, I realize this is painful for both of you. Neither of you knows how to handle this. And you're not the only ones who are suffering: We all belong to the same community of suffering. Of course it's your generation that's been saddled with the cruelest fate—but so many people . . . the aging mothers whose sons are taken as soldiers, women whose husbands are sent to the front lines . . . so many people are having their normal activities, their very lives crushed by the violent acts of an invisible 'nation.' And most tragic of all are the people who can't express their anger toward these contradictions, who have to keep telling themselves that 'It's all for the good of our country.' You'll find those kinds of people all over Japan."

"You're saying that those people . . . they are what you'd call our 'country'?"

"That's right. You young people endure suffering in the same way as all those people. So what I ask you to do is to go to war for those people."

"For them?" At first I wasn't really sure what Mr. Chūjō was saying. "For those people?"

"Well, perhaps it's better to say that you go to war because you stand along with those people. Think of it as going to war to suffer just as they are suffering."

Ōhashi and I stared at the floor. Sat-chan, today was the first time I'd ever heard anyone express the kinds of views that Mr. Chūjō did. Not one person ever did me the favor of sharing ideas like this—not my teachers at school, not Sugii at my dorm, not even the priests at church.

"I know this is still probably very hard for you to understand. But I can't come up with any other way to say it."

"Thank you very much."

Mrs. Chūjō interjected, "Well, this seems like a good place to take a break. Why don't we all go for a walk?"

We all went walking along a narrow path surrounded by the forest. On both sides of the path black cottages, their doors shut tight, maintained a stubborn silence.

Mr. Chūjō was a real expert with the names of plants and birds, and when he saw a bird fly over some withered branches, he said, "Ah, that's a brown-headed thrush. It has a red breast."

In an attempt to give Ōhashi some time alone with Hideko, I joined Mr. and Mrs. Chūjō and we set out ahead of the couple. After a door-to-door salesman with a crew cut rode past us on a bicycle and disappeared into the forest, Mr. Chūjō stopped and with an impish smile asked, "Do you know who that fellow is? He's a military policeman."

He said it so casually that I was startled. "Why is a military policeman dressed up like that?"

"I can't mention any names, but there's a politician who lives around here who's being watched by the military. And I'm honored to say that I'm under observation as well. The military police go around dressed up as salesmen or farmers. And Karuizawa is also one of the places where foreigners from enemy nations have been rounded up and forced to live."

Occasionally I would steal a glance behind me and see that Ōhashi and Hideko were following us, engaged in some kind of conversation. Looking at the two of them, I thought back on the time I spent with you at Kuchinotsu. We spent the day there, acting "as though there was no war," and I wanted to give Ōhashi the opportunity to spend an hour or two the same way. But finally we approached the time when we had to leave. We returned from our walk and said our farewells.

"This isn't much, but . . ." Mrs. Chūjō said, giving each of us a bag filled with potatoes. And the whole family went with us to the Kusakaru Line train station to see us off.

Hideko continued waving her hand when the train set out. Ōhashi stuck his head out the window and stared at her for a long time.

As the train left Karuizawa Station, he muttered as though greatly relieved, "Now I have no regrets."

My own thoughts were elsewhere. Mount Asama, now a purplish color, was clearly visible in the darkening sky. Mr. Chūjō had said, "I want you to think of the country as a collection of people who suffer due to the violence of the nation without understanding anything, unable to accept what is going on." I think what he must have been telling us was that we must suffer together with all those others who are suffering.

"Do you suppose he meant that we have to join that community of sufferers?" I asked Ōhashi.

"It seems that way. But I don't care about any of those confusing problems. I have no regrets leaving behind this world now that I was able to see Hideko."

I nodded. Yes, romantic love ends with nothing more than this for our generation. It felt to me as though, for that reason alone, we were experiencing a pain and a beauty that no other generation could understand . . .

19

DARK DAYS

EARLY ONE MORNING at the beginning of December, Sachiko attended mass at the Ōura Church. Although it was a midweek mass, nearly twenty Christians knelt in the chapel, including Shūhei, who faced the altar dressed in his black school uniform. After mass he was to take a train from Nagasaki Station to enlist in his naval unit at Sasebo.

The priest at the altar spread out both arms and in a solemn voice encouraged the congregation to offer special prayers. "Let us all pray for Shūhei's continued success in the cause of war. And that God will protect him in all situations . . ."

Please let Shūhei return alive. Please don't let him meet with any danger.

Sachiko turned to face the statue of the Blessed Mother.

I don't care what happens to me as long as Shūhei can come back alive.

She repeated the words over and over again in her mind. Tears began to well up against her eyelids as she prayed. The statue of the Immaculata looked down at Sachiko with a never-changing, faultless gaze.

When the mass ended Shūhei went outside, surrounded by his parents and relatives and joined by the Christians who had come to see him off. It was a chilly morning, and a cool breeze blew up from Nagasaki Bay.

One middle-aged Christian man with a self-satisfied look on his face explained to Shūhei, "This afternoon you'll probably have a physical exam. After that, they'll issue you your naval uniform. If things haven't changed since I was in the navy, the first thing you'll be taught is how to hang your hammock and how to fold up your clothing to create a pillow."

At the front of the chapel, the entire congregation gave three shouts of "BANZAI!" Before anyone really noticed them arrive, apron-wearing women from the National Defense Women's League, representatives of the local Soldiers Association, and members of the Neighborhood Alliance had joined the worshippers. Holding Rising Sun flags made of paper, they lined up in two rows, placing Shūhei, who wore his school cap, in the center of their procession. The group descended the stone steps and headed down the hill in front of the church. It was the same slope that Kiku, Father Kolbe, and Itō Seizaemon[1] had climbed and descended, the thoughts going through their heads as varied as their circumstances.

The sky was overcast and leaden in color and the sea was rough. In spite of the depths of his anguish, for the moment Shūhei was smiling and conversing with people in the group who came up to talk with him. Sachiko, knowing as well as she did what was really roiling in his heart, had no idea what she might say, since her own chest had tightened with anxiety. Even had she wanted to speak to him along with everyone else, she had no opportunity, and she detested the fact that Shūhei was overly conscious of the gaze of others.

By the time they reached the train station, a group of students had already gathered inside. Voices singing school songs and songs of encouragement echoed through the building, and the platform was packed with people saying their farewells. Along

---

1 Itō is a major character in Endō's *Kiku's Prayer*.

with the other students heading off for enlistment, Shūhei stuck his head out of the train window, bowing in gratitude over and over to those who had come to see him off. He cast a quick glance toward Sachiko and flashed her his characteristically clumsy smile. The departure bell rang, and with a screech the decrepit train car slowly began to move. Sachiko, no longer concerned what others might think, began running down the platform.

"Sat-chan! That's enough! Enough!" a red-faced Shūhei shouted.

Sachiko's response also came loudly. "I'll be praying for you! I'll go to mass every morning and pray for you!"

That year in Nagasaki, a city fond of festivals and lively events, December and January were cold, forlorn, and subdued. Record stores in the neighborhood blared out such songs as "Katō Hayabusa's Flying Squadron" and "The Messenger Boy Rides His Bike,"[2] but the stalls that, in normal years, stood on every street corner selling New Year's mirror mochi and decorative ropes for the holidays had disappeared, and there was little pedestrian traffic. Going out into the countryside to shop was strictly prohibited, and once in a while a person shouldering a rucksack or holding a large cloth-wrapped parcel was seen being arrested by the police at a bus stop.

Despite the restrictions, when Sachiko got her hands on something even a little unusual, she would think, *I want to send this to Shūhei.*

Recently she had decided she wanted to send him food, even if it meant cutting back on what she ate herself.

Frustratingly enough, there was no communication from Shūhei. Having heard that right after enlisting a soldier had no time to write letters, Sachiko was not particularly worried, but she was lonesome. Then one evening, when she came back home

---

2 Two very popular songs during the war. The first deals directly with the fighting; the second is a bouncy, diverting song.

weary from her work at the rationing office, her father, who had returned home from work unusually early, said as he looked out into the garden, "By the way, a postcard has come for you." Unlike her mother, it felt as though her father tacitly approved of her relationship with Shūhei.

"INSPECTED" had been stamped on the government-issued postcard. Shūhei's familiar handwriting totally buried the back of the card, and the characters seemed to leap up for her to read.

The card said that he was enthusiastically living each day. He wrote that every day was a succession of stressful moments because, unlike what he was accustomed to in the civilian world, here he had to remember everything he heard. In the navy, he explained, they have to call an *ofuro* the "bath," the washbasin "oshitappu," a cleaning cloth is "starboard match," and a bucket a "chinkēsu." The test for student cadets was coming up soon. On the day he enlisted, he was declared fit to fly planes, so even if he passed the test to become a student sailor, he might be transferred over to the flight corps . . .

"Every morning we strip to the waist and do naval exercises, but when we get to learn how to row cutters, our foul moods vanish and we feel invigorated."

She could tell that Shūhei's postcard was written with the awareness that it would be inspected by his superior officers. Sachiko strained to decipher not so much what was written on the card but what Shūhei was trying to say between the lines.

"Dad, what is a student cadet?"

"It's the pathway to becoming an officer without even graduating from the naval academy."

"If a man becomes an officer, does that mean his life is a little easier than when he was a sailor?"

"Yes, but his responsibilities are greater."

Each morning Sachiko never failed to make her way in the dark along the frozen path to attend early morning mass. One day, passing by a Shinto shrine, she noticed a solitary woman performing the ritual of walking back and forth in front of the shrine one hundred times in the hope of having her prayers answered.[3] Did she have a son who had been drafted, which is why she came to the shrine early in the morning to pray for his safety? Although they believed in different religions, there was no difference in the feelings they had as women concerned about a loved one.

At early morning mass—

Sachiko prayed fervently to the statue of the Blessed Mother Mary. Just as, many years before, Kiku had prayed fervently for the safety of Seikichi, who was imprisoned in Tsuwano . . .

"Please don't let Shūhei meet with any danger. Please help him to pass the student cadet examination."

During the three days of the New Year celebration, through the diligent efforts of her mother they were able to prepare the special New Year's foods, though in a restrained fashion, and they were even able to entertain guests with their rationed saké. But even while she assisted her mother, Sachiko's mind was elsewhere. She had received another postcard from Shūhei, which served both as a New Year's greeting and to notify her that January 13 would be the first visitation day.

But I won't be able to go by myself. That was a source of uneasiness for her. Shūhei had no siblings, and since she wasn't his fiancée, she could hardly go to the naval station alone. Shūhei's parents would of course be present on that day, but what could she say by way of greeting to them? That thought left her at even more of a loss. Her mind was absorbed with these thoughts as she served saké to their New Year's guests.

---

3 A ritual in both Buddhist and Shinto folk traditions, this practice is performed by walking up to the temple or shrine altar, then returning to the main entrance. This is repeated one hundred times.

As the January 13 approached, she got up her courage and said to her mother, "It's visiting day at the naval station on the thirteenth."

"The naval station? What's that got to do with anything?"

"What's it got . . . ?" Sachiko reddened. "Shūhei enlisted there. Didn't you hear that from the people at church?"

As she so often did, her mother raised her voice by an octave. "You're still thinking about him? I know I told you that you aren't to do that."

"Why is that so wrong? I have no idea why you would say it's bad without any reason at all." Even though she answered with her customarily churlish face, inwardly she knew she was going to have to give up her plan to visit on the thirteenth, and it made her sad.

On Sunday the thirteenth, her mother was busy working in the kitchen from early morning. Visiting hours at the naval station began at noon. When Sachiko returned from the earliest mass of day and saw her mother still working in the kitchen, she asked, "What are you doing? If you don't hurry and leave you'll be late for the nine o'clock mass."

From the kitchen, her mother turned toward her and quietly said, "You're the one who has to hurry and leave. Otherwise you won't make it during visiting hours. Visiting is only between 12:00 and 2:00, you know."

Stunned, Sachiko stared at her mother, who feigned indifference and said to her daughter, "This isn't much of anything, but give it to Shūhei to eat. Tell him it's steamed buns that your mother made, and that your mother was planning to come but wound up unable to and so you came by yourself. Tell him that."

"Okay." Struggling to hold back the warm something that was trying to seep from her eyes, Sachiko stood up. A mother is, after all, a mother. She had grasped everything that undergirded her daughter's feelings.

"Hurry and go. You'll miss the bus."

Sachiko left the house and trotted to the bus stop in front of the station. A row of families that were also going to the naval station for a visit had lined up to wait for the bus.

Sachiko got off the bus at the long, thread-thin town of Ainoura and set off walking toward the naval station with the rest of the visitors.

About that same hour her father returned home from mass with a dark look on his face.

"Something terrible has happened."

"What is it?"

Sachiko's mother, who had been in the garden, stepped up onto the veranda. Her husband lowered his voice and said, "You remember Father Bois, don't you?"

"Yes, wasn't he the French priest who stayed for a short time at the Urakami Cathedral years ago? What's happened to him?"

"After mass today, Tajima told me that he'd been arrested by the police in Fukuoka."

Sachiko's father reported that Father Bois had been laboring at the church in Fukuoka, but during mass he had made a comment in opposition to the war, and he was arrested for encouraging the congregation to pray for the war to end quickly and for peace to come.

"And Father Bois isn't the only one. A German priest in Tsuruoka made the same kind of comment, and he was arrested, too. The police here in Nagasaki have stepped up their surveillance, so we Christians have been told to exercise great caution." Sachiko's father brought the tea cup to his lips and loudly sipped his tea.

"I heard there was a big disagreement at Urakami about the funeral for a Christian who was killed in battle," Sachiko's mother added. "The head of the town council announced that it would be conducted either as a Buddhist service or a Shinto service. But they said that the Christians at Urakami kept insisting that it be done in the Christian way."

"Those people at Urakami are really tough. But where has Sachiko gone?"

✳ ✳ ✳

At around the same time, the entrance to the naval station was crowded with fathers and brothers who had come to visit. They were led to a visiting area to the right of the gate and sat in chairs arranged in a row, but when they saw their sons or their brothers arrive one after another they rose to their feet, clearly moved. They had now verified with their own eyes the reality that their sons, who until very recently had been dressed in student uniforms, came in waving their hands, decked out in naval uniforms and wearing sailor caps.

Eventually they began to hear from tables placed in the room comments such as, "I'm not having any difficulty," or "I'm doing my very best." In that group of sailors Sachiko located Shūhei surrounded by his parents and relatives.

Sachiko had arrived before noon, but she waited quietly in a corner of the room so she wouldn't disturb Shūhei's parents. Finally finding a good opportunity, she timidly went over and stood in front of Shūhei.

"Actually, my mother was supposed to come with me but she ended up having to do something for my brother, so I came by myself," she lied with a red face. "This isn't much of anything, but since my mother made it . . ."

Shūhei's parents expressed their appreciation and made room for Sachiko to sit down.

Shūhei in his sailor uniform looked less heroic than heartbreaking to her. Especially when she noticed his frostbitten hands poking, darkly brown and swollen, out of his baggy jacket,

Sachiko felt a pain in her chest like flames being fanned. In no time at all visiting hours ended. Even if she had wanted to say something at parting, she could scarcely interrupt while his parents were speaking to him.

Deflated, she walked alone to the bus stop along the road as a dust devil swirled in the air.

✳ ✳ ✳

About a month after visiting day, Shūhei passed the examination to become a student cadet qualified for officer training. As he had anticipated, he was ordered in addition to join the Tsuchiura aviation corps for flight training.

> In high spirits, I have become one who bears the burden of protecting the homeland—I burn with the excitement of being able to offer myself for my fatherland.

A postcard with those sentiments arrived at the church, but Sachiko received no communication from him. Because the postcard was addressed to "All the members at the church," following Sunday mass the priest posted it on the bulletin board.

This isn't how Shūhei writes! Sachiko recognized at a single glance. It wasn't like Shūhei to write sentences so devoid of personality. Having read so many of his letters over a long period of time, that was patently obvious to Sachiko.

Because Shūhei couldn't write honestly about his true feelings, since the postcard would be inspected, he had written these hackneyed, lifeless words. Sachiko knew in that moment that none of his torment had been resolved. In that unsettled state, he had become a candidate for officer training and was now being forced into preparation as a pilot to fight against the enemy. . . . During mass that day, a man no one had ever seen before stood at the back of the chapel. He neither sat down nor knelt. He did not hold a prayer book. When the mass was over, he stood next to the door as everyone headed outside and peered searchingly into each individual face.

Someone whispered to Sachiko's mother, "A detective from the Nagasaki Police Station is here. He's come to scrutinize all of us . . ."

For a detective, the man had neither the rugged body nor the stern face one might expect. His eyes, however, were piercing, and he had a crooked scar on his forehead.

A few minutes later the detective noticed a Christian named Inada, sidled up to him, and with a smile on his lips said a few words to him. Inada's face turned pale, as though all the blood had drained from it. The two men went outside the church together. Inada was taken away by the detective.

"What an awful thing to do! There's no way they could suspect that a person as good as Inada was a spy." Sachiko's father, hearing what had happened, returned home and explained everything to his wife and to Sachiko. Inada had sent a letter of encouragement and some gifts to Father Bois, who had recently been arrested in Fukuoka, and that had aroused the suspicion of the police. Worst of all, in his letter of encouragement, Inada had written some things that could be interpreted as antiwar, and that heightened the suspicions of the police considerably.

Inada was interrogated for nearly a month, then released, after having lost a considerable amount of weight.

"I ask all of you in all sincerity to be careful not to stir up any unnecessary discord." After this incident, the priest quietly went around cautioning the Christians. "If the police ask you whether you worship the emperor or Christ, tell them that as a Japanese you revere the emperor. And that as a Christian you believe in Christ. These two things are in no way contradictory. That's how you should respond."

Sachiko wanted to notify Shūhei about the ways in which the church was suffering, but she could hardly send such a letter to the aviation corps. There was no telling how much trouble it would create for Shūhei were she to write about such things.

Sachiko had recently taken to visiting the deserted house at Ōura on her way home from church or after completing her work at the rationing bureau.

She could see Nagasaki Bay from the withered garden. The doors of the deserted house, their paint peeled off, creaked as the wind blew from the bay, but as she listened to that monotonous sound, it brought back almost achingly a series of memories from those youthful days when they had played here.

With Jim and Van and Shūhei taking the lead, they had explored the pitch-dark house. Hearing strange voices in the kitchen she had fearfully clung to Shūhei's arm. They had discovered cats in the kitchen, and every day the children had secretly fed them.

Jim and Shūhei laughing as they played catch. Until the sun set they had pretended to be on board a battleship.

Where were Jim and Van now, and what were they doing? Back then, Sachiko had never once dreamed that their country and her own country would be at war, the war that Shūhei was writing about in his letters. No one had criticized them for playing with Jim or Van. Not a single adult had pointed to Jim or Van and called them the enemy.

All the many poems that Shūhei had taught her about in this place. Poems by Satō Haruo. A beautiful world woven with words. And one unforgettable, distasteful memory that had shattered that world.

That distasteful memory . . . the tanned, square faced military policeman who had torn up the collection of Satō's poems and stood before them with his fist raised as blood oozed from Shūhei's lip.

From that moment forward, everything had changed. The pleasing days were over. The stench of war and death began to smother the daily lives of Shūhei and Sachiko.

As she stood in the garden of the deserted house, these scenes twirled like a kaleidoscope before her eyes.

At nightfall, she heard the sound of a faint rumble in the sky over Nagasaki Bay. It must have been the sound of the training flights that took off from the Ōmura airport. Of course, there wasn't any way that Shūhei was already flying an airplane.

"They start out at first practicing in gliders. It's called 'sailplane training,' but they only sail for about two seconds." Sachiko learned this from a Christian named Minami who had been in the aviation corps at Ōmura. She assumed that right about now Shūhei must be devoting himself to that kind of training.

One evening as Sachiko was walking down the slope headed toward the deserted house, she passed in front of the Ōura Church just as a man was exiting through the church gate. It was the policeman who had stood at the back of the chapel during mass and taken Mr. Inada off for questioning.

Seeing her walking down the slope, the man stopped and looked searchingly at her. "Off for a stroll, are you? I suppose you're headed for that empty house. Fine, that's fine. Are you impressed that the police know everything?"

He began walking alongside Sachiko. "Young lady, would you mind talking with me for a few minutes? I'm afraid that someone like me who has no connection to Christianity finds discussions of your faith too hard to understand." He smiled as he spoke.

"I don't understand hard things myself . . ."

"Why, there wouldn't be any point in having you tell me about anything hard. What I'd like to know, for instance, is how you Christians feel about the current war."

"That's not something I can answer as a woman. Please ask a man." Sachiko prepared to flee so that she wouldn't give an injudicious answer, but the detective smiled and said, "Your priest told you to answer that way, didn't he? I'll tell you what he said. He told you that if you were questioned by the police, you should reply, 'As a Japanese I revere the emperor and as a Christian I believe in God.'" The detective gave a simpering smile and said to Sachiko, whose face contorted nervously, "That's all well and good, but what about you yourself, deep down in your heart—which would you follow, something your Christ said, or an order from His Majesty?"

Sachiko stopped and scowled at the detective, who still had traces of a smile on his lips. The insubordinate blood of the people from Urakami that flowed in her veins induced her to say, "His Majesty would not issue an incorrect order, would he? I don't think that Christ would teach anything that was incorrect, so it seems to me that following the teachings of Christ could not go against an order from His Majesty."

The detective laughed out loud in delight. "Young lady, you have a good head on your shoulders. My name is Ono, and in my assignment as a policeman I've been dealing with situations relating to Christianity for a long time, but this is the first time I've heard such an intelligent answer. Young lady, I think you know that on this slope a long time ago there was a building belonging to the Knights of the Immaculata, and that a priest named Kolbe worked there."

"Yes, I know that."

"Why do you think a priest like him died? It's because he persisted in maintaining a way of life unsuited to our times. I'm pretty sure a young lady as intelligent as you can understand that it's forbidden to do anything to the extreme. They say that there can be too much of a good thing. It's fine to believe in Christianity, but when push comes to shove you have to make some compromises with the world around you. Otherwise, the church and you Christians will end up in even more painful circumstances. Will you please not make light of what I'm telling you and really think it over?"

Just now there was sympathy and gentleness in his voice, and though it lasted only a moment, Sachiko felt kindly toward him.

"If you don't think this over, it will cause problems for me. To be honest with you, I don't like investigating and arresting Christians. So then, take care." With that, Detective Ono turned to the right and disappeared.

Alone now, Sachiko guardedly watched him go. Curiously enough, she felt neither fear nor trepidation. Instead she sensed courage burgeoning within her. She wanted to write a letter to Shūhei in some form or other informing him about what had just happened. She wanted to write, *I think the police will leave us alone if we express our feelings candidly.*

✳ ✳ ✳

Detective Ono returned to the police station, sat down at his desk, and began writing a report to his superiors.

> *In educating the Catholics regarding the war, we must take care in both word and action.*
>
> *Regarding the various attitudes of Catholics toward the war, recently some reports have stated that "Following instructions that Japanese Catholics received from the Vatican, for a full week last summer secret prayers were offered for peace to prevail."*
>
> *The following are statements taken from the Bible: "But I say to you not to resist evil: but if one strikes thee on thy right cheek, turn to him also the other." "And if a man will contend with thee in judgment, and take away thy coat, let go thy cloak also unto him." "Love your enemies: do good to them that hate you: and pray for them that persecute and calumniate*

you . . ." "But if thy enemy be hungry, give him to eat; if he thirst, give him to drink . . ." Vigilance is called for, since it is easy to interpret these passages from the Bible in a way that emphasizes pacifism or makes an antiwar statement.

One example. A Catholic man, Yamano Shigeru, who currently resides at 2–5 Daimyō-machi in Fukuoka, has told his neighbors, "The world is one family, and God is our parent. The Japanese, the Germans, the British, and the Americans are all God's children. We all differ in personality, but that does not alter the fact that we are brothers, so even if we get into arguments, it is absolutely wrong to argue continually," and has made other antiwar statements such as, "If we could just put God at the center of our lives, we would never have wars. Wars occur when we ignore the existence of God."

Once he had made corrections and adjusted wording, he set about making a clean copy. When that copy was finished, he stretched and sipped some tea from his cup. His coworkers were standing around the hibachi engaged in idle chatter; one of them looked toward him and said, "Mr. Ono, they say it's going to snow tonight. It's suddenly gotten very cold."

Ono nodded and said, "Yes, it has. When I went to the Ōura Church this evening, the wind from the sea was quite strong. I noticed that it's getting cold after the sun goes down." He took a pack of Asahi cigarettes from his pocket.

His coworker responded, "You went to Ōura? The 'Amens' seem rather subdued lately. I haven't seen any signs of opposition from them. Way back when, the peasants from Urakami rebelled against the government and defended their faith, but nothing like that's going to happen in times like these."

"No, I don't suppose it will. I've been investigating religious movements for a long time now, but the only problem we've had was last year when a bunch of Protestants raised a ruckus in Okayama Prefecture, but they've all quieted down now. The Catholics in particular, except for, well, two or three who make trouble, are generally silent."

"They're all afraid of us, so they display a cooperative attitude. Nice that it gives you a little break, isn't it, Ono?"

"Yeah." The detective picked at his teeth with a matchstick. "They've all been rendered spineless. The old Kirishitans had a bit more backbone."

✳ ✳ ✳

It felt as though Shūhei was not free to write letters even though he had become an officer candidate, and all he managed to send was one postcard a month to Sachiko. He faithfully sent postcards with similar content to the church at Ōura, and she was able to find out more about his activities when she ran into his mother at church.

She learned that Shūhei, thanks to his regulated life and intense training every day, had become so muscular that she probably wouldn't recognize him if she saw him. Signs of spring had finally started appearing at the base, the cherry blossoms that surrounded the aviation base had begun to plump out, and every day he and his contemporaries in the squadron enjoyed guessing when the flowers might bloom. Memories of times in the past when he had gone cherry blossom viewing by night suddenly flashed across his mind after he finished the day's training. Most likely by the time these cherries had finished blooming, he and the other men would be assessed for their fitness to either fly or work in reconnaissance. He intended to give his all for his country—these were the kinds of things that he wrote in the postcards that arrived at the church and those addressed to Sachiko.

Every time Sachiko received one of those postcards, she was overwhelmed by a mixture of joy and indefinable sorrow. Nowhere in any of these cards were Shūhei's true feelings expressed. It was as though he had deliberately written these postcards in an effort to conceal his honest feelings.

Sachiko could not believe that Shūhei, who had suffered so much over the contradiction between the war and his identity as a Christian, could so easily conform himself to military life.

As she quietly placed each postcard in her chocolate box, it pained her to imagine how Shūhei must be feeling, since he had to hide his real emotions from his parents, the priest, and even from her. And it saddened her to think of how he felt as he forced himself to don a ready-made attitude of patriotism.

The war situation worsened with each passing day. In February, two islands in the Marshall Islands chain were seized by US forces, and every member of the defending Japanese division died in the fighting; in March, Marshal Admiral Koga Mineichi, who had succeeded Admiral Yamamoto Isoroku as commander-in-chief of the Combined Fleet, was killed in the line of duty near Davao.

In April, as though it were the only spot where "as though there were no war" could be applied, warm breezes blew through Nagasaki, the blossoms opened, and spring arrived, the aroma of flowers scenting the silent backstreets of the city. It was also the month of the Easter celebration for the Christians.

After mass on Easter Sunday, Sachiko met up with Shūhei's mother at the door of the church. She told Sachiko, "I'm only telling this to you and the Father, but Shūhei is moving from Tsuchiura to the Izumi aviation squadron very soon. He said this is secret, so I don't think I should be telling anyone else."

Izumi was located in Kagoshima Prefecture, but Sachiko had no idea what sort of place it might be. It hurt her to have Shūhei moved from one unfamiliar location to another.

The fate of someone she loved was being manipulated by some force completely unrelated to herself. There was nothing she could do in response to help him or lend him any support. Worse, he couldn't even tell her anything that was happening to him.

To young Sachiko, it seemed unfair that every woman in these times had to shoulder the same sorrows. She resented Shūhei for having surrendered himself to that force, and she despised the nation that had so utterly changed him.

✳ ✳ ✳

The season of fresh growth arrived. The pervasive aroma of the new leaves jabbed at Sachiko's nose as she walked through Tera-machi in the afternoon. Both Mount Kazagashira and Mount Inasa were blanketed with young leaves. But no one was flying kites on those mountains the way they did in peacetime.

In the latter part of May, a student mobilization unit was newly established at the Mitsubishi Nagasaki Shipyard, and students were pressed into labor service. Mitsuo, Sachiko's younger brother who was still of middle-school age, ended up working in the same location as his father instead of attending school.

In June, a special edition of the newspaper reported that Japanese troops on Saipan were engaged in a fierce battle with American forces. But a separate event that occurred in Kyushu on the sixteenth of that month alarmed the citizenry of Nagasaki. Forty-seven B-29s had bombed the industrial region of northern Kyushu.

The bombers had flown in from the city of Chengdu in the Chinese interior and dropped their bombs from a very high altitude, so the damage was not that great, but the people of Kyushu sustained a tremendous psychological shock. They realized that they could not know when or at what hour their own town might be attacked from the air.

The rainy season began. The mood of everyone was gloomy.

"It seems as though Japan is losing everywhere. Even Saipan is in danger," Sachiko's father said with an exhausted look on his face; only her younger brother Mitsuo remained enthusiastically positive. "But rumor has it that the navy is building a special weapon at the shipyard. Once that weapon is ready, the workers are all saying that the war situation will totally change."

It was only later that they learned the special weapon, known as *shin'yō*, an "ocean shaker," was a small, one-man planing boat made of plywood. It was an ill-fated weapon, in which both boat and pilot were dashed against the enemy.

Each time Sachiko heard news that grew worse with each passing day, she thought of Shūhei. Whenever she thought about what lay ahead for him, this man who had been compelled to join in a hopeless war, her heart was on the verge of breaking.

If the worst possible thing happens to Shūhei . . . she thought, and felt as though freezing cold water had been poured down her back. She couldn't imagine what would become of her were he to die. *If he dies, I don't know if I can go on living.*

Not for the first time, she asked her mother, "Mom, was Kiku really grandma's cousin?"

"Why are you asking something like that out of the blue?" Her mother looked suspicious. But Sachiko wanted to learn all she could about Kiku's life. Kiku, who died for the man she loved. The man she loved was persecuted by the nation because he was a Christian. Sachiko felt as though she and Shūhei bore some kind of resemblance to them.

"I think maybe I'll pay a visit to Kiku's grave," she said, and asked her mother where it was.

✳ ✳ ✳

That Sunday, Sachiko took Mitsuo along and visited Gentio Valley—the Valley of the Gentiles—where Kiku's grave was located.

"Why are we going there? What's this Kiku person got to do with us?" Puzzled, Mitsuo asked after they boarded the bus. He couldn't understand why Sachiko would go to such a place when it was a Sunday meant for leisure.

"I'm sure you've heard about it from granny or mom, the story about the journey to Urakami."

"I've heard about it, but I've forgotten almost everything. I don't remember anything except that this Kiku was granny's cousin."

As the bus swerved along the country roads, Sachiko explained everything she knew about the fourth raid on Urakami. She told him how, from the final days of the shogunate until the early Meiji period, their ancestors, merely because they were Christian, had been driven from their homes in Urakami village and exiled to various places in Japan, left there to bemoan their fate; and how one of the Christians, a young man by the name of Seikichi, had been imprisoned in Tsuwano, and that Kiku sent him letters and money the whole time he was in captivity . . .

"And Kiku wasn't a Christian?"

"She wasn't. And she worked with granny in Nagasaki." Sachiko had heard that Kiku worked with her grandmother in Nagasaki, but she had no idea what sort of work Kiku had done. "Apparently she did some kind of apprentice work at a shop. But because the work was so hard, she contracted a lung disease. And as the story goes, one wintry day when snow was falling, she coughed up blood in the Ōura Church and died."

"If she wasn't even a Christian, why did she die in the Ōura Church?"

"I suppose it was because she wanted to pray there for that man named Seikichi. That's how women are, even if they aren't Christians."

"Hmm." Mitsuo, a typical middle-school student, seemed to some degree to understand and yet not understand. He said nothing. Inwardly, Sachiko sensed the similarities between the story of Kiku, praying to the statue of Blessed Mother Mary, and herself, kneeling in prayer for Shūhei . . .

After passing through Fukahori-machi, the bus headed toward a mountain road, where the heat was intense. The winding road was barely wide enough for the bus to negotiate, but panting the entire way, it made the slow climb. Sachiko and Mitsuo got off the bus at the terminus, at a tiny village called Ōkago, and following their mother's directions they ascended the mountain path. Her mother and grandmother had come many times to pay their respects at Kiku's grave.

From the opposite direction a female farmworker carrying a sickle was coming down the path. When Sachiko asked, "I was told that this is a Catholic village, is that correct?" The woman answered "Yes," and graciously directed them toward Kiku's grave.

There was still a small stone cross beneath a large camphor tree. It was flecked with pockmarks that looked like those on the peeling surfaces of seashells. Her mother had said that this was Kiku's grave. Sachiko pressed her hands together and offered a prayer, after which she wiped the perspiration from her forehead and took turns with Mitsuo drinking water from a canteen. The remaining water she poured over the grave.

She had a view of Nagasaki Bay. An airplane that looked very much like a drill plane flew over with a faint roar of its engines. It was a reminder that Shūhei was now a member of the aviation corps at Izumi.

20

1944

THE DAILY SCHEDULE was grueling. Morning began for Shūhei and the other student officer cadets at 5:30. When the bugle sounded to awaken all personnel, the cadets leapt from their beds, folded their blankets, pulled on their boots, and quickly raced outside. They had two minutes to be in proper formation. If they were the least bit slow they received correction from the previous class of cadets or from the squadron leader. The correction, though delivered with honeyed words, consisted of slaps across each face.

About a month after their arrival here, training began in formation flying, with the goal of accustoming them to being aboard a plane. Their initial time in the plane was approximately seven or eight minutes, but Shūhei and the other cadets, who of course were not allowed to pilot the plane, rode alongside an instructor. But once they had put on the flight uniform, cap, and the combat boots they were issued, attached the flight goggles to their face, and inserted their hands into their gloves, they felt as though they had become full-fledged members of the crew, which was a peculiar feeling.

From an altitude of about 650 feet, the fields, mountains, and villages were tinged with a variety of colors, and the sensation that their feet were not touching the ground filled them with emotions that included an instinctive uneasiness.

Will I really be able to fly through the skies this way all on my own? That seemed to Shūhei almost like it would be a miracle.

But when the plane turned and he saw the ocean stretching out beneath him, he thought, *It's so beautiful!*

He could see boats floating on the water. Fishing boats, most likely. The shoreline inscribed a vivid line as it stretched along-side white waves that looked very much like shaved ice. The scene inadvertently reminded Shūhei of the sea at Shimabara.

That day when he had enjoyed the beach at Kuchinotsu with Sachiko, he could not have even dreamed that after eight months he would be flying through the sky. And he couldn't begin to imagine what might be happening eight months from today. It was pointless even to consider it.

Most frightening were the occasional sudden changes in the direction of the wind as the plane turned to make its landing, and at those times his field of vision would shift in an instant. There were moments when he thought it was all over for him. Their instructors explained that by the middle of July at the lat-est, Shūhei and his squadron would be able to take over flying themselves, but to that end they must prepare themselves for in-tense training.

Shūhei did not dislike flight duty. Because there was no greater danger than to let your attention be diverted elsewhere, either during glider training or as part of the flight crew, he man-aged to suppress the long-standing anguish that would flit across his heart.

But during instruction in navigation and the procedures for torpedo attack, the anguish would unexpectedly resurface in his mind.

His torment was something he alone was experiencing, not something any of the other cadets had to cope with. When he belonged to the Tsuchiura aviation corps, there had been another Catholic in his class, but he never found the time or opportunity to open his heart to his fellow Christian. That man had been transferred to the aviation unit at Miho, so Shūhei was the only Christian here at Izumi.

Everything they were being taught was linked to killing the enemy. The goal of training for torpedo attacks was the sinking and annihilation of enemy ships. What it came down to was that destroying the enemy was the ultimate order given to Shūhei, and it became his sole objective.

Even though I was taught at church "Thou shalt not kill," right now I am receiving intensive training to kill other human beings.

During the hours of instruction, he was seized by the urge to burst into sudden cynical laughter over the fate he had been forced into, and he wondered whether he was the only cadet who was seized by that dark urge.

It was the rainy season, but it was an unusually rainless, hot, and humid rainy season. Shūhei and the other cadets, their bodies encased in flight uniform and caps with boots on their feet, were literally bathed in sweat.

In the latter part of the month, training gradually shifted from flying with an instructor to solo flight.

At this point, thanks to the fact that an officer who had returned from the Battle of Midway became their senior flight instructor, the cadets knew in much greater detail than when they had been civilians that the war situation had turned completely against Japan.

Contrary to reports in the newspapers, the material resources of the United States and its advancements in radar technology were formidable, while the Japanese Navy had lost a great many of its aircraft carriers in the Midway naval battle. To compensate for these losses, rumors spread that the navy was building planing boats packed with explosives as well as manned suicide torpedoes. A naval battle had been fought in the Marianas in June, and in Europe, German forces had retreated from Rome.

In July, even darker news reports came in rapid succession. Beginning with the news that the army's battle for Imphal had failed, one member of the squadron came racing in and loudly announced, "Listen everyone, there's been a mass resignation of the Tōjō cabinet!"

At mention of Prime Minister Tōjō, the men conjured up the image of the man who had saluted the students who kicked up puddles of water as they marched around the Meiji Shrine competition field, rendered opaque by the steady rain. Even though General Tōjō had incited the war himself, he was free to resign his post as soon as the situation reached an impasse, but the students who had been forced into battle did not have the option of stepping down from their role as soldiers.

The men were granted their first leave at the beginning of July. Shūhei boarded the train along with the others but disembarked alone at Yatsushiro. He had sent word ahead, and his father and mother met him there. Seeing their son in the uniform of a student cadet with a short sword at his hip, his parents initially looked shocked. Until recently he had been a student at Keiō University, and when he enlisted at Sasebo he had been dressed in a baggy sailor's uniform, so it had not occurred to them that their son would step off the train so tanned and strapping.

They went to the inn at the river's edge where his parents had stayed the previous evening. Because his father had once lived in Yatsushiro, he had some influence there, so at the inn they were served both smelt and some hard-to-obtain meat.

After Shūhei had bathed and changed into a yukata, he sat down by the window, stretched out, and began to converse with his parents in Nagasaki dialect. The realization—"So this is the civilian world!"—surged up within his breast.

"What a wonderful view!"

He could see mountains in the distance and a clear river flowing directly beneath his gaze. He noticed a man on the riverbank catching smelt with a long pole. There was no stench of the war here.

"Now, don't you go doing anything dangerous!" His naïve mother kept repeating the same thing over and over to Shūhei as he tore pieces of flesh from the fish and brought them to his mouth. His father, holding a glass of rationed beer that he had saved to open on this occasion, merely gazed at his son with satisfaction.

The next time we meet here, please bring Sat-chan with you. Although Shūhei wanted to say that to his parents, he hesitated until they were preparing to leave. Even then, however, he ultimately couldn't bring himself to say it.

It was not embarrassment that kept Shūhei from making that request of his parents. He had, in fact, started to ask, but then he remembered that he was a student officer cadet with no idea of when he might die. It wasn't simply that he might die in battle. There was no way to predict when an accident might happen during training. In fact, he had been told that two men had died in accidents during the training of the previous class of student cadets.

With even tomorrow an uncertainty for me, is it really right to ask Sachiko to come here, as though she were my fiancée? Shūhei had to ask himself that question. To refrain from inviting her to come was a bitter, painful act of self-restraint. But his Catholic upbringing impelled him to feel that such a sacrifice was necessary.

At three o'clock he boarded the train. Even after the train began to move, his father and mother remained standing on the platform. Their tiny, forlorn figures lingered in his mind's eye.

✳ ✳ ✳

In mid-July, around the time Shūhei's class began attempting solo flights, the war situation worsened considerably: according to reports relayed to them, enemy forces had landed on Guam, and at the conclusion of a series of fierce battles on Tinian Island, eight thousand Japanese troops lay dead.

Their instructor, a former naval officer, began asking them such questions as, "Do you men have the courage to fight to the death? The war has reached the stage where you will be required to hurl yourselves against enemy ships in special submarines equipped with torpedoes. Do you cadets with college training have the naval spirit that we navy officers exhibited in the attack on Pearl Harbor?"

"We have!" someone responded, his voice almost angry, as though he was ready to strike a blow. Shūhei did not answer, but that evening he pondered what sort of reply he would give when the time came that he would receive such an order.

As a Catholic, he had been instructed by the priests and his parents from the time he was a child that committing suicide was a sin. Just as one must not snatch away the life of another person, one must not selfishly obliterate one's own life, since it was a gift from God—that was one of the Church's teachings.

What should he do when he was ordered by his superiors to perform an act that went against those teachings?

There was not a single person in his squadron with whom Shūhei could discuss this problem, since he was the only Christian here.

Besides the contradiction between the Christian teaching "Thou shalt not kill" and the mission of a soldier, a different conflict now stabbed at him painfully . . .

It was a problem he would have to resolve on his own. He knew that there was not a single priest in Japan who could respond in any fashion to this contradiction.

Suddenly, at midnight on August 11, an initial air raid alert was sounded. Twenty-nine B-29s had launched the very first attack on Nagasaki.

The enemy planes targeted Nagasaki's factory area, but they missed their objective, and word was that the bombs had torched some neighborhoods in Inasa-machi and Furukawa-machi.

When he heard the news, Shūhei was relieved that no harm had come to his family or friends, but looking at this from the viewpoint that Kyushu had now been bombed three times, he was keenly aware that Japan's defense preparedness was severely lacking.

On the next leave day, he again took a train to meet his father and mother. The summer sun blazed down on the platform when he got off the train, but when he went to the familiar inn, he was told that his parents had gone ahead to meet him at the station.

As he had before, he changed into a yukata, sat by the window, and gazed at the river where people were fishing for smelt, and at the cumulonimbus clouds that were edged in gold.

Soon he spotted his father coming back toward the inn, wiping sweat from his face. When Shūhei leaned out the window to wave, he suddenly felt as though a gigantic hand was crushing his heart: his mother, dressed in work pants, was walking behind her husband, but next to her he saw Sachiko, also wearing a blouse with her work pants.

What is she doing here? My mother shouldn't have done this. Though he clicked his tongue in exasperation, an inexpressible joy surged through his breast.

At the entrance he listened to his parents' voices explaining to the owner of the inn how they had missed Shūhei at the station.

Soon he heard the stairs creaking. "The bus leaving the station was late so we couldn't find you," his father, still wiping away the sweat, apologized. Behind him Sachiko smiled with embarrassment. Unlike in former days, he couldn't come up with any words on the spot to tease her.

Somewhat awkwardly he said to his mother, "How did you deal with the attack on Nagasaki? You must have been startled since it came in the middle of the night."

The conversation continued for a short time until his mother said, "Shūhei, you haven't even said hello to Sachiko. She went to all the trouble to come here. It's rude of you not to even say 'Thank you,'" she scolded him.

Dinner was brought out, once again some of the smelt caught in the river below. His mother went on to say that he mustn't do anything dangerous, but then a thought suddenly occurred to her, and she said, "Why don't you two take a little walk along the riverbank?"

The katydids chirped loudly in the heat, and as the two strolled the riverbank, Shūhei spoke to her for the first time. "So, Sat-chan, you've been well?"

The two stopped and watched people fishing off in the distance.

"What do you think? I've become a lot manlier, haven't I?"

"Uh-huh, but I was really surprised how dark your skin's become." She was amazed Shūhei had turned into such an impressive recruit. When she'd seen him at the naval station, he had seemed merely pitiful, his frostbitten hands poking out of an ill-fitting sailor uniform. "I guess the training is pretty demanding."

"It really is. It would surprise you if you could see it."

Wondering whether Shūhei had finally forgotten his torment, she peered at his profile, but his tanned face gave no clues. "I pray for you every day. That you won't get sick or be injured."

"I'm really just fine."

Sachiko sensed some vagueness in his words. It made her feel forlorn that he would not tell her everything.

If, for instance, he had told her that everyday life for a soldier was difficult, or that he hated war—even if he had told her that he was cowardly and spineless, she could never feel contempt for him. It was a forgone conclusion that she would be pleased that she was the only one to whom he would reveal his true feelings.

"Sat-chan." Suddenly Shūhei was staring at her. She stiffened, waiting for him to hug her.

"I'm worried about Ōhashi. I haven't had any letters from him. Sat-chan, would you be willing to send a letter to his home? Given the kind of person he is, I'm pretty sure he's dealing well with his situation, but . . ."

So in the final result, is he never going to treat me as anything more than a childhood friend? Will he never think of me as a grown woman? She felt bitter. The sun beat down mercilessly, and in a clump of bushes the katydids shrilled incessantly. The two listened to the clamor without saying a word.

After Shūhei had left for the station, his mother asked her husband, "Dear, when is his next leave day?"

"I'm not sure, probably in about another month."

"Why do you think he wanted to be an airplane pilot? There surely are lots of other things he could do that aren't so dangerous."

"He's doing it for his country."

Sachiko listened to one side as the couple conversed, closing her eyes and continuing to pray: *Please don't let Shūhei be sent to the battlefield . . .*

In the fall, the training became increasingly demanding, and during this time a number of casualties emerged. One day while Shūhei and his squadron were studying, outside the window there was a sudden explosion, as though something had struck the earth, and they saw black smoke billowing into the sky. When the student cadets raced outside, they saw a crashed plane, engulfed in flames.

Oddly enough, the men felt hardly any fear. What they felt was, *So these kinds of things can happen, too.*

Wordlessly, they returned to their classroom and continued their studies.

In September they began training in formation flying. Flying behind the first plane, which carried their instructor, a thought that had occurred to Shūhei when he had been on board a formation flight for the first time suddenly popped back into his head. Back then, it had seemed like a dream that he might someday be able to fly a plane solo, but now it was a reality. Once he became accustomed to the perilous formation flying, Shūhei surprised himself by how unexpectedly daring he felt.

Around this same time, someone got wind of the news that they would be leaving this base and joining another aviation squadron. Confirming that rumor, in the latter half of the month the type of plane that each man would be flying was announced. Shūhei was assigned a battleship attack bomber. The men were not yet allowed to inform their families of their whereabouts.

A letter from Shūhei at around this time—

Sachiko,

Sorry I haven't written for a long while. Thank you for that time you came to see me. It never occurred to me that you might visit, so I was surprised, so surprised that I regret we weren't able to talk more leisurely.

Since then, my abilities as a pilot have improved, though I'm not yet at the top of the game, but I might be about a third of the way toward becoming a great pilot. Of course, it's still possible to cause an accident by slacking off mentally, so tension continues to pile on top of tension, but thanks to that tension I feel a sense of satisfaction that I never felt in the civilian world.

I did want to talk to you more when you were here, but now that I think about it, it probably turned out the way it was supposed to.

Our instructors keep telling us that a man who would be a
soldier must not have his heart drawn away by feelings of
kindness and affection, that we have to simplify our lives and
our surroundings, and that we must not form relationships
beyond those that are essential.

Since I've been here, I started believing that they're right.

I haven't forgotten the memories of my young days that I
spent with you. I will never forget the many ways you
befriended me when I was in the civilian world. But now
that I'm a soldier, I've convinced myself that my relationship
with you must not turn into anything beyond what it was
then.

So, Sachiko, if you find a good man, please marry him.

It was early October when she received this letter, and as she read it Sachiko began to weep loudly.

She was grieved by his exceedingly self-willed declaration. He had one-sidedly made up his mind and was forcing his decision on her—he had been the same way when they had played together as children, and she realized that that part of his nature still had not changed.

Selfish child! She couldn't understand his insensitivity, always twisting her feelings to his own advantage, and thinking only of his own convenience when he wrote, "If you find a good man, please marry him."

That night she took all of his letters from her chocolate box and tried rereading them over and over again. Her eyes swept across each line so many times she could almost have memorized them. As she read in order, starting with his earliest letters up to his current one, her feelings of anger gradually subsided, accompanied by a torrent of new tears. Shūhei had not written a single word about his true feelings in his letters. Things that were somehow disconnected from his real feelings had forced him to write those letters the way he had. And wasn't it possible that the self-serving content of this most recent letter didn't represent his true feelings, either? Wasn't it possible that his real feelings lay elsewhere?

Just as a drowning person grasps for a straw, Sachiko clung to this thought. Waking and sleeping, waking and sleeping until dawn, she kept thinking, *That could be it, I'm sure that could be it!*

She could hardly wait for Sunday to come. She was only able to see Shūhei's mother at mass at the Ōura Church. His mother was Sachiko's only source for knowing what Shūhei was doing right now.

That Sunday—

Following the mass, Shūhei's mother whispered to her, "Sachiko, he isn't in Izumi anymore. But you can't say anything about this to anybody else."

"Then, where . . . ?"

His mother sadly shook her head. Sachiko couldn't tell whether she didn't know or whether she was forbidden to talk about it, but she couldn't ask anything further.

But she couldn't shake the insistent feeling that Shūhei had been moved to a location even more distant than Izumi, and that a deep gulf she increasingly could not traverse had opened between them.

That day she descended the slope from the church with her head hung low. How many times had she climbed up and down this slope since childhood? It was here that she had met Brother Zeno and Father Kolbe. It was here on an Easter Sunday, as petals from the cherry blossoms danced in the wind, that she had come to receive her first communion. It was this slope she had climbed with her family, seeing her breath each time she exhaled, to attend Christmas Eve mass.

Many long years of memories of her times with Shūhei clung to every step along this road.

As she gazed at the ocean, Sachiko wondered what she might do now in an attempt to bury the deep gulf that had been created against her will between herself and Shūhei. Praying, praying for Shūhei—nothing would come from that alone. Since Shūhei was undergoing cruel training, she wanted to be able to experience the same sort of suffering herself.

That day, she made the decision to quit her comfortable job at the rationing bureau . . .

✳ ✳ ✳

That day, the student cadets set aside their normal flight activities and listened to a description of a kamikaze Special Attack Unit[1] from an instructor who had just returned from Clark Air Base in the Philippines.

In the fighting to defend the Philippines, both sides had sustained tremendous casualties, but the Japanese Navy, who were the inferior force, had developed a strategy of using suicide pilots who flew special attack planes, which were the brainchild of Vice Admiral Ōnishi, supreme commander of the First Carrier Division.

In the latter part of October, eleven suicide bombers had taken off from the Davao and Mabalacat airfields and from Cebu Base and attacked their targets: American battleships.

At the time of the launch, the instructor who was describing this to the cadets had been at the Mabalacat airfield, where he watched the departure of the kamikaze Special Attack Unit.

Because of his wounds, Commander Ōnishi had walked with a cane, his body also supported by his deputy so that he could

---

1 At this initial stage of the suicide attacks, the characters that are now customarily read "kamikaze" were pronounced "shinpū," but I have chosen to use the more familiar pronunciation to avoid confusion.

witness the attack group, led by Lieutenant Seki. At 7:30 a.m., five of the planes selected to act as "body attack" planes flew in formation and vanished into the blue sky, escorted by four Zero fighters assigned to protect the suicide bombers so that they could safely reach their targets and subsequently confirm their effectiveness in battle.

To the east of Leyte Island, the attack force located an American battleship unit, comprising aircraft carriers, cruisers, and destroyers. The four Zero fighters engaged American fighter planes while the suicide bombers led by Lieutenant Seki sank an aircraft carrier and an escort cruiser and set another carrier on fire.

As they listened to this narrative from the instructor, Shūhei and the other student cadets in the classroom fell deadly silent. The silence was not simply the result of hearing this story of heroism; it was also caused by their realization of the inferiority of the Japanese Navy that had been forced to resort to such tactics.

We may end up flying those kamikaze planes ourselves. Shūhei wondered whether the instructor had canceled their flight training and taken the opportunity to tell them about these planes as a means to firm up their resolution in advance of imminent orders.

Once again he was forced to consider the contradiction between the situation in which he was now placed and the Christian faith in which he had been raised. Indelibly etched in Shūhei's heart was the church's teaching that one cannot of one's own volition cut off a life that God had granted.

So when your comrades board their special attack planes will you use the teachings of the church as a shield and end up as the only survivor? Don't you just make use of religious doctrine when it's convenient for you? A voice was whispering this mercilessly in Shūhei's ears. It was, to put a name on it, the voice of his superiors, the voice of the nation of Japan. *In the end you may simply wind up as fate dictates. When you enlisted, because of your struggles you entered the navy without any sort of confidence, didn't you? Besides which, now you're being trained to blow up battleships. Even the feeblest kind of resistance is hopeless. You're simply going to have to accept what happens.*

Perhaps it would be much easier to forget all about the teachings of the church—"Thou shalt not kill," "Suicide is forbidden"—and approach this with the same attitude that the other student cadets had. But Shūhei knew full well that this dilemma could not be resolved so simply.

Because of the way the instructor had related the story, he gave the cadets the impression that Lieutenant Seki, who had started out as an ordinary sailor himself, had led the very first kamikaze Special Attack Unit, so Shūhei and the other student recruits never learned the truth. In reality, the very first group, which included two officers who had started out as student cadets, had boarded their suicide bombers as a Special Attack Unit only four days before Lieutenant Seki and his unit had died in glory like falling blossoms.

It is not known whether officers who had started out their military careers as ordinary sailors and then worked their way up through the ranks did not want to grant student cadets the honor of being part of a Special Attack Unit. However, one theory maintains that these officers, who had graduated from the Etajima Naval Academy, regarded those who rose from the ranks of student cadets as inferior to those such as themselves who had started as regular sailors.[2] Some claim that student cadets were

---

2 Endō here has identified a significant problem in the Japanese military during World War II: the jealousy of uneducated "regular sailors" who despised the student cadets who had attended college. This conflict between country/ city and uneducated/educated explains a good deal of the physical abuse that characterized the treatment of younger, better-educated recruits in all the branches of the Japanese military.

assigned to perilous locations at the very front of the battle lines as disposable goods, while those who attended the Naval Academy, even if they were posted to the same kind of locations, were posted to the commander's headquarters or as a headquarters staff officer and were not directly exposed to the flames of war.

Shūhei and his squadron were told at every opportunity, "You student cadets have sullied the honorable traditions of the navy!" and they were subject to stern correction. Sometimes they also received humiliating punishments.

When they had completed their training in formation flying, special solo flight training was conducted. They learned such maneuvers as vertical turns, stalled rolls, aileron rolls, climbing rolls, and spins. They were also trained in night flight, with the emphasis on landing and takeoff. It was a real challenge to master night flying, which, since it commenced at nightfall, relied solely on red and green lantern lights. The slightest error resulted in the instructor on board beating them mercilessly with tightly clenched fists.

This training was referred to as the mid-level curriculum. In the autumn of the year, just as they finished the sixty-hour mid-level curriculum, a shortage developed in the supplies of gasoline necessary to fly planes, and flight operations were canceled; until they were resumed, Shūhei and his squadron passed the time maintaining the airport and studying in their classrooms.

They were told that promotion and graduation ceremonies would be held on December 25, but ten days before that date, a plane being flown by one of their classmates was involved in an accident that occurred during night flight training. Flames erupted from the left engine and the plane stalled and plunged into a grove of pine trees. The student cadet and all the other men on board were severely burned, but they were transported to a hospital and survived.

On December 25, the members of Shūhei's class were promoted to ensign. Coincidentally, it was also Christmas Day.

At 9:00, immediately following the raising of the battleship flag and the ritual of worshipping the emperor from afar, the student cadets were once again immediately called back into service, this time as advanced student cadets. During these ceremonies, Shūhei was thinking back to Christmas Day two years before. A mass was held at the Ōura Church the night of December 24. During the mass, the priest of the church had said that, for a long while, Christmas had taught people the joy of peace. And he said that the purity of Christmas Eve conveys the hope that someday there will be a world in which there is no hatred between people, no hatred between countries.

But being part of this aviation squadron, where again today the roar of airplane engines could be heard across the skies, Shūhei began to wonder whether this memory from the past had actually been a part of his own life's experience . . .

21

AND SACHIKO . . .

WHILE SHŪHEI WAS receiving mid-level training . . .

Like other members of the Women's Volunteer Corps, Sachiko worked at her job wearing black work pants and a headband that read "Absolute Victory."

At this factory, between the sounds of the crane that moved along the ceiling and the rumble of rotating machinery, a worker had to speak in a very loud voice or conversation was impossible.

In a temporary office built right in the middle of the thunderous roar of the factory, Sachiko's job was to create graphs displaying the number of machines in actual operation and the inventory of warehouse parts, and to prepare a list of parts materials, but on occasion she would also be found working at the lathe, after a worker instructed her how to use it.

"You had such an easy job at the rationing bureau, why would you want to work at a factory?" her mother said with an exasperated look when her daughter returned home exhausted.

In the latter part of August, when a law was passed requiring members of the Women's Volunteer Corps to perform labor service, women who were able to find employment at a place such as the rationing bureau where Sachiko had worked were considered the most fortunate of all. Sachiko's mother could not understand why her daughter would deliberately forsake her own good fortune.

The factory where she worked, located in Urakami, produced parts. It was in an area where a variety of factories operated by Mitsubishi were strung out all the way to the Urakami Station.

Initially her exhaustion at the end of the working day was so extreme she felt dizzy. Her nerves were nearly frayed from performing manual labor for the first time in her life and from the deafening noise of the factory. But after about ten days, she slowly grew accustomed to her surroundings.

"You really work hard!" one young woman said, impressed by Sachiko's diligence. She identified herself as Katō Hiroe from the village of Kurosaki.

Sachiko merely smiled and replied, "I suppose."

She was well aware that Shūhei was enduring hardships far greater than the work she was doing. The thought made her feel somewhat closer to him. As a result, boarding a crowded bus from Nagasaki Station early in the morning to go to the factory actually brought her joy.

Additionally, she was able to work on the outskirts of Urakami, which was the village of her ancestors and the place where her grandmother Mitsu had been born, as well as the hometown of Kiku. Of course, Urakami now looked almost nothing like it had when her grandmother was a young girl. But the river flowed in the same location as before, and place names such as Yamazato-machi, Hon'o-machi, Uenshuku, and Shitan-shuku summoned up memories of stories her grandmother had told her as a child.

During her lunch break at the factory, she sometimes climbed the slope leading to the Urakami Cathedral, which was located in Hon'o-machi. There, she would recall what Granny had told her about the origin of the cathedral.

"After making the long journey home from our places of ex-
ile, we discovered that our houses and fields were a total wreck.
But, with our drinking water being only what sprang up after a
terrible storm and with nothing but potatoes to eat, we worked
ourselves to the bone and saved up money and built the church
with our own hands. That's the Urakami Cathedral."

Just as the flesh and shell of a snail adhere to each other, Sachiko and the Ōura Church were tightly jointed together, even
up to the present day. The bond was so strong that Sachiko could
not even think of herself without that church. So she was able
to understand how important a place this Urakami Cathedral
was to the locals.

The Urakami Cathedral was much larger and far more imposing than the Ōura Church. Compared to the starkly white
Ōura Church, which, if anything, was feminine in nature, the
Urakami Cathedral, made of brick, stood solidly at the top of a
hill like a burly man with his muscular arms folded.

Surrounding the hill, a few farmhouses and groves and grave-
yards reminiscent of the past still remained. Looking at those
farmhouses, Sachiko contemplated the youthful days of her aunt
and Kiku. She wondered whether Kiku had walked along this
road.

Katō Hiroe struck up a conversation with Sachiko, who disappeared every lunch break. "You're lucky. Your house is close
by, so you can go home at lunch time." Hiroe seemed to be under
the impression that Sachiko returned home to have lunch.

"No, during lunch break I take walks around Urakami. My
ancestors lived at Urakami a long time ago."

"So then . . ." Hiroe cried out happily, "you're a Catholic?"

"That's right."

"So am I! My gramps talked a lot about Urakami. The Kirishitans at Kurosaki had to stay in hiding for a long time, and we're
Catholic too."

Following this conversation, the two quickly became friends.

"When I walk around Urakami, I think a lot about a woman named Kiku," Sachiko confided to her new friend, as though she were giving her a glimpse into a secret jewelry box. Then she told Hiroe everything she knew about Kiku's life.

"So that really happened to her. . . ." Hiroe gave a deep sigh. "I wish I could have a love affair like that. But with a face like mine, no man's going to give me even a second glance. So, Sachiko, do you have somebody you love?"

Sachiko blushed and nodded faintly, to which Hiroe, her eyes flashing, exclaimed, "Wow! What does he do?"

"He's in the naval air corps. So I'm really worried about him. The training for the aviation corps is really intense. Every day I worry that he might be in danger."

"I'll bet you do," Hiroe nodded.

Hiroe lived in the women's dormitory at the factory, so Sachiko invited her to her own house the following Sunday. Although they had little to offer, she wanted Hiroe to have a chance to eat something that at least had some nourishment in it.

"Would you like to see my treasures?" After dinner, Sachiko privately showed Hiroe her chocolate box.

Of course, she didn't tell Hiroe about the content of any of Shūhei's letters, but when she showed her the poem (after admitting, "No matter how I look at it, I can hardly call it skillful") that Shūhei had sent from Tokyo, Hiroe gave an envious, heartfelt sigh and said, "How wonderful!"

Sachiko was pleased at the praise directed toward Shūhei's poem and asked, "Do you really think so?"

"Really wonderful!"

"So you think this poem is that wonderful?"

"I'm not talking about the poem. I think it's wonderful that you have someone who will send you a love letter." The look on her face made Hiroe appear as though she were in a dream.

Hiroe, who was from Kurosaki, told Sachiko all about her village, which had mountains behind it and faced the ocean. There were many Kakure—hidden Christians—in her village who had been there for a very long time. They believed that the unique religion they had inherited from their ancestors, which was intermingled with Buddhism and Shinto, was true Christianity. Hiroe said that no matter how often the Catholic priests talked with them or tried to persuade them to be rebaptized, they stubbornly shook their heads and persistently refused.

"That's why the relationship in my village between the Kakure and the Catholics is so bad. We even celebrate Christmas and Easter separately. The Kakure, using an old calendar, celebrate Easter but they call it the Flower Festival . . ."[1]

Sachiko had also heard that this was the area where Father de Rotz[2] had performed his missionary labors. Father de Rotz, who had ministered at the Ōura Church many years ago alongside Father Petitjean, had taught agricultural methods in many fishing villages, and as a physician he had healed the sick. As a result he was loved by both the fishermen and the peasants.

Hiroe was a fan of the singers Takada Kōkichi and Ōtomo Ryūtarō and knew a lot of popular songs. In Sachiko's room, she sang a catalogue of songs such as "Nagasaki March," "Tokyo Dance," and "Vroom, Vroom, Fighting Eagle." After she had finished singing "Aizen Wig," she was mesmerized, as though intoxicated on her own singing, and said, "I'm so jealous of you, Sat-chan. Having a boyfriend and all. I'm always praying for Lord Jesus and the Blessed Mary to hurry and introduce me to

---

1 Ironic, since the Hanamatsuri, the Flower Festival in Japan, commemorates the birth of Sakyamuni, the historical Buddha.

2 Father Marc Marie de Rotz (1840–1914) was a French priest who went to Japan in 1869 and lived out his life there, ministering to the poor and with his own funds building factories where the peasant women produced textiles, macaroni, bread, and soy sauce.

a boyfriend, but nobody has shown up yet. I wonder if Lord Jesus and the Blessed Mary disapprove of love," she muttered with a serious face.

Sachiko stifled her amusement and said encouragingly, "I don't think they do. I'm sure they'll provide someone for you."

Sachiko thought Hiroe was wonderful. She didn't have a malicious bone in her body, and her face, tanned by the sun and the salty ocean breezes, always displayed a broad, affable smile. Watching her as she sang popular songs, Sachiko thought that a young woman like this was certain to go to heaven.

Sachiko walked Hiroe to the bus stop when it was time for her to leave. Along the way, Hiroe asked, "So, do you still get letters from your boyfriend in the air corps?"

Sachiko shook her head. The city of Nagasaki that night was dreary, as though drained of all energy, and since the issuance of strict blackout orders, the houses were as dark as death.

B-29s attacked Tokyo starting in late November, and at Ōmura even tighter restrictions were imposed after a large number of students doing volunteer labor were killed in the October air raid. Shūhei sent no word, and 1944 was winding to a close in less than a month.

Christmas that year was a lonely event at every church, and because of the blackout restrictions, midnight mass was canceled.

January, too, was bleak. Sachiko's father was able to obtain about two liters of his favorite sake in January, but thereafter only a little over half a liter was rationed out.

Although Nagasaki had thus far been spared, beginning about a month earlier many regions of Japan, starting with Tokyo, were mercilessly bombed by B-29s. Some said that almost every neighborhood in Tokyo had been bombarded.

However, following a mass in late January, Sachiko received unexpectedly happy news from Shūhei's mother.

"Sat-chan, Shūhei says he's going to get two days leave starting February 10 and is coming back to Nagasaki."

Sachiko's face turned crimson from joy and embarrassment. Largely because she had been so sad that he had not sent her a single postcard, her feelings of happiness came flowing like a fountain from every part of her body.

What made her the happiest was what Shūhei's mother then said: "When he gets back to Nagasaki, I'm sure Shūhei will want to see you before anyone else."

Sachiko wasted no time giving the good news to Hiroe at the factory.

"Terrific!" Hiroe was as pleased as if this were happening to herself, and every day thereafter when she bumped into Sachiko she would count on her fingers and say, "It won't be long," or "Just ten more days."

"You have to introduce him to me, too," Hiroe insisted, and Sachiko promised she would.

It was not surprising that, the night before Shūhei was to return home, Sachiko's happiness kept her from sleep. But she couldn't neglect her work at the factory, so she said to her mother "Mom, I may be a little late coming home tonight."

With a suspicious look, her mother asked "Why?"

"Well . . . Shūhei's coming back to Nagasaki after a long absence so I thought I'd go say hello." Her answer was daring and honest.

Sarcastically, her mother said, "Listen, I haven't given my consent to anything. What exactly are you to Shūhei?" But Sachiko still remembered the warm affection her mother had displayed when she went to see Shūhei at the Sasebo naval base.

Sachiko worked until noon, until finally Hiroe had to press her to leave at once. "I often use this as an excuse: just tell them that you have a headache."

Sachiko lied to the assistant manager and got a permission slip to leave work early.

She hobbled as though in terrible pain until she passed through the factory gate. Between the gate and the bus stop her pace naturally picked up. Before long she was scrambling toward the bus stop.

"As though there were no war. . . ." While she waited for the bus, she muttered to herself the poem that Shūhei had written.

When she opened the door to the house at Kotohira-machi, Shūhei, wearing a splash-pattern kimono, slowly emerged. There was no question that he was more powerfully built now, but without his military uniform, he still bore some of the look of the bookish youth from his school days.

"Oh!" He raised one hand almost reverently and said, "My mom said you'd be coming, so we waited for you to start lunch." He grinned, displaying his white teeth.

In the parlor, however, sat a number of his relatives who had come to see Shūhei, making it impossible for the two of them to talk alone.

"I really never thought that someone like me could become a pilot," Shūhei said as though mystified, inviting a laugh from everyone.

"How about you sink some of the enemy's aircraft carriers with your bombs?" one drunken relative crowed, "No need to worry about us here on the home front. But would you boys be kind enough to shoot down all them B-29s? All these air raid sirens are disturbing my sleep."

"What's going on with Japan's airplanes? They're letting the enemy bomb Japan at will."

Shūhei looked up and shouted angrily, "Listen, just hold on a little longer! Then I'll be whipping across the skies and making it so you can all sleep peacefully!"

His comic remark once again filled the parlor with laughter, but Sachiko stole a glance at Shūhei's face. It was obvious to her that Shūhei was forcing himself to put on an act. She couldn't

bear looking at him knowing that he had to suppress the things
he so earnestly wanted to express.

Soon she made her way quietly to the kitchen and said to
Shūhei's mother, "I . . . It's getting dark, so I'd better go home.
Thank you so much." She felt as though it was best to leave early
so that Shūhei and his parents could have some time alone that
evening.

"Wait, Sat-chan, you're leaving?" Shūhei, who had been in the
bathroom, ran after her. "Why . . . ?"

"Nagasaki's more deserted than it used to be. If I don't go
home early, I'll get in trouble."

"Should I walk you home?"

"Of course not. You've got all these guests here to see you."

Shūhei glanced over his shoulder and listened to the laughter
from the parlor. Then he said, "Then, Sachiko, can we meet at
2 o'clock tomorrow? At that house." "That house," of course,
meant the Western-style home behind the church.

"Why should we meet? I think it might be better if we don't
see each other anymore. Childhood friends don't keep on meeting," she said emphatically and then fled outside.

And yet she knew, after all was said and done, that she would
be going to that house tomorrow. She felt certain Shūhei would
be there as well.

On a day unusually warm for February, she went to the garden of the deserted house. Shūhei was on the veranda, which
was surrounded by walls with peeling plaster. He was dressed,
as he had been yesterday, in a kimono, and the scarf around his
shoulders caught the bright sunlight.

"I figured you'd come." When he saw Sachiko, a teasing look
glinted in his eyes. "What was wrong with you yesterday? You
were like a blowfish in distress."

"A blowfish in—?"

"You puff up and get all huffy very quickly."

"Well, I mean . . . You haven't written me for a very long time, and besides . . . in your last letter . . ."

"We can't write much of anything in letters since they have to pass through the censors. And to be honest, things aren't like they used to be, our training is so intense that I haven't even been able to write my parents more than once a month . . ."

"But still . . . that's terrible, though. Why do they forbid pilots to write a simple letter?"

Shūhei looked at her grimly in reaction to the embittered expression on her face. "Sat-chan, let's not talk about the air corps today. Yesterday those people made me talk about it until I was sick of it. Just for today I'd like to go back to being the young man I was a long time ago. I want to be the Shūhei who read poetry here with you."

Sachiko could not complain or grumble at such a suggestion.

"Sat-chan, listen to this." Just as he had three years earlier, Shūhei opened the book that rested on his lap and began to read:

My love,
Think of it, of that land—
The joy of living there, just we two.
There we will love in peace;
Let us love, then let us die . . .

"That's by the poet Baudelaire. It's called 'Invitation to a Voyage.'"

"'Invitation to a Voyage'?"

"Right. . . . An invitation . . . to a voyage . . ."

His eyes closed, Shūhei softly enunciated the words "invitation to a voyage" as though he were muttering a sincere prayer. He kept his eyes shut and said nothing for a brief while.

Sachiko sensed that he had read her this poem in connection with the future that lay ahead for the two of them. Had he perhaps, in place of his letters that passed through censorship, deliberately chosen this poem to express his own feelings . . . ?

Shūhei lifted his face and abruptly said, "Sat-chan. I really love this poem. . . . I want us to always remember this poem."

"Always? What do you mean?"

"To help us remember today."

Sachiko's heart suddenly began to pound. It was an ominous, unanticipated drumming.

"Shū-chan, surely you're not . . . you're not being transferred again, are you?" she cried. "This time to somewhere far away from Japan?"

"Transferred?" Shūhei looked surprised, then gave a strained smile. "No. I'm not being transferred."

"If you're not being transferred, then what's all this formal nonsense about creating memories?!"

"Damn! You're really being strange today, Sat-chan."

Still, Sachiko's intuition convinced her that Shūhei was hiding something from her. "Shū-chan, why won't you be truthful with me?" She sounded bitter. "Are you just trying to be kind to me?"

"No, I'm not."

"Then why have you decided to hate me and won't tell me? It would be kinder, if you truly hate me, to just come out and say so. . . . That would be more like you than writing things like, 'Let's just spend time together like brother and sister,' or ' If you find a good man, you should marry him.'"

His arms folded, Shūhei smiled in amusement. "Hey, could you just be quiet? I didn't ask you to come here so we could argue. To begin with, there's no reason at this point to hate you."

"Then you love me?"

"Yes, I love you."

"Then promise me you won't ever write anything like that to me again . . ."

Shūhei did not respond, but a shadow of pain appeared between his brows. In his situation he could not tell the truth even to a young woman to whom he had just clearly expressed his love.

"Sat-chan." The look on his face was that of an older brother remonstrating with a much younger sister. "I can't promise that. You couldn't realize this, but training for members of the air corps isn't a game. Pilots more experienced at flying than me have made mistakes and died in accidents. Some of my classmates have been seriously injured. We have no idea when we might be sent to the battlefield. A man like that . . . he doesn't have the right to promise . . . love or marriage."

Sachiko could not think of anything to say.

"You understand, don't you, Sat-chan?"

As he spoke, Sachiko stared at Shūhei, her eyes opened wide. Her eyes grew moist and cloudy, then drops of silvery tears trickled down her cheeks.

"Don't die!" She cried in a strained voice. "Stay alive. Come back!"

She threw herself at Shūhei's chest like a bouncing ball and pressed her face against his body. "Come back. I'll be waiting. I'll wait as long as it takes."

Her soft hair was fragrant. Shūhei inhaled the aroma as he held her.

With her eyes closed, Sachiko felt the strength in his arms. She would give him everything if he were to ask for it now. This was Shūhei, so she would do anything he wanted. It no longer mattered to her whether her mother or the priests would be angry with her.

Shūhei pressed his face strongly against her uplifted face.

In that moment, a scene was revived before his eyes, something that had happened to him and the other student cadets a week before.

That day, after the cadets heard a lecture on wireless homing guidance, their instructor casually launched into a lengthy report.

He began with a candid description of the battle situation in the Philippines. In total contradiction to the announcements from military headquarters, Shūhei and his comrades learned for the first time that the Battle of Leyte in October of the previous year had ended in total defeat for the Japanese Army, and that the attempted strike by the navy had also failed, resulting in the loss of the main force of the Japanese combined fleet.

It was as they anticipated, but now they heard directly from their instructor's mouth, "Japan has lost more than half of the battleships we have been relying on."

An indescribably oppressive air encircled everyone in the room at those words. No one even coughed.

"At this point the enemy controls both the sea and the air. The proof of that lies in the fact that B-29s are dropping their bombs wherever they please without any resistance. What I'm going to tell you now falls under the category of secret information. In the air raids on Ōmura in October, our navy lost many of our most advanced fighter planes. In December, the aircraft carrier Junyō was hit by torpedoes from enemy submarines a mere fifty miles from Nagasaki and has sustained major damage."

Initially it seemed odd to them that at this juncture their instructor was revealing to his cadets these highly classified matters.

The instructor dispassionately described the hopeless situation to them. His manner of speaking was so matter-of-fact that it had the reverse effect of gradually increasing the anxiety of his men.

"In order to break out of this position of weakness, the navy has established a new Fifth Air Fleet, concentrating all the forces in their possession and firming up their determination to regain the upper hand with a single stroke. But success will rely to a great extent on the special attack forces that we have talked about on many occasions. I suspect you probably have some sense of this, but during the battles to retain the Philippines, many of the men from the thirteenth class of student cadets participated in the kamikaze Special Attack Unit with remarkable military success."

The men began to realize what their instructor was now trying to say. The room was utterly silent.

"This is neither compulsory nor an order. Make no mistake: this will be entirely voluntary for each of you. I would like any of you who wish to volunteer to be part of the Special Attack Unit to raise your hands."

The instructor peered intently at his men. The silence was so painful it was difficult to endure. One man raised his hand. Then another three men raised their hands. Finally another four did the same.

Then Shūhei closed his eyes and did just as they had done . . .

That was the scene, like recalling a wasteland desiccated by winter, that was bleakly revived in Shūhei's mind when he pressed his lips against Sachiko's. "This is neither compulsory nor an order," the instructor had said, but after a moment of hesitation Shūhei had raised his hand. He had his reasons . . .

✳ ✳ ✳

"We should be going, Sat-chan." Shūhei stood, hoping to drive from his mind that scene of secrecy that neither his parents nor anyone else yet knew about.

When the two started through the opening behind the deserted house to go out onto the road, as they always had . . .

A military policeman came walking up the hill. Coincidentally enough, it was exactly the same situation as three years earlier.

For a year now, it was not at all unusual to run into a military policeman here in Yamate-machi. Security had tightened rapidly since the antiaircraft artillery corps headquarters was set up in Minami Yamate-machi, and aerial searchlights were located on Mount Konpira, Mount Inasa, Mount Hoshitori, Mount Kazagashira, and Mount Tōhakkei.

The military policeman was, of course, not the same man who had beaten Shūhei in the past. But his face, with its strong protruding cheekbones, shared many characteristics with the earlier man. And his piercing gaze, after he came to a stop and stared at the two emerging from the abandoned house, was identical to that of the earlier policeman.

"Stop right there!" he called out to Shūhei and Sachiko. "What were you doing in there?"

Shūhei pointed to the paperback poetry collection that he had earlier handed to Sachiko and replied, "We were reading a book."

"Reading a book? This house . . . does it belong to you?"

"It doesn't."

"In an abandoned house that doesn't belong to you . . . you were reading a book, were you? Dressed like that?"

Sachiko was wearing work pants, but Shūhei was dressed in a kimono. By this time, it was highly unusual to see a man out into the streets of Nagasaki without puttees wrapped around his legs.

"What's the book?"

Shūhei looked at the man with defiance in his eyes, thrust out his chest and barked, "It's a collection of poetry." His voice, as he uttered that one sentence, was filled with the resentment and sadness of that day when he had been the victim of senseless violence in this same location . . .

"Poetry? So you were reading poetry with a woman in this abandoned house, were you? In this sloppy outfit."

"Is there something wrong with reading poetry?"

"What did you say? Listen, you bastard, what's your occupation?"

"I'm a student."

"A student where?" The policeman approached the two and planted his feet, preparing for a fight.

Slowly, emphasizing each word, Shūhei said, "I . . . I am Ensign Kōda, a student in special training with the naval air corps."

The policeman's body instantly snapped to attention.

"I have come back to Nagasaki on special leave. I won't be telling you the name of my base because it's secret. However, if you wish to take responsibility, I'll give you the name."

"You have my sincere apologies." The policeman saluted and retreated two or three steps.

"Sat-chan, let's go."

Trembling, Sachiko set off behind Shūhei. She could feel, to an almost painful degree, the gaze of the military policeman, still harboring suspicions, behind her. But Shūhei's body had never seemed as imposing and dependable as it did now.

As they approached the church, Sachiko asked, "So you're not a student cadet?" There was still a shrillness in her voice.

"Why do you ask?"

"You just said that you're a student cadet in special training."

"It's pretty much the same thing," Shūhei muttered, staring forward.

✳ ✳ ✳

The following day, Shūhei returned to his unit. Sachiko mingled unobtrusively among his relatives who had come to see him off at the station. Just as when he had gone to enlist in the Navy Second Division at Sasebo, the dilapidated train car in which he was riding creaked and surged forward, slowly moving past the platform.

Sachiko said her farewells at the station and headed straight to the factory. The assistant manager seemed to have heard from Hiroe the reason Sachiko had taken two days off work and he said nothing other than, "You made sure to see him off, didn't you?"

Hiroe, who had been lying in wait, dragged Sachiko behind a noisy machine and asked, "How was it?"

With just one exception, Sachiko sketched out the events of the last two days for her new friend. The part she left out . . . was her first kiss with Shūhei.

Sachiko crouched down beside the machine and wrote out the poem that Shūhei had taught her so that she could have Hiroe also memorize it:

My love,
Think of it, of that land—
The joy of living there, just we two.
There we will love in peace;
Let us love, then let us die . . .

Here in the factory filled with deafening sounds from the transport cranes, she inscribed the poem, which hadn't struck her all that powerfully when she first heard it. But now each word, each line of the poem felt to her as though it was emitting light.

"Your boyfriend taught you this poem, didn't he, Sat-chan?" Hiroe seemed to be looking far off into the distance. "I want to have a boyfriend like that," she sighed.

Sachiko was enveloped in feelings of happiness she could not put into words. Since that day she had spent with Shūhei, the loneliness of last year, when she had no letters from him, along with her resulting paranoia, had been swept away.

On the train platform, Shūhei had said to his parents and Sachiko, "I'm going to be very busy from now on, so when there isn't a letter from me, please consider that good news."

✳ ✳ ✳

Not long after Shūhei returned to his unit, more than a thousand carrier-based planes launched from a US mechanized unit surged like waves over Tokyo. In the January 27 air raid, a section of the downtown Shitamachi area was reduced to ashes. According to reports, just as in the previous air raid, the gigantic B-29s floated slowly across the skies of Tokyo for an hour and a half. It was also rumored that the number of Japanese fighter planes sent on a counterattack was minimal.

"It won't be long before Nagasaki is a burned-out ruin, too," Sachiko's father grumbled as he read the newspaper. "We started a hopeless war."

On February 4, the leaders of United States, the United Kingdom, and the Soviet Union held a conference at Yalta, but the Japanese public had no idea of the enormous significance of that meeting.

There was nothing Sachiko could do other than pray each morning for Shūhei. Without fail, she set out for mass at the Ōura Church in the darkness of early morning with temperatures still frigid. One such morning she again noticed the elderly woman who was probably a soldier's mother performing her ritual of one hundred steps at the Shinto shrine along her way.

Sachiko stopped and studied the woman for a short time. She felt an indescribable sorrow for this soldier's mother, and realized that her own situation was the same.

At this stage of the war, virtually everyone, including Sachiko, had a clear awareness that Japan was approaching annihilation.

Even when she went to the factory, materials were in short supply. More than half the machines had stopped running, so the workers were enlisted to dig air raid shelters. Sachiko and the other women had been given the grandiose name of Women's Volunteer Corps, but some of the female workers living in the factory dormitory, including Katō Hiroe, grew faint and collapsed from hunger and exhaustion as they worked.

Following successive days of air raids in Tokyo, US forces landed on Iwo Jima in a series of unbroken assaults. It came as a terrible shock. Territory that heretofore had belonged to Japan had finally become a battleground. A grim atmosphere hovered over the factory on the day that news arrived.

"But they say that right now Mitsubishi is producing a new weapon, so we'll be okay." Once again, Sachiko's younger brother Mitsuo voiced his confidence that the new weapon would reverse Japan's weakened position in a single stroke, but to Sachiko, Japan appeared like a man who has been punched and punched again and is on the verge of breathing his last.

It seemed, however, that Mitsuo's claim was not a total fabrication. There were workers at Sachiko's factory who insisted that a wondrous new weapon had been built at the Mitsubishi shipyard, and that the war situation would be reversed in March. The weapon actually was a five-man submarine which was designed so that, like the special attack planes, it could smash itself against enemy battleships.

But even after the highly anticipated month of March arrived, there was no change in the war situation; in fact, on the seventeenth day of that month, Iwo Jima fell, with twenty-three thousand Japanese soldiers annihilated.

Only nature had not changed from normal years, delivering warm breezes. A springlike aroma could be sensed even along the ruined streets of Nagasaki, and shoots on the willow trees turned greener each day.

Just as warmth began to offer a small reprieve to the frayed emotions of the citizens of Nagasaki, twenty B-29s unexpectedly attacked Sasebo and Ōmura.

The city of Nagasaki, where the next air raid was likely to occur, ordered compulsory evacuation of government offices and of citizens living near train stations. The majority of those ordered to evacuate streamed into the neighborhoods of Aburaki, Shiroyama, and Urakami, where Sachiko worked.

"Sat-chan, they're saying half the buildings have been destroyed in Uchinaka-machi, Yachiyo-machi, and Tsukimachi," a stunned Mitsuo came home to report. Recently he had announced that he wanted to attend the Naval Flight Academy, much to the dismay of his mother.

The cherry blossoms began to plump out.

Seeing those swelling blossoms, Sachiko naturally recalled the postcard that Shūhei had sent her the previous year. He had written that the cherry trees had blossomed even at the air corps base; as she had done with all his other communications to her, Sachiko carefully placed it in her chocolate box.

How many times had she reread those postcards?

On April 1, enemy troops landed on Okinawa. When Sachiko went to the factory on the day that piece of news arrived, dark, hopeless expressions were written across every face. Even Hiroe, normally cheerful, privately asked Sachiko, "What's going to happen with this war? Japan's going to lose, don't you think?"

A week later—

When Sachiko returned home from the factory, she was handed a thick envelope by Mitsuo, who said, "Letter for you, Sat-chan."

It was the first letter she had received from Shūhei in a long, long time.

22

REQUIEM

SHE WAS SO HAPPY.

Unlike his previous communications, which had been either a postcard or just one sheet of stationery, this envelope from Shūhei felt bulky in Sachiko's hands.

The weight of the envelope gave Sachiko the impression that, for the first time since his enlistment in the navy, he had finally written his true, honest feelings.

Once her brother left the room, Sachiko, not bothering to change out of her work clothes, took the letter from the envelope, her fingers quivering with joy. She could hear the voices of children as they played outside. Shūhei's clumsy handwriting danced across the surface of the white paper.

> *Sat-chan.*
>
> *Thank you for everything over these many years.*
>
> *Thank you for being my companion in poetry and stories for such a long time, and for spending time with me for so many years. Right now I'm thinking back over all that we shared together for so many years and relishing each moment.*
>
> *It's raining outside.*

*Tomorrow, I'll be setting out on a little journey. But
unlike the time we strolled along the Shimabara Peninsula,
this time I won't be able to invite you along.*

I enjoyed that trip very much.

How wonderful it would be if the war would end soon.

*If there had been no war, Kōda Shūhei would have become
a literary genius.*

Do you still remember that poem?

> My love,
> Think of it, of that land—
> The joy of living there, just we two.
> There we will love in peace;
> Let us love, then let us die.
> There we will find order and beauty
> And luxury and peace and joy and . . .

*P.S. Please forward the enclosed letter addressed to
Reverend Takagi at 31 Yotsuya Shinano-machi, Shinjuku-ku.
But please know that the letter is also written for you.*

Now, this time in earnest, a true goodbye.

from Kōda Shūhei

The clumsy characters resembling ants crawling across the white paper sprang up and went blurry before her eyes.

It was evening, and outside her house children were singing. When one young girl finished her song, a different girl followed and sang her own song. The songs were the same that Sachiko and her friends had sung in the same way when they were young.

Sachiko's hands that held the sheets of stationery trembled slightly.

Dear Reverend Takagi:

Forgive me for sending you this letter out of the blue. I am Ensign Kōda of the kamikaze Special Attack Unit and the National Salvation Corps.

You may not recall this, but I met you about two years ago. Do you remember a student who came into your church one evening without even requesting permission, and asked you a rather self-serving question?

That was me. I apologize once again for my rudeness back then.

Given that I met you only once, and only very briefly, I should explain that I decided to send you this letter on the day before I set off on my mission because that night you gave a little punk like me an honest answer to my question, free of any lies or deception.

Since childhood, I never once dreamed I'd become a soldier. Born and raised in Nagasaki in a Christian home, not once did I imagine a day would come when I would dress in a military uniform and head into the battlefield.

When I got swept up in this war, coerced into abandoning my studies and joining the military—I'm embarrassed to say it, but every part of me was in a state of confusion.

Part of the reason I felt so confused was that the war had forced a detour in the entire direction of my life. But something even more extreme sent my mind into turmoil. It was the fact that I somehow or other ended up being raised in a family of Christian believers.

From the time I was a child, at church I was made to recite one of the Ten Commandments, "Thou shalt not kill." The concept didn't mean anything to me as a child, but that was because I thought it was impossible that I could ever end up killing another person in my entire lifetime.

But then came the day when I found out that my beliefs were all an illusion. It was the day I learned that student draft deferments had been eliminated. Once you enter the military, there's no way of knowing when you'll be sent into battle. And you have no idea when you might end up firing a rifle at an enemy or stabbing him to death with a bayonet.

When I realized that, I panicked. I was shaken. I had no idea what I should do as a Christian believer.

But as you know, with the exception of only a small number of people, the Japanese church has been totally silent on this question. They have given me no guidance. That's one of the things I've been confused about.

In addition . . . I love literature. The reason I enrolled at Keiō University was because of my hope that, if at all possible, someday in the future I'd like to write even just one poem, just one story.

Through my reading of literature, I came to understand that every person has a life of real depth. Even if it seems like there's nothing in a person's exterior to recommend them, I learned that each person, along with their pains and sorrows and joys, has hopes and prayers that accumulate like a geological layer in the depths of their swamp-like core.

Killing a person isn't simply a matter of taking his life away. It's unconscionably wiping out that person's earnest hopes and prayers. There is no way I can do that. Even if I weren't a Christian . . .

But I wound up being drafted into the navy. There wasn't anything I could do about it. I enlisted not out of duty, but out of resignation. Not from patriotism, but from fear.

My one salvation was the fact that all the other students who had been drafted had the same kind of anxieties. And it isn't just students—it's the majority of the Japanese people.

The person who made me aware of that was a diplomat I met prior to my enlistment.

"Everyone is suffering just as you are," he told me.

But even if that is the case, it doesn't mean that my mind has been freed from all doubts. I still had to find some way to resolve the struggles in my heart.

The brutal training I received day after day became my salvation. Life as a member of a naval corps allows you almost no time to think.

Having your body driven to the point of total exhaustion—thanks to that, for a time after my enlistment I didn't have even a moment to agonize over anything.

Thinking, or suffering over unnecessary things—they say that a soldier who does that is too entrenched in the outside world.

Even so, the dilemmas deep within my mind didn't just evaporate. Sometimes they'd suddenly raise their heads and stab at my heart. If I were to list out those dilemmas, here's what it would look like:

1. *Why does a nation have the right to force us to kill other people?*
2. *Why does the church not approve of killing people in a war?*
3. *What should a Christian do when he has to kill an enemy on the battlefield?*

Of course I know that some Christian theologians have promoted the idea of a "holy war," the idea that if it's a war fought in the interest of justice or a war against evil or villainy, then that makes it a "holy war."

But that doesn't apply to the current war. American Christians and Japanese Christians each insist that they're the ones fighting a holy war, so they kill each other—What could be more paradoxical? And I doubt that there's even one Japanese Christian who has gone off to fight believing that this is a holy war.

Now that I've written this much, I notice that it has grown lighter outside my window. Maybe the rain has stopped. It's so quiet. I'm staying in a room at an elementary school. Some of my buddies from the same training class are writing their final letters, just as I am. Some are lying down with their eyes closed. One man is opening up a can of pineapple with reverent care. Somebody is playing the organ in another room . . .

From the day I enlisted right up to the present day, I've been pondering these questions from every possible angle. But no matter how much I think about them, there's no way a green young man like me can answer them.

I have always remembered the pained look on your face that night. You were kind enough to tell me in all honesty that you didn't have the answer, either. But your face in that moment looked truly distressed.

If I were to claim that it was only after careful consideration that I requested permission from my superior officers to join the special attack force and pilot one of their planes, that would only be so much lip service. In my mind, I felt the same sort of resignation to a hopeless fate that the other student pilots felt.

But I can't say that I didn't have other feelings as well. For one thing, I wanted to share in the same fate as my comrades from my training class. Having shared my daily life with them, even though at times our views about some things differed, I feel as though I want to spend my last moments with them, sharing a common fate. Can you understand that feeling?

And then . . . it's embarrassing to put it this way, but even though this is a war, once I have killed someone (assuming that I succeed at ramming my plane into a ship tomorrow) and stolen away another person's life, I must make restitution for doing that. And so I, too, must die. That was what I decided.

That is what drove me to be part of the special attack force. If I had not made this decision based on the feelings I've just described to you, there would be no way I could resolve these contradictions in my mind.

Even if the war is to blame, if I were to kill someone, in the unlikely event that I returned home alive, I would never be able to forget what I had done for the rest of my life. I have no doubt that the form and features of the person whose life I stole away would appear before my eyes every waking moment.

The war is totally to blame for all of this. I could probably make excuses to myself, claiming that it wasn't my decision, but somewhere in my mind I would know that such an excuse would be a deception, a lie. It may be that I'm that much of a coward, but wiping out the life and the daily existence of a person is something that I could not bear as one who was, after a fashion, a Christian.

So if I'm going to kill someone, it's best in the end that I should die, too. There is no other solution. I keep telling myself this ever since I joined the special attack force. I repeat and repeat it, trying to convince myself. And it's possible that by doing so I'm trying to justify the sin of suicide, which the church also prohibits.

I don't think I know what I'm writing anymore.

The fact is, what I've told you here stems from a futile struggle to make some sense of things in my own mind. Maybe

*these are just things I've invented to give some meaning to my
own death.*

*But I'm not alone in this. I think all the men about to set
out feel the same way. I'm sure that in their letters they will
write such phrases as "Eternal loyalty to His Majesty forever!"
or "I shall scatter like the falling blossoms for my country,
placing my trust in those who will follow after me." But I'm
sure that's nothing more than a line of reasoning they are
forcing themselves to believe in to convince themselves that
their own deaths have meaning.*

*What it comes down to is that we were unable to escape the
surge of this gloomy fate. We were a generation of pain.
Truly . . . a generation of pain.*

*But there is one thing I can say with confidence. Chris-
tianity in Japan has been negligent. It has offered us no words
of truth that would help us respond when we are faced with
the predicament of having to kill another person. Yet, I
imagine that the church is suffering just as I am. I imagine
they have no answers.*

*This has turned out to be very long, so I'll stop here. Please
continue to live and stay in good health. I wrote this letter for
you and for one other person to read. That other person is a
woman who was a childhood friend. Thank you for everything.*

*Kōda Shūhei
Navy Special Attack Unit*

*P.S. Please burn this letter immediately. I don't want it to
cause any trouble for you.*

Outside, children were singing their songs. The sun gradually set, and little by little the room where Sachiko sat grew dark.

With the two letters resting on her lap, Sachiko sat motion-less, like a stone statue. She stared at a single point in space.

"Yukiko, don't you do anything sneaky!" She could hear the children arguing.

Someone called Sachiko's name from the kitchen doorway. It was her mother, who had just returned from running some errands.

"What's going on? It's pitch black in the house!"

Her mother came inside, looked into Sachiko's room, and saw her daughter sitting there.

"What in the world are you doing?" She turned on the lights and saw Sachiko sitting in a daze. There was a letter on her lap.

"Is that . . ." She started to ask. But then her mother under-stood everything.

23

AUGUST 9

MORNINGS ON THE island of Tinian in the South Pacific always began with a wake-up call from small birds in the jungle.

Each morning at nearly the same hour, as night yielded to the light of day, and as the beach where waves crashed with monotonous regularity and the groves of palm trees appeared faintly through the mist, the jungle suddenly grew boisterous. The tiny birds had begun to chirp.

August 8. It felt as though it would be another hot day. At North Field, lit by the orange rays of the morning sun, mechanics dressed in white work uniforms were performing inspections on three B-29s, crawling around like insects swarming on a piece of candy.

Before long, the bomb was delivered in a trailer. The bomb was spherical in shape, resembling a balloon or a dirigible. The mechanics had nicknamed it "Fat Man."

When Lieutenant Colonel Paul Tibbets, commander of the 509th Composite Group, and physicist Dr. Norman Ramsey finished their breakfast, Tibbets put on his sunglasses and the two men walked to a corner of the airfield to watch as "Fat Man" was loaded onto the plane.

"It's a different shape than the Little Boy that we dropped on Hiroshima, isn't it, Norman? That first one looked like a tiny

whale," the Lieutenant Colonel said to the physicist. "'Fat Boy'
here looks like a middle-aged woman."

"But she's a scary woman, carrying enough plutonium to blast
apart a city." Dr. Ramsey smiled bitterly. "What sort of town is
your target of KO-KU-RA?"

"It's an industrial area in the northern part of the island of
KYU-SHU in Japan. Given this weather, we may want to take
off ahead of schedule. The reports from the observation station
indicate that the weather will be good through tomorrow, but
for a five-day period starting on the tenth, there could be storms.
On the outside chance that we had an accident due to a storm,
we'd be in a helluva mess."

"Will you delay departure, then?"

"No, I'd rather move it up. I'm considering tomorrow." As he
answered, the lieutenant colonel looked up at the sky, which on
this hot day had cleared up. Thanks perhaps to a small breeze,
the branches of the palm trees along the beach were swaying,
and they could hear the roar of the ocean here at the airfield.
"I'll talk it over with Major Sweeney, the plane's captain . . . but
the men we plan to put on board are in excellent health."

"Jim is complaining of a little back pain."

"Damn! He's the only member of the crew who speaks Japanese. He told me that when he was little, he lived on KYU-SHU
in Japan."

The physicist nodded and walked away from the commander.
He was prone to sweat, and he didn't like standing endlessly in
the direct rays of the sun on the airfield.

*I imagine over fifty thousand Japanese in Hiroshima were
wounded by the explosion of Little Boy. This time around, the fat
lady is going to blow up in the skies above KO-KU-RA . . .*

The scientist in him felt a faint stabbing pain in his chest. But
at once another voice—speaking tranquilizing words to soothe
the pain of Ramsey and all of his colleagues—interceded to
eliminate his pain: "Without these bombs, countless numbers

of additional people will die. This is a measure we take to end the war quickly. If the end is justified, the means can be rationalized away."

An updated report from the weather station on August 8 warned that the region would be hit with bad weather after the tenth, so it was decided that the attack on Kokura using the new bomb, "Fat Man," would take place on the ninth. Still, as though in an effort to cast doubt on that forecast, not a single cloud could be seen in the August skies over Tinian. The wind was rather strong and the ocean was rough, producing whitecaps, but just as it had been, day after day, the sun blazed down during the daytime, and in the evening the palm trees and the beach were painted rose by the setting sun.

"Jim, are you familiar with KO-KU-RA?" At a small party thrown to offer encouragement to the flight crew that evening, the physicist Ramsey asked Lieutenant Colonel Jim Walker. He had learned that morning from Colonel Tibbets that Jim had lived in Japan.

"I've only passed through it a couple of times. I was still a kid, so I hardly remember anything about it. I do remember, though, that it was an industrial area. I was brought up in a city called NA-GA-SA-KI."

"NA-GA-SA-KI? What kind of city is that?"

"It has a large shipbuilding facility. But it's surrounded by beautiful mountains and the ocean. Even during the many years when the doors to Japan were closed, it was the only place where Dutch ships could land. And a section of the city called U-RA-KA-MI even has a connection with President Ulysses S. Grant."[1] With relish Jim described the history of Nagasaki—especially the history of US-Japan relations centering around

---

1 Toward the end of his post-presidential world tour, Grant stopped in Japan, where he greeted the emperor; during their visit to Nagasaki, he and his wife Julia each planted a banyan tree in Suwa Park.

Nagasaki—to Dr. Ramsey. That had been the topic of his studies at Harvard.

After describing the persecution of the Christians at Urakami, Jim brought his narrative to a close with, "And that's why Japan was able to take its first steps toward becoming a modern nation, thanks to the sacrifices of the farmers of Urakami."

Apparently disinterested, Dr. Ramsey merely nodded and left to discuss something with Major Sweeney, the captain for tomorrow's sortie. In a soft voice, he asked Sweeney, "How much . . . how much does your crew know . . . about the atomic bomb you're dropping tomorrow?"

"Well, of course specialists like Frederick and Phillip know all about it. Jacob is also aware. The other men talk a lot about how much power they think this bomb has, but in reality I don't think they can even begin to imagine. I think they consider it about the same as a large-scale conventional bomb."

Ramsey appeared satisfied with this response. Even though the first strike had already been dropped on Hiroshima, in fact nobody knew much about its awful destructive force. It was better that they not know. Especially someone like Jim, who had lived in Japan as a youth . . .

"I agree," Major Sweeney nodded. "If Jim knew, it could cause him a lot of grief. He speaks very fondly of the Japanese people he knew in the past."

"Was it really necessary to have him on board?"

"It is. He's very good at Japanese. We have orders not to use radar for the attack, but to do visual bombing."

✳ ✳ ✳

09 *August*, *0300 hours Tinian time*
It was an hour when the island was still swathed in darkness and its citizens in a deep sleep.

But lights were already on in the buildings and along the runways at North Field, floodlights were beaming, and the engines in the three airplanes hummed faintly. Especially on Runway Alpha, mechanics swarmed around the B-29 nicknamed the "Bockscar"[2] and the two other planes, making final inspections.

The twelve crewmen, led by Major Sweeney, came out of the administration building. They shook hands with Lieutenant Colonel Tibbets, Dr. Ramsey, and others who were waiting to see them off, then headed toward the gigantic silver planes. The time was approaching 0330 hours.

The men disappeared into the planes and the mechanics scattered and withdrew, by which time morning had finally started to color the sky a pale white. Before too much longer, the small birds in the jungle would awaken and start to make their racket, just as they did every morning.

At present the only sound was the waves pounding languidly, monotonously.

One after the other, the three planes began to glide forward, building up speed as they dashed toward the end of the runway. Suddenly they were aloft in the brightening sky, and swiftly they disappeared from sight.

"Very different, isn't it?" Dr. Ramsey said sardonically to Major Tibbets. "Three days ago when Little Boy took off from here carrying a similar atomic bomb, cameramen who didn't even know what was going on were snapping away, taking pictures of the crew members getting ready to set off on their mission. But there's none of that ruckus today."

---

2   The specially modified B-29 was nicknamed after its original commander, Captain Frederick C. Bock, but was flown on this bombing mission under the command of Major Charles W. Sweeney. Captain Bock flew the observation plane.

He was rather disappointed that the revolutionary bomb they had finally managed to build was now being given short shrift.

The major responded in an ill-tempered voice, "But today's bombing attack on KO-KU-RA is even more important from a strategic standpoint. With one blast, we'll be wiping out the largest industrial region in Japan." His foul mood could be traced to his concern that the pump for one of the reserve fuel tanks on the just-departed Bockscar had been malfunctioning and was removed only this morning.

If they can't use that fuel tank, their range of operations will be limited. As he climbed the stairs into the administration building, he suspected that the captain of the plane, Major Sweeney, was feeling just as anxious as he was right now.

But among the three planes proceeding toward Japan, inside Bockscar, which was carrying the bomb, an even more serious, heart-stopping moment of panic had just occurred.

Twenty minutes after takeoff, a red warning lamp suddenly began to flash as though it had been given a scare.

"Lieutenant Colonel!" Lieutenant Barnes, who had been at the rear of the plane, hurried forward with a pale face to report to Commander Ashworth. The flashing warning light could be an indication of problems with one of Fat Man's fuses.

"Say nothing to anyone," the lieutenant colonel said, his finger to his lips. Lieutenant Barnes hurried back to inspect.

✳ ✳ ✳

Nagasaki, August 9, 7:00 a.m.

They were listening to the morning news on their old-fashioned radio. Mitsuo went out into the tiny garden, stripped to the waist, and began his exercise routine. His father appeared from the vegetable garden holding several dew-glistening tomatoes and handed one to Mitsuo.

"It's going to be another hot one today, . . ." his father muttered as he looked up at the cloudless sky.

The radio announcer repeated warnings that, because of the tremendous power of the new type of bomb dropped three days earlier on Hiroshima, citizens must take appropriate precautions even if only one enemy plane was sighted; they must wrap their bodies in white cloth; and they must not let light rays shower down on them.

"Do you think there'll be another air raid today?" Mitsuo, his arms waving, asked his father, who had started reading the morning paper.

"Ever since the beginning of August they've been attacking Nagasaki every day."

Mitsuo's mother, who was setting out bowls and chopsticks on the table, said, "Mitsuo, if the alarms sound, no matter where you are, you go straight to an air raid shelter, and don't you do anything stupid."

"Got it."

In reality, starting in the latter part of July, B-29s had been incessantly attacking Nagasaki, which until then had been the target of fewer air raids than other regional cities.

On August 1 in particular, a total of fifty planes, including both B-29s and B-25s, had bombed Nagasaki, their targets focused on the shipbuilding and steelmaking facilities. A bomb had also fallen with a terrible blast that shook the ground very near the plant where Sachiko worked. The air raid shelter trembled, sand dropped from the ceiling, and Sachiko shielded Hiroe, who clung to her as they waited for the enemy planes to leave.

Thereafter, sirens sounded almost every day. Warning alerts alone had sounded four times yesterday.

"Sat-chan, take this to Hiroe." Her mother handed something wrapped in newspaper to Sachiko, who was sitting at the breakfast table. Inside were several of the tomatoes her father had just picked from the garden. Sachiko's mother was well aware that Hiroe, who lived in a dormitory, had little to eat.

"Okay."

"How is your aunt doing?" Sachiko's mother inquired after her older sister, who worked as a nun at the Ōura Church. She had been bedridden for about two weeks with a heart condition.

"She seems about the same." Every morning, Sachiko quietly got out of bed while her family was still asleep and went to mass at the Ōura Church. Her parents knew from other sources why she was doing that.

As she ate, Sachiko was deep in thought.

Ever since Shūhei had joined the aviation corps, she had gone to early morning mass each day without fail. At a shrine along her route to Ōura, she had invariably seen an elderly woman performing the ritual of one hundred steps. She's probably offering prayers in that manner hoping that her son will return alive from the war—Sachiko had watched the woman and likened her situation to her own . . .

Beginning yesterday, the woman was nowhere to be seen. Had she fallen ill? Or had she received notice that her son had been killed in battle?

Already four months had passed since Shūhei had died in battle.

The church was always quiet and attendees few in number at early morning mass on weekdays. Sachiko took her usual seat on the right side of the chapel. From there, she could look directly at the statue of the Holy Mother Mary.

The flickering flame from the candles projected the shadow of the priest, whose head was bowed, onto the wall. An aged nun coughed painfully.

"Please help me understand." Sachiko spoke to the statue of the Blessed Mother that was right in front of her. For so many years, so many women—including Kiku—had pled for help amid the many varied trials they were suffering as women . . .

"Why did Shū-chan have to die? I still don't understand why this has happened to him. Please tell me why Shū-chan had to go off to that far-distant land."

The Blessed Mother gazed at Sachiko and said not a word.

"I've hardly had the strength to go on living since that day. I've tried to act cheerful, as though nothing had happened, so that I don't cause my father and mother to worry. . . . But to be honest, as soon as I can I want to go to that place where Shū-chan is . . ."

Sachiko closed her eyes and tried to control her emotions. She could dimly see the flames at the altar. And in the depths of her ears, she could once again hear Shūhei's jubilant voice as he read "Invitation to a Voyage" to her.

My love,
Think of it, of that land—
The joy of living there, just we two.
There we will love in peace;
Let us love, then let us die.

The mass ended. She went outside along with the nuns, struggling to conceal her tear-streaked face from just moments before. She greeted the other worshippers with a smile, and went to speak to her ailing aunt . . .

"Sachiko, if you sit there staring off into space, you'll be late for the factory."

Sachiko nodded and grunted her assent, then left the house.

August 9. It was hot and humid again today. It felt as though it would be another suffocating day. Even though it was still morning, she could hear the shrill cries of the cicadas, so near at hand they seemed to be swarming along the ground. The leaves of the tomato and corn plants in their diminutive garden sweltered in the heat.

"Hey, did you hear?" Inside the bus bound for Urakami, a man was speaking with his friend. "The news is saying that the Soviet Union just invaded Manchuria."

"The Soviets did?"

"Yep." He apparently worked for a newspaper and wanted to share the news he had just heard with everyone on the bus.

But the faces of the passengers displayed no surprise or alarm. They were all silent, total exhaustion inscribed into their expressions. All were worn and weary from the long war, so their reactions to every event were muted.

About the time Sachiko arrived at the factory, a report came in that B-29s were flying reconnaissance over Kita Kyushu. No one paid any attention to the report.

✳ ✳ ✳

Iwo Jima, 0800 hours

Lieutenant Barnes spent some time examining the wiring on the plane, in an attempt to determine the cause of the frantic flashing of the warning light. Finally, in a voice filled with relief, he said to Commander Ashworth, who stood beside him with a worried look, "Commander, I've found the problem. The rotary switch is in the wrong position."

When the lieutenant flipped the switch back to the correct position, the warning light stopped flashing. The two men wiped the sweat from their faces with their hands. Their chests were still pounding. Soon they caught sight of a dark reddish-brown, conical-shaped island in the silvery ocean beneath them. It was Iwo Jima, where American forces had landed on February 19 and, after nearly a month of fierce fighting had finally wrested it from the control of the Japanese Army.

A weather report came in over the wireless. It was sent from the reconnaissance plane surveying KO-KU-RA. The skies over the city, the report said, were "crystal clear."

They were approaching Yakushima. This was the arranged rendezvous point where Bockscar was to meet up with the observation plane and the camera plane that had departed at the same time from Tinian. Captain Van Pelt, who sat in the navigator's seat, announced "Captain, one plane sighted."

The plane that was spotted was the one carrying observation instruments, but the essential camera plane was nowhere to be seen.

Ten minutes passed. Twenty minutes passed. But the camera plane still had not arrived. The only addition to the scenery was two US submarines that had surfaced near Yakushima.

"What do you want to do?" Captain Van Pelt asked nervously. "Do you want to wait? We'll be wasting fuel."

The pump that delivered auxiliary fuel had malfunctioned prior to takeoff, so it had been removed, leaving the plane without reserve fuel. They could not afford to waste a single drop.

"We'll wait another forty-five minutes." Captain Sweeney, clicking his tongue, was clearly furious over the late arrival of the camera plane.

The wasteful circling over Yakushima continued for forty-five minutes. But there was no sign of the absent plane in the clear blue sky.

"Let's go." Captain Sweeney wanted to waste no additional fuel or time.

Lieutenant Colonel Jim Walker, who was assigned communications, notified Captain Bock's observation plane that they were departing.

"Proceed to KO-KU-RA."

KO-KU-RA—

Jim remembered passing through that city when he had traveled with his father and mother from Nagasaki to Yokohama. But he had no clear memory of what the city was like.

Nagasaki was the only Japan he knew. A city with two promontories that enfolded the narrow bay like two embracing arms. The dark, low roofs of the Japanese houses. The heat of summer and the cries of the cicadas. The Ōura Church and the Japanese friends he had played with.

"I'm pretty sure the boy's name was SHŪ-HEI. And there was the girl, named SA-CHI-KO." Were the Japanese children he and his younger brother Van had played with still living in Nagasaki?

Those were wonderful memories.

Those two Japanese would be about his age.

✳ ✳ ✳

Kyushu, just before 1000 hours

Maintaining an altitude of 31,500 feet, Bockscar leisurely proceeded north in the skies above Kyushu.

The sky was so blue it stung their eyes to look at it. The only interruption to their view was a bank of thin clouds floating across, looking as though they had been styled with a hairbrush.

Did these mountains and valleys stretch out endlessly along their path? The scenery that opened up before their eyes looked like a map colored only in yellow and green hues.

For some reason, Japanese fighter planes did not show up to engage them. They couldn't see any bursts from antiaircraft artillery. Although of course, at this altitude, shells from antiaircraft guns wouldn't reach them.

Jim felt as though he were in a world beyond time. He had even begun to forget that he was in a B-29 that was about to bomb Kokura.

The Japan he remembered so fondly. How many years had passed since he had visited this country? During summer vacation in Nagasaki, the ocean and the sky had been as gleamingly blue as today's sky. That day he had gone swimming in the ocean at Nezumi Island with Shūhei and Sachiko. No doubt those two were living somewhere below him at this very moment.

A buzzer sounded. They were approaching their target of Kokura.

Those two Japanese couldn't even dream that their young friend was in a B-29 flying through the skies above them, Jim thought. On this plane that was about to drop a bomb on their country that he remembered with such great affection.

In truth, he did not feel the slightest hatred toward the Japanese. Fighting against people he did not despise was not a fate he had chosen for himself.

I was put into this plane by a tremendous force that cared nothing about my wishes. And I'm not the only one. Lieutenant Barnes in the rear of the plane and Commander Ashworth don't know anything about Japan or the Japanese people. How can you love or hate someone you don't even know?

The tremendous power that is forcing me to do this. Could it be that Shūhei and Sachiko have been ensnared by that same power?

The second buzzer sounded.

They had sighted Kokura. Bockscar reduced its altitude. Thin clouds swept by the windows on both sides of the plane.

"The bastards got it wrong!" Captain Van Pelt growled to Captain Sweeney. "The report said not a cloud in the sky over KO-KU-RA. But look at it!"

The captain's frustration was understandable. Patches of clouds blanketed Kokura and its vicinity.

As the plane descended, thatched-roof houses, rice paddies, and factories, looking tiny from their altitude, appeared through breaks in the clouds.

The buzzer blared repeatedly, demanding preparations to drop the bomb. The bomb bay doors opened, and the crew members—except for the bombardier, the pilot, and the engineer—put on dark black Polaroid goggles. Bombardier Beahan put on his Norden bombsight.

They spotted a river. Then railroad tracks.

But whitish smoke came floating in from the west. The heart of Kokura, which they had finally gotten in their sights after so much effort, was no longer clearly visible because of the smoke.

The clouds were not the problem. A turbid white smoke veiled the sky over the city. There seemed to be a massive fire somewhere that had not yet been extinguished.

"Shit!" Bombardier Beahan lifted his face from the bombsight and cursed. "I can't see the target with this stuff in the air."

Their target in KO-KU-RA was a huge armory. With smoke blocking their vision, there was no way to determine its exact location.

Although the crew of Bockscar did not know this, three days earlier the Yahata Steelworks plant located adjacent to Kokura City had been bombed. The lingering smoke from that attack still had not dissipated and had drifted to its present position.

"Captain, what do you want to do?"

"We'll circle for a while and wait to see if the wind can do anything with that smoke," Captain Sweeney muttered dispiritedly. But what he was most concerned about was fuel. Even under normal circumstances he wouldn't have wanted to use up fuel that was in short supply, but with this setback . . .

"The Japs have started shooting!" Beahan jerked his eyes from the bombsight and shouted. With each flash from the Japanese antiaircraft positions, smoke clouds shaped like cabbages materialized outside the plane.

"Climb!" The B-29, which had been ready to begin the bombing attack, rapidly climbed back to its earlier altitude of 30,000 feet.

"Captain," Jim reported. He had been listening in on intercepted Japanese radio communications and watching the radar screen, and over the wireless he picked up sounds that seemed to be coming from Japanese fighter planes, sounds that were growing louder. "Zero fighters approaching!"

It was unusual for fighter planes of the Japanese Navy, which was on the verge of collapse, to still be pressing forward with a battle. Yet here at Kokura they were attempting to attack using the few fighter planes they had left. The number of cabbage-shaped clouds fired from the antiaircraft artillery increased around them. Apparently the enemy's antiaircraft fire had been re-aimed to the altitude of the B-29 as it circled.

"What's the status of the smoke?" Captain Sweeney shouted to Beahan.

"No good!" Beahan responded. "It's not moving at all."

Commander Ashworth came running from the rear of the plane. "We can't delay any longer." Captain Sweeney nodded. "Should we abandon KO-KU-RA?"

"That's the smart thing to do, since we're under strict orders to do a visual bombing. There's nothing we can do here."

"And we're short on fuel . . ."

"We'll drop Fat Man on NA-GA-SA-KI." Of the crew, only the captain and Commander Ashworth knew about the order to use Nagasaki as the secondary target if weather conditions rendered the dropping of Fat Man on Kokura impossible.

"Proceed to NA-GA-SA-KI," Captain Sweeney ordered the navigator, Captain Van Pelt.

✳ ✳ ✳

Nagasaki, 10:00 a.m.

It was getting hotter.

At the factory, four or five men who had heard about the Soviet Union entering the war were discussing it together.

"Manchukuo will be fine. The Kantō Army there is the strongest of our forces," one of them said reassuringly.

"Will it really? General Yamashita was in command in the Philippines, so I didn't worry about it, either, but . . ."

Another of the men looked uneasy. The Japanese people were beginning to doubt this seemingly heroic war and the rallying cries of the Imperial Military Headquarters.

The workers had a twenty-minute break. The members of the Women's Volunteer Corps removed their headbands and wiped away the sweat. Their foreheads were dripping with perspiration.

The rays of the sun reflected like melted tin outside the factory.

Sachiko walked out into the bright sunlight and sat in the shade of a pile of lumber. Two dust-covered sunflowers faced her.

Katō Hiroe came over, wiping her neck with a towel.

"Hot again today, huh?"

"So hot!" Sachiko handed Hiroe a package with the tomatoes her mother had sent. "This is from my mom."

"Thanks. She's always so nice."

"You should eat some now. Your throat's dry, isn't it?"

"Naw. I'll save them for later."

They heard a sound like an explosion somewhere in the sky. But the air raid alert had been lifted some time before, so it was unlikely to be an enemy plane.

Hiroe knew that whenever Sachiko heard an explosion, she shut her eyes and struggled to endure it. At such times she knew to leave her friend alone.

Each time she heard an explosion, Sachiko pictured the plane carrying Shūhei.

The base, at morning.

Shūhei was one of several men with his body encased in a flight suit. They stood in ranks, saluted their commander, and split up to board their planes. The planes were already prepared.

They climbed into their planes.

The explosions grew louder, the signal flag waved, and one after another the planes taxied away.

My love,
Think of it, of that land—

Shūhei was not the only one who had gone off to that land. Young men of around the same age as Shūhei had also gone to that land, leaving their mothers and wives and lovers here in this land.

You're too selfish! Shū-chan, you always have to do things your own way! Sachiko felt that deep in her heart. And resented it. What are the mothers and wives and lovers left behind supposed to do with themselves? How are they supposed to go on living?

"Hey, we should go swimming at Kurosaki," Hiroe encouraged Sachiko.

At the end of the twenty-minute break, Sachiko and Hiroe got up from behind the stacked lumber and were about to go back into the factory when Mr. Hachimi came out of the office and called, "Okukawa-san! Sachiko-san!" Mr. Hachimi had been drafted and in earlier days had opened a small restaurant in Sasebo.

"Okukawa-san, you have a phone call from your family."

"Thank you." Phone calls from the family were highly unusual. Her heart pounding, Sachiko raced to the office.

"Hello? Mom, what's going on? Talk loudly! I'm in the office at the factory, so I can't hear you very well . . ."

The noises from the machines began to echo through the building. The sounds of smashing metal and of whirling bores made it very difficult to hear her mother's voice through the receiver.

". . . condition has gotten really worse."

"What? Whose condition?"

"Your aunt's." Her aunt, a nun at the Ōura Church, had been having trouble with her heart and had been in and out of bed, so Sachiko had called on her every morning after she attended mass. She hadn't seemed so bad this morning, but . . .

"Can you come right away? I'm hurrying over there right now."

"Okay." Sachiko hung up the phone and went to talk to the assistant manager.

"If that's the case, then you can go," he nodded gently. Perhaps because he had a daughter about the same age as Sachiko, he was always obliging with her.

She went to tell Hiroe where she was going. Her friend was standing in front of a machine, already in a sweat. "You'd better hurry and go!" she nodded, wiping at the sweat.

"Okay. I'll see you later." Sachiko took two or three steps and then turned back. Hiroe was waving her hand and smiling at her. It was a warmhearted smile, the sort Sachiko liked very much.

When she went outside, the bright sun, the sweltering heat, and the cries of the cicadas all slapped her in the forehead at the same time.

The weeds growing along the fence of the factory were caked white with dust. Hurrying down that long, gray dusty path, she arrived at the stop just as the bus was arriving.

She sat down on the bus, closed her eyes, and again thought of Shūhei. The special attack plane carrying Shūhei disappeared into the sky . . .

"Damn, an air raid alert!"

The bus had driven only a short distance when the air raid siren blared. The bus came to a stop and the passengers, guided by a man on a bicycle who was from the air defense team, raced to a bomb shelter.

The bomb shelter was deserted. Holding her breath in the shelter, Sachiko again thought about Shūhei and began praying.

✳ ✳ ✳

"What?!"

When the order was given to the crew to proceed to NA-GA-SA-KI, Lieutenant Colonel Jim Walker cried out in shock. Seeing the look on his face, Captain Sweeney understood how Jim was feeling.

"Jim, let's talk for a minute." He came over beside Jim. "I understand, I really do. I know how much NA-GA-SA-KI means to you . . ."

"It's the city where I grew up."

"But for the Japanese, it's a city with a shipyard where battleships are built and a plant producing weapons. It's as important a target to strike as KO-KU-RA."

Jim was silent, so Major Sweeney kept trying to assure him. "We've got to put an end to this war as quickly as we can. We can't afford to shed any more blood in vain or lose any more lives than we already have. You can see that, can't you, Jim?"

Jim still said nothing.

"Our bombing raid today is different from normal raids. This attack has sufficient power to force the Japanese to abandon their will to resist. That's how much destructive power Fat Man has. With one blow we'll probably wipe out the shipbuilding facility and the factories without leaving a trace. And we'll be able to save the lives of hundreds of thousands of GIs."

No response from Jim.

"If we don't drop this bomb . . . how many lives will be lost if we have to invade Japan?"

Jim did not look up, but he nodded his head almost imperceptibly. Not that he agreed with the captain's arguments. He simply couldn't control his feelings if he didn't think along the same lines.

"Cheer up, Jim." Captain Sweeney slapped Jim's shoulder and returned to the cockpit.

What an unbelievable series of coincidences! Jim thought. If the auxiliary fuel pump hadn't malfunctioned at Tinian, there wouldn't have been any need to change course to NA-GA-SA-KI. They wouldn't be bound for NA-GA-SA-KI if the smoke from a fire hadn't concealed their target in KO-KU-RA.

Considered from that perspective, Jim could see that Nagasaki was an ill-fated city.

You've run out of luck, he muttered—to himself, and to Nagasaki.

✳ ✳ ✳

Nagasaki, 11:00 a.m.

It smelled of dank soil and straw mats. The air raid shelter, its floors and walls covered with woven matting, was crowded with only ten people in it.

In the shelter, Sachiko and the others crouched silently, waiting for the enemy plane to leave the skies over Nagasaki.

The heat in the shelter and the smell of the soil had made her feel a bit nauseous.

"Hot, isn't it?" a middle-aged woman beside her sighed and struck up a conversation. "I hate the air raids at night, but when an enemy plane shows up at this hour, I can't take care of anything I need to get done." She grumbled at the inconvenience.

"Lady, the enemy doesn't take our situation into consideration when they decide to attack!" An elderly woman seated nearby said, her face clearly betraying the effort she was making to conceal her amusement. Everyone in the shelter chuckled at this exchange, and the oppressive atmosphere lightened up a bit.

"If this warning isn't lifted soon, we're gonna be in trouble," the middle-aged woman again complained. She explained that her nephew had received a draft notice, and they were supposed to be heading to Mogi right now. They'd been told that if her nephew didn't arrive in Mogi by 1:00 P.M., he'd be taken off to Honshu by boat.

As she listened to this subdued conversation, Sachiko worried about her ailing aunt, and in her heart she prayed the rosary for her aunt and for Shūhei.

Without warning a memory of the time she had spent with Shūhei at Hara Castle was reawakened in her mind. He had proudly displayed to Sachiko and Takeda Mieko a pottery fragment he had picked up and boasted that it came from around the time of the Shimabara Rebellion, but a local farm woman had told them that it was a piece of a night-soil bucket. Even now she could almost see the deflated look on Shūhei's face.

He was so funny!

A mixture of longing and sorrow beyond words surged up like a torrent in her heart. She could not bring herself to believe that a day would come in her lifetime when her memories of Shūhei's unique face would dissolve away.

Climbing into that special attack plane . . . it must have been so painful for him.

Though she knew it was pointless, feelings of regret, compassion, and heartache blended together and clamped down on her chest.

✳ ✳ ✳

A siren blasted.

"Ah, finally the alert has been lifted!" Several people standing near the entrance left the shelter, but one of them returned and grunted, "No good. The bus driver hasn't come back yet."

Sachiko also climbed out, but she hated the thought of having to stand motionless at the roadside beneath the direct white beams of the sun that felt like rays from a blast furnace, so she headed back to the entrance of the bomb shelter.

Just then, she heard a sound like an explosion in the distance. But she must have been hearing things, because no further sound reached her ears.

"What time is it now?" In response to the question from the middle-aged woman, Sachiko looked at her wristwatch. It was barely past 11:00.

"Just a little after 11:00," she replied.

✳ ✳ ✳

Nagasaki, 1101 hours

As they reduced their altitude, they could see the glistening ocean directly beneath them. Several fishing boats floated on the surface. There was a peninsula dotted with a number of small fishing harbors. A conical-shaped mountain that might have been a volcano stood at the highest point on the peninsula.

Captain Sweeney thought, *It's like the country of Lilliput in* Gulliver's Travels. *And the little people of this Lilliput dared to undertake a war against America, the country of giants . . .*

When they passed Shimabara, a thin layer of clouds began to veil the ground. It looked as though those thin clouds completely shrouded their secondary target of Nagasaki. The wind was blowing from the east . . .

"Captain, this isn't what the weather plane reported . . ." Captain Van Pelt sounded discouraged. "It's cloudy here, too."

Conditions for the bombing attack appeared to be as poor as they had been in the skies over Kokura. Captain Sweeney went to consult with Commander Ashworth, who had ultimate responsibility for this attack.

"Do we cancel the attack?"

"No, we can't do that. If we fly away from here carrying Fat Man, we don't know whether we'll have enough fuel to reach Okinawa. It would be dangerous to land at Okinawa with barely enough fuel. If the landing fails, the plane and the entire base would be blown to bits."

"Then do we abandon Fat Man over the ocean?"

"Don't be ridiculous! We'd be wasting several million dollars and the work of a few thousand people."

Jim could hear their conversation.

To be truthful, when he heard the report from Captain Van Pelt that the clouds covering Nagasaki would make it difficult to drop the bomb, Jim was relieved. Now Nagasaki, the city imbued with memories for him, would be spared . . .

He paid careful attention to the exchange between the Captain and the lieutenant colonel.

"Should we use the radar?" the lieutenant colonel asked. But Captain Sweeney shook his head.

"We've been ordered not to use radar. Our instructions are to carry out the attack using only visual identification."

One of only a small handful of available atomic bombs must not be dropped onto a mountain or into the ocean. So the direction from the top brass was to adhere strictly to visual bombing in order to assure accuracy.

"Then what shall we do?"

"Shall we try to make it back to Okinawa?"

Yes! Jim smiled. *Nagasaki, you're saved!*

"We'll circle one last time, and if we can't drop the bomb, we'll head back to Okinawa."

The decision had been made. Jim stared at the radar screen, Captain Van Pelt gripped the joystick, and the plane made its final loop.

Then it happened. The wind blowing from the east opened a tiny break in the clouds. Bombardier Beahan discovered it and shouted, "Eureka! I can see blue sky!"

The buzzer sounded repeatedly. The crew members all put on their Polaroid goggles.

Such a . . . such a sorry fate. . . . Jim shut his eyes and muttered.

The bomb bay opened. The bombsight located the Mitsubishi weapons production plant. The time was 1102 hours.

24

AFTERMATH

SOME THIRTY YEARS LATER . . .

This area that ran alongside a private railway line in the Tokyo suburbs had also changed dramatically. During the war there had been only five or six small shops in front of the train station, but today an upscale supermarket and bank had opened, lively music flowed from a pachinko parlor, and young people clustered in the record shops and tearooms.

In the evening . . .

A housewife carrying a shopping basket stopped at a green-grocer's located in a corner of the plaza in front of the station.

At the doorway to the shop, she had spotted a discarded man-darin orange box, with "Mogi Oranges" written in large black letters on the side.

"Excuse me, do you have any Mogi oranges inside?"

"Mogi? Oh, this? These aren't for sale. A friend from Kyushu sent them to me," the young shop manager replied. "Are you from Kyushu, ma'am?"

"Nagasaki. Mogi is right next to Nagasaki. It's been a long time since I've had any of those oranges."

"Wait just a moment, please." The kindly young shop man-ager disappeared inside and soon came out holding two of the Mogi oranges his friend had sent. "These aren't for sale, so please just take them. Only two left, I'm afraid."

"Oh, I couldn't do that. It's really all right."

After haggling, the woman bought a red delicious apple to thank him for the gift and placed it and the oranges in her basket.

Weaving her way across the plaza, the woman was heading in the direction of the bus stop when a high-school-aged girl waiting for a bus called out to her, "Mom! Oh, I'm glad I ran into you. Can you give me some bus money?"

"Don't be silly. You can walk home. You're in high school, aren't you? See, your mother is walking home."

"I had a killer ballet rehearsal after class, and I'm beat. Besides . . . you need the walk. You're putting on weight."

Nevertheless, young Harue set off on foot beside her mother.

"I got a wonderful gift at a shop back there."

"What is it?"

"Oranges. Nagasaki oranges."

"What? Only two? Nothing to be grateful for even if they were a gift." She cast a scornful glance at her mother. Her daughter wasn't alone in showing disdain for the oranges. That evening when her son, who was busy studying so he wouldn't fail his college entrance exams a second time, came downstairs for dinner, he said, "I'd rather have the apple." Bored, he turned on the television and showed no interest in eating an orange.

"You kids, during the war and the Occupation, if we'd had even one orange, . . ." the mother started to say, but then stopped herself. It was a foregone conclusion that making a statement along those lines would elicit only a counterattack from her children: "It's not the war or the Occupation anymore!"

After dinner, her son fled back to his room to study, and her daughter listened for a few minutes to a popular song on the television, but she soon slipped out of the dining room.

Around 9:30, her husband, who had eaten dinner out, returned home. Her husband was Tokyo-born, so he had no fond feelings for Mogi oranges, either. In the end, only the housewife, Sachiko, ate them.

She savored each section of the orange. With each section she ate, a resonant memory sprang back to life in her mind.

The taste of the orange revived so many different recollections and memories of Nagasaki. . . . Those memories were hidden away deep in Sachiko's heart. Among the many experiences of her youth spent in that city, she had shared with her husband and children only those she didn't mind revealing, but those submerged deep inside her she kept locked away in a box within her heart.

That box within her heart resembled the chocolate box in which she had stashed away items of greatest importance to her during her youth. She was the only one who ever opened that box, inside which she had not placed anything connected to her daily activities with her husband and children, but things that related to her life alone.

Having changed his clothes, her husband sipped on the tea that Sachiko had poured for him while he sat alone lining up stones on his *go* board. His hobbies were playing *go* and fishing, and every night before he went to bed, he practiced various patterns of stone arrangement on his *go* board.

The children were in their rooms. In the distance, she could hear the sound of a train racing by. It was definitely peaceful and quiet inside her home. As she ate her orange, Sachiko acknowledged that her present life was not an unhappy one.

But not being unhappy and feeling completely content in her heart were not the same thing.

Her husband was more the strait-laced, serious type who had never deviated from his life's course. Thirty years had passed since Sachiko married him. She had been twenty-six at the time. She married him not out of passionate love for him; rather, she had agreed to a meeting to consider him as a potential spouse in order to set her ailing father's heart at ease, even though prior to then she had repeatedly turned down a series of candidates for trumped-up reasons.

Her husband's goodness and seriousness had been the salvation of Sachiko, who had felt empty over the loss of something of tremendous value to her. She had never told her Tokyo-born husband many details of her experiences in her younger days.

Her heart was always governed by the feeling that, even were she to tell him, he wouldn't be able to understand, and by the desire not to have to remember what had happened the day the bomb was dropped.

11:02 a.m. on that ninth day in August. The blinding flash of light that struck Sachiko's forehead even though she had been in a bomb shelter at a place in the city far removed from Ground Zero. The horrific rumbling of the earth. Sand had fallen through the roof of the shelter.

When she emerged along with several others from the shelter, she was shocked that the world could be transformed into a veritable hell in a mere instant. The factory where she had been working only minutes earlier had been totally destroyed, but that was only the beginning. It had never crossed her mind that Urakami, in many ways her hometown, could become an inferno racked with the agonized shrieks of the dying. She couldn't have imagined that Hiroe and her assistant manager and Mr. Hachimi, all of whom she had talked with just that morning, would no longer be alive in this world.

No! Enough! I don't want to remember any more!

That is why she had not told her children about that day in any detail. It wasn't something that could be conveyed in words.

Those memories, too, were locked away in a box—not the chocolate box, but the box inside her heart.

There was one more painful memory in that box. Of Shūhei.

She had not told her husband about Shūhei. She hadn't wanted to hurt this gentle man for no good reason. She had only discussed her relationship with Shūhei with the priest at the Ōura Church before her wedding. The priest had responded, "Don't tell your husband as long as you live."

And so her husband had no idea that in her youth, she had loved a young man with every fiber of her being. Neither did her son or daughter know. Her daughter mocked her mother, "Mom, your life has been really dull, hasn't it? I'd hate to have a life like yours!"

Certainly in the eyes of her son Tsuneo and her daughter Harue, she was nothing more than an outdated matriarch who knew virtually nothing about what was going on in today's society.

"Mom, you've never heard of Olivia Newton-John either?!" Sachiko couldn't associate anything with the name Newton other than the man who had discovered gravity. Harue just laughed at her.

"She's more out of it than dad! The other day she called the Green Car on trains 'First Class!'" Tsuneo smirked.

Occasionally Sachiko went on the defensive and retorted to her insolent children, "If you want to discuss actors, how about Ingrid Bergman and Cary Grant! To me, you two seem like foreigners without a country. I have to regard you as foreigners with different manners and customs and ways of thinking just so I don't get mad at you!"

What was saddest for Sachiko, however, was the fact that, at some point in time, both Tsuneo and Harue had stopped attending church. She had taught Tsuneo when he was a child how to hold his hands to pray, but once he became a high school student, he said, "I don't get why you still believe in this stuff. If there is a God, why did he murder so many Nagasaki Christians with an atomic bomb?"

"So, for instance, do you children think that what happened at Auschwitz was God's doing? A great many believers were killed there, too. Isn't the atomic bomb the same?" Sachiko retorted. "You're just making a blameless God shoulder the burden of sin."

But gradually her children stopped attending church, even on Sundays.

Each time she had to stand up to her children as they matured, Sachiko felt an ever-increasing disconnect between generations. At such times, she wondered to herself what Shūhei would say in such situations, if he were still alive.

No doubt Tsuneo and Harue would regard the love that she and Shūhei had felt for one another as a musty, old-fashioned romance. When she listened to her children having interminable phone conversations with their boyfriends and girlfriends, she felt as though "love" in its truest sense had been lost to the Japanese. Anyone could be in a love-like relationship, but none of them could experience real love. In today's age, love had become too effortless, an activity all too easy to participate in. But Sachiko knew to the depths of her soul how difficult love could be.

"One of my relatives was a woman named Kiku . . ." But when she told Harue about Kiku's life in an attempt to explain the meaning of real love, her daughter was not emotionally stirred the way she had hoped she would be.

"If that had been me, I'd never have done anything like that. To tell you the truth, I would have given up on a man like that. I wouldn't have any choice other than to abandon him."

"Being in love isn't what you think it is." At such times, Sachiko lost her temper and got into an argument with her high-school-aged daughter. There was, in the final analysis, a disconnect between mother and daughter at a very deep level.

✳ ✳ ✳

She hadn't been back to Nagasaki in a very long time.

When her mother died fifteen years previously, after discussing it with her brother Mitsuo, she moved her parents' graves to a Catholic cemetery at Fuchū in the suburbs of Tokyo.[1] Thereafter there was no need to go to Nagasaki to visit their graves.

She didn't return to Nagasaki, because every street, every slope triggered painful memories for her. Half of her relatives and many of her classmates at Junshin had died one after the other in the wake of that August 9. And were she to visit the Ōura Church, one man's face would come achingly to mind.

The Nagasaki that Sachiko knew was locked away in the box inside her heart, looking just as it had in former days. It was a secret that belonged to her alone.

There were other things she didn't tell her husband or children.

Once each year, when the day arrived, she would leave her house in the afternoon. That day when she received her final letter from Shūhei, it had been evening. She had made up her mind to consider that day the anniversary of Shūhei's death.

On that day, she rode the train to Yotsuya and, walking among the throngs of pedestrians, she headed toward Sophia University on the road that paralleled the riverbank. With permission from a guard at the university gate, she crossed the campus, which was crowded with students scrambling cheerfully in all directions, and went into the Western-style building that was the only completely quiet spot on the campus.

The building was the Kultur Heim that Shūhei had often written about in his letters. Climbing the noiseless stairs, she came to the chapel, which was unchanged from the days when Shūhei had sat there next to Ōhashi.

---

1 When Endō died in September of 1996, he joined his elder brother, Shōsuke, and his mother in a burial site at a Catholic cemetery at Fuchū in the suburbs of Tokyo. In December of 2015, all three graves were moved to an underground crypt at St. Ignatius Church, located on the campus of Sophia University in Tokyo, where his funeral service had been held.

Occasionally a foreign priest would be in the chapel praying by himself. Often, no one was there besides Sachiko.

Sitting alone in the chapel, she pictured Shūhei, who would have been here more than thirty years earlier.

Through the window she could see the garden with its many trees, their branches crowded with birds. Just as she had spoken to the statue of the Blessed Mother in the Ōura Church when she was a girl, she spoke again.

Dear God, I am nothing more than an ordinary housewife. The simple, common sort of housewife you can find all over Japan. But, dear God, you have given so much to this ordinary housewife during her lifetime. The joy of having a family, the pleasures of having children, and I have known true love. But it hasn't been all joy and happiness. . . . You also granted me the pain and sorrow that came from the war and from losing someone so very precious to me. You also gave me the opportunity to meet a saintly man like Father Kolbe. Those pains and sorrows sometimes made me doubt what was truly your will, but those doubts even now prod me to seek after you. You've given me far too many tasks to perform in this life, but . . . thank you.

When she concluded that prayer that wasn't really a prayer, a portly man came timidly tiptoeing into the chapel.

He was bald and wore thick glasses, but Sachiko gave a start when she saw his sheepish figure from behind. She realized that it was Shūhei's friend, Ōhashi Shin'ya . . .

Ōhashi sat down and bowed his head. He remained unmoving in that position for about ten minutes and then, timid still, left the chapel. She heard his footsteps on the stairs; that sound soon ceased, and the building was once again silent . . .

Sachiko did not follow him. She held back, thinking that this was how life should be.

AUTHOR'S AFTERWORD

EACH TIME I see a housewife about my same age, whether on a train or a bus or standing in front of the train station, I feel a sudden undefinable affinity with her.

That sense of affinity comes from the fact that she and I are from the same generation, and that we have lived through the same period of history. We survived that great, torturous war and somehow made it through the postwar era so filled with change—while it's true that we are of the same generation, maybe what I feel toward that person isn't anything all that complicated, but perhaps just the honest feeling, *We did well to survive, didn't we?*

We did well to survive—but there are more complex feelings underlying that emotion. Concealed beneath the fact that we survived is all the sorrow and suffering that come from having lost those dear to us, those we loved, those we were close to in the war or in the wake of the war.

Naturally, every person has some dramas in his or her life that merit being written about, but in addition to those individual dramas, our generation also has a great drama we share in common.

I tried to write about that great shared drama in the life of this novel's protagonist, Sachiko.

"Ah, this is me! She's just like me!" I can say that it was worth my efforts writing this novel if a housewife kind enough to read it finds a character resembling herself in it.

Of course, another motivation for writing this novel came five years ago, when I visited the Auschwitz concentration camp in Poland. In that hellish place of mass slaughter, I stood before the starvation chamber where Father Kolbe demonstrated the majesty of human life. (Regrettably, even though many tourists visit the rainswept Dutch Slope in Nagasaki, few are aware of the location in that city where Father Kolbe worked.)

I'm certain that again today, Sachiko will pass by me on the street. In the evening, at the exit of the supermarket, on a rainy day in front of the greengrocer's, at midday by the gate of a house in a residential development—in the eyes of her children, she may appear to be old-fashioned, behind the times, a woman who has led a pathetic life. But she is one who experienced true love, and who lived in a real-life drama, though now she says nothing, maintaining an anguished silence . . .

Endō Shūsaku

1982

APPENDIX:
SYNOPSIS OF *KIKU'S PRAYER*

FRAGMENTS OF THE life of Kiku, who was the cousin of Sachiko's grandmother, are referred to at several points throughout *Sachiko*, often in comparison to Sachiko's experiences. To assist readers unfamiliar with Kiku's story, a summary of the novel follows.

The story begins around 1860 when Kiku, a young girl from a farming village on the outskirts of Nagasaki, meets and begins to fall in love with a young man, Seikichi, from a neighboring village. But she is disappointed when she discovers he is a Kirishitan, one of the underground Christians who practices his religion away from the eyes of the government.

In 1863 Father Bernard-Thadée Petitjean, a French missionary priest, arrives in Nagasaki. In addition to helping build a small Catholic church at Ōura, in 1865 he makes contact with a group of "hidden Christians," descendants of the original Japanese Christians from the seventeenth century who were forced to abandon their faith. But spies are following Petitjean and, after discovering where the hidden Christians worship, officers of the government raid the building and arrest sixty-eight of them, Seikichi included.

Kiku, who had met up again with Seikichi and fallen even more in love with him, turns to Father Petitjean, and in the Ōura Church she offers her very first prayer to the Blessed Mother, the beginning of many prayers she offers on Seikichi's behalf at the feet of the statue of Mary in the small church. The captured Christians are tortured until they disavow their beliefs. Those who recant, including Seikichi, are released.

The shogunal government that has ruled Japan since the start of the seventeenth century collapses in November of 1867, and under the influence of Western culture, reforms known as the Meiji Restoration usher in a period of what appears will be new freedoms for the people—except for Christians. The ban on the foreign religion is maintained by the new government.

Seikichi withdraws his recantation and is once again arrested and exiled to a distant part of Japan, where he and other Christians are jailed, exposed to harsh weather conditions, and often tortured.

Kiku, who is now working as a servant at a teahouse in Nagasaki's entertainment district, meets a petty government official named Itō Seizaemon who tells her he knows where Seikichi has been imprisoned. Itō is a sadistic, unscrupulous man of unbridled lusts, and he tells Kiku that he will help her get money to Seikichi if she will surrender her body to him. She resists, but ultimately gives in out of the belief that she will be able to make Seikichi's time in prison a bit better if she sacrifices her virtue. Itō of course keeps the money to buy himself liquor and other women. Recognizing that she is now tainted and feeling unworthy to marry Seikichi once he is released, Kiku continues selling her body so that she can send more money to the man she truly loves. Her health eventually fails, and one snowy night she goes again to pray for Seikichi before the statue of the Blessed Mother in the Ōura Church. She collapses there, and Father Petitjean finds her dead at the base of the statue.

It is not until 1873 that pressure from foreign governments in Europe and North America forces the Japanese authorities to lift the ban on Christianity, and Seikichi and the others are allowed to return to their homes.

WEATHERHEAD BOOKS ON ASIA

Weatherhead East Asian Institute, Columbia University

Endō Shūsaku, *Kiku's Prayer: A Novel*, translated by Van Gessel (2013)

Li Rui, *Trees Without Wind: A Novel*, translated by John Balcom (2013)

Abe Kōbō, *The Frontier Within: Essays by Abe Kōbō*, edited, translated, and with an introduction by Richard F. Calichman (2013)

Zhu Wen, *The Matchmaker, the Apprentice, and the Football Fan: More Stories of China*, translated by Julia Lovell (2013)

The Columbia Anthology of Modern Chinese Drama, Abridged Edition, edited by Xiaomei Chen (2013)

Natsume Sōseki, *Light and Dark*, translated by John Nathan (2013)

Seirai Yūichi, *Ground Zero, Nagasaki: Stories*, translated by Paul Warham (2015)

Hideo Furukawa, *Horses, Horses, in the End the Light Remains Pure: A Tale That Begins with Fukushima*, translated by Doug Slaymaker with Akiko Takenaka (2016)

Abe Kōbō, *Beasts Head for Home: A Novel*, translated by Richard F. Calichman (2017)

Yi Mun-yol, *Meeting with My Brother: A Novella*, translated by Heinz Insu Fenkl with Yoosup Chang (2017)

Ch'ae Manshik, *Sunset: A Ch'ae Manshik Reader*, edited and translated by Bruce and Ju-Chan Fulton (2017)

Tanizaki Jun'ichiro, *In Black and White: A Novel*, translated by Phyllis I. Lyons (2018)

Yi T'aejun, *Dust and Other Stories*, translated by Janet Poole (2018)

Tsering Döndrup, *The Handsome Monk and Other Stories*, translated by Christopher Peacock (2019)

Kimura Yūsuke, Sacred Cesium Ground *and* Isa's Deluge*: Two Novellas of Japan's 3/11 Disaster*, translated by Doug Slaymaker (2019)

Wang Anyi, *Fu Ping: A Novel*, translated by Howard Goldblatt (2019)

Paek Nam-nyong, *Friend: A Novel from North Korea*, translated by Immanuel Kim (2020)

HISTORY, SOCIETY, AND CULTURE
Carol Gluck, Editor

Takeuchi Yoshimi, *What Is Modernity? Writings of Takeuchi Yoshimi*, edited and translated, with an introduction, by Richard F. Calichman (2005)

Contemporary Japanese Thought, edited and translated by Richard F. Calichman (2005)

Overcoming Modernity, edited and translated by Richard F. Calichman (2008)

Natsume Sōseki, *Theory of Literature and Other Critical Writings*, edited and translated by Michael Bourdaghs, Atsuko Ueda, and Joseph A. Murphy (2009)

Kojin Karatani, *History and Repetition*, edited by Seiji M. Lippit (2012)

The Birth of Chinese Feminism: Essential Texts in Transnational Theory, edited by Lydia H. Liu, Rebecca E. Karl, and Dorothy Ko (2013)

Yoshiaki Yoshimi, *Grassroots Fascism: The War Experience of the Japanese People*, translated by Ethan Mark (2015)

This publication has been supported by the Richard W. Weatherhead Publication Fund of the Weatherhead East Asian Institute, Columbia University.

The translator and Columbia University Press wish to express their appreciation for the generous grant given by the College of Humanities at Brigham Young University toward the cost of publishing this book.

Columbia University Press wishes to express its appreciation for assistance given by the Pushkin Fund in the publication of this book.

Columbia University Press wishes to express its appreciation for assistance given by The Japan Foundation in the publication of this book.

JAPANFOUNDATION